Praise for MAGS AT ~~~~ ~~~~~~~~~~

From the icy rivers of Pittsburgh to the sunny shores of Daytona Beach, this novel is a wild ride, ranging from quirky to other-worldly—especially when Mags takes us behind the doors of the Genius House. A self-professed Nancy Drew, she loves nothing more than a good mystery to solve, and she's aided and abetted in her quest by sidekicks including an opinionated invisible cat and people-size talking mushrooms. Intrigued yet?

Judith A. Levine
Writing Professor, Collins College, Plano/Frisco, TX

I love the voice ... and the amazing path that Mags's life takes. She's genuinely funny, reads like the Southern essayists I love, and her characters are as interesting as, if not more hilarious than, Carl Hiaasen's.

Denise Ousley Exum
Associate Professor, University of North Carolina, Wilmington

This novel is interesting, fun, insightful, with great characters. I especially love the incorporation of so much about writing, about literature, about language, even about feminism and feminist theory. And Jim Crow!

Linda A. Bell
Director of Women's Studies Institute (Retired),
Georgia State University, Atlanta

What does a non-book reader do? He opens out of curiosity to the middle of the book and reads a few lines. [Then] he becomes immediately attached to the book and cannot put it down.

Eugene S. Strickland
City Manager (Retired), Lakeland, FL

This is one helluva novel. Especially in its engagement of such important issues as overpopulation; the mind/body concepts that go back to Jung's theory of the Collective Unconscious; and current followers of the Corpus Hermeticum.

Marvin "Skip" Lowery
Professor (retired), Daytona State College at Daytona Beach,
Florida

I liked the recurring symbols—the memory box and the ["technicolor"] car especially. All readers could definitely identify with objects from their childhood that symbolize important milestones and memories. [I also like the idea] of tying classic novels or pieces of literature to illustrate a character's life.

Dee Pollard Beasley-Schultz
Heartbeat Center for Writing, Literacy and the Arts. Inc.
Osseo, Wisconsin

MAGS BOOKS

The Mags Chronicles - Book 1

MAGS
at
THE GENIUS HOUSE
A Composite Novel

S. O'Duinn Magee

MAGS BOOKS
A Division of S. O'Duinn Magee, LLC
136 W. Granada Blvd.
Ormond Beach, FL 32174
386.956.4529
www.soduinnmagee.com

Printed and Distributed by
MyBookOrders.com (MBO)
Website Fulfillment Order Services
Fulfillment Division of Salem Author Services
Mill City Press, Inc.
2301 Lucien Way #415
Maitland, FL 32751
407.339.4217

Printed in the United States of America

Paperback ISBN-13: 978-0-9905-4142-4
Ebook ISBN-13: 978-0-9905-4143-1

DEDICATION

For
Wesley, Kelley, Christine, Julie

FOREWARNING!

- This book is a *composite novel*. A what? A "composite novel" is a group of titled stories which, when combined under one cover, form a single narrative arc. And that—"a single narrative arc"—is how we define any novel, whether comprised traditionally of numbered chapters or otherwise.

- This novel, the first book in a five-novel series called *The Mags Chronicles*, contains two major parts:

  o Part One, "THEN: The Backstory," and
  o Part Two, "NOW: It Begins with a House."

- This novel contains LOTS of characters, most of whom you'll encounter again in future volumes of *The Mags Chronicles*. To help you keep track of who's who while you're reading, I include a "List of Characters" at the back of the book.

- This book is fiction, except for the parts that aren't.

S. O'Duinn Magee
a.k.a. Mags

TABLE OF CONTENTS

PART ONE
THEN: THE BACKSTORY

PROLOGUE

Once
    Upon
        a
            Time . . . there was a girl who loved stories.

At first the girl thought stories only lived in books. But that was when she was very young and inexperienced. That was when she saw, as they say, *through a glass darkly.*

As she grew, the girl found that stories lived everywhere, in people she knew and even in herself. That was when she began, as they say, to see things *face to face.*

Moving into adulthood and looking back, the girl realized that stories—like life—are all about doors and windows, about chance and choice. That was when she became a woman and, as they say, *put away childish things.*

And that was when she knew, finally, that there are really only two stories:

You go *or* You stay.
You walk through a door *or* You watch through a window.
You follow the Yellow Brick Road *or* You wait in your Tower
By The Sea.

PITTSBURGH

IM·MI·GRANT

-noun

1. a person who migrates to another country, usually for permanent residence.

2. an organism found in a new habitat.

dictionary.com

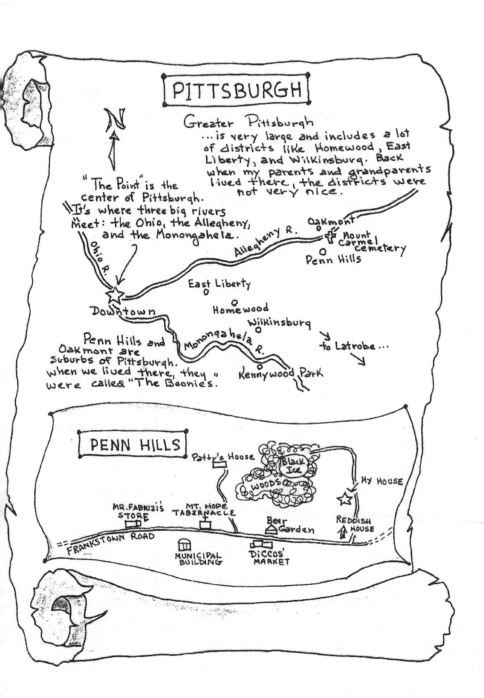

PITTSBURGH

Greater Pittsburgh ...is very large and includes a lot of districts like Homewood, East Liberty, and Wilkinsburg. Back when my parents and grandparents lived there, the districts were not very nice.

"The Point" is the center of Pittsburgh. It's where three big rivers meet: the Ohio, the Allegheny, and the Monongahela.

Ohio R.

Allegheny R.

Oakmont
Mount Carmel Cemetery
Penn Hills

East Liberty

Downtown

Homewood
Wilkinsburg

Monongahela R.

to Latrobe...

Penn Hills and Oakmont are suburbs of Pittsburgh. When we lived there, they were called "The Boonies."

Kennywood Park

PENN HILLS

Patty's House

Black Ice

WOODS

MY HOUSE

MR. FABRIZI'S STORE
MT. HOPE TABERNACLE

Beer Garden

REDDISH HOUSE

FRANKSTOWN ROAD

MUNICIPAL BUILDING

DICCOS' MARKET

BLACK ICE

It's my scariest early memory—looking up at the dark ceiling of ice, seeing the cracks in it, knowing I'd fallen through. I was suspended under that frosty ceiling, but my coat, leggings, mittens, boots were pulling me down, and I was cold. It got dark, darker, and I was sinking. Then light found my face, came close to my face, in my eyes.

No no, too bright, too bright! It hurts, blinding me! BLINDING ME! NO!

Somehow they pulled me out. *It's cold! Watch out! She's too heavy!*

They took me home. *It's not our fault! She fell through black ice! We saved her!*

"Home" was thirty miles northeast of Pittsburgh, in Penn Hills. Penn Hills was really small back then, basically a municipality in a township. We had just one main road with a few buildings strung along it. The only new one was the Municipal Building, where I caught my school bus. The other buildings were old: DiCiccos' roadside vegetable market, the Beer Garden, Mt. Hope Tabernacle Church, and Mr. Fabrizi's general store.

One thing for sure, though, Penn Hills had a lot of them. Hills, I mean. The houses were all built into a hill or on top of a hill or at the bottom of a hill. In front of our house the road sloped down past us like the Big Dipper roller coaster at Kennywood Park—steep, practically straight down, then bottoming out at the very end. After that were woods and the lake where I fell through black ice.

Everyone thought my dad was crazy for moving us to The Boonies. *There's nothing to do there, and there aren't any jobs*, everyone said. But my dad was a traveling salesman, so he didn't have to worry about having a job close to where we lived, and he loved the idea of owning land. I knew we were rich. We owned the meadow out back where violets and goldenrod grew all summer long, a big yard filled with apple trees, and part of the woods that extended down to a creek beyond. And we had the only house on our street with two bathrooms, one on the first floor and one upstairs, where my grandma and I had bedrooms.

But my dad was proudest of the game room down by the cellar. It had a shiny wood floor like a basketball court and big mirrors on the walls and a chrome-and-formica bar with skinny red barstools. He kept barbells and a weightlifting bench there, and a saddle for when he went horseback riding, and rifles for when he went hunting. And there was a record player on a shelf behind the bar with stacks of records for parties.

I loved it when they had parties in the game room because I could hear the music even in my upstairs bedroom and because my mom would bring me a special bedtime treat like cookies and hot cocoa. She'd bring my grandma a treat too, a Hot Toddy if it was wintertime or a Gee n' Tee if it was summer.

Muti (that's what I called my grandma) would be in a bad mood anyway because what she wanted was to be invited to the parties. She'd stomp around her bedroom, and sometimes she'd stand at the top of our stairs and holler really loud, something like *For Christ's sake, can't y'uns be quiet? We're trying to sleep up here!* Then she'd go down to the kitchen and make herself another treat.

At school in first grade I was a celebrity. My mom had a red velvet coat with a fluffy white fur collar, and when she visited my classroom the kids would whistle and say *Your mom's a hubba hubba!* I had a green velvet coat with a brown fur collar and a matching fur muff, and I wore black patent leather Mary Janes instead of lace-up shoes. And I got every kind of lesson available. Piano, tap, ballet, baton twirling, hula dancing.

It didn't occur to me until way later that learning to dance the hula when you lived in the coal country of western Pennsylvania was a little odd. I don't remember much of what I learned, either, except that the teacher called us *wahines*. (That's pronounced vah-HEE-nee, in case you didn't know, which I sort of guessed because back then nobody else knew how to pronounce it.)

You're spoiled rotten, Muti would say to me when I was getting dressed up in new clothes or going for yet another lesson. *Well,* I'd think to myself indignantly, *I know I'm not spoiled like bad eggs or moldy bread or the rug that got wet when the cellar flooded.* In fact, everything seemed wonderful then: velvet coats with fur collars and patent leather shoes and lessons and the best house in the neighborhood. *You must be rich!* the kids said at school, and I knew it was true.

I worried, though, about that black ice. The ice had seemed wonderful too—sparkly white, shiny where sunlight hit it, smooth with a light covering of snow. I ran and slid, laughing and falling down, picking myself up and shaking off the snow before I started running and sliding all over again.

But that black ice was hiding under the white snow, waiting for someone to step on it.

Waiting for me.

So there I was, in the middle of having fun, when the ice broke and I plunged through it into the freezing water below. I'd never heard the term *foreshadowing,* and if I had, I'm not sure I would have understood it. But I knew about lessons. That treacherous black ice was a lesson, and I knew I needed to remember it.

ODE TO LUIGI

Uncle Walter and Aunt Cissy lived Downtown in a redbrick rowhouse that was built into the side of a hill. Their rowhouse was just like all the others, but I knew they were rich because they owned the vacant lot next to their house. and it had grass and a tree. Tucked between all the dirty redbrick buildings, their vacant lot was a patch of bright green. In the middle of the patch of green, jutting up from dead center, they had one skinny tree with a circle of chicken wire around the trunk to keep neighborhood dogs from using it as their pee place.

The steel mills nearby smoked day and night, sending black sticky soot into the air. Aunt Cissy hated soot. She was a fanatical housekeeper, just like Muti. She'd wash windowsills and banisters, stoops and steps. But next day the soot would be back, powdery black dust covering every surface it could reach.

In front of their rowhouse the redbrick street was a hive of activity. I loved going out for a walk with my cousin Wally, peering into store windows, pooling our coins to buy kosher pickles and stick-pretzels that looked like big cigars.

The sidewalks were dirty with cigarette butts and gum wrappers and gobs of phlegm in the storm drain gulleys. Old men smelling like wet wool would shamble by or be asleep sitting up in corners and alleys. The streetcars were clean, rolling along on metal tracks cut into the redbrick streets, but cars and buses farted exhaust fumes that choked you if they blew in your face. Pushcarts vied with horse carts for street space, and if you were in a car, driving behind a horse cart, you watched the horse squeeze out turds that dropped to the street.

The city's filthy, my dad said.

I don't understand why Cissy wants to live downtown, my mom said.

I knew why.

The city was electric, exciting, exotic.

Wally and I would wait on the corner down from his house, talking, playing rock-paper-scissors. He knew the Italian words—*roccia, carta, forbici*—but I was slow in Italian, so he always won. I didn't mind because we were waiting for Luigi and his cart with a block of ice on top, listening for the bells that jingled every time his horse took a step.

If the sun was shining, the bottles of flavored syrups on Luigi's horse cart shone with the colors of stained glass, just like the windows in Holy Rosary Church: red, green, orange, yellow, purple. Luigi would shave the ice into paper cones and, just for Wally and me, mix the flavors by pouring a little of each one on the ice in our cones: cherry, lime, orange, pineapple, grape. Then greedily, our hands sticky with syrup, we'd suck the bright sweet jewels of the city while we walked along the street with Luigi.

Luigi liked us because we were respectful to him, so he'd let us give sugar cubes to his horse Pucci while we were walking. Luigi had a monkey, too. The monkey wore a black felt hat with tassels on it and his name was Mussolini. Sometimes if Luigi was in an especially good mood, he'd play songs on his mouth organ while we were walking, and when he did that Mussolini would take off his hat and hold it out for tips. That's when I'd notice that Luigi kept Mussolini on a chain. Wally said it was because the monkey couldn't be trusted. *Otherwise,* he said, *why name a monkey Mussolini?*

Wally knew lots of history because he read *The Encyclopedia Britannica* for fun, so he was smart about lots of things. Adults didn't pay much attention to his ideas, though. Aunt Cissy and

Uncle Walter were always trying to shush him, and Muti said Wally was too smart for his britches. But I figured he was right about the monkey's name.

We probably looked pretty bad when we got back to Wally's house, especially if we'd wandered through alleys and backlots on our way home, searching for lost coins and treasures. *Look at you two, you're a mess!* Aunt Cissy would scold. If Muti was there too, she'd spit on a handkerchief and wipe our faces with it.

We didn't care. We loved Luigi and Pucci and Mussolini and sno cones, and we knew that in the city, syrup and soot go together.

WEDNESDAY'S CHILD IS FULL OF WOE

It's no fun being a thumb-sucker and a bed-wetter. I was both of those, and Muti never let me forget it. She put iodine on my thumbs to make them taste bad, and she tied mittens on my hands at night, and she'd call out *Pee-Baby, Pee-Baby!* when she was hanging sheets outside on the clothesline.

My mom tried to apologize sometimes for Muti. *She was different before the Great Depression,* Mom would say. *Muti used to laugh a lot.* Mom also said it wasn't her fault that her mother lived with us. *I never asked her,* she said. *Your dad was too good-hearted. When Muti lost her house in the Depression, your dad invited her to live with us.*

At our house Muti was always working—cooking, canning, sweeping, scrubbing floors, doing laundry in a wringer-washer in the cellar, hanging clothes outside on clotheslines to dry.

Doing laundry back then was no joke. I can picture her even now, hefting the big heavy clothes poles and carrying them outside to prop up the clotheslines, going back and forth with baskets of wet wash to hang up with big wooden clothespins, then later, taking everything down and bringing it in. If she didn't have anything else to do, she would iron . . . and iron . . . and iron some more.

Spring cleaning, after the snow finally melted, was the worst job of all. Storm windows had to be taken down and washed and stacked in the cellar, window screens for summer had to be cleaned and jimmied into the window frames, carpets and rugs had to be hauled outside and hung on a clothesline so you could beat them with a broom.

Muti cried a lot while she was working. I remember her on hands and knees in our kitchen, washing the blue-and-white checkerboard linoleum floor with a bristle brush, dipping the brush in and out of a bucket of soapy water. Scrubbing. Wailing.

Someday I'll leave this godforsaken place. Y'uns will all be sorry when I'm gone, she would cry. My mother would be quiet and calm during scenes like this. *Let me know when you're leaving,* she'd say, and *Make sure you don't miss the bus.*

But I got nervous when Muti cried. It made me feel guilty, like it was my fault she had to move to The Boonies and live with us.

It made me feel guilty for hating her.

THE REDDISH HOUSE

The Reddish House sat way back from the road and up on a hill. It was a decrepit old two-story wooden house, tall and skinny with tiny windows, and if you looked at it straight-on you'd see that it leaned to one side like it was ready to fall over. If I saw a house like that now I'd call it the Norman Bates house or the Boo Radley house. But this was way back before Norman Bates and Boo Radley were famous, so I just called it the Reddish house.

The Reddish family lived there. Mister, Missus, Joan, and Joan's cat Boots. When Muti would go to visit Missus, I'd go too. Joan was already a teenager, but she was *slow*, so she didn't mind that I was much younger than she was. We played Chinese Checkers and Parcheesi, and I'd let her win. Winning made Joan happy. She'd bounce up and down in her wheelchair, hugging the cat, clapping and laughing.

At my house we didn't have any pets, so I was very interested in Joan's cat. He was black except for his chest and his feet which were white. If he'd been my cat. I might have named him "Boots" just like Joan did, because he looked like he was wearing white boots on his feet. But Joan told me she didn't name him because of how he looked. She named him after her all-time favorite story "Puss in Boots." *I love Puss in Boots because he tricks everybody,* Joan said. *They all think they're smarter than he is, but in the end he always wins.*

It made sense to me that Joan would love the story about a smart trickster cat who wins all the time. After all, she never got to win anything except when I let her win at Chinese Checkers and Parcheesi, and I was sure nobody told her she was smart. Oh, and there was one other interesting thing about Boots. He had only a nub, not a tail. *It got cut off on accident,* Joan said. But the "accident" part sounded strange to me, and I noticed that when Mister was around, Boots hissed at him and hid under the sofa.

Sometimes when we were visiting at the Reddish house, I'd play their big upright piano so Muti and Missus could sing religious songs like "Ave Maria" and "Our Lady of Fatima." Their singing didn't sound very good, so after one or two religious songs I'd play songs without words. Joan liked that because she could pretend she had drums, beating time on the table. Then Missus would give us homemade pie, and she'd make tea for herself and Muti. I remember the tea because Missus would pour it into cups that had saucers. The two of them would dump their tea into the saucers, then dump it back into their cups to cool it off. *We don't want to burn our tongues* Missus would say, and they would laugh.

Mister didn't like tea, so Missus made coffee for him, and he poured Uncle Jack in it from a bottle. Mister was particular about pie, too, and he didn't often like the kind Missus gave us, especially if it was vinegar pie. But vinegar pie was Muti's favorite because it reminded her of Germany. *It's just like my mum used to make,* she'd say. *Vinegar pie was for special holidays like Easter, after we fasted during Lent.* Joan liked vinegar pie too, but for once I agreed with Mister. When no one was looking, I'd trade plates with Joan so she could have two pieces. Otherwise she never got two pieces of anything, only one.

Once Joan's mother made cherry pie, but it was sour, and she forgot to remove the pits from the cherries. Joan's father yelled and threw his plate on the floor, then smashed his hand down hard on the piano and made Joan cry.

It always puzzled me that Joan's mother seemed so old, older than Mister, maybe as old as Muti. When I asked about "old" Missus and "young" Mister, Muti said *Don't be a nosy parker!* But I still wondered. Sometimes, walking home from my bus stop after school, I'd hear hollering and crashes inside their house. When I told Muti about the noises, she said *Little pitchers have big ears.*

Joan got a double whammy. Missus died, and Boots ran away, all in the same week.

Missus didn't have a funeral, either. The only reason we knew she died was because Mena at the DiCiccos' market told my mom. Then Muti and I took cookies to the Reddish house. I told Joan I was sorry about Missus. *I miss my mum,* she said. *Mum always took care of me. I don't like having a man give me a bath and dress me.* That's when she told me she was double-sad because Boots was gone too.

My grandmother only liked Missus, not Mister, so we never went back.

Joan wasn't allowed outside so I didn't see her after that, but lots of times I saw Mister going in the Beer Garden. One time I saw him coming out of the Beer Garden with a Lady in a Red Dress, and sometimes I'd see the Lady going in the Reddish house. Another time I saw Mister burying something in their yard, but when I went closer to see what he was doing, he yelled at me and told me to go home.

I thought if I could find Boots for Joan, I'd take him to her in secret and smuggle him into their house. Every morning I put a bowl of milk out on our front porch, expecting the cat to show up, repentant like the prodigal son who ran away from home and then came back. I liked that prodigal son story, but I had to admit there wasn't a place in it for Joan and Mister. Or Boots, either.

Boots never came back.

THE LITTLE MATCH GIRL

Life was quiet before television was invented. If you lived in The Boonies and you didn't play cards like my mom or read books like my dad, your other main choice once nighttime came was listening to radio. The Green Hornet and the Shadow were my favorite radio characters. Of course I also liked the

Lone Ranger, but it was harder for me to identify with him. He roamed the wide-open spaces Out West, but I could never make those spaces real in my mind because in Penn Hills we didn't have them. We didn't have wide-open spaces, I mean.

Or Indians like Tonto.

I'd never seen a cactus, either. And the closest I could come to picturing a tumbleweed was a dandelion when its petals got all fluffy. If you blew on the dandelion when it was fluffy, the fluff came loose and tiny pieces went floating off in the wind, like tiny parasols.

The Green Hornet and the Shadow were different, though. They were City Crusaders so I could picture them in my head, sort of like Italians in black capes and Lone Ranger masks. I could imagine them fighting crime in the downtown streets after criminals punched out the streetlights. There they'd be in their flowing black capes, saving Aunt Cissy and Uncle Walter from kidnappers, then chasing crooks and thugs through alleyways and warehouses and ending up in the steel mills with their thundering red-hot furnaces that made the air red and orange.

Sometimes before I was ready to go to sleep at night Muti would read to me. I always wanted to hear fairy tales, so that's what she'd read, but the ones she picked were all about snow and ice, about being cold and freezing. Her favorite story was "The Ice Queen," about a mysterious woman who travels around at night in a magical sleigh pulled by white wolves. In the daytime she lives in a castle made of ice with the orphans she rescues when she's out at night, dashing through the snow in her sleigh.

Muti liked to read the parts about how beautiful the Ice Queen is, in her purple velvet robe and white fur cape and a crown made of icicles, and how she helps all the poor orphans by giving them a home. But I never trusted that story. I always thought the Ice Queen kidnapped those children, and bad things happened back in the castle made of ice.

Another story Muti picked a lot was "The Little Match Girl," about a girl who has to sell matches door-to-door in the city because she's so poor. One day she doesn't sell enough matches to buy food, so she has to continue knocking on doors even though the sun has already gone down, and lamplighters are lighting the streetlamps. Finally, in the dead of night, she freezes to death on the doorstep of a rich man's house because he won't open his door and let her come inside to get warm.

Muti and I would be sad when she finished the story and closed the book, and I'd drift off to sleep thinking if I wrote that story I'd send the Green Hornet to rescue the Little Match Girl and burn down the rich man's house.

Or maybe I'd send the Shadow to appear mysteriously with a document proving the Match Girl is the long-lost daughter of the rich man, the daughter who'd been kidnapped years ago by a beautiful but mysterious woman in a sleigh pulled by wolves.

Or maybe I'd just send Robin Hood and his Merrie Men to steal all the rich man's money so he has to sell Fuller Brushes door-to-door and live in the attic because his house has been turned into a luxurious orphanage for all the children who'd been kidnapped by the Ice Queen.

I didn't think Muti would approve of changing the stories, so I didn't tell her my ideas. I didn't try to analyze her choice of stories back then, either. I just wondered whether the stories she picked reminded her of being back in Germany, where it was really cold and there was lots of snow and ice. I kept on wondering, too, about castles made of ice and doors that stay locked and why they're in so many stories.

There's something important going on here, I thought to myself. *Someday I'll figure it out.*

KNIGHTS AND LADIES

Muti did cleaning for the Knights of Columbus at their meeting hall in East Liberty. She also cleaned for the Catholic Ladies Underwriters and Benevolent Association—the CLUBA—who held their meetings at the Knights of Columbus Hall where she cleaned. I thought CLUBA was a fancy way of saying "club" because that's what they were. But that was before I understood acronyms.

Twice a month I'd go with Muti to the Knights of Columbus Hall in East Liberty so she could clean. We'd get there early because she cleaned the hall twice: first so the place was nice and neat for the CLUBA meeting, and when that meeting was over she would clean up again to leave things nice and neat for the Knights of Columbus to meet. She didn't get any money from the Knights or the Ladies for all the work she did. Instead of paying her the Knights let her come to Wednesday bingo for free, and the Ladies let her belong to their CLUBA without paying dues.

Muti wanted the Knights and the Ladies to like her, but I knew they didn't. If the Knights really liked her, they would have let her come to Saturday bingo for free instead of Wednesday bingo because Saturday bingo was when they gave the good prizes. And if the Ladies really liked her, they would have invited her to their "card parties" and "social teas." Probably Muti didn't have the right clothes to wear to their uppity events anyway, but I figured it wouldn't hurt them just to invite her and make her feel wanted.

I loved stories about real Knights and Ladies, like Lancelot and Guinevere in Camelot, but I didn't like the East Liberty Knights and Ladies at all. I had to pretend I did, though, because Muti was proud to think she was one of them. *We do good works for the poor,* she would say. *We raise money at bingos and rummage sales so we can buy babushkas and galoshes and donate them to the war orphans.*

I always wondered what a war orphan looked like.

Then I found some pictures.

My dad kept his books downstairs in our game room, whole sets of books by Mark Twain and Zane Grey and his favorite, Edgar Rice Burroughs, and a lot of *Life Magazine* books that were full of pictures. One book was *A War in Photographs,* about the bombings in World War II in Europe. That's where I found the war orphan pictures.

One was a photo of two kids, a boy and a girl, walking through rubble and smoke. They were wearing coats too big for them, and they were holding hands. Another picture was just a baby in a diaper, all dirty or maybe burned, sitting alone in the middle of a bombed-out house and crying with its face scrunched up. *If that's what war orphans look like,* I thought, *they sure need a lot more than babushkas and galoshes.*

I knew what babushkas and galoshes were. In Pittsburghese (it's the way you talk if you're from Pittsburgh), babushkas were headscarves and galoshes were boots, but back then I didn't realize their significance to Muti. The idea was, if you could stay warm and dry by covering your head and your feet, then you were protected and safe. You might not be rich, you might be really poor, but at least your head was warm and your feet were dry.

Realizing this when I got a little older, I tried to imagine how awful life must have been in Germany to make Muti's parents decide to come to America. *Maybe they were always cold and wet in Germany,* I thought. *Maybe they were so poor they didn't even have babushkas and galoshes.*

By then I'd heard some of the stories about the early arriving-in-America years. I knew that Muti grew up with four families in one house, that she had to quit school and be a live-in maid in a rich man's house when she was still a kid. *I bet the rich man's family wasn't nice to her,* I would think. *I bet that's why she likes the Little Match Girl story, because rich people were mean to her just like the man who wouldn't let the Little Match Girl come inside and get warm.*

Muti ended up better than the Little Match Girl. Better for a while, anyway, because she didn't freeze to death before she got to be a teenager. She worked and saved money and got a good husband with a job, and they bought their own house with lots of room for their children and extra space for relatives from Germany.

One of my mom's favorite framed photos shows all of them together in front of their house. Mom and Aunt Cissy are wearing ruffly white dresses with big bows in their hair, their little brother Jake is all gussied up in a sailor suit, their dad's wearing a three-piece suit and a fedora, and Muti's dressed up like Eleanor Roosevelt in a fancy dress and necklaces and a hat with beads and feathers.

Everybody looks happy in that picture, including Muti. But that's the way photographs work, isn't it? They freeze you in an instant of time, which is okay, I guess. Except if everything changes, the frozen instant in the photo is a constant reminder of what you lost.

What they didn't know when they posed for that picture was that The Great Depression was coming, and that's when everything changed because the banks failed. Muti lost it all—their savings, her husband, the house. First their savings were wiped out. Then her husband got fired from his job at the

Railroad and keeled over dead from a heart attack, and before he was dead even a year, the bank took their house.

I always wondered about that bank failure thing. If the banks failed and ran out of money and had to close their doors, then how could they come back a couple of years later and take people's houses? It makes the bank sound like Lazarus in the story where he's dead, but then he comes back to life, and it's a miracle. According to the Bible story Jesus helped Lazarus come back to life, so I wondered if Jesus helped those banks just like he helped Lazarus.

I really wondered about Jesus helping the banks, so I figured I'd ask Muti sometime when she was in a good mood, but she never was. It didn't matter, though, because her money and husband and house were long gone.

They came here from Germany expecting to find Camelot, I'd think to myself, *and look what they found instead.* Thinking about this made me dislike the Knights and Ladies of East Liberty all over again.

GHOSTIES AND GHOULIES

I hated our cellar. To get to the cellar in our house you went down a narrow wooden stairway from the kitchen ("cellar" is Pittsburghese for "basement," which I'm sure you figured out). The cellar's where the coal furnace was, and the wringer-washing-machine, and the laundry tub where Muti gave me a bath in cold water when I got muddy from playing in the creek behind our house, and the apple and potato bins, and the dirt-pantry for home-canned vegetables and chowchow relish and tomato jelly. None of that was why I hated the cellar, though.

The reason why I hated the cellar was it had only one light—a bulb above the laundry tub you turned on and off by pulling a string that broke at inconvenient times. And without the light, the cellar was dark. This was a problem because I knew *bad things* lived there in the dark. I knew all about banshees and goblins and leprechauns and changelings, and I knew no matter how fast I ran, they would be right behind me.

I knew about those bad creatures because of my name and the fact it's Irish even though the rest of my family are German. It's Irish (my name, that is) because my dad's father was Irish, and *his* name was Michael O'Duinn Magee. And that's the only thing my dad knew about his dad because my dad wasn't even born when his father got killed. So my dad's name was Raymond O'Duinn Magee, and that's where I got the "O'Duinn Magee" part of my name.

Besides his name, my dad only got one other thing from his father, and it was an old book that was practically falling apart. The book was all about the family tree of Irish fairies, and it's where I read about banshees and leprechauns and the rest.

Now here's the thing about those Irish fairies: they're not nice at all. My friend Patty didn't believe me when I told her so because Patty thought all fairies were cute like Tinker Bell. No matter how hard I tried, I couldn't convince her. But I knew better. I knew those Irish fairies lived in dark places like our cellar, and I knew they did bad things to mortals.

I also knew I needed a charm to protect myself. That's when I made myself an amulet which I had read about on a Pocahontas Indian Guide Card that came in a box of Kellogg's Shredded Wheat Biscuits.

I did the best I could about ingredients for my amulet. First I snitched an old pair of Muti's rosary beads (she had lots so I didn't feel bad about taking some old ones). Then I got some long hairs from the tail of Luigi's horse Pucci.

Luigi was glad for me to have the horse-tail-hairs for my amulet because he was not foolish about fairies like my friend Patty. Luigi called the fairies *diabolici pericolosi,* and he agreed I should protect myself. Whenever we talked about them. he made me whisper. Then he'd make The Sign of the Cross, turn around three times, and kiss the crucifix that he wore on a chain around his neck.

I needed a garlic clove for my amulet too, but since we didn't cook with garlic at my house, I had to settle for a crabapple from one of the trees in our yard. I worried about the substitution at first—the crabapple for the garlic—but after I wore the amulet a few times and didn't get snatched by *bad things* when I ran through our cellar in the dark, I didn't worry quite as much.

When I wasn't wearing the amulet I kept it in my Commonplace Box. I'd read that lots of people in Olden Times had Commonplace *Books*—like a combination scrapbook and diary. I wanted to be different so as soon as I started accumulating secret treasures, I decided to have a box instead of a book. I figured a box made more sense than a book because in a box you had room for things like dried rose-beetles and clothespin dolls. And your amulet, when you weren't wearing it.

I don't collect beetles or clothespin dolls anymore, but I still have the amulet in my Commonplace Box along with other treasured possessions. Nothing big, things that are significant to me. The falling-apart book of Irish fairies is there, along with a tiny wall plaque that's inscribed with an old Scottish prayer:

> *From ghosties and ghoulies*
> *And long-leggety beasties,*
> *And things that go bump in the night—*
> *Good Lord, deliver us. Amen.*

Maybe if I'd had the prayer back when I was terrified of being in our dark cellar, I wouldn't have worried about the crabapple-substitution. Then again, maybe worrying is just part of my nature.

I'll try not to worry about that.

BETHIE JEAN

We had so many Elizabeths in our family, they all had to have nicknames. My mom was Elizabeth Margaret, so she got to use her middle name and be called Peg, but all the other Elizabeths had to be some variation of Liz or Beth.

Mom's mom, my Muti, was Bess.

Mom's sister-in-law was Aunt Betty.

Mom's sister was Aunt Cissy (she didn't want to be one of the Elizabeths).

My cousin was Bethie Jean.

Bethie Jean's father was Uncle Jake, my mom's little brother. In the old photos Uncle Jake looks like a movie star—tall, good-looking in his starched white Navy uniform, with a big grin on his face. *Jake could have had any girl he wanted,* my mom said. *He was going steady with a sweet French girl, but Aunt Betty got herself in trouble, and Jake had to marry her.*

I didn't think Aunt Betty could get in trouble all by herself, but when I asked how it happened, no one would tell me.

Bethie Jean was always skinny but always eating candy. She embarrassed everyone, making up words that sounded dirty, putting her hands in her underpants and pulling them down. Uncle Jake would smack her and say, *For God's sake, Bethie Jean,*

stop that! Then Aunt Betty would cry, and Bethie Jean would curl herself all up in a ball on the sofa or on the floor and shut her eyes tight and suck her thumb. My mom would roll her eyes and do that *tsk tsk tsk* noise with her tongue. *Betty puts up with a lot from Jake,* Mom would say.

Bethie Jean's cravings for sweets, pulling down her panties, making up those words and calling attention to herself—these were all symptoms. "Acting out." A cry for help. But I didn't know that then.

Bethie Jean was twelve when she and Aunt Betty went away. As the story goes, they just slipped away, leaving for California without telling anyone they were going. *I hope they don't end up on the streets,* Muti said, but I knew she expected them to do exactly that. *Wherever they are, I bet they're better off,* I thought to myself.

A few years later Uncle Jake married Aunt Lizzie and got a stepdaughter, but they didn't stay with him very long.

SAINTS AND MARTYRS

Muti said we lived *in the middle of nowhere.* If you rode a bus in one direction you got to the movie theater. If you rode a bus in the other direction you got to the dairy where we bought milk and butter. You had to take three buses, at least, and then transfer to a streetcar to get somewhere Muti liked: Mount Carmel Cemetery, or Aunt Cissy's rowhouse downtown, or the big Wilkinsburg Bingo Parlor where Uncle Jake fixed bingo games so she could win. (Uncle Jake also *ran numbers,* but I thought fixing bingo games was a lot more interesting because how they did it was mysterious.)

When I'd go to bingo with Muti, I wasn't allowed to play for real, so instead I'd try my best to pay attention, but I could never spot the fix. She'd play one game after another without winning until it was time for the fixer-game and suddenly she'd shout "Bingo!" Then Uncle Jake would pick up her card and call out the winning numbers, and she'd get prize money in cash. *I always give half of the prize money back,* she would protest. But I never saw her do it.

On the bus rides back from bingo she grumbled a lot. *I deserve to win something once in a while in this shitty excuse for a life,* she would say. *Your Uncle Jake is the only one who looks out for me.* She said that a lot about Uncle Jake, and I would always think *Well then, why doesn't he ask you to come live with him and Aunt Betty instead of with us?*

But I never said it out loud.

Even more than Mount Carmel Cemetery and Wilkinsburg Bingo, the place Muti liked best was Holy Rosary Catholic Church in Homewood. I was baptized there because it was the family church while my mom was growing up. I don't remember being baptized, but I sure remember those long bus-and-streetcar trips with Muti when she was going to confession at Holy Rosary Church. Mom always wondered why Muti had to go to confession all the time, so I guess she didn't know about Uncle Jake fixing the bingos.

Sometimes while Muti was in the confessional box I waited for her in the pew, but sometimes I waited in the vestibule. If I waited in the vestibule by the votive candles, I could read the holy cards that had titles like *The Seven Dolors of the Blessed Virgin Mary.* I liked that one a lot because it sounded like the Virgin Mary had a really big family and seven of them all had the same name, "Dolores."

This made sense to me because it was like our next-door neighbors who had to have nicknames because they had so many Doloreses. They had Dots and Dotties and Dees and

Deedees. They even had a Dolly. So while I was waiting in the vestibule I would speculate about the nicknames in the Virgin Mary's family, and I'd figure what a good thing it was that she didn't get one of the Dolores nicknames.

I mean, think about it. *The Blessed Virgin Deedee.* It just doesn't work, does it? Even Muti would have trouble praying to *The Blessed Virgin Deedee,* and the poor person who made all those holy cards would be out of a job.

There was one holy card that really confused me, though—the one called *Miracles Performed by the Infant Jesus of Prague.* It confused me because I knew the Infant Jesus got born in Bethlehem, and I didn't think in Ancient Days it was easy to get from one place to another in a hurry. Especially if you were an infant.

When I asked Wally about it, he said *Prague's in Czechoslovakia, which is about 1500 miles from Bethlehem,* and that's when I was sure the holy card must be wrong. I mean, if it took Muti and me three buses and a trolley car to get to Holy Rosary Church from Penn Hills, how could the Infant Jesus just pop on over to Prague once in a while to do miracles?

My favorite holy cards, though, were the ones about saints and martyrs. There was Saint Lena who plucked out her own eyes and carried them around on a plate just so she could make a point about being pure in mind and body. And there was Saint Simeon Stylites who sat high up on a pole for his whole life. I didn't understand what *his* point was, but I told Wally I thought living on a pole for your whole life was a good way to get noticed.

There were actually two Saint Simeons, the Elder and the Younger, Wally told me. *They were the most famous of the group of ascetics who called themselves "pillar hermits," and they were quite influential in Eastern Christianity during the Medieval period.* Wally talked like that because he was always reading

29

his encyclopedia. Lots of people made fun of the way he talked, but I thought he was interesting.

Some holy card saints were heroes because they were Martyrs as well as Saints. Their stories were the best of all, like Saint Peter the First Pope, getting crucified upside down. And how about Saint Genesius, the patron saint of clowns and actors who got born again for Jesus while he was onstage in a play that was not exactly religious? When he changed his lines and started preaching right there and then, the Emperor got mad and beheaded him for real.

My favorite, though, was Saint Sebastian who got a double whammy and died twice. First he was shot full of arrows like a pincushion, and later he got beaten to death and thrown into a toilet. *It was a "latrine,"* Wally told me, *not a "toilet." Technically speaking, a "toilet" is a modern invention. In fact, our English word "toilet" comes from the French word "toilette," and it only dates back to the Sixteenth Century, long after the death of Saint Sebastian.*

Sometimes Wally can be very know-it-all and annoying.

Riding back from Holy Rosary Church on the bus, I would think about the saints and martyrs, imagining how brave they were and how sad it was that they had to be dead a long time before anyone appreciated them. Like Joan of Arc, my favorite saint of all, who had to wait six hundred years to get officially sanctified.

I hope you learn something from those holy cards, Muti would say while we were riding the bus back home. *You should read something besides fairy tales all the time.*

THE BEER GARDEN

Walking to my school bus stop, I passed the Beer Garden every day. It was a big log cabin with smeary windows and

ADULTS ONLY printed in red on a dirty-white sign by the door. I never understood how you could grow beer. Did it grow in the ground, like carrots? Or above the ground, like cabbage? Or maybe on vines, like grapes? And anyway, where was the garden? Was it out back? Or did they grow stuff *inside* the building?

The night the Beer Garden burned down was better than Fourth of July. That old wooden building went up in *whooshes* as high as fireworks, catching the trees on fire and sending showers of sparks as far as Frankstown Road, our main road out front. We were all there, us and all of our neighbors except for the Reddishes. We wondered if they were watching from their high windows, but we couldn't see because the windows were dirty. I wondered, too, about the Lady in the Red Dress and where she was when the fire started, but I knew better than to ask Muti about her.

Muti liked the fire. She said it was *good riddance to bad rubbish*, smiling the whole time while the building went up in smoke and laughing out loud when the roof caved in.

People were excited, whispering, forming in groups, re-forming into new groups. *The Fire Chief saw Big Tony DiCicco running out the back door,* someone said.

No, someone else said, *it wasn't Big Tony who was running. The Fire Chief saw Sonny DiCicco running into the woods.*

Maybe it was Big Tony <u>and</u> Sonny, someone whispered.

Those DiCiccos set the fire to get the insurance money, someone whispered back.

That Sonny DiCicco's no good, just like the rest of them, everyone agreed.

31

We stayed until the firetrucks left.

My dad was friends with Big Tony, so when the crowd was breaking up the two of them went back to Big Tony's market. *We'll just shoot the breeze for a while,* my dad said. I wanted to go to the DiCiccos' market too, but I had to go home with Mom and Muti.

Your father didn't come home last night, Muti said the next morning. She seemed pleased about it, like she knew some kind of secret, but she didn't tell me what it was.

DiCiccos' market was closed all the next week. I remember because Muti wanted cantaloupe, and when we couldn't get any, she threw a hissy fit.

Then on Saturday Big Tony's nephew Ralphie brought us our first TV.

It fell off a truck, Ralphie said.

WHERE'S SONNY?

After a bad fire in the woods near Turtle Crick ("crick" is the way you say "creek" in Pittsburghese), Sonny wasn't at the DiCiccos' market anymore because he got sent away to military school. *"Military School," my ass!* Muti sniffed, meaning she knew where he was instead of military school but couldn't tell.

I was a little confused, though. At the DiCiccos' market there was a huge framed picture of Sonny on the wall, and it sure looked like he was wearing a military school uniform. When we were there to buy vegetables and fruit, he'd stare back at us from his portrait, standing at attention and saluting—all decked out in dress blues, white gloves, fancy hat, lots of gold braid. Muti hinted that the portrait was a fake. *I wouldn't put anything past those DiCiccos,* she'd say, rolling her eyes. Well, real or fake, the portrait didn't keep people from talking, saying

Sonny was in Juvenile Detention or Reform School or Jail, or he got sent to Italy and good riddance.

At first I couldn't understand why people were so interested in Sonny's whereabouts.

I mean, why did it matter to anyone else where Sonny really was? Especially since he wasn't around anymore to cause trouble. Then I realized they didn't care about Sonny at all. What they really cared about was why they didn't like Big Tony. And they didn't like Big Tony because they were jealous.

Like Mrs. Fabrizi, for instance, who was jealous because the DiCiccos lived in a nice house next to their market instead of upstairs in the same building. (Mr. and Mrs. Fabrizi lived above their General Store with their five kids.)

Or like Patty's mom, who was French-Armenian and didn't like Italians just on principle. Patty's mom was always talking about her "principles" and said Italians caused the Armenian Genocide. But when I asked Wally about it, he said *Your friend's mother is wrong. The Armenian Genocide was perpetrated by the Ottoman Empire, not the Italians.* I was glad to know that, but I knew better than to correct Patty's mom.

Or like Muti, who sniffed about *those no-good Italians* and their *skeletons in the closet.* Muti was always mad about something on principle, sort of like Patty's mom, so I didn't pay much attention. At the time I just wondered why it mattered so much where Big Tony kept his Halloween decorations (we kept ours in the cellar). But that was before I understood metaphor.

Sonny never came back from wherever he was. Then Big Tony's orphan niece Mena (her real name's Philomena) stayed at the market for a whole week and ran it while Tony and his wife went to Italy, and everyone kind of assumed they went there for Sonny's funeral.

AND THEY LIVED HAPPILY EVER AFTER

Penn Hills had a huge wedding one summer, and my mom and dad were in it. Mom looked beautiful in a long pink dress, and Dad was handsome in a white dinner jacket and pink cummerbund. Mom carried pink roses, and Dad had a pink boutonniere pinned on his jacket.

Actually the wedding was in Latrobe, not Pittsburgh. Which made sense because Latrobe's famous for its Brewery and its Benedictine Abbey Church, two good reasons to have a big wedding there. Plus the DiCicco family is distantly related to the chief priest at the Abbey, Father Vincenzo Parlapiano. The wedding ceremony was a nuptial mass, of course, and the all-night reception afterward was at the Fire Hall, with men in black shirts and ties playing accordions so everyone could dance.

The bride and groom, Mena and Frankie, were beautiful like Cinderella and Prince Charming. Everyone said Frankie looked just like Clark Gable, and Mena looked like Vivien Leigh except blonde.

When the reception was over and everyone was throwing rice, Frankie grabbed Mena, picked her up, and walked up the stairs with her in his arms—the long satin dress trailing behind. *It's just like that scene in "Gone with the Wind" when Rhett Butler carries Scarlett up the stairs,* everyone said. Even Muti got all teary and sentimental.

Since Mena was Big Tony's orphan niece and Frankie was a DiCicco-by-marriage, Big Tony paid for the wedding and reception. *The whole kit and kaboodle,* as he was fond of saying.

He also was fond of saying the first baby would be named after him, and they'd call him "Sonny Two Shoes" for a nickname.

I thought that was creepy because why would they want to jinx a new baby with the old Sonny's name, especially when the old Sonny was a jerk? Even my mom and dad didn't think Sonny Two Shoes was a good idea for a name, but they kept quiet about it because Big Tony was determined.

The first baby, Lynn, was adorable, blonde and beautiful like Mena. *The first one's for practice,* Big Tony joked.

The second baby, Angela, had dark curls and dimples like Frankie. *Not to worry, third time's the charm,* Big Tony said.

They named the third baby Phyllis. *Call her "Phil" and to hell with it!* said Big Tony.

Mom and I would visit Mena, always sick with mysterious ailments. Each time we went to visit they were in a different house, worse than the one before. Frankie was never there, always off somewhere "on family business." The girls stayed together, away from us, like they were triplets or something. And like Mena, they were always sick. *I wonder what's wrong with those girls?* my mother would say.

Things got worse instead of better. Lynn left home early, dropping out of high school to get married and have a premature baby. Angela left too, without telling anyone where she was going. Phyllis tried to stay, but Frankie kicked her out when he came home unexpectedly one day and found her with her boyfriend. That left nobody in the house to be with Mena because Frankie was hardly ever home. When Mena died, all alone, they didn't find her until two days later.

Mom stayed sad for Mena. I guess she couldn't help thinking about that fairy-tale wedding in Latrobe, wishing her friend could have lived happily ever after like Cinderella. But I wondered. I thought about fairy tales, how the story always ends with the wedding and the fancy dress ball, and then I understood. Because in real life after the ball is over, you have to clean up, have your fancy dress dry-cleaned and stored in a clothes bag, and go back to your job. Which is not exactly in a castle. So the stories don't really lie, but they're misleading because they leave out the hard parts.

It's a mistake to concentrate on the Cinderella story, I'd think to myself. *Scarlett O'Hara went from riches to rags instead of the other way around, but she cleaned up when the party was over.* And the most important thing to remember about Scarlett is her final statement: *After all, tomorrow's another day.* In other words, she never gave up on her story.

THE SADNESS OF RHUBARB

Mainly I remember the rhubarb, stringy and sour, stewed but bitter because she couldn't afford sugar. Nothing else would grow in the backyard garden that stopped abruptly at the fence. If you climbed over that fence, you'd fall straight down a precipice—a vertical sheet of solidified coal slag, ebony black and diamond hard. She'd pull up the rhubarb, look over the fence, and walk back to the house with her arms full.

Rhubarb keeps you regular, she'd say. My dad always laughed, but I couldn't swallow the stuff. "She" was my dad's mother, my other grandmother. The one I called "Groossma" because she was Pennsylvania Dutch and that's how they say grandmother.

To me she was an enigma, a formidable figure always dressed in black, long hair pulled back severely and twisted into a knot.

Except for her wedding ring (a plain gold band), her only personal decoration was the rococo-looking hairpin she stuck in the knot of her hair. It was at least six inches long, black like her dress, and studded with multicolored stones.

I liked to imagine the hairpin was a priceless treasure, part of the Romanov crown jewels. And she herself was royalty, a refugee who fled for her life from Tsarist persecution. I knew deep down, of course, that the hairpin wasn't valuable, and she wasn't a refugee from Tsarist oppression, much less royal. But I didn't ask anyone because I loved making up stories and letting them come alive for me.

Years later I pieced together Groossma's real story, and I realized that, like Muti, her life was not easy. When Groosma was a child, her mother disappeared without a word. Left unprotected with a tyrannical father and a no-good brother, she eloped with Mick Magee, and they moved to Pittsburgh.

Then the unthinkable happened. Pregnant with my father Raymond, she got the news that her husband Mick had been killed on his job at the rail yard—squashed like a bug between two train cars. *It was an accident, an honest mistake*, Groossma's brother Jasper Junior said. Jasper Junior worked for the railroad, and he convinced her to waive liability.

She got two dollars.

Jasper Junior got a promotion.

She managed to keep her house by taking in laundry, boiling clothes and sheets and towels in huge iron tubs set on the dirt floor of the cellar. First she'd start wood fires underneath the tubs, then stir the steaming laundry with big wooden paddles.

I remember that cellar with the dirt floor. I remember the dampness, the smell of dirt. I can still picture those huge tubs for boiling the clothes, the long metal washboards for scrubbing out stains, the hand-crank wringer for squeezing out wash water. Clotheslines crisscrossed the entire space, and at one end were the "ironing boards"—wide planks laid across sawhorses—with flatirons that she heated on a potbellied wood stove.

Thinking back on all this I try to imagine how awful it must have been, working in that cellar. Cold in the winter, hot in the summer. Damp and smoky all the time. She survived it somehow, but life eventually took its toll on Groossma. By the time I knew her she'd retreated into her own head, into a quiet distant land where she could hum to her parakeet and tend the African violets that lived in pots upstairs in *The Sitting Room* where I was never allowed to go.

It's funny the way memory works, isn't it? We forget some things and remember others. When I think of Groossma I seldom recall the African violets or the parakeet. But to this day, stewed rhubarb makes me gag.

LIFE ACCORDING TO NANCY DREW

The road to my friend Patty's house was the steepest of all. Walking down, you slanted yourself backward so you wouldn't fall forward, on your face. Walking up, you bent forward and stayed on the balls of your feet so you wouldn't fall backward, on your butt. Patty's family lived at the very bottom of the road, in the foundation of their house.

It looked like those pictures you see of World War I bunkers, just a concrete-block box, long and low, a few feet above the ground and flat on top with tar paper spread over it. There were two skinny scrinched-up windows on the front, one on each side, and the only door was in the back. To get in, you walked down a narrow pathway made of cinders and knocked on their door.

There were woods in the back and lots more cinders in a flat place where Patty's dad kept old cars and trucks that he was *detailing*. Her father was building their house when he got time off from his job as an auto mechanic. So far all they could afford was the cellar, so that's where they lived.

My mom felt sorry for them because they didn't have a nice house like we had, and Patty was embarrassed about living in a foundation. Instead of walls they had partitions and a concrete floor that sloped toward a big drain in the middle, which was where they put their sofa and chairs. But none of that mattered to me because I loved being there. They had a complete set of Nancy Drew mysteries and all the Oz books. Patty and I played duets on their enormous gargoyle-carved upright piano, and her mother cooked beautiful exotic things. At my house we had fried baloney, boiled pork, endless sauerkraut. But at Patty's house they had pilafs, croquettes, croissants.

Ruth Winston thinks she's better than everybody else, my mom said.

Her brother's a big shot politician in Lancaster, my dad said.

She should have stayed in Lancaster and not married a garage mechanic, my mom answered.

Then suddenly Patty's mother was gone.

Ruth Winston's in the hospital with a nervous breakdown, people whispered.

Patty's mother was in the hospital a long time. She came back with black circles around her eyes like a raccoon.

Ruth Winston went god-crazy, my mom said.

I knew my mom was right about the god-crazy bit. Patty's mom was always at Mt. Hope Tabernacle Church at the top of their road, at Bible study or choir practice or a mission drive. I liked to go there with Patty for Sunday service because I liked to sing and because the songs at their church were all about stories and adventure.

"Onward Christian Soldiers" sounded like valiant knights going off to the Crusades, and "The Church in the Wildwood" made me think about Hansel and Gretel lost in the woods, but instead of finding a witch in a gingerbread house, they find a little brown church where they're safe until their father comes and rescues them.

To this day I remember that my favorite song of all was "Love Lifted Me", and it went like this:

> *I was sinking deep in sin,*
> *Far from the misty shore,*

I pictured quicksand, which I had read about in the Nancy Drew book where Nancy's tomboy friend George ignored WARNING signs and got herself trapped. (*That quicksand's just like black ice,* I would think to myself.)

> *Very deeply stained within,*
> *Sinking to rise no more;*

I pictured Nancy's friend George stuck in the quicksand, sinking slowly but hollering for help like crazy, furious at herself for being so stupid when she should have watched where she was walking! (*George was lucky,* I'd think to myself. *I couldn't holler while I was sinking in the lake under black ice, plus I was freezing cold.*)

> *Then the Master of my Fate*
> *Heard my despairing cry;*

I pictured Nancy's always-dependable father, running with Nancy to the edge of the bog and throwing George a rope; then the two of them slowly pulling George out of the treacherous sucking sand. (*I wish Mr. Drew had pulled me out of the lake instead of those stupid boys,* I would think to myself.)

From the waters lifted me,
Then saved was I!

I pictured the exhausted George, a sandy mess but getting hugs all around, then cookies and cocoa for everyone back at Nancy's beautiful house. (*I didn't get hugs or cocoa,* I'd think to myself disgustedly, *just a scolding from Muti.*)

Patty's mother recovered from her nervous breakdown, and Patty's father got their house built. He even bought a suit and became a deacon in the church. *Too little, too late,* said my mom, raising her eyebrows and doing that *tsk tsk tsk* thing with her tongue. I guess my mom was right, though, because before long Patty's mom ran off with a Doctor of Theology.

Later we heard that Patty's mom and the Doctor of Theology were living in Florida when a hurricane blew their whole town away and sank it in the ocean. *Wow,* I thought. *That quicksand will get you if you're not careful.*

It was around that time when I was beginning to understand metaphor.

FUN WITH THE SUNDAY FUNNIES

My cousin Wally and I were the family misfits. We were smart and fat, but fat was what everybody noticed.

Fat people know they have to stick together. Wally and I loved plots and intrigues, so we were natural co-conspirators. At my house I'd have a secret stash of fig newtons snitched from the cookie jar in our game room. At his house he'd have a secret stash of milk duds that he'd get from his friend whose father owned a market near their house. Whenever our parents visited at each other's houses, we'd say *no thanks* to offers of fresh fruit snacks. Then we'd go hide out with his stash or mine.

In between visits Wally and I would memorize the comic strip sections of the Sunday papers: mine from the *Pittsburgh Press* and his from the *Post-Gazette*. Back then "the Sunday funnies," as they were called, were a big deal. That's where, in full color, you could keep up with the adventures of your favorite characters: Dick Tracy, Little Orphan Annie, Superman, Flash Gordon, Prince Valiant.

There were other popular characters in the Sunday strips too, like Archie & Friends and the Katzenjammer Kids. But stories about home and school were too tame for Wally and me. We much preferred stories of high adventure. In our imaginations we'd be Dick Tracy and Tess Trueheart, sending secrets back and forth on two-way wrist radios while we unearthed deadly plots and saved imperiled citizenry from horrible villains like Prunehead or Little Face Finney.

Or we'd be Superman and Lois Lane, flying through the sky on the track of dastardly criminals. Well, actually, Superman would be flying, and Lois would be hanging on for dear life. Which is why I always wanted to be Superman, not Lois.

My favorite comic strip was Flash Gordon because Flash hung out with the gorgeous and super-smart Dale Arden while they fought the sinister plots of the abominably insane Dr. Zarkov. Wally's favorite comic strip was Prince Valiant, which was fine with me too because I could be Lady Aleta if I was feeling glamorous, or I could be any number of other exotic characters like Merlin or Gawaine or Morgan le Fay if I was feeling adventurous.

And the great thing about Wally was, he didn't care if we switched identities when we playacted one of those superhero-plus-adoring-female duos. If I wanted to be Dick Tracy for a change, he'd be Tess. And if I wanted to be Superman, he'd be Lois Lane.

I guess you could say, in that regard, Wally was way ahead of his time.

I should have known that real life wasn't likely to live up to those adventures in the Sunday funnies. Later, whenever I'd hear about Wally, though, I'd think he came close. I knew, for example, that he went to Yale and won all kinds of grants and fellowships. In the summer he was always in Europe, reading obscure archives in dead languages and working on his dissertation about Saint Julian.

Through the years I often pictured Wally in some ancient medieval ruin, maybe like the monastery in *The Name of the Rose*. In my imagination Wally would be wearing a hooded monk's robe, looking gaunt and glamorous like Sean Connery, working all night by candlelight in the tower library where only the ecclesiastical *cognoscenti* were allowed to go.

I knew, of course, that even in my wildest imaginings Wally wouldn't look like the handsome and mysterious William of Baskerville, Sean Connery's character in the movie. If we have to be precise about it, Wally would look more like the fat assistant librarian Brother Berengar who was always sweating, huffing and puffing up and down stairs while his monk's hood kept slipping off his sweaty bald head.

But that's not the point. The point is that Wally was doing the adventurous thing, the romantic thing, the thing we imagined ourselves doing when we hid out with the Sunday funnies.

After Yale, Wally got an important job as curator of a rare book library at Berkeley, and he kept on plugging away at his dissertation, always "on the brink" of a truly original discovery about Saint Julian. *Mags*, he told me once on the phone, *it's all about historicity, about the historical record. Discovering whether Saint Julian was a real historical figure or just a legend is as important as finding out whether King Arthur was a real person or a fiction. If I can do this, I'll be famous!*

Some people might have taken shortcuts, jumped the gun and made a preliminary announcement about being "on the trail" of Saint Julian. But not Wally. He's always been a true scholar, insisting on absolute accuracy. If there was just one more obscure source that needed to be checked and verified, Wally would do it, even if it meant traveling to an out-of-the-way collapsed catacomb, huffing and puffing and sweating bullets while he tunneled in.

We talked once a year or so, and it seemed to me that the longer he worked, the farther he had to go. He didn't get discouraged, though, and we always joked that when he finally finished his doctoral thesis it would be the biggest, fattest dissertation ever written.

Well, that would be appropriate, he'd laugh.

MAY AND DECEMBER

Her name really was "May." It was spelled just like that, too, with a "y" on the end instead of an "e." May Louisa Gottschalk was known to everybody as "Maisie." His name was not "December," of course. That's just what everybody called them—May and December—because he was fifty years older than she was. Maisie, still a teenager, was Groossma's stepmother.

I know, I know. I couldn't believe it either, at first. But here's what happened: Groossma's tyrannical father, Jasper Senior, found himself a young woman with a great body. In the old photos Maisie is tall and lithe, wearing slinky clothes and high-heeled shoes, always with her arm tucked snugly in his or around his shoulders. She had beautiful hair, too, sort of blondish and wavy, and she had a real flair for scarves and jewelry—big rings and long dangly necklaces.

The only problem was her face. Her upper lip looked like someone had run a sewing machine over it, back and forth, back and forth. *The doctor who operated on Maisie's harelip was a quack,* my mom said. *He messed up her face, and now it's too late to fix it.*

Maisie and Jasper Senior went through his money in three years, and then Maisie left him. She blindsided him, actually, but no one else was surprised. Especially my mom. *There's no fool like an old fool,* she'd say, shaking her head and raising her eyebrows.

I always wondered what it would be like to have a stepmother lots of years younger than you. I knew better than to ask Groossma what she thought about it, though. Later, Maisie met Stella, and they moved in together. *Birds of a feather,* said my mom. *They should be ashamed,* said Muti. Groossma never commented, but her silence on the subject said volumes.

The thing is, even though everyone had opinions about Maisie, nobody seemed surprised. Not when she married Jasper Senior, and not after that, when she moved in with Stella. And that started me thinking about their stories, trying to fit them with the story patterns that I already knew.

Maisie and Jasper Senior, I'd think. Then *Maisie and Stella.* They sure weren't like Cinderella and Prince Charming, or Scarlett O'Hara and Rhett Butler, or Samson and Delilah, or Dick Tracy and Tess Trueheart. They didn't fit into fairy tales or movies or Bible stories, or for sure not in the Sunday funnies. They didn't even fit in my dad's favorite adventure books by Edgar Rice Burroughs, which by then I loved as much as he did—

Tarzan and Jane in the jungle? Nope.

John Carter and Dejah Thoris on Mars? Nope.

David Innes and Dian the Beautiful in Pellucidar? Don't be silly.

Okay, I asked myself, what's going on here? What am I missing? And that's when I realized I was focusing on details and missing the big picture.

Oh my gosh, I said to myself, Maisie and Jasper Senior might not *look* like Scarlett O'Hara and Rhett Butler, but their stories are the same. It's all about two people being attracted to each other. It's the story of the Romantic Couple.

Think about it. Rhett was dashingly handsome, and Scarlett was enticingly beautiful. What difference does it make that Jasper Senior was a geezer (with pots of money), and Maisie had a ruined face (but a fabulous body)? It's still the same story as Rhett and Scarlett except, in the end, Maisie dumped Jasper instead of vice versa. And Maisie and Stella? Nobody could mistake them for David Innes and Dian the Beautiful, but their stories are *really* the same because Maisie and Stella are living happily ever after, just like David and Dian.

Mags, I said to myself, you need to remember this.

My dad never said anything bad about Maisie. I think he admired her for living as she pleased, for making no excuses.

And I thought she was funny, always cracking jokes in that "buzzy" kind of cleft-palate voice.

She'd say things like *Honey, the way to get ahead in life is to always be sincere. Take it from me, ya gotta be sincere, even if ya have to fake it.* Then she'd smile and wait for you to figure out the joke, and by the time you did, she'd be started on another one.

Dad and I would stop by to see Maisie and Stella once in a while, when we were on our way to Kennywood Park. *Groossma won't know,* he'd say, winking at me conspiratorially because he knew I'd keep our secret.

Maisie and Stella always seemed happy, glad to see us— hugging us, laughing, telling funny stories. Doing their *schtick,* as Maisie would say.

Buzzing at Dad and me, buzzing at each other.

AUNT SASA

When my dad and Uncle Walter played golf at the country club, they'd take Wally and me with them because Aunt Cissy insisted they take us. She was always nagging at the two of us to lose weight and "walk off some of those pounds." The thing is, Aunt Cissy was tall and skinny like Olive Oyl, so she didn't understand how anyone could be fat. She also didn't understand that Wally and I always jinxed her plan.

Dad and Uncle Walter didn't like us hanging around when they were focusing on their swings and putts and things. They'd give us money to buy slurpees and candy at the clubhouse, and then we'd go over the hill behind the golf course to Aunt Sasa's house. We had to fib about where we went, of course, because we weren't allowed to visit Aunt Sasa.

That old gypsy woman's crazy, Uncle Walter would say. And Aunt Cissy would chime in with warnings about how somebody's sister told somebody's mother who told *her* that the gypsy woman boils cats. *My parents are ridiculous*, Wally would say. *They subscribe to common prejudices about the Rom, stories about sorcery and witchcraft that are wholly unfounded.*

So Aunt Sasa's a "Rom"? I asked. *Is that the same as a gypsy?*

Not exactly, Wally said. *"Gypsy" is the colloquial term for an enormous group of people with a shared racial, cultural, and linguistic heritage. The Rom, a sub-group, came to this country from Serbia, Russia, and Austria-Hungary in order to escape persecution.*

Naturally I wanted to know why the Rom were persecuted, and Wally was glad to explain it all to me at length, how they were nomads and artisans with colorful languages and costumes and traditions.

Finally he said, *There's nothing diabolical about them. They're different, that's all, and that's why uninformed people are afraid of them.*

Wally was interested in Aunt Sasa because of the way she talked. *Her people are from Vojvodina in Serbia*, Wally told me. *Aunt Sasa's the only one left, so she has no one else to talk to in her native language, which is Schtokavian—the prestige dialect of Serbo-Croatian. She's teaching me her language so it won't be lost.*

I loved it when Wally talked like a history book because then I didn't have to go hunt up the book and read it myself. Plus it wasn't Aunt Sasa's family history that interested me the most. I was fascinated by her jewelry and scarves and tambourines, and I loved her little house that looked like a Conestoga wagon would look if you built it out of wood about three times as big and took off the wheels.

Most of all I loved the old smoky mirror that hung inside on the big wall, between a pair of crossed sabers with gold tassels and a gorgeous antique satin quilt—big black and white checks with a heavy red fringe all around it. It was always a little smoky inside her house because of the wood-burning parlor stove in one corner, but that's not what I mean when I say the mirror was "smoky." It wasn't dirty, that is, and you couldn't clean the smokiness off it. It was more like the mirror had smoke *inside* it, smoke you could see, curling and drifting, when you looked into it.

Aunt Sasa was mysterious about her mirror. *If you're born strong with the Sight, you can see into the mirror,* she'd say. And sure enough, when I looked into it I saw cloudy shapes floating, but slowly, the way spider webs float and flutter if they aren't attached to anything.

Mags, you're imagining things, Wally said when I told him what I saw, but I figured he was jealous because the only thing he saw when he looked into the mirror was his own face, looking back at him. Besides, Aunt Sasa believed me. Sometimes she'd peer into the mirror with me, saying *Look there! What colors do you see? What's that in the corner?*—helping me distinguish one shape from another.

Wally said he was going to write a book about Aunt Sasa and make her famous. *Her real name is Sasastré Zupančič of the Romany Nation, and her Tribe are The Kur. She's royalty among her people,* is what Wally said.

I already knew that Wally wasn't good about finishing things he started, so I didn't hold out much hope for the book about Aunt Sasa. Anyway, since I was planning to be The Famous

Writer In The Family, I figured I'd write the book myself, and I knew Aunt Sasa's mirror would be important in the story.

I'd been going to Bible class with my friend Patty at Mt. Hope Tabernacle in Penn Hills, and I loved the passage we'd just memorized out of Corinthians, the one about seeing now *through a glass darkly, but then face to face.*

That's it! I thought to myself. *A glass darkly. That's Aunt Sasa's mirror. When I write the book about Aunt Sasa the title will be something about a looking glass or a mirror, something like "Through a Glass Darkly" or "A Mirror Darkly."*

Then I got stuck, trying to figure how I'd write Aunt Sasa into a mirror story. The only two mirror stories I knew were "Snow White," where the Wicked Queen turns homicidal when the mirror tells her she's not beautiful any more, and the "Wonderland" stories where Alice goes through the parlor mirror and has weird adventures. But Snow White and Alice weren't the least bit similar to Aunt Sasa, and I certainly didn't want to make her a Wicked Queen. Plus neither story seemed to fit Corinthians very well, and I couldn't talk to Wally about any of this because he'd say I was stealing his book about Aunt Sasa.

Okay, I said to myself, *I bet there are some good mirror stories out there, so I'll just keep my eyes and ears open. And when an Aunt-Sasa type of mirror story comes along, I'll tuck it away for future reference.*

THE TURNING POINT

It was summertime, just after the Fourth of July. I was on our front porch with Mom and Muti, looking up at the sky and waiting.

I remember being excited when I saw it, first just a dot in the sky, then getting bigger and bigger as I watched. Then it was so close I could see the red-and-white writing on the side. The plane dipped down over our house, and he waved to us out of the window. It was his first solo flight, and he was proud. We waved back and watched the plane rise up, heading away from us.

I didn't hear the crash.

I remember Mom putting her hands to her face, though. *It's Ray!* she hollered, and she started to cry. Then Muti told me to go inside.

The single-engine plane had gone down in the woods at the bottom end of our street, right by the lake where I fell through black ice. The newspaper story said a wing of the plane caught on a tree as the pilot was attempting to gain altitude.

He was lucky, everyone said.

It was just his leg. It could have been worse, they all agreed.

I guess they were right, that it could have been worse. But that's when everything changed. That's when things went away. Like piano lessons and dance recitals, parties downstairs in the game room, patent leather shoes and velvet coats with fur collars. My mother quit all her card clubs and became a waitress, working nights. *I can make better tips if I work dinners,* she explained.

He came home, finally. To a hospital bed in the living room. To Muti, in a smoldering rage because of her new role as nurse and bedpan-emptier. To the news that his company, Ringsdorff Carbon, had had to let him go.

Dad and I talked then, sometimes.

It wasn't my fault, he said. *They say I was flying too low, but I wasn't. The altimeter was wrong. It showed that I was twenty feet above that tree.*

Telling me, my dad replayed it, over and over. *They always blame me,* he said. *The plane crash wasn't my fault. I always get blamed for everything.*

We talked about other things, too. Like the time he and his friend Danny were racing on Danny's sled, down the steep icy street in front of Danny's house, when an out-of-control car came sliding toward them and ran Danny over. *They blamed me for that,* my dad said, *but it wasn't my fault. I jumped off the sled in time, but Danny didn't.*

Or like the time he took Big Tony and Sonny hunting and Sonny got shot in the foot. *They blamed me for that,* my dad said, *but it was Sonny's fault. I told Tony not to trust Sonny with a shotgun, but Tony wouldn't listen. And then Sonny shot himself.*

Or like the time he borrowed Uncle Walter's brand new car and crashed it into a ditch. *They blamed me for that,* my dad said, *but it was the road crew's fault. They should have put barriers around that ditch before they knocked off work for the day.*

One time after we talked, I walked down to the bottom of our street and into the woods where he crashed. The trees were sparse, not dense. And they didn't look very tall, not at all like craggy giants ready to snag errant aircraft on their towering spires. It was then that I began to think seriously about the stories we tell ourselves.

Stories about Fate and Chance and Luck. And Responsibility.

MY APPLE TREE

It was my favorite tree, the biggest thickest one in our yard, and Muti liked it too because it grew the best apples for making vinegar. She and I would pick the apples in the fall, whole bushel baskets full, once the weather was cold but before the first snowfall. Sometimes I'd help make the vinegar too, but I mainly helped just in the early stages because I liked mashing the apples and straining the juice with our big old wooden press that came from Germany.

After we mashed the apples, we'd make applesauce with the pulp, cooking it with lots of sugar and cinnamon, and then she'd keep some of the juice for cider. After that she'd spend weeks doing the rest of the vinegar-making—stirring, filtering, tasting, and then storing the finished product in big jars downstairs in the cellar.

Muti never made apple pie, just vinegar pie which I didn't like. But when we got tired of mashing apples, we'd keep some of them to make apple dumplings. Apple dumplings are easy. You just peel and core the apples, set each one on a big square of homemade pie dough, pour on lots of sugar and cinnamon before you close up the pie dough squares around the apples, top each one with a pat of real butter, and bake them.

When the apple dumplings were baking, that's when our house smelled like heaven. I remember wishing it smelled like that all the time, but it didn't. Most of the time our house smelled like vinegar, just like most of the time the Italians' houses smelled like garlic.

Dad didn't like my apple tree because it grew too many apples. They fell off and rotted on the ground, and then we had to throw them into the woods behind our house.

But I didn't mind. That tree was my special place. Good for climbing. Good for sitting on a branch and hiding, high up, pretending I was Fritzie in the Swiss Family Robinson, taking my turn as lookout, protecting the family from vagabonds and pirates.

I went to my tree when they told me we were moving to Florida.

Dad's leg hurts when the weather's cold, my mother said. *You'll like it in Florida. You'll make lots of new friends. You can take piano lessons again, and we'll go to the beach!*

I thought I could see everywhere from the high branch up in my tree, but I couldn't see Florida.

I didn't think apple trees grew there.

DAYTONA BEACH

I dwell in Possibility—
A fairer house than Prose—
More numerous of Windows
Superior—for Doors—

Emily Dickinson

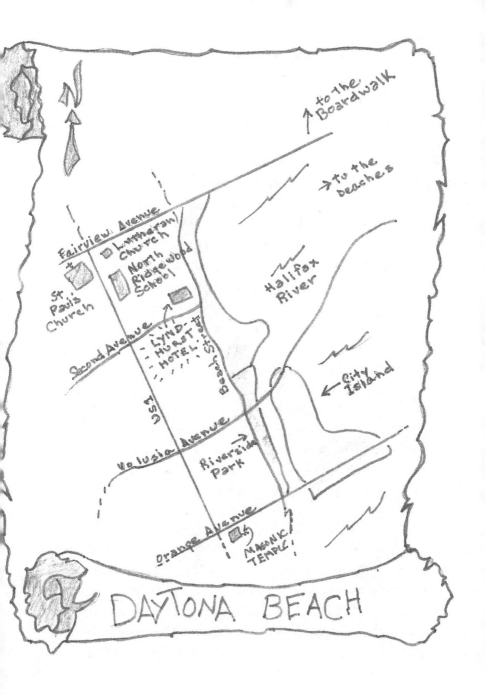

to the
Boardwalk

→ to the
beaches

Fairview Avenue

Lutheran
Church

North
Ridgewood
School

St.
Paul's
Church

Halifax
River

Second Avenue

LYND-
HURST
HOTEL

Beach St.

City
Island

USI

Volusia Avenue

Riverside
Park

Orange Avenue

MASONIC
TEMPLE

DAYTONA BEACH

WELCOME TO PARADISE

As a business venture it was crazy. A Yankee with a bad leg and a dream falls in love with Florida, buys an old wooden three-story hotel with a tin roof, and moves his wife, daughter, and mother-in-law to a world they can't comprehend.

Our first sight of Daytona Beach was the tiny airport. It had two runways and a few board-and-batten buildings that resembled leftover World War II barracks. There was no air conditioning, of course. That would come decades later with Florida's elevation to a climate-controlled tourist magnet.

My dad picked us up at the airport in an old beat-up Pontiac. I was hoping he'd borrowed it, but no such luck. That car belonged to us. It would be our sole means of transportation for the next four years.

During the ride to our new home, Muti was uncharacteristically quiet, maybe because she was so hot and sweaty in her long-sleeved dress and cardigan sweater and stockings and hat. Mom had told her to dress lighter, that it would be warmer in Florida than she was used to, but she'd worn her Pittsburgh clothes anyway.

Soon we got a glimpse of our future—the Lyndhurst Hotel, part boarding house, part halfway house. A few regulars lived there year-round, transients rented weekly, snowbirds rented occasionally, and, as we would soon find out, not enough people rented anytime.

Without trees for shade, the blazing sunshine blinded us. *That's why they call Florida THE SUNSHINE STATE!* my dad exulted.

Looking like flesh-eating plants from a *Flash Gordon* comic strip, two six-foot-tall Spanish Bayonet plants flanked the hotel's wide wooden front porch. *Those spiky plants greeted PONCE DE LEON when his Conquistadores discovered Florida!* my dad crowed in delight.

Walking around the side of the hotel, we saw sandspurs and patches of dead grass that looked like dried-up scabs on the sand. *That sand is pristine, just like the sand on THE WORLD'S MOST FAMOUS BEACH!* my dad cheered.

In back of the hotel there was a low place that stayed filled up with water and tree frogs that croaked all day and all night. Especially all night. *They won't hurt you, FROGS JUST LOVE TO SING!* my dad chirped.

Inside was no better. Looking around, we saw mildewed wallpaper and faded paint, exposed pipes, rusty window screens with rips where mosquitoes would come in. And right away, we saw cockroaches. *They're "palmetto bugs" from the palm trees,* my dad laughed. *They're survivors! THEY WERE HERE BEFORE THE DINOSAURS!*

I'd never seen a dinosaur, but I'd never seen bugs as big or disgusting as those cockroaches, either. Not only did they look bad. They smelled bad, too, and they could fly. And when they flew, they buzzed.

Mom stayed quiet, but not Muti. She hated it, and she told me she hated my dad, too.

This is a godforsaken hellhole that your father has brought us to, she said.

BARBARA OUT BACK

Barbara Out Back was my first Florida friend. She and her mother and her little sister Vickie lived in one of those tiny Airstream trailers called a Silver Bullet. Their trailer park was out back of the hotel and around a corner on First Avenue, sort of tucked away where you didn't see it unless you looked for it.

We would see them out walking lots of times, coming down a path by the side of the hotel on their way to Riverfront Park and back. Barbara's mom would be pushing Vickie in a stroller, and Barbara would have Dam Dog Leo on a leash. Leo was a nice friendly dog, a beautiful Dalmatian, but they called him Dam Dog Leo because they didn't want him. They had to keep him, though, because he belonged to Barbara's stepdad who was off making a fortune in South America.

Muti took a dislike to Barbara's mom right away because she didn't wear many clothes. I tried to tell her that it didn't make sense in Florida to wear lots of clothes, but Muti wouldn't listen to reason. *That hussy from out back thinks she's hot shit!* she'd say. Or, *There goes the trash from out back!*

Or if Barbara came to get me because we were going to the movies, Muti would call out really loud, *Out Back's waiting for you!* When I said indignantly that my new friend had a name and it was *Barbara*, she started calling her *Barbara Out Back* just to annoy me. Barbara laughed it off, though, and anyway my mom was extra nice to Barbara. I think Mom was glad I'd found a friend right away in Florida.

Barbara was beautiful. Not just pretty, beautiful. Very pale and blonde and petite. And she wasn't stuck-up at all. I thought she looked just like Lana Turner, and that's how we started talking about the famous soda shop story, how Lana Turner skipped school and got "discovered" in a soda shop in

Hollywood and then became a big star. Barbara was already planning that when she was sixteen she'd go to Hollywood and get discovered. *My mom won't need me anymore to take care of Vickie,* she said, *so I'll just get on a bus and go.*

It sounded like a good plan to me. Barbara even had her stage name picked out: *Diana DuPree*, which I agreed sounded glamorous and elegant. The only hitch was, before she could leave for Hollywood her stepdad had to come back to buy them a house and support them so her mom didn't have to work anymore in the buffet line at Morrison's Cafeteria. That worried me a little bit, but Barbara was sure everything would happen the way she planned it.

Barbara and I loved movie stars and movies, and movies were really cheap, just ten cents for a matinee. We'd walk downtown, watch our favorite stars up on the screen—Janet Leigh and Esther Williams and of course Lana Turner—and then talk about them all the way back.

It was different back then because nobody worried that we were out alone, by ourselves. Barbara was so pretty she attracted attention, but if a strange man said something to her, we'd just walk fast away from him. And in the movie theater, if a man tried to grab her hand or talk to her, we got up and moved.

After that summer we had to stop being friends. She was going into seventh grade, and I was going into sixth grade, and that made mountains of difference. In sixth grade at North Ridgewood School we had one teacher all year long, carried lunchboxes, and went outside to the playground for recess. In seventh grade at Mainland Junior High they changed classes, ate lunch in the cafeteria, and went to the gym for "phys ed."

The biggest difference, though, was that sixth graders went home right after school. Seventh graders had clubs and practices after school, and at night they went to dances and jayvee football games. After our summer as newfound friends, Barbara I and lived in two different worlds.

I figured Barbara would be really popular in school because she was so beautiful, and I was right. She got to be a jayvee cheerleader right away and before long she had a boyfriend. Every day I'd see them walking together, going down the path by the hotel.

Then one day there was a new family living in the Silver Bullet. *Good riddance to bad rubbish!* Muti said. But I was glad for Barbara because I was sure her stepdad came back and bought them a house. *I hope they moved somewhere fabulous,* I thought. *I hope they moved to Hollywood so Barbara can get discovered.*

I thought about Barbara every once in a while after she moved away. Occasionally I'd flip through a movie magazine, looking for "Diana Dupree" among the ingénues. Eventually, though, I got busy with my own projects and didn't read movie magazines anymore.

Several years later, home from college for a weekend, I decided to go to a Saturday matinee to see *Gigi*, which was the big romantic hit movie that year. I was just about to buy my ticket at the Daytona Theater downtown when I spotted Barbara walking Dam Dog Leo on a leash. She was with an older woman pushing a stroller, and there were two little kids walking with them.

Wow, I remember thinking, *Barbara's mom sure looks bad. There's no way I would've recognized her!* But Barbara looked great—the same petite figure, the same blonde hair. I started to call *Barbara Out Back!* to see if she'd turn around and recognize me.

Then I held back. The petite blonde was trying to control one of the kids who was screaming bloody murder, and when she turned around, I saw that she wasn't Barbara after all. When the older woman turned around also, trying to grab the screaming kid without dropping the cigarette that was stuck in her mouth, I realized that *she* looked like Barbara. Sort of.

But the older woman couldn't be Barbara, could she? She was pudgy and drab, not petite, not blonde. Certainly not beautiful. No, she couldn't be Barbara. I was so glad I hadn't called *Barbara Out Back!* to a stranger. There's nothing more embarrassing than going up to someone and saying "Hi, do you remember me?" and then feeling like an idiot because it was clearly a case of mistaken identity.

By that time the two women had changed direction and started walking toward me, and now both kids and the baby in the stroller were screaming. As they went by, I heard the drab pudgy one say to the petite blonde, *For God's sake, Vickie, stop daydreaming and help me with these damn kids!* As they passed by the Dalmatian looked at me with his big soulful eyes, as if to say *Don't worry, I'll take care of them.*

Hi, Leo, I said under my breath.

Then I decided I wasn't in the mood, after all, for a romantic movie.

HALLOWEEN WITH THE HOUYHNHNMS

Up North, Halloween was the best of all holidays. By then the weather was frosty, not snowing, yet so cold you could see your breath when you blew in and out. On Halloween we'd go house to house in our neighborhood, getting home-baked *pizelles* and real hot chocolate with marshmallows floating on top. There'd be candied apples brought out on trays, still warm, covered with chopped walnuts. And popcorn balls, sweet and buttery, wrapped in waxed paper. Everyone knew our names, praised our costumes, and invited us in to get warm before going to the next house.

My first Halloween in Florida was not like that. In Florida it was hot. Really, really hot. We didn't know anyone, and anyway you can't trick or treat in a hotel. *There's a Halloween party across the street at the YMCA,* my mom said. *Why don't you go to the party and have fun?*

So there I sat, high up on bleachers in a cavernous gymnasium, watching kids throw darts at balloons and play ring toss, listening to people laughing and screaming in the Haunted House. I was embarrassed to enter the costume contest because mine was a pathetic last-minute throw-together, just something to get me free admission to the party. For what seemed like hours I sat on the bleachers alone, wishing someone would look my way, ask me to play a game or go through the Haunted House. Wishing someone would talk to me.

No one did.

It was still hot when I walked back to the hotel. Mom was sitting on the porch with Pauline, one of our regulars who lived there year-round, so I sat down in one of the big wooden rocking chairs.

Did you have fun? my mother asked. *I had a great time,* I lied, *and I even won a prize!*

Then I got up, went in my room, and closed the door, and cried.

You know how an incident in the past will stick in your memory? How you'll have an image, a mental picture so sharp that when you think about it, it seems you've jumped back in time? That it's happening all over again?

That hot Halloween night in Florida is one of those images for me. It's not the party at the YMCA that I see, though. It's Mom and Pauline and me, sitting on the hotel porch, and what I remember is telling a lie about the great time I had at the Halloween party. The thing about that lie is this: it wasn't mean or petty. It was a good lie. If I'd told the truth and let my mom know how unhappy I was, she would have felt worse than she already did about moving to Florida.

The other thing about that lie is, I had to protect myself because Pauline was there and because she loved saying hurtful things. Especially about being fat. Pauline was like Aunt Cissy, as tall and skinny as Olive Oyl. *I tell it like it is,* Pauline would say, and *I call a spade, a spade.* Well, sometimes that's a good policy, but other times it's not.

We'd just finished reading *Gulliver's Travels* in school, the fourth section about Gulliver in the land of the talking horses, the Houyhnhnms. (That's what the talking horses are called, and it's pronounced HWIN-ums, which is genius because it sounds like the voice a horse would have if it could talk. All breath-y and whoosh-y and whinnying.)

Anyway, the Houyhnhnms are supremely rational beings. They live according to *Reason,* and they're so noble they won't tell a lie. Not ever. Their language doesn't even have a word for lying and so they can't understand why anyone would want to say "the thing which is *not.*"

All of this makes the Houyhnhnms sound very noble. But the Houyhnhnms aren't noble. They're dense, just like Pauline. Because it's not about telling the truth or lying. It's about making yourself feel righteous even if you hurt someone else in the process. Understanding the Houyhnhnms helped me understand Pauline. So that night, before Pauline had time to work up an insult about my fat self or my pathetic costume, I told a lie.

In case you don't remember, Gulliver was really happy to leave the land of the Houyhnhnms. I've noticed that, just like Gulliver getting away from the talking horses, people are really happy to get away from Pauline. I wonder if she notices?

THE HOTEL CAT

I called him Ranger because he had a black "Lone Ranger" mask on his face. Otherwise he was all black except for a white chest that went all the way up on his nose and white feet that looked like spats.

I almost named him Tux because of those white markings, not that I'd ever seen a tuxedo for real but because of a book. Our librarian at North Ridgewood School was proud that we had the book called *Old Possum's Cats*, so I'd check it out every chance I got, and that's where I found the Jellicle Cats (they're black and white) and Bustopher Jones (a tuxedo cat with white spats). I named our hotel cat Ranger, though, because of the black Lone Ranger mask.

Because I only saw him from the back at first and noticed his nub tail, I thought *Oh my gosh, how did Boots get to Florida?* But he wasn't Boots, of course, and, since I didn't know much about cats, I thought maybe Ranger's tail got cut off "on accident" like Boots in Pittsburgh. But then one of our snowbird guests at the hotel saw Ranger and told me he's a Manx. *Manx cats don't have tails*, she said, *and they're rare, especially tuxedo*

Manx like this one. Then she told me the Biblical story of how the Manx cat lost his tail.

As the story goes, it was already raining like crazy when Noah had to slam the door of the Ark and *accidentally* cut off the tails of the two Manx cats who'd almost been left behind. One of the almost-left-behind-cats was farther through the doorway than the other one was when Noah had to slam the door, however. And that's why some Manx cats have only a small nub of a tail while others are entirely tailless.

Well, I was skeptical about the Noah story, but I was curious as to why a supposedly rare cat like this one would hang around our fleabag hotel. I mean, if you were a smart rare cat, wouldn't you choose a better hotel where you'd get great handouts and snacks? I mean, I get it that you wouldn't pick a hotel on the beach where you'd get sand in your fur, but why not an elegant old place like the Troy Hotel on Volusia Avenue downtown? I was really curious about this, so I decided to study our Lyndhurst cat.

Every time I'd see him near the hotel I'd do my invisible-against-the-wall trick and watch where he was going. Which is how I learned where he sleeps at night—under our rickety three-story fire escape out back. In the daytime he mainly slept on the hotel's front porch, but sometimes he'd bestir himself to check out the trailer park where my friend Barbara lived or the YMCA across the street.

Once in a while, though, he'd disappear like *zip* and be gone for hours. I was hugely curious, of course, so that's when I put on my Nancy Drew hat and made a plan. But I had to be secretive about my plan and that wasn't easy. Our maid Dorothy had quit on Christmas Eve, and we couldn't afford to hire a replacement (actually Dorothy *died* on Christmas Eve, but that's another story), so we had to take over the work in the hotel. Mom was quiet about it, as usual, but Muti drove me crazy, nagging at me all the time to help with laundry and cleaning.

Anyway, it was almost three months later, in March, before I could put my "plan" into action. I'd been observing Ranger's comings and goings so I knew, if he was going to roam far from the hotel, it would be on a Monday.

Sure enough, one Monday morning on my way to school I followed him on my bike and saw him run into the "tunnel" that lay underneath North Ridgewood Avenue between North Ridgewood School and St. Paul's Catholic Church (the tunnel was a scary place, not at all safe like an airy overpass, and the City closed it a few years later).

I couldn't *wait* for school to be over that day so I could assume my Nancy Drew persona and determine whether Ranger had gone in the church after running through the tunnel. I couldn't just walk into St. Paul's like a tourist, though, because I had to look as though I *belonged* there. Cleverly, non-chalantly, I sidled in with a handkerchief bobby-pinned to my hair (female Catholics in those days had to cover their heads) and wandered around. Eventually I found him hunkered down on a side aisle—staring at a statue of St. Patrick.

Except he wasn't staring at St. Patrick at all. Instead he was gazing at a small shrine with a single framed painting on it, flanked by candles. I noticed a brass plaque mounted on the wall above the shrine, and when I moved closer to read the plaque Ranger looked right at me. He didn't move or startle, though, and I could've sworn he was trying to tell me something. Then two people came to light candles to St. Patrick and, faster than I could see, the cat vanished.

Okay, I asked myself, is it creepy that a cat visits a church? Yeah, I answered back, it's pretty creepy, but since I'm here I might as well investigate (I was *loving* Nancy Drew mysteries at that point!). First I read the brass plaque that was mounted on the wall above the shrine:

St. Gertrude of Nivelles
Patron Saint of Cats: Feast Day March 17
Gift of the Krauthammer Family

Then I looked closely at the painting on the shrine, and I couldn't believe what I was seeing: the figure in the painting was a nun, and she was holding a cat. A tuxedo cat.

When I told Muti what happened at the church she turned it around and made it all about her own self, just like she always did. *You should have reminded me about St. Patrick's Day,* she scolded. *I always went to mass on St. Patrick's Day in Pittsburgh, before your father brought us to this shithole town.* I tried to tell her I didn't know it was St. Patrick's Day when I followed Ranger to St. Paul's, but she wouldn't listen. Anyway, she hated cats, and she was glad Ranger never came back.

Our snowbird guest at the hotel felt sorry for me, though, because she knew I missed Ranger. *Dollink,* she said in her New Jersey accent, *at least this way he's always alive in your memory. If he's dead or alive, who knows? Does it matter?* I guessed she was right, that the important thing is for me to remember Ranger.

But her question also started me thinking about that day in the church, especially when Ranger looked at me as though he was trying to tell me something. I mean, what's possible and what's just coincidence? Was it possible that a cat could know about a Saint's Feast Day? Or was it just a coincidence that Ranger visited St. Gertrude's shrine on that particular day? I didn't know.

PLUCK YOUR MAGIC TWANGER

I always had a good relationship with frogs. My friend Patty was squeamish about them, but I wasn't. I liked to watch them jump and swim in the creek near our house in Penn Hills, and sometimes I'd bring one home in a bucket. That's when Muti would have a fit. *They're nasty,* she'd say, and *They make warts on you if you touch them.* Then she'd dump out my bucket when I wasn't looking.

But she didn't get mad if I listened to Froggy the Gremlin on Smilin' Ed's Buster Brown Radio Show on Saturdays. I'd curl up on our pink sofa, sitting as close as I could to the radio that was on the end table, waiting for the program to start. When I heard Smilin' Ed say *Pluck your magic twanger, Froggy!* I'd crack up. Then while Froggy plucked on his twanger, I'd sing along with Smilin' Ed's Gang.

Florida had lots more frogs than Penn Hills. In fact, frog gigging was a local pastime, and it wasn't long before my dad's new friend Max invited him to go on a frogging trip. Max had a little boat he kept on a trailer behind our hotel, and my dad loved going with Max when he took his boat out. They'd hitch the trailer onto Max's beat-up old truck and away they'd go, any time of the day or night. Fishing was in the daytime and so was oystering down at Ponce Inlet. But frog gigging—when you take your boat out in shallow water on the river and spear frogs—happens at night.

The thing is, my dad loved water because when he was a kid in Pittsburgh he roamed wherever he wanted to, and one of his favorite places to roam was the Monongahela River. Just like Huckleberry Finn he built rafts, fished for food and cooked it over a campfire, and he had great water adventures. Mom and Muti, on the other hand, were terrified of water and boats, and I guessed that's why they didn't like seafood. Because they couldn't imagine their food coming from anything but a garden or a farm.

When Max's wife Myrtle would cook up what Max and Dad brought home, neither Mom nor Muti would touch it. Especially frog legs. *Tastes just like chicken,* Max would say, but Muti wouldn't budge. *I'd rather eat fried baloney,* she'd say, and that's what she'd cook while Myrtle cooked frog legs for Max and Dad. I never ate Myrtle's frog legs, either, only because it'd be like munching on Froggy the Gremlin. I mean, just imagine that you're biting into a frog leg and in your head you hear Smilin' Ed say *Pluck your magic twanger, Froggy!* It would bring you to tears.

Besides that, I'd found my own favorite Florida food which I got from Jim Ed Clifton, the redneck who rented our cheapest room out back. Jim Ed always had a stash of MoonPies in the saddlebag on Stormin' Norman, his big green motorcycle, and he was generous about sharing with me. We'd go up on the fire escape and sit there talking, munching on MoonPies and sipping our drinks. (He always drank Jim Beam which he kept in his saddlebag with the MoonPies, and I'd have my Orange Crush.)

Jim Ed, you and MoonPies are saving my life, I'd say to him, and he'd just smile. When I told him about Smilin' Ed and explained that eating frog legs would be like biting into Froggy the Gremlin, Jim Ed broke out in a great big belly buster of a laugh, slapped his leg, and hollered *Fa-a-a-r out!*

Jim Ed didn't eat frog legs either.

ALWAYS CHASING RAINBOWS

My dad's favorite thing about being a Shriner was wearing his fez. It was maroon velvet with a gold tassel and on the front it had an insignia embroidered in gold—two crossed sabers and the words *Order of the Mystic Shrine.* I loved his fez, too. Even then I was a sucker for ceremony and costumes, the mysterious and the exotic.

In Daytona Beach the Masonic Temple was on Orange Avenue, about six blocks from the hotel. My dad loved going there for meetings and card games, so I was glad when he signed me up for the Rainbow Girls. But you couldn't just join. First you had to read *The Rainbow Book* and pass a test. Then you could be initiated and go to secret meetings, and at the meetings you had to wear *an evening gown.*

As high scorer on the rainbow test, I got to be a Signifier. The Seven Signifiers were the colors of the rainbow: Red, Orange, Yellow, Green, Blue, Indigo, and Violet. I got to be Green, so I had to wear a green evening gown. It would be my first evening gown ever, and I couldn't wait to go with my mom to Lerner's on Beach Street to shop for it. I shudder now, remembering, but back then I loved it. My evening gown was lime green, a garishly bright mid-calf-length creation of stiff nylon net over taffeta, disastrously accessorized by yours truly with flat white leather sandals and an unfortunate chiffon stole.

I put my gown on every morning when I got up and every night before I went to bed so I could practice in the mirror being Isadora Duncan, flinging the stole over my shoulder and rakishly angling my head. Appropriately posed, I would then raise my eyes as if looking straight at the assembled dignitaries and practice my Green Signifier recitation. Concluding my Signifier speech, I would imagine the applause of the elec-trified crowd while I improvised a few Isadora-type twirls.

While I was practicing, I got Isadora's biography from the City Island Library for inspiration. The first parts were amazing, all about her life in glamorous places like Paris and London and New York, wearing diaphanous gowns and flowing scarves and one time even dancing naked in front of a waterfall. Isadora didn't get a happy ending, though, because she was riding in a convertible with the top down when her long flowing scarf wrapped around a rear tire and choked her to death.

Uh oh. I looked suspiciously at my chiffon stole, but figured I'd be safe wearing it since I wouldn't be riding in a convertible any time soon. Then I started thinking about the driver of the car Isadora died in and imagining how awful he felt about it. Especially if Isadora was decapitated.

That's when I was inspired to write my first story, all about beautiful people riding in a convertible and having a glamorous glorious time until one of the passengers gets her long chiffon stole caught in a tire and chokes to death before she's decapi-tated. I couldn't figure out how to write the decapitation part, though. I just couldn't picture it, you know? Anyway, it wasn't a very good story.

I didn't exactly electrify the Masonic dignitaries, either.

Mainly I remember marching around the room with the other Signifiers while Exalted Mother Margaret, our Grand Chaperone, played the first white baby grand piano I'd ever seen. There we were, all the Colors of the Rainbow in stiff nylon net and mismatched shoes, circling the room to the strains of Chopin's "Fantaisie-Impromptu in C-Sharp Minor"—the one we always recognize because someone made the popular song "I'm Always Chasing Rainbows" out of the middle part.

I couldn't stay in the Rainbow Girls for very long because the owner of the building evicted the Masonic Temple and made it a Greyhound Bus Station. The next-closest Masonic Temple was in Jacksonville, but my dad couldn't travel there so he didn't get to wear his fez.

Oh, well. It's probably good that it got packed away with my evening gown, since you sure can't wear a fez *or* a lime green evening gown just on a whim.

STICKS AND STONES

You know that old saying, *Sticks and stones can break your bones, but words will never hurt you?* It's a lie. Words cut worse than knives, worse than razor blades.

And not only that—those are the cuts that never heal.

At school Up North I got teased a lot about being fat. Kids said awful things, ugly things, and they'd sing that song "Fatty, Fatty, Two-by-Four" on the playground. I guess now we'd say I was bullied a lot, but back then we just called it teasing.

I hated it but I pretended I didn't care. Because that's all you can do. You pretend not to care, and maybe you can even fool yourself into thinking how you look isn't the most important thing. Especially if you're a girl.

By the time I moved to Florida, though, it was hard to fool myself that looks don't matter. By then there were lots of TV shows with beautiful people in them, and it was the same with movies. That was the era of tiny, wasp-waisted movie stars like Debbie Reynolds and, a little later, Sandra Dee who starred in the *Gidget* movies. Unfortunately for me, my body type didn't jibe one bit with the teeny-tiny teenage ideal. I was already taller than anyone else in my family, and worse than that, my weight matched my height.

It's just baby fat, my mom would say. *You'll grow out of it.*

Mom was always sweet like that, not getting on my case about being fat. But the popular girls at school looked like the movie stars up on the screen, and I didn't look like any of them. I tried to compensate by stuffing my too-fat self into the currently favored teen fashion: gathered skirts and waist-cincher belts. "Stuffed" is probably a good word, though, for the way I looked.

And speaking of stuffing, the shoe style at that time—for tiny girls with tiny feet to match their tiny waists—was soft-sole ballerinas. They didn't even make them in my size, so I stuffed my big feet into a small size and pretended my feet didn't hurt. That was when I developed an appreciation for the ugly stepsisters in the Cinderella story, the ones with big feet. *You know,* I'd think to myself, *somebody needs to give those stepsisters a break instead of making fun of them all the time.* Making friends in Florida was a slow process, partly because I was naturally shy but also because I kept myself aloof, afraid of cruel remarks and insults. So I guess it's no surprise that books were my salvation.

When we moved to the hotel, we put all my dad's books on shelves in the lobby. That's when I discovered *Frankenstein,* which I read over and over. It sounds strange to say that Mary Shelley's monster is a real human being, not a caricature, but it's true. He's smart (he teaches himself to read) and ethical (he understands good and evil) and kind (he saves a poor family from starving to death in wintertime).

All those things happen in the middle of the book where the monster wanders into the woods and watches the family, looking through their windows but not letting them know he's there. He knows how ugly he is, and he knows they'd hate him on sight. So he hides, and listens, and watches, and he tries to imagine what it would be like to love and be loved. Then the old grandfather of the family, a blind man, befriends the monster. The monster lets the old man touch his face, so the blind man realizes the monster is truly hideous. But the grandfather doesn't care because he realizes how extraordinarily smart and good and kind the monster is.

In the end, though, the monster's good qualities don't matter. Once the blind man's sighted son sees the monster, panic takes over, and after that things go downhill like crazy.

Mary Shelley subtitled her novel *The Modern Prometheus*, implying that for her the story was about prideful humanity overreaching itself. But the Frankenstein story always makes me think about the power of words and wonder about writing a story where everyone's blind. How would an entire world full of blind people find ways to make themselves feel superior? Would they use words? They couldn't say *The color of my skin is better than yours* because they couldn't see it. And it'd be hard to make fun of fat people unless everyone went around poking and prodding each other. It would even be hard to judge people because of where they lived or the clothes they wore or the foods they ate.

Maybe they'd have to say things like *Ewww . . . You don't smell good.*

Or *You have an accent when you talk, and I don't like it.*

Or *My sweater feels softer than yours.*

Yes, even if they couldn't say hurtful things about the way other people looked because they couldn't see them, they'd still find ways to judge.

They'd sniff and listen and touch, and then they'd use words to assert their superiority, just like the people in a fully-sighted world. Just like us. *I will never underestimate the power of words,* I vow to myself. *Never.*

NIGHTTIME AT THE BOARDWALK

When my dad scouted Florida, he tried out Miami and Naples and Tampa and Panama City before deciding on Daytona Beach. The reason he could scout around was because Big Tony DiCicco won bookoo bucks on the horses and decided he wanted to buy a hotel in Florida, so my dad tagged along on Tony's trips. Dad never told me exactly why he didn't choose the other places, but I guessed Daytona's beach and the Boardwalk had a lot to do with it.

My mom didn't like a lot of things about Florida, but she did like the Boardwalk. I think it reminded her of the Boardwalk at Atlantic City where they used to go sometimes when they lived Up North. They'd take the bus there, *a whole gang of us,* my dad would say. They'd gamble all night and come back the next day.

In Florida Muti never went to the Boardwalk even one time, but Mom and Dad and I went there a lot. When Mom wanted to stop at a candy booth and buy salt-water taffy like they had at Atlantic City, I knew she was missing things Up North. She'd get quiet and just want to sit on a bench and wait for us while my dad and I played skee ball and rode the bumper cars. Then he and I would walk along the souvenir booths near the Bandshell and stop to watch the artists painting on velvet.

Some of the artists painted horses on velvet, and some of them painted portraits. But we always watched one artist in particular, the one who specialized in beachscapes and seascapes. He'd look out beyond us at the moon and the ocean, then turn back to add yet one more gleaming brushstroke to the black velvet on his easel.

One night when Dad and I were watching *our* artist, I began to sense a connection between painting and poetry. We were studying poetry in school, and I'd written a few poems of my own, but I wasn't excited about them. Not excited, that is, until the night at the Boardwalk when I realized what lay lurking in the artist's painting.

After we got home that night, I wrote a very bad poem about an artist painting on velvet. It was okay that my poem was bad, though, because it taught me about the need for revision. I carried that poem around in my head and whenever I got a chance, I revised it on paper. I'd put in a word, then take it out. I'd take out a line, then put it back in. Then I'd crumple the page, throw it away, and start all over again from scratch.

The thing is, I knew my poem wasn't right.

I also knew that when I got it right, I'd know that too.

So I put it away until I was ready to get it right, and then I forgot about it.

I finally remembered my poem when I was in high school and read Matthew Arnold's "Dover Beach" in Miss Gatch's senior English class. Arnold's poem is solemn and sad, reflecting the spiritual *angst* of the Victorian period he lived in.

But it's beautiful, too, and evocative, and reading it sparked memories in me of being at the Boardwalk with my dad—looking out at the ocean when the artist did, then looking back at the luminescent beachscape as he painted it. There we'd be, Dad and I, watching the artist bring a fairytale setting to life, stroke by stroke.

That's how my dad fell in love with Florida, I realized. *To him, Florida is a silver-on-velvet place, a magical place where dreams can come true. That's why he moved us to Daytona Beach.*

And that's when I finally finished my poem . . . while acknowledging my debt to Matthew Arnold:

> <u>*Painting on Velvet*</u>
> *The sea is calm tonight.*
> *The tide is high, the moon shines full*
> *Upon the water.*
>
> *On the easel all is black,*
> *Soft black,*
> *Inky black.*
>
> *I follow the artist's eye, the artist's brush.*
> *One line, horizontal, limns a horizon*
> *Where sky meets moon-blanched sea.*
>
> *The brush gleams briefly . . .*
> *Tips a wave with streaks of blue and green and*
> *silver, iridescent,*
> *Sends moonlight filtering through feathery palms,*
> *Scatters points of faery light on sand.*
>
> *This beach, this shore . . .*
> *What thoughts, what dreams did they provoke in*
> *early minds?*

What yearnings did they inspire,
This ebb and flow of time and tide that waits for none?

I never showed the poem to my dad because he didn't like poetry, just adventure fiction. But early on, after he had to move back to Pittsburgh to work, I saved my money and bought him one of those paint-on-velvet beachscapes for Christmas. I wanted him to have it with him Up North in his apartment, so he could look at it and remember.

He opened it on Christmas morning at the hotel, and that was the only time I ever saw my father cry.

CRUEL SHOES

Unlike Muti, Mom tried to be happy. She'd always say *I'm no Pollyanna, but things could certainly be worse.* Well, that goody-goody Pollyanna story was never a favorite of mine, but I had to admit it was at least cheerful, not morbid like Muti's favorite stories about the Ice Queen and the Little Match Girl.

Sometimes when we'd be sitting on the hotel porch Mom would tell me stories about how it was during the Depression. One time she wanted to go to a high school dance, but she didn't have any nice shoes to wear. So her dad gave her a government shoe coupon he'd been saving, and she took it downtown to cash it in. She was so excited, she said, when they had her size. But when she got home and opened the box she realized the shoes were clunky brown oxfords, like nurses wear.

She didn't go to that dance, but she made up her mind she'd have nice shoes someday, and I always figured that her obsession with having matching shoes for every outfit was related somehow to those clunky brown oxfords.

What is it about women and shoes? I wondered to myself.

I was really curious, so I talked to the librarian at school, who turned out to be an expert on fairy tales. She knew all about shoe stories, especially the old versions that were so-o-o brutal. All those "red shoes" stories, for example, where the dancer puts on the shoes and has to dance until she dies. And early versions of the Cinderella story, where the stepsisters cut off their toes (in some stories they cut off their heels) to fit in the glass slipper, but they still don't get the Prince because they bleed to death.

Not only that, the Cinderella story goes all the way back to the ninth century in China where having tiny feet was a major priority and where foot-binding was invented. You don't know about foot-binding? The terrible thing about foot-binding was that girls didn't have any choice in the matter. Their mothers or grandmothers or aunts just started doing it to them while the girls were very young, and by the time they were grown up they had crushed feet that would fit in shoes just three inches long!

It's true. Try to picture your foot so curled up and mashed, it'll fit in a shoe that's three inches long. The tiny foot was called a "Lotus," and it was all done to girls in the name of beauty. Ouch.

After reading about all of that, I decided I was done squishing my feet in those stupid little ballerina soft-sole shoes that didn't even come in my size. I couldn't wait, though, for Easter Sunday to arrive so I could get all dressed up in my brand-new outfit from Lerner's and wear my first-ever pair of high heels . . . Uh oh. I know what you're thinking, and you're right.

In principle, there's no difference between squeezing your feet into tiny tight shoes and forcing your feet into tipsy

high-heeled shoes. Tight shoes give you toe-bumps and bun-
ions. (Trust me, I know.) High heels make it impossible for you
to run, *and* they increase the odds that you'll trip and sprain an
ankle. (I know about that, too.)

That's why the phrase "fashion sense" is an oxymoron. If
you strive to meet the dictates of fashion, you have to abandon
common sense. Particularly in regard to shoes, that is, and particularly if you're a woman.

I wasn't thinking this through, of course, back when I was
tottering around in the hotel lobby in my first pair of high
heels, then practicing how to walk up and down stairs without
falling on my butt. No, back then I needed desperately to fit in,
so fitting in—not deciphering the hidden agendas of fashion
and power—was my uppermost concern. As Groossma would
say in her heavy Pennsylvania Dutch accent: *Vee get too soon old,
und too late schmart.*

ROAD TRIPS

When he came to visit Florida, Big Tony always stayed in
his fancy hotel over on the beach instead of our low-rent hotel.
My dad didn't worry about being snubbed, though, because he
loved it when people from Up North came to visit. He'd save
up his vacation days from Ringsdorff so he could be in Florida
when his friends were there.

I remember one time when Ralphie Marbles Junior (Tony's
cousin) drove Big Tony's huge white Cadillac all the way from
Pittsburgh to Daytona Beach, with stopovers at places like
Atlantic City so Tony could gamble. Once Tony arrived at his
own hotel on the beach at Daytona, though, he got busy with
big-stakes poker games and trips to the dog track with his cronies, so Ralphie'd hang out with us.

Ralphie loved Florida's "attractions," so Dad would plan day-trips in our old beat-up Pontiac, and they'd take me along. We'd drive to Silver Springs so we could ride the glass-bottom boats and watch catfish play football with doughballs. Or we'd drive to Marineland to marvel at the porpoise show, then walk on the beach with slurpees. One day we even drove to Weeki Wachee Springs over near the Gulf Coast to see mermaids swim and breathe underwater. (They breathed real air out of hoses, of course, but it was still amazing to see them diving and posing and performing in fishtails.)

Mom never wanted to go with us on one of our trips, but she'd pack up a big lunch so the three of us could stop on the way back and eat at a roadside picnic place. The thing is that back then, fast food eateries were few and far between. Even Howard Johnson's restaurants were hard to find. Remember those? Roadside restaurants with orange tile roofs? And yummy fried clams? And 28 flavors of ice cream???

Well, all good things must come to an end, and day-trips that included me ended abruptly one summer when Big Tony decided he wanted to go to Cuba to gamble. I figured he must have won bigtime at the dog track or poker because he asked my dad to plan a trip to Cuba for the three of them—Dad, Tony, and Ralphie—all expenses paid. What you have to remember here is this was *not* Cuba-after-Castro-and-Communism. Far from it. Instead, this was pre-Castro-Cuba as depicted in *The Godfather, Part II*—a tropical paradise that drew tourists from near and far, especially to Havana with its exotic, erotic night life and high-stakes gambling.

Dad was excited about the trip, and I couldn't blame him. Muti was jealous, though, so Mom and I tried to placate her by treating her to dinners at Morrison's Cafeteria and Johnson's Coffeeshop while Dad was gone. *No, I'll just fix fried baloney for myself,* she'd sniff, so Mom and I left her to be miserable all by her lonesome.

When the guys got back from their Cuba trip, Ralphie took us all out for barbecue at Buck's Barn. Then, afterward, Dad and Ralphie sat on our hotel porch with Mom, talking about their trip. I wasn't exactly eavesdropping, but they didn't exactly know I could hear them, either, and that's when I overheard the news that Sonny DiCicco lived in Miami with a bunch of "girly boys." They didn't use the word "gay." Back then "gay" wasn't connected with sexual preference. It just meant happy. Dad was talking about "Queers," though, and Ralphie used some Italian words that sounded like "Gabagool" and "Fanook."

Mom was just weird, like she couldn't believe what she was hearing about Sonny. After all, he *was* supposed to be dead, she said, not alive and well. And certainly not living in Miami Beach. And how could someone *she* knew be a homosexual? She finally got it, though. *So Sonny's a homosexual?* she'd say. It was funny, too, the way she said "homosexual," making it a long drawn-out five-syllable word: *ho – mo – secks – you – all.* Like even though she was saying it, she couldn't get her head around the concept.

Mom and I took Tony and Ralphie to the Winn-Dixie for groceries so we could pack them a "lunch" for the drive back to Pittsburgh, and Tony was a hoot in the store. *What is this grits???* he'd say, and *Is not any good salami here, no good prosciutto!* Grumble, grumble. He complained at the top of his voice, of course, but in spite of all his kvetching we cobbled together an acceptable assortment of munchies they could pack in their cooler for the drive back home.

The next day Big Tony and Ralphie stopped by our hotel to say goodbye, and I was glad Muti hadn't been sitting on the hotel porch the night Mom got the news about Sonny. Being as Muti never liked Sonny, and subtlety not exactly being her forte, I was glad she didn't get an opportunity to say something snide to Tony about Sonny being *one of them queers.*

A DOOR OPENS

They never talked about money in front of me, but I knew we didn't have much. I knew the "Vacancy" sign was always lit.

It had been three years since Uncle Walter died, and my dad went back Up North to take Walter's job at Ringgsdorf Carbon. Mom had gone back to waitressing, working in the buffet line at Morrison's Cafeteria, and we never spent money on anything that wasn't a necessity. But no matter how much we scrimped, it wasn't enough.

I went with Mom to a loan shark's office on Beach Street, upstairs above Kress's Five and Dime store. There was only one chair, so I sat on the floor below the window. He ignored me, but he called my mother *Honey* and *Sweetie.*

I was ashamed for us. I wanted to kill him.

Afterward Mom would sit with her friend Edna on the porch late at night, talking. Edna had a good job as a bookkeeper, and she knew a lot about financial things. I heard "sell at auction" and "file for bankruptcy." I never heard laughter. When my dad came to Florida unexpectedly, I suspected something bad was about to happen.

Then the O'Malleys showed up out of nowhere. Kathleen and Bill. They saw the auction notice and decided to come look at the hotel. For one whole week they came by every day. After talking for a while with Mom and Dad, Kathleen would play on our upright piano in the lobby for Bill to sing. An old-fashioned Irish tenor, Bill sang all my favorites like "Danny Boy" and "When Irish Eyes Are Smiling" in a thrillingly sweet high voice.

He sang some Irish songs I hadn't heard before, too. Like that funny one about "a grand old shillelagh" and one that always started my imagination working overtime: "The Harp That Once Thro' Tara's Halls."

I loved his voice. I loved the music. And I started thinking about Tara, Ireland's version of Camelot. I knew about Tara because I read about it in my dad's old falling-apart book about Irish fairies, plus I'd read *Gone with the Wind,* and I knew that Scarlett O'Hara's mansion was named "Tara" in honor of the mythical kingdom in Ireland.

I guessed that for my dad, the Lyndhurst Hotel was supposed to be Tara. *We all want to find Tara,* I thought. *We all want to find the Camelot of our dreams.* Then I'd get mad, thinking about those stories and how everyone gets them wrong because they forget that every story has two sides. *Scarlett O'Hara survives, but barely,* I'd think to myself. *And Camelot doesn't survive at all, not after Mordred destroys the Round Table, and Arthur has to throw Excalibur back to the Lady of the Lake.*

I thought about all that because I hated the loan shark in his dark office above Kress's Five and Dime, and because I was scared of *selling at auction* and *filing for bankruptcy,* and because I was tired of being poor. But I was being too pessimistic.

As things turned out, we'd be just like Scarlett O'Hara. We would survive.

Old-time vaudevillians, longtime supper-club entertainers, retired with enough money—Kathleen and Bill were bored. They'd just sold their house in Holly Hill for a big profit, and they wanted to be partners in the hotel—we'd continue to run it while they lived there and made the hotel a success by staging "entertainments" in the lobby. After a lot of talking about "licenses" and "permits," we took the deal.

Maybe my dad was right, I thought. *Maybe we're going to find Tara after all.*

SURFACE TENSION

My best friends in high school were Mark and Merril. Mark's family lived in a big Spanish-style house with a red tile roof and lots of arches. From the attic window of their house you could see all the way to the river. That was where Mark kept his Sunfish sailboat tied up. Whenever we got a chance, the three of us would take Mark's Sunfish out on the river. Anyone who lives in Daytona Beach knows the Halifax River is part of the Atlantic Intracoastal system that begins at Norfolk, Virginia, and ends at Miami. So our "river" was actually a saltwater inlet.

A Sunfish can fit one or two people easily, or three if you don't mind being crowded. So when we all got in it we didn't have a lot of extra space. Plus we had to take brooms with us. Why? Because most people just boated or skied on the Halifax. If you swam in it like we did, you had to beat the water first with brooms so you could scare off any creatures that might be lurking near your boat, like sharks or stingrays or jellyfish.

Sometimes after we tied up Mark's Sunfish, we'd go to Merril's house to get something to eat. I loved her house. Everything was new and expensive and *fashionable*, like a set in a movie, and they collected expensive stuff, like *Steuben Glass* and artsy-looking statues. And they always had wonderful food. I never told Merril's mom about fried baloney. She wouldn't have believed it.

I don't think I was jealous of Mark or Merril. Not exactly. But I knew the houses they lived in were grand, and money was not a problem for them, like it was for my family. I couldn't look *into* their lives, though, the way you can look through a window. I could only look at their lives from the outside and then try to imagine the rest.

I had to imagine what it was like when Merril's stepdad was home, for example. He was a big man with a loud voice, and he scared me to death. When he was home, which wasn't very often, Mark and I knew to stay away. Merril said it was because her stepdad was so exhausted from being on the road, he needed peace and quiet. But that always sounded suspicious to me.

And then there was Mark's mother. She was always *resting* when we were at Mark's house, so we never saw her, and I tried to imagine what she looked like. Was she tired because she'd been out running marathons? Or was she an albino who had to avoid daylight? Or did she do embarrassing things so they had to keep her locked up?

Looking at their lives from the outside was like looking at the water from the deck of Mark's Sunfish, seeing a surface that glittered with sunlight, smooth and serene, not revealing the currents that raged and eddied, hiding life-forms that roiled and moiled underneath. *They call it "surface tension,"* I said to myself.

Then I'd think about surfaces like black ice, literal surfaces that deceive because they hide what's below them. But there are other surfaces, too, like buildings and facades and masks and even stories. All of them can hide more than they reveal. I'd think about Joan Reddish, never allowed outside. And Sonny DiCicco, mysteriously disappearing. And Patty's mom, running away with a Doctor of Theology. I'd think about Uncle Jake and Aunt Betty and Bethie Jean, even Boots and Ranger, gone forever. All those facades, all those smooth exteriors—what were their stories? What transpired behind closed doors?

Back on the Halifax River with Mark and Merril, peering at the smooth sunlit surface of the water surrounding the sailboat, I'd wonder what dark surprises lay hidden below. Even if you throw a rock or a pebble that breaks the surface, ripples hide what's underneath. You have to go through—like my friends and me diving into the river—to see what the surface tension hides.

That's what Lewis Carroll's Alice had to do, I said to myself.

I'd never really thought before about Alice being brave, but she was. Going through the looking glass was a courageous thing to do. Yes, her first trip to the land of the Mad Hatter was an accident, when she fell down the rabbit hole. But the second time, when she went through the looking glass, she did it on purpose.

I knew I'd do that too, someday. And I knew it would be scary on the other side. Because once you're there you can't hide from anything, not even yourself.

And that's why you go.

ME AND MY AMAZING
TECHNICOLOR DREAMCAR

My dad got it in a trade. It was only eight years old, but it looked like it had been through at least one war, maybe two. As long as a boat and heavy as a tank, "it" was a 1948 two-door Chrysler Town and Country convertible with wooden doors. The convertible canvas top was so threadbare and tattered that I used band-aids and adhesive tape to hold it together, and I had to put a piece of plywood over a big hole in the passenger-side floorboard.

But it ran—thirty-five to forty miles per hour, max.

And it roared—you could hear it coming a block away.

Let's paint it, my dad said. We bought half-pint cans of paint at Sears: red, pink, orange, royal blue, mint green, forest green. If you can picture the 1948 Town and Country, you'll remember that the doors were solid wood: dark mahogany for the recessed inside panels, lighter oak for the raised framing. When we finished painting them, the doors and trunk lid looked like checkerboards: pink and red panels on the doors, orange and blue panels on the lid of the trunk. Then we painted mint green on the front and back fenders, and forest green on the hood.

Before we painted the front fenders, though, and to my great dismay, we had to take off the air horns. Long and slender, gleaming chrome, they looked like Gabriel's trumpets. The problem was, they were illegal. *If you blow them too close to the drawbridge, the Bridgetender might open it,* Dad said. *And then there'd be all heck to pay.* (My dad never swore. "Heck" and "Dang it!" were the closest he ever came.) I was sorry to give up the air horns. But when the paint dried . . . even without Gabriel's trumpets perched on the front fenders . . . my car was a glorious sight.

And wonder of wonders, seemingly overnight, I went from misfit to popular. Well, to be absolutely honest about it, I went from misfit to *somewhat* popular. After all, in real life you couldn't expect to become Miss Teen Queen overnight. That only happened in movies, and even then you had to be Debbie Reynolds or Sandra Dee.

But you have to understand. In my high school most kids didn't have cars, especially girls. So in my group of girlfriends I was unusual, the only one with wheels. I could pick everyone up and go driving on the beach with the top down. Or take a crowd to the Volusia Drive-In Theater. Gas cost twenty or thirty cents a gallon, sometimes ten cents a gallon if a gas war was going on. So if everyone chipped in a quarter for gas, we'd be in business.

That year, *The Year Of My Amazing Technicolor Dreamcar*, was a landmark year for me. That year, I came to terms with Florida. For the rest of high school and until I went away to college, my Amazing Technicolor Dreamcar was as special to me as Cinderella's coach was to her.

One of my prize possessions for many years was a precise 1:24 scale replica of a 1948 Chrysler Town and Country convertible. Pristinely perfect in its acrylic display case, it had pride of place on any desk where I found myself working.

At one time I had a notion to paint this diminutive version of my old car. I even went to Dunn Toys and Hobbies downtown and bought tiny jars of model paint in six colors: red, pink, orange, royal blue, mint green, forest green. *Such is the power of symbols*, I think.

I wish now, years later, that I'd talked to my dad about symbols. Everything that car symbolized was important to him:

Taking a chance. Daring to be different. Playing the hand you're dealt and making the best of it.

That's it! I think to myself. *Painting that car was an act of defiance. It was just like moving to Florida in search of his dream.* Then I felt better. *It's okay,* I think to myself. *Maybe my dad understood about symbols after all.*

THE BAD GIRL

Reenie was from Philadelphia, but she got sent to live with her granddad in Florida after she got expelled from her expensive boarding school the third time. I thought she was fascinating. She always had beer and cigarettes, "fags," she called them, in her backpack. She said she started drinking when she was nine but didn't get in trouble for it until she was twelve when she packed her summer camp suitcase full of beer and got caught. It wasn't smoking or drinking that got her expelled from boarding school, though. She got expelled for fighting.

In Florida she was in Catholic school because it was her *last chance*, is what her dad told her. She said Catholic school was okay, though, because the nuns were always taking kids back and forth to church, and it gave her lots of chances to sneak a fag. The thing she hated was the uniforms. *Mags,* she told me, *those uniforms are UGLY.* (She pronounced it *yoo-glee.*) *I think those nuns went to Jay-Cee-Pen-AY and said "Sign us up for the butt-ugliest uniforms in the store."* (Reenie was always saying funny things.)

Every day when school was over she'd change clothes in the boys' bathroom. *The nuns don't look for me in the Boys' Head,* she laughed. Then she'd put on red lipstick and blue eye shadow, spray herself with Jungle Gardenia (her favorite cologne plus it hid the smell of beer), and ride her bicycle to a secret hideaway.

I rode my bike a lot after school and that's how I first met Reenie, when I was looking for a shady spot to rest for a minute and stumbled into her hideaway. It was off Riverside Drive, down a path and under an oak tree, and behind the oak tree she'd piled up some blocks to make a jetty so she could sit there with her feet in the water.

She didn't mind that I'd found her hideaway as long as I didn't tell anyone, so when I was out on my bike I'd stop to see if she was there. Most times she was. I'd have my Orange Crush to drink, and she'd share her stash of the day with me: boiled peanuts or her favorite, fried pork rinds.

Sometimes when I got there, she'd be sunbathing on the jetty in a bikini. Reenie's was the first bikini bathing suit I ever saw, and this was another fascinating thing about her—she didn't look good in a bikini, but she didn't care. *Frak 'em if they can't take a joke,* she'd say. (Reenie made up her own f-word, "frak," which was somehow funnier than the real one.)

At first I didn't think Reenie would like me because I was so boring, compared to her. But she was interested in me because I was from Pittsburgh, which was really low-class to people from Philadelphia, and because I lived in a hotel. I'd tell her Pittsburgh stories and hotel stories, and she'd tell me stories about her super-rich family: her poofy dad who judged Miss America pageants in his spare time and her mom who was a ballerina before she got polio and her brother Timmy who was retarded but the family wouldn't admit it and her sister Zilla who had a port wine birthmark and two illegitimate children.

Reenie's attitude about being rich was strange. She was obviously a snob about a lot of things I did, like singing in a church choir and having meat loaf for dinner and watching *I Love Lucy* on TV. *Mags, that's so BOOR-jwah*, she'd say, *so pluh-BEE-yun!* I didn't feel insulted, though, because she was never mean, just funny.

At the same time she was totally contemptuous of her family's lifestyle—their house in Philly that was so big it had a name instead of a street number, her parents' fancy-dress parties with real celebrities like Grace Kelly, things like that. *It's all so Mosaic*, she would say, *so frakkin' Lapidary!* (That's another funny thing she did, picking words like "mosaic" and "lapidary" and using them totally out of context, on purpose.)

We didn't see each other much after we both acquired motorized vehicles. I got my Amazing Technicolor Dreamcar, and she got Scary Mary, the purple motorcycle she built in her granddad's garage out of spare parts. I guessed she'd settled down some, though, because as far as I knew, she hadn't been expelled from Catholic school.

Then one day I saw Reenie with Jim Ed at the beach, and that's when I found out she quit school so they couldn't expel her. *Frak that Catholic school shit*, Reenie said. *It's so go-SHAY!* (She was being funny, mispronouncing *gauche* on purpose, but I didn't think Jim Ed caught on.)

It turned out that Jim Ed and Reenie were a couple ever since they met at a biker bar in Samsula called Sopotnik's Cabbage Patch. Jim Ed sang there with his band, and Reenie danced on tables for tips, and the way Jim Ed told their story it was love at first sight. *She came roarin' in on Scary Mary*, Jim Ed said, *and I fell hook, line, and sinker!*

Oh yeah, Reenie laughed, *Scary Mary hooked up with Stormin' Norman, and they've been stuck together like glue ever since.* Then she laughed again and punched me, said *How's THAT for a frakkin' double ahn-TAHN-druh?* and planted a big smacker kiss on Jim Ed.

He left then for a few minutes to talk with a couple of his buddies, and that gave Reenie a chance to fill me in about their life together. Jim Ed's mom died suddenly, she said, so the two of them moved in the big old family house in Samsula. Before long they started taking in strays, just folks who were generally needy, letting them stay for free until they got on their feet.

It wasn't long, though, before Reenie's dysfunctional siblings started showing up, so she and Jim Ed took them in too. *Yeah,* Reenie said, *first we got God-Zilla and the Rug-Rats* (her sister Zilla and Zilla's two kids by different fathers). *Then,* she laughed, *we got Tim the 'Tard* (her retarded brother Timmy). *And then, wouldn't you just know it, PeePeePop wandered in. What a frakkin' zoo!*

I knew, of course, that Reenie's bluster was just that. Bluster.

She and Jim Ed were good-hearted souls, and I was glad they'd made themselves a family. And except for being fatter, Reenie was just the same: smoking like a fiend, saying funny outrageous things. *By the way,* she said, *I graduated from Budweiser to Jim Beam, but I still love Jungle Gardenia. And Jim Ed got me hooked on MoonPies.*

I felt really good that day, watching them roar away on Scary Mary and Stormin' Norman, because they seemed so happy. *Come party with us at Sopotnik's,* they said. *It's halfway between New Smyrna and DeLand, just a little off State Road 44. You can't miss it because out by the road there's a big green concrete cabbage with a bench built into it and a neon sign on top that says Cole Slaw Wrestling.* I said sure, I'd come to Sopotnik's sometime soon.

I didn't go, and I'll always regret that I didn't.

I didn't think any more about Reenie or Jim Ed until one day when I saw a headline in the local section of the *Daytona Beach News-Journal* that said SLAIN BIKER TO BE HONORED. Underneath the headline was a photo of Reenie posing proudly with Scary Mary, and under the photo was a caption that said *Bye Bye, Miss American Pie.*

The story was short.

Reenie had become a fixture in Daytona's biker society. During Bike Week and Biketoberfest and year-round she was everybody's favorite Biker Chick, a soft touch for anyone who needed help: transients, migrant workers, single moms, run-aways. The night she died, that's what she was doing—trying to help someone.

The paper quoted her partner Jim Ed Clifton that several weeks earlier they'd taken in an old homeless woman named Edith. One night at Sopotnik's Edith went psychotic, grabbed a knife, and bloodied several people including Reenie. The bartender wanted to call the cops, but Reenie said no, if Edith got put back in the looney bin she'd never get out. *She'll be fine,* Reenie told everybody. *She just needs a little time, a little space.* Then Reenie took Edith outside so she could talk to her and calm her down.

Reenie and Edith were out by the road, sitting on the cabbage bench and talking, when the truck hit them. *The driver of the truck veered off the road to avoid hitting a deer,* the paper said. *No one was at fault. It was a freak accident.*

That's when I finally went to Sopotnik's—for Reenie's memorial. When I got there, motorcycles were everywhere. Acres of motorcycles, a sea of motorcycles. Up by the front door a platform was set up for the band. Bikers wearing badges saying "We love you, Reenie" passed out MoonPies and flyers with Reenie's picture on them. Jim Ed couldn't keep from crying, so he didn't say much into the microphone.

Then the band played "Proud Mary" and "Amazing Grace," and so many people sang with them, it sounded like the Mormon Tabernacle Choir had come to Samsula. Finally, Jim Ed announced that Reenie's family would leave with her ashes, taking them to be scattered at her secret hideaway by the river. As the band started in on "Bye Bye, Miss American Pie," we watched them drive away:

Jim Ed on Stormin' Norman, with Reenie's ashes in a Jim Beam canister;

Zilla with Timmy on Scary Mary;

Two biker friends ferrying Zilla's kids Pistol and Solo;

And Cedric the Saxon, a legendary old-time biker who'd bundled PeePeePop into the sidecar of his motorcycle Posse Comitatus (Posse's the bike, Comitatus is the sidecar).

The band sang one verse after another, the crowd joined in on every chorus, and once again the massed voices sounded like a cathedral choir:

> *So bye bye, Miss American Pie,*
> *Drove my Chevy to the levee, but the levee was dry.*
> *Them good old boys were drinkin' whiskey and rye,*
> *Singing, "This'll be the day that I die.*

"This'll be the day that I die . . .

The sun was low on the horizon when I left Sopotnik's, and it was dark by the time I got home. I knew that Reenie's parents still lived in Philadelphia, so I tried to call them and tell them what they missed. But they were hosting a party at their house and couldn't come to the phone, so I left a message with the snooty person who answered.

They never called me back.

BEING SANCHO PANZA

Before the days of cheap portable boomboxes, ubiquitous amplification, and wireless stage equipment, there were lots of small jobs for piano players. Since I always needed money and hated waiting tables, I took every piano or organ job I could get: funerals and weddings, dance studio rehearsals, background-music events like fashion shows and receptions.

Mainly, though, I substituted at local churches when their regular organists were sick or on vacation. Which means I accompanied a lot of vocal solos. And *that* leads me to an analogy, to-wit: *If solo vocalists are the Don Quixotes of music, the brave ones who take the chance of failing every time they perform, then accompanists are the Sancho Panzas of music, the faithful followers.*

I mean "follower" in the literal sense. When you accompany someone on the piano, you have to let the singer be the leader. If they go fast, you play fast and keep up with them. If they slow down, you do the same. Even if they totally mess up, like forgetting a whole part of the song, you have to go along with the mistake and make it sound like it was supposed to happen that way.

Once at St. Paul's Church I was playing for Mrs. Krauthammer to sing when she started singing the wrong hymn, not the one I was playing. It was awful, like a tug of war, because she kept on singing the wrong song instead of taking the cues I was frantically trying to give her. The tug of war couldn't last long, though. I had to give in, so I subsided into some background figures and a few chords so we could get through the song. Then, of course, she blamed me for the mistake and said she wanted another organist the next time she sang a solo. That was all right with me because I never liked her anyway, and that's when I started thinking about Sancho Panza.

Have you ever read *Don Quixote?* Don't worry if you haven't. It's way too long and pretty much crazy, as stories go. I started thinking about it because in the story Don Quixote, a prima donna like Mrs. Krauthammer and demented to boot, coerces Sancho Panza to be his squire and follow along after him while Quixote gets involved in one insane scheme after another. Sancho "knows his place," as they say, so he always defers to the Don, even when they both get in trouble because of Quixote's craziness. Finally by the end of Book Two (like I said, the whole thing together is a *really* long story), Sancho decides he's had enough, and he goes home.

Now, it's true that Sancho Panza has enough gumption to go on a journey instead of just hanging around at home and going nowhere. But here's the catch: it's Don Quixote's journey, not Sancho's. And that's what I decided to remember. That in the long run, tagging along on someone else's trip can be a lot more trouble than figuring out what *you* want to do—and then doing it yourself. From then on I didn't take every accompanist job that came along, and I never saw Mrs. Krauthammer again. I heard, though, that other organists got so exasperated with her, she had to start singing *a cappella*.

YOU HAVE TO PICK A STORY

I think some people get in trouble because they get their stories mixed up. Take my girlfriend Merril, for example. She was very talented musically, and her big ambition in life was to be a concert pianist. When her stepdad realized Merril was serious, he sold their Baldwin spinet piano and bought her a white baby grand.

Merril's mom got into the act too and redecorated a spare room just for the piano, with a black-and-white tile floor like a giant chessboard and floor-to-ceiling red draperies. She said the draperies were for good acoustics, but I figured she just wanted to make a statement. Merril's mom was all about statements and treatments—she made *statements* with house decorations and she was always inventing new *window treatments*.

To get back to Merril's story.

Merril's mom got Mrs. Ludovici as Merril's piano teacher, the one all the rich kids took lessons from. But the situation fell apart when Mrs. Ludovici dropped Merril as a student because of fingernails. Merril wanted to play the piano, but she wanted to keep her long fingernails too, so when she played, her fingernails were always click-click-clicking on the keys.

Merril and her mom got manicures whenever they wanted, and I have to admit, Merril's hands and long fingernails were beautiful. Everyone admired them. Her nails were hard, the kind you can shape into ovals and buff to a shine, and her hands always looked like a magazine advertisement for Jergens Lotion.

Not like mine. My fingernails were soft, always peeling and splitting. I guess if we're describing my hands next to Merril's hands, the best we could say for mine is that they were functional. I didn't worry about nail beauty at the time, just clipped my nails short so they wouldn't make clicking noises on the piano keys.

I understood, though, that Merril had a hard choice. Her mom had fabulous, expensive rings, and she let Merril wear any of them she wanted to. Wearing rings like those, especially if you had beautiful hands like Merril's, would make anyone feel like a princess. But here's where the story mix-up comes in. Because princesses in stories don't *do* anything or *go* anywhere. They just wait. Cinderella waits. Snow White waits. Sleeping Beauty waits. All those princesses shut up in towers just wait and wait and wait.

I've been thinking a lot about this princess-stuck-in-a-tower thing lately and wondering why there are so many variations on the same story. In fact, I started wondering whether stuck-in-a-tower is the flip side of yellow-brick-road. In the stuck-in-a-tower story you stay and wait, but in the yellow-brick-road story you go out and do stuff.

Think about it. I dare you to find a story that doesn't boil down to one of these—waiting in a tower or going on the road.

Getting back to Merril's story: the thing is, you have to choose. Merril had to choose between being a Pianist and a Princess, but she couldn't make up her mind. And not making up her mind was a big problem because if you don't choose between doing and not-doing, your options go away, and you end up—by default—with not-doing.

That's what happened to Merril. She got more teachers after Mrs. Ludovici, but none of them lasted very long because of the long fingernails which Merril refused to clip. Eventually Merril quit taking lessons, her stepdad sold the white baby grand piano, and her mom redecorated the piano room for a giant TV and a popcorn machine.

As Muti was fond of saying, *You can't have your cake and eat it too.* Which, I guess, is another way of saying you'd better pick a story before a story picks you.

ANOTHER DOOR OPENS

When I wasn't filling in as a substitute organist at one of the other local churches, I sang in the choir at Resurrection Lutheran. It was a small stucco-box-of-a-church on the corner of US1 and Fairview Avenue, nothing grand like St. Paul's Catholic Church on the next block or First Baptist downtown.

So there I was at choir rehearsal on a dismal-yet-typical Wednesday—our only good tenor was absent, the sopranos were swamping the altos, and our regular organist Mr. Ratzinger was wetting his whistle too often from his thermos. We were droning our way through "A Mighty Fortress Is Our God," which was written by Martin Luther himself and would be *The Big Number* on Sunday, being that Lent had just started and things had to be gloomy for awhile.

Then Kara Andresson came in late, apologizing, and sat down in the back row. When she started singing the rest of us stopped, the whole front row turned around and stared, and Mr. Ratzinger got such a coughing fit he had to wet his whistle until his thermos went dry. Our pastor's wife stood up and said *Folks, I'd like you to welcome Kara Andresson. The Andressons are our newest family at Resurrection Lutheran.*

We got right back to singing, but we all knew *Something Important* had just happened.

Kara Andresson's voice was like nothing I'd ever heard: warm, rich, thick like honey. Golden. She'd had a professional career, she told us, and what she sang during her professional career was opera. Real opera. Grand opera. There was no opera company in Daytona Beach, of course. At that time there wasn't an opera company anywhere in Florida, not even Palm Beach or Miami. But there was a local impresario who'd met Kara in New York City and remembered her, and he signed her up to sing in a series of concerts at the Bandshell, on the beach just north of the Boardwalk

Kara needed an accompanist and asked me if I'd be interested in working with her. Naturally, I jumped at the chance. The concerts were set to begin in a few weeks, so I started practicing the piano-vocal scores she gave me. I also got opera books from City Island Library so I could read the stories that went along with the arias Kara would sing. (My friend Booker worked weekends in the library. and she'd extend the due-dates for as long as I needed.)

And right away, Kara and I started rehearsing together. Playing for her, I heard her *become* the roles she sang—Mimi and Butterfly (in Italian), Carmen and Marguerite (in French) Rosina (in German). Even if you didn't understand the words, when you heard her sing you lived the story with her.

My memories of being onstage at the Bandshell are a blur. I can still hear the music in my head, but I see only a few image-fragments—the Emcee in a white dinner jacket, crowds of people seated in front of the stage on benches, colored lights going around and around on the Ferris wheel at the Boardwalk in the distance.

I remember Kara at the microphone, though, wearing the most spectacular gowns I'd ever seen. One, a waterfall of sequins, shimmered like sunlight at dusk. Another was stiff red satin with a long gold train, and one was the color of night, soft black velvet with iridescent silver sprinkles like droplets of water.

And I remember roses. Kara's husband Lars presented her with a huge bouquet of roses onstage at every performance, a different color each time, while the audience cheered, and she took her bows. *I wish your dad would send me roses once in a while,*, my mom always said wistfully. I knew, though, that Mom didn't trust those roses, just like the people at Resurrection Lutheran didn't trust Lars. *He'll dump her someday,* the wives would whisper when they thought Kara couldn't hear. And *He thinks he's hot shit,* the husbands would say when Lars picked Kara up in his big Cadillac after choir practice. Me, I figured they were all jealous because Kara was beautiful and Lars was super-rich. None of that mattered to me, though, because Kara opened a door for me that revealed a vista I'd never imagined.

I'd always loved stories, always loved music. Now, because of her, I saw that stories and music could complement each other in opera: the ultimate art-in-performance.

I never played at the Bandshell again after our series of concerts was over, and it wasn't long before the Andressons left Daytona Beach. First Lars ran off with his secretary, then Kara moved back Up North with the kids. So my mom was right not to trust Lars and his roses, and the people at Resurrection Lutheran got their poetic justice. Our choir went back to its usual level of comfortable mediocrity, and it was around that same time when we got a new music director who announced right away that any music written before 1800 was "secular."

The more things change, the more they stay the same, I thought to myself. Yet I knew beyond a doubt that, for me, Kara Andresson opened a door that revealed a previously unknown and magical world.

GOLDILOCKS: A PRINCIPLE OR A STORY?

Mark and Merril were just friends, not a romantic couple, so I wasn't a third wheel when we did things together. And Merril and I could be best girlfriends because I was no competition in the boyfriend department. She always had a boyfriend. Some were long term, like a year or more, and some were short term. That didn't matter. Whoever she was with, she'd be totally engrossed in him. Maybe it was because I was an only child that I didn't know how to do the boyfriend thing. I was used to being alone and I liked being alone. Besides that, I didn't know how to talk to boys, didn't even know what they were interested in.

If you were a girl back then, fitting in was all about "going steady"—wearing a boy's ring on a chain around your neck, being stuck to him like glue. If you were really lucky and he had a varsity letter sweater, you got to wear that all the time too, even if it was ridiculous in the Florida heat to be wearing a wool sweater. And there was no way to escape the fact that school events were always boy-girl date-occasions. The idea that a bunch of girls (or a bunch of boys) could go together to a party or a dance hadn't happened yet.

I did get a steady boyfriend finally, thanks to Merril. She explained to me that it wasn't going to happen like a bolt of lightning out of the sky, that I had to work at it. *Mags,* she'd say, *remember Goldilocks. Don't be too much or too little. Be just right.* What she meant was I had to quit being too smart about books and too dumb about sports. And I had to start listening instead of talking. In other words, I had to learn to be "girly." I knew I wasn't Cinderella, but I didn't want to be one of the stepsisters either, so I took Merril's advice.

The good news about this is for many years I concentrated on being "just right" and I did indeed fit in. I guess you could say that I chose a story, and it worked for me for a long time. The bad news is, when I had to give up on that story years later, it took an even longer time to un-learn everything and pick a new one. But that was because I didn't understand the Goldilocks Principle.

You know the Goldilocks story, I'm sure:

Goldilocks, walking in the forest, sees the house of the three bears. She knocks but no one answers, so she goes on in and makes herself at home—tasting porridge, sitting in chairs, and trying out the beds. In all three cases she picks the one that's "just right," including the bed in which she falls asleep. When the bears get home, they're not happy, especially Baby Bear who has an empty bowl, a broken chair, and a stranger in his own wee bed. Just then Goldilocks wakes up to find three very annoyed bears standing over her. She jumps up, runs out the door and into the forest, and never again returns to the house of the three bears. The End.

There's a lot of philosophizing about the Goldilocks Principle, and it's actually called that—the "Goldilocks Principle"—in astronomy and economics. If you look it up in economics, you'll find this: *A Goldilocks Market occurs when the price of commodities sits between a bear market and a bull market.* And if you look it up in astronomy, you'll find this: *The Goldilocks Principle is the idea that an ideal amount of some measurable substance is "just right" for a life-supporting condition to exist.*

Well, when I thought about all this, I realized that people confuse "principle" with "story." The Goldilocks "principle" works just fine for economies that need stability and for exoplanets that need to sustain life. But the Goldilocks "story" encodes a double standard, and I'll tell you why.

Like everyone else, I thought this story was a cautionary tale about the dangers of excess and the importance of choosing a sensible mid-point. But when I looked more closely, I realized that the "message" of this story is what I'd been hearing my whole life: *Be a nice girl* and *Play nice* and *Don't be a nosy parker* and *Don't be bossy.* Especially *Don't be bossy.* Which really means *Defer to other people all the time so they will like you.* And that's where The Goldilocks Principle becomes The Double Standard.

Think about it.

When the story begins, Goldilocks acts like she's never heard of a double standard. She doesn't just hang around outside the bears' house, politely waiting for them to come home and invite her in. Knowing that the house is unoccupied, she goes inside and tests everything—hot and cold, high and low, hard and soft. Then she decides what she wants to do, and she does it. Here's the kicker: When she wakes up and sees the bears looming over her, disapproving if not actually threatening, she runs out of the house and never returns.

Lesson learned—nice girls do not go out adventuring.

Whether the bears should have left their door unlocked is not the issue in this story. The issue is whether Goldilocks should have minded her own business and not messed about with the bears' stuff. In fact, the *real* issue is whether she should or shouldn't have had the freedom to be out exploring and walking through doors in the first place. And that's what I didn't understand. You have to pick sides, and everyone sides with the bears instead of Goldilocks. If you side with the bears, you accept authority. But if you side with Goldilocks, you have to buck convention and assert your independence. Especially if you're a girl.

Hmm, I thought to myself. If I ever write a Goldilocks-story, I'll keep her curly blonde hair because after all that's what her name's all about, but I'll change the ending. Instead of running away, my Goldilocks will be a Neighborhood Watch Deputy, and she'll lecture the bears about locking their doors when they leave their house.

Not only that. My Goldilocks won't be intimidated. She might be tiny and petite and girly, but she'll also have brass balls.

THE OTHER ALICE

I used to fantasize I was adopted, that my real family had to leave me on a doorstep in Pittsburgh because they were Royal Refugees who had to travel incognito (the Romanov Jewels story again). Or they had to give me away because they were Triple Agents who were engaged in fantastically dangerous international conspiracies that might have put me in harm's way. Or my amazingly talented and beautiful parents were murdered by an Agent of Evil, leaving me an orphan. I liked the orphan scenario best.

Orphans are the stuff of mystery and romance: Oliver Twist, Jane Eyre, Little Orphan Annie, David Copperfield, Heathcliff. You're already thinking about Harry Potter, I'm sure. And don't forget Frodo. Do we get any information at all about Frodo's parents? *Au contraire.* The closest Frodo comes to having a family is Bilbo, and the two of them are just first cousins once removed. (I know this for sure because I checked it in *The Silmarillion.*) After reviewing likely orphan-options for my own story, I'd always decide magnanimously that I wouldn't go looking for my birth family. After all, I'd say to myself, I couldn't hurt my dad and mom, the adoptive parents who'd so unselfishly taken me in and cared for me as best they could.

It was true, though, that my family was seriously lacking in female role-models, and that's what I needed. Alas, my grandmothers were the original hard-luck cases, my aunts weren't much better, and neither were the adult females I'd met so far, Up North and in Florida. In other words, there wasn't one Rocket Scientist or Famous Writer or Private Detective or Musical Prodigy in the bunch.

Then I found a model. Her name was Miss Fortunato. Miss Alicia Fortunato. She was a last-minute substitute to teach junior-year physics at Mainland High School when Mr. Yoakum had to get an emergency appendectomy, and when he came back in January she was gone. But that one half-year was enough.

I expected physics and math to be my least favorite subjects because I wanted to read Victorian novels and Romantic poetry and plan my future career as a writer and storyteller. But Miss Fortunato was a romantic heroine in the flesh. She was beautiful and smart and mysterious, and I fell totally in love with her.

She was striking—obviously proud of being tall because she always wore high heels, sometimes high-heeled boots, and she walked like a man, like she wasn't afraid to go anywhere, anytime. She was very thin, very pale, with hair so dark it looked jet black, and with an abrupt asymmetrical haircut that nobody in Daytona Beach had ever seen before. She wore a lot of black and white, or black and red, and she always wore silver jewelry—big chunky silver rings, and a silver cuff bracelet engraved with the first seven numbers of the Fibonacci series. Also dangly silver earrings shaped like the infinity symbol.

She wasn't young, but she wasn't old either. And she was mysterious. Where was she from? She had an accent that sounded vaguely French, but she never explained. And where did she live? She never said. Why wasn't she married? Or was she? How did she end up in Daytona Beach, of all places?

Stories abounded. Rumors flew. That she was a fabulously rich heiress from Chicago. That she'd been a big game hunter in Africa. That she was a CIA agent. That she was a famous artist in disguise. That she had an affair with F. Scott Fitzgerald. That she was in a witness protection program. That she was really a man.

Fortunately for me she was a spellbinding teacher who knew math and physics inside and out, and she really cared about teaching. When she conscripted me to be her de facto teacher's assistant, I was thrilled. I went to school early and stayed late, helping her file papers and organize slides and photos, and, while we were working, we'd talk. She was interested in radial forms among plants (it's where the importance of the Fibonacci series comes in) and in Gestalt psychology (she was concerned about *the problem of wholeness* and *the structural integrity of complex systems*).

And she was so-o-o-o smart. She knew words I'd never heard of, and I knew a lot of words. One day she said we should indulge in *abstract rodomontades,* where you blurt out anything and everything that's good about yourself. *You mean like indulging in "braggadocio"?* I asked, and she said that was it exactly, so that's what we did. (I have to admit that it felt good.)

Sometimes we talked about mysteries because she loved them, and I did too, especially the kind of "puzzle books" that Agatha Christie made famous. *Life's messy,* she'd say. *Life follows the second law of thermodynamics, but a well-written mystery reverses it.* I knew exactly what she meant. The second law of thermodynamics, sometimes called "The Arrow of Time," says all systems are entropic. That is, as they lose energy they move from order to chaos. The problem is that we love order, not chaos, so when an Agatha-Christie-type mystery tidies up the chaos and restores order at the end, it makes us happy.

Most of all I loved it when we played "what if" games while we worked, games where you could just let your imagination run wild.

For example, *What if Homo Sapiens is Planet Earth's most invasive species?*

Or, *What if our timebound classical universe has a doppelgänger—a quantum universe where time constricts and dilates and runs backward?*

Or, *What if Neanderthals are not really extinct, but just hiding out?*

After we decided on a concept, we'd talk about how it might take shape as a scenario, how it might be worked out as a story.

There's something you need to remember here—science fiction has never been a "respectable" literary genre. When Kurt Vonnegut was labeled a "sci-fi writer" (*Player Piano* and *The Sirens of Titan* were his first novels), he said it was like being in "the file drawer that was regularly mistaken for a urinal." He wasn't exaggerating. Science fiction was the piss pot of literature, metaphorically speaking. And if it was bad for a guy like Kurt Vonnegut to be a sci-fi writer, it was even worse to be a woman writing sci-fi.

I knew all that and it's why I didn't talk to anyone at school about loving science fiction. Then Alicia Fortunato came along and gave me permission—not just to like sci-fi but also to believe I'd write it someday. In my mind's eye I'd look into the future and see myself in a huge auditorium, accepting an award from The Science Fiction Writers of America. And on the Selection Panel, applauding like crazy, is—you guessed it! Alicia Fortunato.

You only need one role model, and I'd found mine.

Miss Fortunato's last day at school loomed large in my imagination. I hoped for a memorable farewell, like the goodbyes you see in movies where you know the characters will meet again in the future because of the intense personal bond they've established. After all, she'd told me I could call her "Alice" just before Thanksgiving break, hadn't she? *You mean like Lewis Carroll's Alice, going through the looking glass?* I asked. But she said no, she was "the other Alice." She said her family called her Alice, or Alli, and she thought of me as family, like a daughter, so I could call her "Alli" too.

And hadn't she consoled me gently when I'd been depressed about not getting asked to the homecoming dance? That's when she said—I'll never forget it—*Mags, you and I are the women men don't see.* Then she gave me one of those conspiratorial looks, and she winked at me.

So, of course, I anticipated a memorable farewell, heavy with implied anticipation of our future comradeship in a world where women march arm-in-arm, on an equal footing with their male compatriots. I should've known better. Nothing happened the way I'd imagined it: no hugs, no tears, no implied future comradeship. Alli—Miss Fortunato—seemed tired and grumpy in class, and she left school early, before the last bell rang.

I was straightening up the science files in the workroom when the principal, Mr. Fenton, came by and said Miss Fortunato had gone, so he'd lock up the room. I hung around for a while anyway, hugely disappointed and hoping she'd come back, but I finally gave up and went to my locker to clean it out for the holidays. That's when I found what she left for me—a brown paper bag on the top shelf of my locker. Inside the bag were three items: a jet-black wig with an asymmetrical haircut, the silver Fibonacci cuff bracelet, and a note.

To say I was stunned is an understatement. *So she really was in hiding?* I thought, looking at the wig. *But hiding from what?*

I went in the girls' bathroom and tried the wig on in the mirror, but I looked ridiculous. I could hear Mr. Fenton calling me, saying he needed to finish locking up, so I hurried back to my locker, got all my stuff including the brown bag, and waved goodbye to Mr. Fenton.

Outside in the parking lot I sat in my Dreamcar for a while not knowing whether to cry because *Miss Alicia Fortunato* had locked me out, or to laugh because *The Other Alice* had invited me in. Either way, I was stuck with a Mysterious Stranger who provoked questions but refused to provide answers. Sitting there, I slipped the bracelet on my wrist (leaving the wig in the bag—it really did look ridiculous on me) and stared at the note:

Dear Mags, always follow the numbers.

Alice

Merril loved the wig so I gave it to her, but I kept the note in my Commonplace Box. Not that I understood the message. *What* numbers? Fibonacci numbers? Those magical numbers that spiral outward or inward, anticipating but never reaching infinity? Are the "numbers" related to radial forms? or Gestalt psychology? Even if they are, what does that mean to me?

I stayed upset about Miss Fortunato's abrupt departure and the mysterious note for a while. Eventually, though, I put both the Fibonacci bracelet and Alli's note in my Commonplace Box and forgot about them.

Years later my friend Talisman gave me a biography of the science fiction writer James Tiptree, Jr. who exploded on the literary scene in the late 1960s as one of the brilliant members of the "New Wave" sci-fi movement. No sooner had I started reading the biography when I practically had a stroke, like a lightning bolt in the brain. Why? Because the sci-fi writer James Tiptree, Jr. was really a woman named Alice B. Sheldon who pulled off one of the biggest double-identity stunts in all literary history. She didn't just publish under a male pseudonym, like the Brontes and lots of other women writers. No indeed.

As a male writer known as "Tip" she corresponded endlessly with fans and other sci-fi writers for almost ten years from a P.O. box in Virginia before the deception was discovered. And until her identity was revealed by accident, "Tip's" fans and fellow writers were wild to find out something—anything— about this exciting recluse who refused public appearances and telephone conversations.

I stayed up all night reading the biography, *The Double Life of Alice B. Sheldon,* and I found out her real life encompassed African safaris, debutante balls, elopement with an alcoholic poet, publication in *The New Yorker,* stints as a WAC and a CIA agent, numerous romantic encounters and entanglements, a PhD in experimental psychology, and an entrepreneurial adventure running a chicken hatchery in New Jersey.

All that was interesting, of course. I mean, how many people have so many fabulous adventures in one lifetime? But here's what really caught my attention: during an emotionally frazzled period in her life, Alice Sheldon disappeared. She *sort of* disappeared, that is. It was as if she'd gone into a witness protection program—adopted an alias, assumed a new personality, rented a house under her new name. But only on weekdays, not on weekends—on weekends she went back to her other life. Eventually she reunited fulltime with her family but only when she herself was ready, and then she enrolled in American University as a graduate student. Her hiatus had lasted several months or, as she herself said, "a short time."

When I read that I thought *Omigod, the timeline's perfect. So is it possible? Is it possible that Alice B. Sheldon was my Alice? Could it really be true? Naw, not hardly,* I decided. *Things like that only happen in books and movies. Only in fiction.*

I spent the next few days in a daze, wandering around and wondering. Then reality set back in, and I regretfully told myself *my* Alice couldn't have been *that* Alice. I decided, though, to get the silver Fibonacci bracelet out of my Commonplace Box and polish it.

I've worn it ever since, any time I feel in need of inspiration.

ALL'S WELL THAT ENDS WELL?

It was my sixteenth birthday, and I was dying to have a slumber party at the hotel. Mom said we could use one of the Snowbird apartments as long as we cleaned up after ourselves, and she knew she could trust me and my friends because we didn't drink or do drugs or anything like that. We didn't intend to slumber, of course, mainly talk, play records, dance, eat a lot.

All of which we did.

By midnight, however, boredom had set in, and Merril, ever the instigator, double-dog-dared us to go investigate "that old haunted house on the beach in Ponce Inlet." I said *No Way!* and I meant it because deserted old houses like that are scary. I mean, what if one of us crashed through a rotten floorboard? Or slipped on rickety stairs? Not to mention that I'd never forgotten the ghosties and ghoulies in the cellar of our house Up North. I couldn't admit to my friends that I believed in fairies, however, so instead I warned them how dangerous such a jaunt could be.

You know how it is, though—everyone wants to do it, you don't want to poop the party, and pretty soon you're driving a car full of giggling girls to a deserted old mansion on the beach way south of town. My idea was oh what the heck, I'll be the Lookout and stay with my Dreamcar while the girls figure out how to break into the house and get back out again, and then I'll drive us all back to the hotel. It was a good plan, but I should've known it wouldn't work.

To back up just a minute, the old beachside mansion is a landmark in Volusia County. It was known for years as "Captain John's Castle" but it's immortalized in the official *Weird Florida* book as "The Genius House" because that's what locals started calling it around the time it got a reputation for being haunted.

The house never become a magnet for tourists, though— partly because it's so out-of-the-way, but also because any brave soul who sets out to investigate the house gets seriously spooked. Including the author of *Weird Florida,* by the way, who includes in his book a warning that *pernicious spirits* are wont to hover and screech when disturbed by snoopers.

Anyway, the house is way south of town, past the Ponce Inlet Lighthouse and the end of Highway A1A along the ocean. It's three stories, an imposing old coquina structure that looks like a castle, with outbuildings and a tower—also coquina—surrounded by acres of ground cover called ice plant. The house and property must've been spectacular in the 1920s, part of Old Florida's building boom, but it fell into disrepair after the Great Depression. Naturally it didn't take long for the old deserted house to get a reputation for being haunted, especially because of the legend surrounding it: (1) that Captain John was the sole survivor when a treasure ship sank off the coast, and (2) the treasure he salvaged to build his castle was cursed.

A shipwreck? A treasure that carried a curse? This is the stuff of legend so pervasive that it takes on a life of its own. And this legend, surely, is why surfers and boaters swear they see strange lights up high in the tower, and why residents of

Ponce Inlet love telling stories about *woo woo* noises and eerie music that wake them in the middle of the night.

All this was going through my mind while my friends and I squeezed in my Dreamcar that night and set out for the beachside. The area's different now, of course, but back then everything south of the Port Orange Bridge was dark and deserted. And creepy.

It seemed to me that I drove forever on A1A along the ocean until finally, when the highway turned to gravel and then dirt, I was completely disoriented. That's when the girl we called Booker chimed in. She knew the beaches better than anyone because she surfed whenever she got a chance, and she warned us that the house would be tough to get into because the Beach Patrol boarded it up to discourage trespassers.

At that point I breathed a sigh of relief, thinking we'd have to abandon our outing, but no such luck. Booker said we could get in the Tower instead of the House, and it'd be easy because the big old tower door was broken. So that's what we decided to do.

Reluctantly and with Booker directing, I drove us to a dirt-road turnoff and followed a trail until we reached the southern-most corner of the property, practically on the beach itself. After I parked my Dreamcar, Booker led the way through palmetto scrub to the Tower.

Like I said, I intended to stay by my car and be the Lookout. *Oh no you don't*, Merril said. When one of the girls hollered *Here! This is the broken door! We can get in this way!* Merril pulled me along with her and the others, and we all went in.

Inside it was pitch black except for some light coming from a trapdoor above the Tower's spiraling stone staircase. *It must be moonlight that's coming in the big windows up top,* Booker said, *so let's push open the trapdoor and climb the stairs.* She had our only flashlight, so with Booker in the lead and Merril right behind, we started climbing single-file.

Oww! My foot!

What? All of us except Joy were already on the stairs, climbing. She was the last one in and hollered because the big wooden door had slammed shut on her foot.

Pull, Joy! Pull!

Those of us on the high stairs heard scuffling and muffled cries, but we couldn't see a thing down below.

Come on, Joy! Pull!

We need the flashlight! Quick, throw us the flashlight! Before Booker could stop her, Merril grabbed the flashlight and tossed it to the group below. And that was unfortunate because Merril was never famous for eye-hand coordination. All of us watched the flashlight arc up, then down, before it hit the stone floor with a crack and went dark.

In the meantime, Joy somehow extricated her foot but lost her shoes in the process. *Ewww, nasty! I'm walking on rat turds!*

Open the front door! Pull the door open! We need light!

Muffles and scuffles. *There's no handle! The door won't budge!* Silence.

This was long before portable communication of any kind, of course. Telephones in that era had rotary dials and corded handsets, and we even had party lines, if you can imagine that (or remember it). So there we were, locked in a musty old tower with no way to contact the outside world. Our only option was to climb the stairs toward the light at the top of the Tower, so that's what we did.

As we climbed, I couldn't shake the feeling that *something* was watching us. It was the same feeling I got when I had to cross that dark cellar in Pittsburgh and climb those steep stairs to our kitchen. *Mags, you're being silly*, I scolded myself, but I still wished I'd brought my amulet with me from my Commonplace Box when I agreed to this crazy adventure.

Finally, we reached the top of the stairs and ducked through a low archway into a circular room. And *that's* when I realized the light we'd been following was shining from the coquina rocks themselves. But how was that possible? *There must be phosphorus in the rocks*, I thought to myself, remembering "The Hound of the Baskervilles"— that terrifying Sherlock Holmes novel about mysterious murders on moonlit moors. I wasn't convinced about phosphorus, though, and anyway I had more pressing matters to worry about. Like the disastrous scene at the hotel come morning when we supposedly slumbering partygoers were obviously missing in action. And it's fair to say that all my friends were experiencing some combination of dread and chagrin, as well.

Everyone except Merril, that is. Merril, typically, was tickled pink with our situation. Right away she started going *woo woo woo*, hooting like an owl out the turret-windows in the Tower. She also managed to find a scrap of paper in her jeans pocket and got busy writing a note: *Help! I'm a prisoner in the tower!* She figured she'd toss the note out of a turret-window and leave a half-empty box of Milk Duds up on the sill, maybe with another note that says *Help! I hear him! He's coming back!* The rest of us were not amused, pointing out to Merril that her joke wouldn't be funny if we remained locked in the tower all night.

Fortunately for Merril, though, Booker remained calm. *We need a plan,* she said. *If we take off our shirts and tie them together, we can make a rope. I'll tie the shirt-rope around my waist and go out the window onto the ledge. Then you all hold tight to the rope while I rappel to the ground. I'll jimmy the Tower door with Mags's lug wrench from her Dreamcar, and I'll let you all out.*

Whew. thank goodness for level-headedness. Even Merril conceded that Booker's plan made sense, but I proposed an addendum because I wasn't interested in doffing one of my very few decent shirts and getting it back torn in half. Instead I volunteered to feel my way down the stairs, wait by the big door for Booker to open it from outside, and hold the door open while we all ran out.

Once I was down by the door, waiting, I started thinking what a great mystery novel this would make. Better than Agatha Christie's *And Then There Were None,* which is the greatest locked-room mystery novel of all time. I mean, think about the possibilities. You could have ten teenage girls locked in an old stone tower, tormented by bats and rats and strange noises while a pockmarked homicidal maniac dressed like Howdy Doody entices them out one by one so he can do dreadful things to them with his woody . . .

I was thinking really hard, inventing details, but I got tired of standing up so I sat down with my back to the door, and that's when I felt Joy's shoe, sticking out from under the door.

Hmm, I wondered, *this is the toe-end of her shoe. How'd it get turned around? Did she walk in backward? And is it really stuck, squashed under the door?* I grabbed the toe of the shoe, jiggling and pulling it, and bingo! the door creaked open.

"The door's open! The door's open!" I shouted, and then several things happened almost simultaneously:

—a siren screamed in the distance, obviously coming closer;

—the shirt-rope broke, dumping Booker and a shower of blouses into a clump of palmettos;

—a crowd of girls in brassieres (plus Merril, topless) came tumbling down the staircase.

While my friends ran out the door and into my Dreamcar, squishing themselves down on the floor and shushing Booker who'd gotten considerably scratched up when she landed in the palmettos, I slammed the Tower door behind me.

Then I jumped in my car and turned onto A1A just as a Beach Patrol vehicle roared past us (a local resident must've reported those *woo woo* noises again). It was fortunate that I'd decided to hang onto my blouse, being as I could wave nonchalantly to the officers while I drove away in my roaring multicolored rattletrap.

Mom seemed puzzled the next morning when my friends left wearing their pajama tops. "And why was the redhead wearing just one shoe and limping?" she asked. "Oh, it's a long story," I said vaguely, and then Mom got distracted when Muti started complaining because someone had used all of our band-aids.

All's well that ends well, I thought, but even back then I knew that Shakespeare was being ironic when he wrote those words. His play's about good people making bad choices, fooling themselves into thinking that things are ending well. They don't realize it at the time, but their bad choices will come back to haunt them.

That's what foreshadowing's all about, of course, and that's why it's such a valuable tool for storytellers. Musing about haunted houses and split-second timing, I replayed our midnight adventure in my mind.

And I thought about those poor befuddled Beach Patrol officers who arrived at the scene to discover an authentic locked-room mystery—a pile of torn shirts on the ground, and upstairs in the Tower a frantic note, a half-empty box of Milk Duds, and a girl's frilly pink blouse. (The blouse was Merril's, and she left it in the Tower on purpose. Merril *never* quits!)

Booker was the last one to leave the hotel the next morning, and I asked her if she'd noticed strange lights in the Tower, possibly something phosphorescent in the coquina rocks?

No, she said, *the only light was moonlight, and it was brilliant. We're lucky there was a full moon last night and not a cloud in the sky. It's like Shakespeare said, all's well that ends well. Right, Mags?*

Absolutely, I agreed.

BETHIE JEAN CAME BACK

Bethie Jean came back just before my high school graduation. Uncle Jake had died Up North in a VA hospital, and they contacted Aunt Betty to do something about a funeral. Aunt Betty refused, but Bethie Jean said after all he *was* her father, so she'd go to Pittsburgh and take care of the arrangements. We didn't see each other, but we talked on the phone a few times because she'd call Florida to talk to Muti, and then, when the two of them ran out of things to say, like in six seconds, Muti would hand me the phone.

During those phone conversations, I found out that Bethie Jean and Aunt Betty never made it to California. They got as far as Steubenville, Ohio, and stayed there for six months, and then they went to Nashville, where Aunt Betty had a cousin.

Not Nashville in Tennessee. Nashville in Indiana.

It's a really small town, Bethie Jean said, *and it has this great place called The Little Nashville Opry, where big country stars practice their acts before they take them to the real Opry.* Bethie Jean kept on talking because she was excited, and I was getting excited for her. *And when the big stars aren't performing*, she said, *they let beginners get up on stage and show what they can do so they can get experience being in the music business.*

Well, that thing she said about "being in the music business" caught my attention so I asked her about it. And that's when she told me she was bored stiff when they got to Nashville, so Aunt Betty's cousin gave her an old guitar. *I never knew I could sing*, she said, *but once I got started everyone said I sounded just like Patsy Cline, and when I tried out at the Little Opry, I got a job right away.*

I was starting to get all prickly, like the hairs were standing up on my arms. *Omigod*, I said. *Do you have a stage name?*

Of course I do, she said. *I'm known on the country music circuit as B.J. Smithfield.*

I couldn't believe what I was hearing.

I mean, I've always loved country music, listened to country stations on the radio whenever I could. And now my very own cousin, my little skinny potty-mouthed cousin, informs me she's *B.J. Smithfield?* With folk-country songs all over the radio, high on the charts? Right up there, in fact, with Arlo Guthrie and Dolly Parton and The Carter Family? Who woulda' thunk it?

The last time we talked on the phone while she was still in Pittsburgh, Bethie Jean and I agreed we'd stay in touch, but of course we never did. She sent me an autographed publicity photo, though, showing Bethie Jean—sorry, B.J.—standing on a stage in front of a microphone and strumming on her signature black-and-white polka-dot guitar.

On the bottom she wrote:

To Cousin Mags,
The past is gone, so let's enjoy the here and now!
                                    Love forever, B.J.

Even though Bethie Jean and I didn't "stay in touch" I always listened for her songs on the radio, and I loved them because they were story-songs, what poets call "narrative songs." Basically she told stories with her music, and a really interesting thing is the kinds of stories her songs were about. They weren't your typical princess-stories that end with the fancy dress ball and everyone living happily ever after.

No, B.J.'s story-songs were adventurous and daring, about girls who went climbing down from their towers, endangering life and limb. Or girls who unlocked their cages, trusting they wouldn't slam into the ground before they learned to fly. There was even one song that revised the *Hansel and Gretel* fairy tale, about a girl who escaped from an oven.

Then one of those uncanny things happened.

Just like Patsy Cline but exactly ten years later, B.J. Smithfield died in a plane crash. By that time my mom and dad were back in Pittsburgh, and news of the plane crash was all over Radio Station KDKA. After Mom called me and told me the news, I listened to the radio whenever I could.

Sure enough, B.J. Smithfield's last song was a number one crossover hit that stayed on the charts for months. It's called "Wolf," and it starts out like this:

Bring me no candy, read me no rhymes,
Sing me no songs of those times when you ravaged
my mind . . .

It wasn't over-produced, with no twangy backup or throbbing bass. Just B.J. singing and accompanying herself on her acoustic guitar.

I heard her song practically every time I turned on the radio, and I'll never forget its haunting refrain:

Lock the door,
Lock the door—
It's midnight, and the Wolf is at the door.

ATLANTA

Either you will
go through this door
or you will not go through.
...
The door itself makes no promises.
It is only a door.

Adrienne Rich

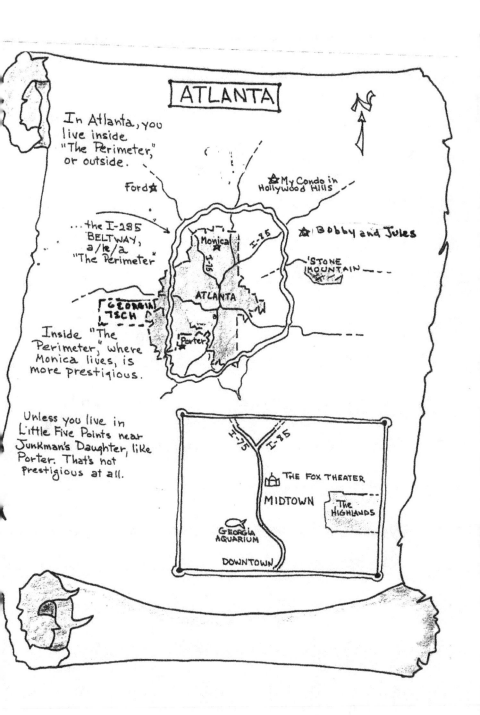

ATLANTA

In Atlanta, you live inside "The Perimeter," or outside.

Ford ☆

☆ My Condo in Hollywood Hills

...the I-285 BELTWAY, a/k/a "The Perimeter"

Monica ☆

☆ Bobby and Jules

'STONE MOUNTAIN

GEORGIA TECH

ATLANTA

Porter ☆

Inside "The Perimeter," where Monica lives, is more prestigious.

Unless you live in Little Five Points near Junkman's Daughter, like Porter. That's not prestigious at all.

I-75   I-85

THE FOX THEATER

MIDTOWN

THE HIGHLANDS

GEORGIA AQUARIUM

DOWNTOWN

PUT THE BLAME ON JANE (AND CATHY)

Atlanta's a big place, so it was pure serendipity that Merril and I ran into each other one day at the High Museum of Art. I was in the top-floor gallery, browsing one of the High's collaborative exhibits with MOMA, when I spied an attractive woman at the far end. The woman in question, dressed and accessorized to the nines, was pointing at a painting and obviously talking about it with two little girls who were maybe ten and twelve.

I could only see the woman from the back and side, couldn't see her face, but something was oddly familiar, and I couldn't stop staring. Jet black hair in an asymmetrical cut, high heeled boots, clingy black dress with a red-and-black flowered scarf draped over one shoulder, heavy silver jewelry . . . *Omigod,* I thought. *It can't possibly be, can it? Am I seeing a ghost? Is that Miss Fortunato?*

No, of course it wasn't Miss Fortunato. It was Merril and the two little girls were her granddaughters. After we screamed and hugged, I told her she looked amazing.

I have an excellent surgeon, she said.

Then I asked her if she was wearing the same wig—Miss Fortunato's wig that I'd passed on to Merril all those years ago.

No, she said. *Miss Fortunato's wig bit the dust years ago. I always loved it, though, so I had a new one made just like it for my wig collection. My collection's top-of-the-line.*

We agreed that we'd meet up a little later in the museum's café, which we did. While the granddaughters ate lunch at their own table, Merril and I followed wine and croissants with strong coffee while we talked and reminisced and talked some more, for hours. Eventually the granddaughters got restless, so after more hugs, Merril and I said good-bye.

Atlanta traffic was impossible, as usual, so to distract myself while I drove back to my condo, I thought about the stories Merril regaled me with at the museum. Gradually my memories of the two of us as teenage girls were overlaid with the outlines of her life story and my own, creating in my mind a palimpsest of images.

By the time we were seniors in high school, Merril and I were avid readers of nineteenth century romantic fiction, especially the Gothic novels. Like the heroines in those books, we wanted the ecstatic romance, the fog-bound moors, the mysterious manor. Most of all, we wanted the unattainable hero, rich and handsome and mysterious like Jane Eyre's Rochester or Catherine Earnshaw's Heathcliff.

Let's start with Merril and her search for Rochester.

If you remember *Jane Eyre*, you'll recall that Jane doesn't exactly have a lot of fun. She nearly starves to death in an orphanage called Lowood after she escapes from an abusive relative at Gateshead and before she gets hired as a Governess at Thornfield Hall (pay attention to the names). Thornfield Hall belongs to the dark and mysterious Mr. Rochester who's hardly ever home, partly because he has *a secret* . . . namely his first wife Bertha who's locked up in the attic.

Eventually Jane deciphers Rochester's secret and runs for her life across the moors. After wandering around in freezing cold weather, Jane gets rescued by a platitudinous missionary known as St. John Rivers (one of those names again and it's pronounced "Sinjin Rivers"). Rivers wants to marry Jane but she—in the nick of time—finds out she's an heiress. Meaning she now has options.

Time passes while Jane exercises her options. Eventually, however, Jane's reunited with Rochester after Bertha causes a catastrophic fire at Thornfield Hall during which Rochester loses his fortune, his eyesight, and one hand. After all that—finally—Jane utters the famous line, *Reader, I married him!*

As I discovered while Merril regaled me with her stories at the museum, her adventure went considerably better than Jane's . . . at least for a while. She didn't have to live in an orphanage or do any moor-wandering, and her Byronic hero seemed to be the answer to every romantic heroine's prayer. It was that famous line, *Reader, I married him*, that did her in. Because Merril married him. And then she married the next one. And the next one. And the one after that.

I guess you could say Merril was a glutton for punishment, serial-monogamously speaking. Except as she told me that day over wine and coffee, at least she figured out while divorcing husband number three that it's best to keep *romance* and *finance* separate. Which she did while she was married to and divorcing husband number four.

Continuing to think about those Gothic novels while driving home that day, I admitted ruefully to myself that unlike Jane Eyre who went looking for love, I was a *Wuthering Heights* kind of heroine like Cathy Earnshaw. I stayed home, in other words, waiting for love to show up on my doorstep.

So there I was, expecting Heathcliff to magically appear while never realizing that in real life your Byronic hero might carry emotional baggage as heavy as a backpack full of rocks. Not noticing all that "baggage," I'd get myself into a relationship and then run like hell when it wasn't working out. To be sure, though, I had some interesting experiences with a Poet, a Pothead, and a Professor, to-wit:

First *The Poet* came to town—tall, dark, passionate, mysterious. Never mind (as I found out later) that he didn't know a trochee from a tracheotomy, and the only mystery was why Interpol hadn't caught up with him yet. It was nevertheless an incendiary romance, fueled by the poems he recited to me in a voice like Antonio Banderas while I imagined castanets clicking and Flamenco guitars playing in the background. I was devastated when he left abruptly after two weeks, but he was full of promises to call me when he got back from Spain.

(He didn't.)

Next there was *The Pothead*—not so tall or dark (pretty short, actually, just 5'6" tall with long wavy red hair and freckles) but very passionate, and I totally adored that *Glaswegian* accent. It was not meant to be, however. We had one romantic weekend in Big Sur and the Monterey Peninsula before the ex-girlfriend from London arrived on the scene. She was a hairdresser for rock stars and the first person I ever met who had fluorescent green hair, and she didn't like me one little bit. By the time they left for London together I was resigned to the situation and agreed we'd all stay in touch *just as friends*.

(We didn't.)

A few years later *The Professor* arrived—tall and dark but not mysterious or passionate, a little whiny actually and prone to high-sounding philosophizing. He was ready to stay "for the long haul" as he put it, presumably doing me a big favor, but this time it was I who made the decision to call it quits. We promised to stay in touch via e-mail, and I assured him I'd read his fabulously provocative new book.

(I didn't.)

After that I changed my e-mail server, finally finished my PhD, got a job at Georgia Tech, and bought my one-bedroom condo in Atlanta.

When Merril and I said good-bye that day in the museum, she told me she'd recently bought a townhouse in Atlanta and would be in town often because she wanted to see the grand-daughters. "That's fabulous," I said, and I invited her to join my neighborhood book club. The club's an interesting group of my longtime Atlanta friends, very eclectic, and I knew they'd all think Merril's a hoot.

Merril said not right now because she was excited about going on a big singles cruise, but after she got back from the cruise, she'd get in touch with me about joining the book club.

(She didn't).

MOVING TO A ROOM WITH A VIEW

It was time to clean out my office at Georgia Tech and get ready to move to a new one. After seven long years in a dingy office in the basement across from the men's bathroom with a broken door, I'd be moving to the third floor after the holidays, just before school goes back into session in January.

I couldn't wait! Already the maintenance crew had started upstairs in my new office—painting, installing carpet, putting in track lighting that I'd picked out at Home Depot. My new space would be three times as large as my old space, and I'd finally have windows and a vista: a panoramic view of down-town Atlanta. In short, I'd finally *arrived*. I had status, respect, a tenured faculty position with benefits, and a cushy office. Not only that, I'd never have to see The Little Wiener again.

Who?

The jerk in the next office. Also known to me as *Nemesis*, because he was always making trouble for me behind my back. *Her courses aren't rigorous, and she gives too many A's,* he'd say to my department chair. Or he'd say to my dean, *She's a terrible committee member, always late or absent.* Or he'd say to students, *You'll be bored stiff in her classes.* Imagine the most awful lies someone might make up about you and think of all the derogatory woman-names someone might call you, and you'll know how he talked about me.

True, it's possible I made the situation worse by confronting him, but who'd blame me? I stayed pissed off because I always had to watch my back, so what was I supposed to do? Turn the other cheek? *Au contraire.* So it was all-out war between The Wiener and me, down in our dingy basement offices. The Wiener never let up, but neither did I, and finally I'd won.

Wait . . . maybe when I'm happily ensconced in my new office, I'll turn the tables on The Wiener. What is it they say about revenge? It's "a dish best served cold"? That's it. It's an old *mafioso* saying, meaning you lay a careful plan to destroy your enemy, but you bide your time and hit when he least expects it.

Yes! I thought. That's what I'll do. I'll concoct a plan as fiendishly clever as anything Agatha Christie ever dreamed up. And while I'm planning and plotting, I'll start spreading a rumor that it's time for The Wiener to retire.

My friend Talisman is a longtime sounding board for my laments about The Wiener. Talisman lives in Florida, and she's a professor, too, but unlike me, she loves everything about academics: committees, politics, publish-or-perish. The whole shebang.

Whenever we talked on the phone and I started complaining about campus politics and stupid committee meetings and endless paperwork, she'd argue back. *Mags*, she'd say, *if you're not happy, you need to make a change. You'll never write that novel you're always talking about while you're an academic. It's not possible, and you know it.*

Deep down I knew she was right but guess what. I had some early lessons about the dangers of taking chances and "following your dream." And I know from sad experience it's not fun to be poor, and I'd be crazy to give up a secure job with a monthly paycheck and benefits. So I always tell Talisman I'll wait until my condo's paid for. and I have a nest egg, and *then* it'll be time to say goodbye to academics for good.

Besides that, in the meantime, I get a reprieve once in a while—along with some extra income—turning out my Kitchen Table Books. Oh, I didn't tell you about Kitchen Table Books? It's a series I dreamed up when I moved to Atlanta. Here's the pitch:

Picture yourself after a hard day at work, sitting at your kitchen table and eating cold lasagna out of a plastic container and wishing you had one of those gorgeous Coffee Table Books to distract yourself. You know what I mean, books with titles like *Mansions in the Hamptons* and *Famous Castles of Europe*.

Time to get real, right? You don't have one single mansion to your name, and you sure don't live in a castle. Not only that, you aren't crazy about blowing an entire paycheck on one of those gorgeous-but-ridiculously-expensive Coffee Table Books

That's when I started thinking about creating a low-cost, scaled-down alternative: *Kitchen Table Books.*

Gorgeous-but-affordable, they're a little bit artsy, a little bit literary, with lots of color photos and quirky artwork, tasty tidbits of gossip, as well as a few recipes with bios of chefs and artists.

When my friend Booker visited me in Atlanta, I pitched the project to her, and she loved it. We both needed something creative we could do in our spare time, and we knew we'd be great collaborators. Which we are.

Our first Kitchen Table Book—*Toasting with Toulouse: Absinthe Makes the Heart Grow Fonder*—was a runaway success, and we have high hopes for the next one that's titled *Proust and His Cookie.* And we have ideas for others including . . .

What? Okay, *okay!* Maybe Kitchen Table Books aren't Great Literature. But sometimes you're not in the mood for a heavy meal like *War and Peace.* Sometimes all you want is dessert: one perfect chocolate fudge petit four, or one marzipan strawberry with a hint of almond. Just a smidgen of sweetness to brighten your day

In a nutshell, that's exactly the way Booker and I envisioned our Kitchen Table Books. And the sales of *Toasting with Toulouse* prove we were right.

BOX IS A BOX IS A BOX IS A BOX

I'd already packed up my textbooks and papers and stashed them in a storage room, but we're advised to take our laptops and important personal belongings home with us over holiday breaks, so that's what I was doing. Packing up my important personal stuff, I mean. And I was glad I still had three days before the holiday weekend so I could pack slowly.

My scale-replica Amazing Technicolor Dreamcar, for example, got its own box and bubble wrap, and I dusted every framed photo and *Star Wars* figurine before wrapping them in heavy paper. Normally I wouldn't have packed up my diplomas and my collection of classic movie and opera posters, but I figured I'd keep them safe at home, then move into my new office like gangbusters with all my stuff.

Hmm, I thought to myself. Maybe I'll even have an office-warming party so The Wiener can eat his heart out. Not that I'll invite him, of course, but he'll hear about it because I'll invite *Everyone Who's Someone* except him.

I thought I'd packed everything except a few desk trays and my Commonplace Box when I noticed something on a high shelf, shoved back into a corner. Oh my gosh, I said to myself, it's the Gertrude stein that a student gave me years ago. What a cool gift! I was laughing while I got it off the shelf and dusted it.

You get it, right? It's a ceramic beer stein in the shape of Gertrude's head. It says *The Gertrude Stein* around the bottom in raised letters, and there's a diminutive Alice B. Toklas figure perched on the handle. I remember the student who gave me the gift, too. I'd included some of Stein's poems in a course on Modernism, and the student, her name was Linda, screamed bloody murder about having to read them. Said they were nonsensical, crazy, screwball.

I couldn't say I blamed my student, either.

I mean, there were valid artistic reasons why Stein wrote the way she did, but when you try to read what she wrote, you realize it's practically impossible. Most everyone's familiar with *Rose is a rose is a rose is a rose*, of course, but other quotes are way more outlandish, like this one:

Out of kindness comes redness
and out of rudeness comes rapid same question,
out of an eye comes research,
out of selection comes painful cattle.
Crazy, right?

Here's the thing, though, and it's something Stein never gets credit for: she's funny. "Painful cattle," for instance. I'm not sure *why* it's funny, I just know that it is. And I love the famous passage where she's describing her childhood home in Oakland, California: *There is no there there.* In a peculiar way it makes perfect sense as a description of a dead-end place, and believe it or not, you'll see it quoted everywhere: *There is no there there.* I kid you not, you'll see it in print media, on the internet, even in TV ads.

Back to me, packing up in my old office.

There they were on my desk, the Gertrude Stein and my Commonplace Box, side by side. And that's when I remembered Stein's famous "rose is a rose is a rose." Hmm, I wondered. Does that mean a box is a box is a box? Looking at my Commonplace Box and thinking back to when I made my first box years ago in Penn Hills, I wasn't sure because it's not literally the same box. And *that's* because my first Commonplace Box in Penn Hills was a Buster Brown shoebox that got mashed when we moved to Florida.

I needed a new one then, so when we lived in the hotel, I transferred the precious contents of the Buster Brown shoebox to a tin MoonPie canister that Jim Ed Clifton gave me. But the MoonPie canister rusted out by the time I left for college, so I switched to Tupperware—a green rectangular container with one of those famous "burping seal" tops that render it airtight. The Tupperware box traveled well, which is good because I moved around a lot after I left home, and I always had it with me.

So there I was in my old office at Georgia Tech, ready to pack up my third Commonplace Box . . . no wait, I thought to myself. It's my third box but it's also the first box *and* the second. Isn't it? Seeing it there on my desk, remembering, I felt a wave of nostalgia. It was late afternoon, at least an hour before security guards came around to lock up the building, so I could indulge myself. I peeled off the burp sealed top and looked at my life in a box.

Everything seemed so small, tumbled together. I picked up the precious book of Irish fairies gently, looked at the frontispiece with its hand-written inscription that says *Property of Michael O'Duinn Magee* in an elegant swooping script, then just as carefully nestled it back. Also dating back to the Penn Hills days were two clothespin dolls I'd carefully hand-painted, lying next to the old "Ghosties and Ghoulies" prayer plaque. My amulet was pretty shabby (ants got the crabapple), but I'd saved Pucci's horsetail hairs in a glassine sleeve.

Other treasures signified a tumble of years: the Fibonacci cuff bracelet and cryptic note from Miss Fortunato; my Mainland High School class ring and Tri Delta sorority pin; my dad's Masonic ring and Mom's bowling medal that says *State Champions* on the front; Muti's seed-pearl rosary beads; Groossma's jeweled hairpin with three stones missing; holy cards from funerals; and some old black-and-white photos in a dingy envelope.

I could hear security guards clinking around in the hallway, so I put everything back in the Tupperware box and sealed it (those burp seals really work), thinking I'd put the old photos in one of my albums later. Then I got a flash of inspiration. Mags, I said to myself, there's a new year coming, and you're moving to a great new office, and it's time for a new box. A beautiful new box, not a shoebox or a cheap tin or a plastic food container.

Yes! I said back to myself. This time I want a box made of sandalwood or teak, with carvings on the lid and brass hinges and a fancy filigree clasp-lock with a key. And I know just where to find it, at Pandora's Emporium. My new Commonplace Box will be a one-of-a-kind creation, hand-crafted and signed by the artist. I couldn't wait to go shopping!

Then I thought again about Gertrude Stein. She'd know what I meant if I said:

Out of Buster Brown comes MoonPie
but Tupperware is burping green,
and out of burps a very little difference is likely
with Pandora box selection.
Worship purple produce.

Oh yes, I said to myself, laughing at my own joke—a box is a box is a box, and they're all here because there's a here here!

I couldn't help thinking, too, about Stein's supposed last words. Have you heard the story? She was dying of cancer in a hospital in Neuilly, a suburb of Paris. As she lay close to death, she said to the room in general, *What is the answer?* When no response was forthcoming from anyone in the room, she said, *In that case, what is the question?* Then she died.

Some authorities think the story of her last words is apocryphal, just part of her legend. But I figure it doesn't matter. If you're so uniquely *you* that a legend grows around you after you die, then who cares if you really said your so-called last words or if someone made up a story?

At that point you're the story and the story is always being here. How cool is *that*?

A CHRISTMAS STORY

I have a holiday ritual that started when I moved to Atlanta. On Christmas-Eve-Eve (two days before Christmas) I decorate my tree and eat a whole box of holiday cookies from Publix. (I can't resist those Publix holiday cookies, so the easiest thing is just to eat a whole box and get it over with.)

On the day after that, the day of Christmas Eve, I treat myself to an afternoon in the Highlands, a quirky area of shops and cafés near Midtown. I always get home from the Highlands before dark, though, because on Christmas Eve in the evening my cat Schrödinger and I watch our favorite holiday movie *A Christmas Story* while we wrap presents and eat Claxton fruitcake. So as I was saying . . .

What? I didn't tell you about my cat Schrödinger? Sorry, I thought I already told you about Schrödy. You remember Boots and Ranger? Boots in Pittsburgh and Ranger in Daytona Beach? Well, I figured I was through with cats forever after Boots and Ranger. I mean, they were hardly success stories being as both cats disappeared when I'd barely gotten acquainted with them. So who could blame me for swearing off cats?

Or at least I *thought* I'd sworn off cats forever, but everything changed when Schrödinger showed up at my condo in Atlanta. I was home one Saturday, grading papers, when I heard a ruckus outside—geezer shouts and cat yowls, to be specific. Upon opening my front door, I was greeted by a standoff: the geezer next door was snapping a towel at a tuxedo Manx while the cat clawed the geezer's potted plants to smithereens.

Then something strange happened—the cat abruptly abandoned the geezer's potted plants, turned toward me, and met my gaze. While he looked at me, I looked at him, and somehow I knew my life was about to change forever. Then my new housemate and I went in my condo, leaving the geezer to survey his ruined front porch.

Not that I was without misgivings, which I'm sure you can well imagine. I mean, sharing your space is *hard*, even with a feline. Nevertheless, Boots and Ranger proved I'm a sucker for smart tuxedo trickster cats, especially if they're Manx tuxedos, so I decided to give this new cat a chance. He needed a name, however.

That's when I remembered our snowbird guest at the Lyndhurst Hotel years ago, and her comment to me when I was sad because Ranger went away: *At least this way he's always alive in your memory. If he's dead or alive, who knows? Does it matter?*

Hmm, I thought. If Ranger can live in my memory, then he can be dead *and* alive at the same time. Because isn't that how someone—anyone—lives in your memory? And the same goes for cats. That's when the famous thought-experiment called "Schrödinger's cat" popped into my head, and that's when I knew this cat's name should be Schrödinger.

The moral of this story is that Schrödinger and I are living happily ever after. He didn't disappear like Boots and Ranger, in other words, and the two of us are boon companions. We talk together, laugh together, and he gives me advice . . . even when I decline to accept it.

Getting back to my holiday ritual: Finally I get up early on Christmas morning to make my famous Hoppin' John (it's black-eyed peas and rice, mainly, but the secret's in the sauce and the Andouille sausage), to take with me when I get together with my book-club friends. We always party on Christmas Day at someone's house and exchange funny gifts.

Hoppin' John's a southern tradition for New Year's Day, the idea being if you eat it on New Year's Day you'll have good luck for the whole year. It worried me a little that I make it for Christmas Day instead of New Year's Day because I sure don't want to tempt fate by tromping on tradition. Everyone laughs at me for being superstitious, but you know what? When I make my Hoppin' John on Christmas morning, I put some aside and freeze it so I can thaw it a week later and eat it on New Year's Day too.

I also throw salt over my shoulder when I sneeze, and I *never* walk under a ladder. Better safe than sorry, is what I always say.

I get nostalgic on the first day of my holiday ritual while I'm decorating the tree, and that's because my ornament collection is a hodgepodge.

I have a few really old ornaments like my treetop angel, for example. I keep her because she dates all the way back to Penn Hills, but I never really liked her. She's chubby and sanctimonious, and she has one of those stupid halos stuck to her head. I've felt better about her since I started my Atlanta Tree Collage, though, because I always make her share the treetop with my Wonder Woman action figure.

I collected a few other ornaments through the years, but the ones I love best really aren't tree ornaments at all except I hang them on my Christmas tree anyway. Like theater tickets and playbills and my very first credit card with a hole punched in one corner for hanging. And keychain mementos from places like The Grand Canyon and Dollywood and Big Sur. And I tie up heavier things in net bags so they'll hang well on lower branches, like seashells from Daytona Beach and the Elson's Pocket Music Dictionary given to me by my very first piano teacher in Penn Hills.

For me, I guess, my Tree Collage is like my Commonplace Box in that both of them hold my history. More than that, though, they encourage me to time-travel in my head. There I'll be in my condo in Atlanta, then *Bingo!* I'm in Daytona Beach, then *Bingo!* I'm in Penn Hills. In a few seconds—no more—I've journeyed along the Yellow Brick Road of memory and staked my claim to the places and events that made me who I am today.

It was the morning of Christmas Eve.

My tree was decorated, the Publix cookies were long-gone (and I enjoyed every single bite, thank you!), the Claxton fruitcake was chilling in the fridge, and it was time to leave for The Highlands. I had three more gifts to purchase, and I'd planned that after getting my Dickens-nostalgia fix while strolling cobblestone streets and enjoying Carolers in their authentically Victorian costumes, I'd head for Pandora's Emporium and pick out my new Commonplace Box.

Humming *We Wish You a Merry Christmas*, I slid my precious Tupperware-Commonplace Box into a shoulder tote, put on my favorite winter coat—it's black wool, long, with a red satin lining and hood—and punched in the security-lock code. The weather forecast was light snow starting in the afternoon, continuing through the night and all day on Christmas, and I was so excited about being out and about that I felt I'd dropped a ton of years and become a kid again.

"Schrödy," I said, "I'll leave the tree lights on all day so you can enjoy them while you're snugged up on the sofa, and I'll be back by dark so we can watch *A Christmas Story* while we wrap presents and drink hot chocolate. Okay okay, *you* can have hot chocolate, and I'll have Glenfiddich on the rocks. What? Sure, we'll share the fruitcake. Deal? Great, it's a deal."

While I was locking my way out, though, he had to get in the last word.

"What, Schrödy? Okay, sure. I'll bring you a bag of boiled peanuts from Blind Willie's, but you *promise* to stay out of my planters, okay? What? If you have to make a promise, I have to make a promise too? All right, *all right*. I promise to stop humming."

The Highlands is one of those places where it's fun just to *be*. You can stroll along the cobblestone streets and enjoy the quirkiness of small Craftsman-style bungalows interspersed with mom n' pop shops, galleries, and every kind of eatery you could want. I'd already planned my shopping trip and knew that once I'd checked off everything on my list I'd hang out for a while at Blind Willie's with an appetizer and a glass of wine (just one!) while grooving on Willie's piano blues. Then as I'm leaving Blind Willie's, I'll buy a bag of those to-die-for boiled peanuts for Schrödy, just like I promised.

First, though, I headed to Wine & Roses for Monica. She's my dean at Georgia Tech, a Professor of French, and she's an expert on French wines. It's a running joke between us that I'm not a good judge of wine because I buy it for the label— the quirkier the better. I knew for sure I wanted a red, which I finally narrowed down to Sexy Red Bomb (a blend) or Mad Housewife (a cabernet). Mad Housewife won, and I declined to consider that there might be some buried Freudian motivation for my choice.

My next stop was a great little indy bookstore for Bobby and Jules. We're book club friends since I moved to Atlanta, and I knew the books I wanted for them: *A Lionel Christmas* for Bobby (a model train enthusiast) and *The Making of Gucci* for Jules (a fan of high-end fashion). Even though they're a couple, it's impossible to find one gift that works equally well for both, so I always do separates.

Before leaving, though, I lingered for a while at an exhibit near the front door that featured sculptural poetry—assemblages of paper and wire that explore the connection between language and art and the body. Then I thought about my Kitchen Table Books. Sigh. Did I mention they fit a mass-market niche, and you can buy them in Hallmark stores as well as the occasional Baskin-Robbins? Eventually I pulled myself together and headed outside into a magical snowfall—flakes of snow fluttering like butterflies in a breeze.

Snow always reminds me of those years long ago in Penn Hills. We don't get snows in Atlanta like those in Pittsburgh, but Atlanta snowfalls never fail to toss me back in time. I remember the crunching noises your boots make, and I remember that wonderful feeling of safety when you come in from the cold to get warm. Most of all, I remember how beautiful the white blanket of snow looked at night when Christmas lights around doorways and windows reflected their chains of colors: red, green, gold, blue.

Colored lights were different back then. They were heavy wires with just a few big colored bulbs that you screwed into individual sockets, not like the multiple strings of mini-lights and LED pinpoints that you see everywhere now. But snow was the same. When it was perfect and new, it fell so softly you could stick out your tongue and catch those tiny flakes, each one unique. When snow was falling softly, you could feel time itself slowing down.

I walked back to my car, catching snowflakes on my tongue. Then I put the Lionel and Gucci books in my car, and I stashed Monica's wine in the wine carrier I always keep in my trunk (a subtle suggestion from Monica after I gave her a bottle of wine that hadn't been properly climate-controlled). Finally, after putting my Tupperware burp-box in its tote bag and locking my car, I headed for Pandora's Emporium.

If hyperbole were a person, she'd be Pandora. Everything about her is excessive, exaggerated, overdone. She talks loud, walks fast and heavy, wears too much of everything including jewelry, cologne, makeup, even hairspray. She caught sight of me as soon as I walked in the door and stomped across the room to hug me. Then she pulled me over to a far counter where we could chat privately. Except you can't chat privately with Pandora because her voice is like a volume knob that's stuck on LOUD.

So, Mags, you got any paintings for me? Any sketches or tchotchkes? It's over a year since you brought me anything to sell, ya know? (In my spare time I draw and paint and create assemblages. Pandora likes my style, calls it *Femikitsch*.) I said no, I'd been busy with classes plus I'm the faculty sponsor for an honor society plus I read papers at two conferences in the fall, all of which I have to do to get promoted—

Mags! Pandora was shouting. *When are you gonna start your real life? I'll give you a job here part-time, watchin' the store. The rest of the time you make things, and we sell them for ridiculous prices. It's a no-brainer! Plus you can write books, and we'll sell those too!* Fortunately at that point Pandora got distracted and stomped off in a cloud of cologne to greet a customer who'd just come in the front door.

I'd already noticed the decorative boxes arranged on shelves against a back wall, so I walked there to browse. One wood box had a patina like brushed gold, with a purple velvet lining and exactly the kind of filigree lock-clasp I'd pictured for my new box. Another one, copper and tin, was in the shape of a castle and encrusted with gemstones. A third had enameled inlays on the lid and sides, and a box next to the castle-box was crafted of brushed green leather with an intricate golden dragon embossed on the lid. And that's not even mentioning at least a dozen others that were fancifully hand-carved and hand-painted.

I sat down on a chair, overwhelmed. All the boxes were beautiful and unusual, as Pandora well knew, but . . . but what? I asked myself. I wasn't worried about money. I knew Pandora would give me a good price and let me pay on time, if I wanted to. So why was I not rushing to judgment here, picking out the gorgeous *objet d'art* that would hereinafter hold my most precious mementos?

I knew why.

Yes, I said to myself, I know why. All the boxes are beautiful, each in its own way, but all of them are wrong. My Commonplace Box is about life, not art. It's about *my* life. My life as a shoebox and a cookie tin and a plastic container designed to hold leftovers. My life as . . . that's when I saw it, on a ledge under a counter at the shop's gift-wrapping station.

It was the perfect Commonplace Box for me and my small treasures. It's certifiably "vintage," just like me, and befitting its status as a Survivor (also just like me), it had obviously stood the test of time. *Yes!* I said to myself as I pulled it out from under the counter and set it on top. *This old tin Wonder Woman lunchbox will go forward with me through all the years to come!*

Then I called to Pandora and said, "This is the one I want!"

Oh fuck no, Honey! she shouted at me, startling the sweet-looking little lady she'd been attending to, on the other side of the store. While the sweet-looking lady backed away from Pandora and surreptitiously headed out the door, Pandora made a beeline for me and the box I was now clutching in both hands, holding it close to my chest as if daring her to snatch it from me. *Darling*, she hollered, *that's a piece of shit! I keep petty cash in it because I think it's a joke. It IS a joke! Look, there's a dent in one corner of the lid, and you have to tie it shut because the clasp's all jiggly. Not only that—*

Uh oh. Pandora turned around, looking back toward the empty counter where the sweet-looking lady was supposed to be waiting for her. *Damn it all!* she said. *I will never understand these prissy southern ladies with their helmet hairdos and their teensy-tinesy voices and how they get offended if you talk above a whisper and god forbid they should step in dog shit.*

I agreed that genteel southern belles take some getting used to, and then I tried to pay for my new box. *Honey, I'll give you the goddam thing*, Pandora groused.

Then she walked over to the beautiful boxes on display, picked up the gemstone-encrusted castle-box, and brought it back to the gift-wrap counter. *Lemme just dump the petty cash in this one*, she said. *It's been in the shop for two years because it's overpriced. Plus the artist's a pain in the ass, always calling and wanting to know why it isn't selling.*

I commiserated with Pandora about artists and their egos while she moved petty cash to the castle-box. Again I tried to pay for my box, but she wasn't having it. *No, Mags*, she said, *I can't take money for crap. And who knows? Maybe someone will want to buy this other one, now that it's the petty cash box. Then I can get Mr. Hot Shit Artist off my back about it.*

Dealing with Pandora usually exhausts me, but that day I wasn't tired because I was thrilled about my new Commonplace Box, and I was ready to transfer the contents, just as I'd planned. Blind Willie's was several blocks away, and I enjoyed every minute of my walk. The temperature was obviously dropping, so I pulled my big satin-lined hood up over my head, making me stand up straight and feel mysteriously provocative. Or provocatively mysterious. Like Meryl Streep in *The French Lieutenant's Woman*, waiting on the fog-bound jetty for Jeremy Irons. I was amusing myself with my *persona mysterioso*, expecting the French Lieutenant to be waiting impatiently in the doorway, ready to jump my bones . . .

But no such luck. No one at Blind Willie's even remotely resembled Jeremy Irons. Oh well, I thought to myself, it's not crowded, and there's a blazing fire in the fireplace, so I'll make myself comfortable. After ordering my wine and appetizer, I sat in a two-person booth near the back where I could change my boxes without being bothered by anyone. The changeover took just a few minutes, and then I leaned back to enjoy the music and watch the fire.

My memory was accelerating into overdrive, watching the flames. It was a gas fire, like the one I have in my condo but very unusual, like maybe they tossed some of those metal salts on the fire to get blue- and green-looking flames. My dad used to build fires like that in our fireplace when we lived in Penn Hills. He'd make colored flames with pinecones by sprinkling boric acid powder on them before he tossed them in the fire. (Boric acid was one of those old-timey remedies you could use in tons of ways, so Muti always had some under our kitchen sink.)

Our Penn Hills fireplace was real, of course, and we burned wood in it. I remember Muti complaining about having to clean the fireplace. She'd wear big heavy gloves while she swept ashes and soot into a bucket and re-arranged the logs. *Mr. Big Man,* she'd complain, *he makes the fire, but he don't clean up.* Then she'd stomp down the steps to the cellar and empty the soot-bucket into the coal furnace.

Thinking about Muti in Penn Hills brought back memories of the Little Match Girl and the Ice Queen, the Shadow and the Green Hornet—images from the past that seemed as real as if they'd been neighbors or relatives, not just story-characters.

Hmmph, I thought to myself. Stories are important, but try telling that to some of my colleagues at Georgia Tech. When you teach English and Humanities at a tech-oriented college, you have to defend yourself all the time. *That stuff you read and teach isn't real,* they'll say, *it's just storytelling.* Then they'll start in about the importance of fiber-optics and nanotechnology and bio-robotics and how they're remaking the world.

But never mind. I know stories are important, and I know why. Because we get them early on and they become part of our lives. They set up our expectations, provide role models, give us patterns for living. There've been civilizations that didn't have fire or the wheel, but there's never been a civilization that didn't have stories.

That's what I always say to my techie friends who just roll their eyes and say *Fine, whatever.* But you know what? I zapped them all last year at commencement when I passed out flyers saying *Four years ago, I didn't know what an engineer was, and now I are one.*

It was time to drive home after my sojourn at Blind Willie's. Again I enjoyed the walk back to my car through the Currier and Ives streetscape—the cobblestones and strolling carolers and colored lights and still-falling snow. It was picture-perfect, like a scene out of Dickens. I could almost hear Tiny Tim calling out *God bless us, every one!* while the Cratchit family celebrated their Christmas dinner of goose and pudding and cider.

I didn't let myself get distracted, though, because I was keeping my promise to Schrödy. I wouldn't be late getting home, and I'd remembered to buy him a bag of those boiled peanuts he loves so much. And I was excited about snuggling with him on our sofa while we watched *A Christmas Story*

I'm not sure he gets it, though, when I crack up over my favorite scene, the one where Ralphie puts on the pink bunny suit that's his horrible Christmas present from Aunt Clara. It's classic, reminding you of every time you got a terrible Christmas gift but had to pretend you liked it.

And I was looking forward to seeing my book club friends tomorrow at Monica's. They're my earliest Atlanta buddies, the group I joined when I moved here: Pandora and her adopted daughter Dorothy Jane; my editor Ford and his cousin Porter; Bobby and Jules (a power couple); and Monica, of course, my dean at Georgia Tech.

And who knows? Maybe tomorrow will be the day Elton John arrives to celebrate with us. We always set out a special Elf-on-the-Shelf with a gift for Sir Elton, just in case he shows up. He never has, but like Porter always says, you want to be ready for the Rapture.

My condo's northeast of Midtown, a short distance off I-285 in a development called Hollywood Hills. The developer's a David Lynch aficionado so the streets have names like Twin Peaks Boulevard, Lost Highway, Blue Velvet Vector. The condo section in Hollywood Hills, where I live, is on Mulholland Drive. People always ask me if I'm kidding, but I always say no, I'm not kidding. It's true. I live on Mulholland Drive.

So while I was driving on the beltway I was thinking about those surrealistic David Lynch films. Then I started wondering how Lynch would adapt "The Night Before Christmas" as a movie. Tim Burton turned it into "The Nightmare Before Christmas," I thought, but I bet David Lynch would make it super-sexy.

I exited I-285 and headed north, amusing myself by picturing Isabella Rossellini as "Ma in her kerchief" and Kyle MacLachlan as "Pa in his cap." The two of them would be buck naked, of course, except for the kerchief and cap, and you'd have a flashback of what they were doing before Pa sprang from his bed to see what was the matter.

And I cracked myself up picturing that whack-a-doodle Dennis Hopper up on the housetop, click click click. There he'd be, dressed up like Jolly Old Saint Nicholas and getting blitzened with Vixen and Rudolf and Olive (the other reindeer) . . . when I realized something was very very wrong. What's going on?

Do I hear sirens?

What are all those flashing lights about, up ahead?

What's happening?

Two hours later I was soaking wet, chilled to the bone, as nasty-dirty as a Dickens chimney sweep. Bawling to beat the band, I trudged through slush and ashes, stopping to holler for Schrödy, then bawling again while I slipped and slid and circled aimlessly around the pitiful shell of my burned-out condo.

I have good insurance, the Developer assured me and my burned-out neighbors.

You'll be compensated for everything you lost.

Dorothy Jane spent the next three days with me at the fire site, sifting through ashes. It was heartbreaking to see that even though some things survived, they were too smoky or singed or water-damaged to be salvageable and had to be trashed. Finally, we assembled a pitiful cache of remnants that included the old Penn Hills Angel from my tree and some water-stained books.

And Schrödinger's box. It was in the basement by his cat flap. Even though Schrödinger didn't come back right away after the fire, I figured he must have gotten out through his flap so I'd just clean his box and get it all ready for him when he arrives, repentant like the Prodigal Son who stayed away too long.

Even though I'd lost my laptop in the fire I knew Georgia Tech would replace it, and I keep all my files on flash-drives in my purse, meaning my school files were intact, and I could start the semester as planned. Monica was great, encouraging me to take a leave of absence if I wanted to, but I said no. Work keeps you sane, gives you a reason to keep going. I knew that's what I had to do.

My friends and I moved our Christmas Day get-together to New Year's Day, and we all tried our best to be festive. Jules even cooked Hoppin' John, but I couldn't eat any of it. I wasn't feeling very trustful about having good luck at that point, and who could blame me? Everyone gave me thoughtful gifts, but there was really only one thing I wanted.

After the party, just like every other day since the fire, I drove to Hollywood Hills so I could walk up and down Mulholland Drive, looking for Schrödy.

SNOW FLURRIES

Do you know what a snow flurry is? It's when you can't count on the snow to fall steadily. It starts, then it stops, then it starts again, and in the meantime there's enough wind (also stopping and starting unpredictably) that you get clouds of snow here and there. Swirling clouds of snow.

That's what a flurry's like after a disaster, too. There's a flurry of activity for a while with people calling and coming to see you and wanting to help, maybe for a week or even several weeks, but then the flurry dies down and you're left with the new situation. Because people, even people who love you like crazy, have to get back to their own lives.

After the flurry over my condo fire subsided, reality set in. I'd lost everything that mattered to me: albums and scrapbooks, my piano and all my sheet music, the Christmas-tree-collage, my dad's adventure books, photographs in frames including the signed photo of Bethie Jean, diplomas and certificates, my collection of classic opera posters, my scale-replica Dreamcar—everything went up in smoke.

How ironic, I thought, that I've always been so afraid of ice. I never forgot that treacherous black ice in Penn Hills, the ice that cracked and dumped me into freezing-cold water. After that I was so-o-o careful, always watching where I walked, trying to play it safe and not take chances. But it wasn't ice that did me in, it was fire.

That fire stole my history, I'd say to myself. Then I'd think no, Mags, be reasonable. The fire didn't steal your history because it couldn't. That's when I'd open my Commonplace Box and get out the envelope of old photos. I'm not even sure why I put them in my box in the first place, instead of in an album. Why these, and not others? Chance, I guess, or maybe serendipity.

We want *so much* to hang on to the past, to have something tangible we can touch and feel and look at. But tangible things aren't our history, I reminded myself. Our history lives in us, in our minds and hearts and memories.

I may have only a few photos left—those frozen instants of time in black and white—but the stories are all in my head, and I'll never lose them. The people are there, too. Whenever I think about them, while I'm remembering them, they're alive in me.

In the meantime, though, I had to think about practical things like where I was going to live. Pandora's daughter Dorothy Jane said I could stay in her spare bedroom until I found my own place. After all, she said, moving in with my few remaining possessions wouldn't be difficult and if I were staying with her, I wouldn't feel pressured to buy a house or condo until

I found one I really liked. So that's what I did. I moved in with Dorothy Jane, I mean.

My friends and I were all back at work at that point, of course, so house-hunting had to be mainly on weekends, and as luck would have it the only person with weekends free was Ford. In case you forgot, Ford's my editor at the publishing house where Kitchen Table Books are printed and marketed. When Booker and I agree that a new KTB title is ready to publish, I send the paste-up to Ford. Who usually opines that the book's a disaster.

Ford's *schtick* is that writers deserve to be treated like crap. Everyone thinks it's funny that Ford and I have a contentious relationship, yet for Ford and me most of the time, it works. He's pushy and obnoxious about deadlines, but I'm just as pushy and obnoxious about quality. If a book isn't ready, in other words, I stall until it is.

Like I said, most times the relationship between Ford and me works. It was definitely *not* working, however, while we were driving around looking at houses. I was distraught, naturally, but Ford chose that inopportune time to needle me about getting the next Kitchen Table Book out.

The new book's titled *Proust and His Cookie*, a catchy title if I say so myself . . .

You don't get it about the title? Marcel Proust is famous for connecting the aroma of a cookie—a *petite madeleine*, specifically—with memories of the past. It's called "the episode of the madeleine" and it's in his novel *À la recherche du temps perdu*. Which believe it or not is in seven volumes. That's right, seven volumes. A total of 3,000 or 4,000 pages (depending on whether you read it in French or English) and 2,000 characters—literally a cast of thousands.

I've always found it interesting that Proust had to write seven books just to get remembered for one episode about a cookie. Like I said, though, it's a *very* famous episode, so famous, you'll see it referenced practically everywhere, even in places where engineers and scientists hang out. Like there's a restaurant at the Gonda Neuroscience and Genetics Research Center at UCLA, for instance, called the Café Synapse, and *Proust's petites madeleines* are always on the menu. I kid you not.

Anyway, Ford had bugged me all during the fall semester to finish the Proust book because he wanted to get it out in time for the Christmas shopping frenzy. I tried to explain to him that I was hopelessly bogged down at school plus I was writing two conference papers, but he kept on bugging me anyway until I finally exploded.

At which point we had a big fight and compromised—I'd finish with the paste-up right after Christmas, and we'd get the book out for Valentine's Day. Which certainly would have happened if the small matter of my life going up in smoke had not intervened.

So the whole time we were looking at houses, Ford and I were needling each other. We were falling into our familiar everyday work-pattern, in other words, but I was only paying half-attention to him, and he was getting pissed off.

Then I saw three houses that I really liked, and I was discovering that realtors loved me. They knew I'd have cash once I got my insurance payout, *and* I was a good mortgage-bet because I had a secure job with benefits, *and* I didn't have an existing house that I needed to sell.

In the world of residential real estate, in other words, I was a hot property. It sounds weird to say this, but I was feeling popular for a change, and any time I wanted a free lunch I could take my pick of realtors who'd be thrilled to pick up the check.

And I was starting to get my spirits up. After all, I'd moved into a great new office, and I loved the view, especially from my big window that faces south. *And* I still had my Commonplace Box because I'd been changing it from Number Three to Number Four while the fire was destroying everything at my condo. *And* a neighbor in an unburned section of Hollywood Hills said she was sure she'd seen Schrödy in the woods behind her house, and knowing what a smart resilient cat he is, I was confident he'd be back when he's good and ready.

So life was starting to look okay again. Not great, but pretty good.

Then The Wiener moved into the office next to mine.

BEST IN SHOW

Dorothy Jane and I were beginning to get on each other's nerves. I certainly appreciated her generosity in offering her guest bedroom to me. But you know, sometimes I wonder if it's easier to live with a stranger than with a friend.

The thing about Dorothy Jane is, she lives and breathes (and would happily bleed) for the University of Georgia. Her whole house is decorated in UGA colors: red, black, and silver/gray. Now I'm a big fan of power-colors, myself, especially red to complement black, which is one of my favorite combinations when I'm choosing outfits. But red-black-gray is not exactly soothing when you're surrounded with it in your house. Can you picture a black toilet? Neither could I, until I moved in with Dorothy Jane. Oh, and gray walls everywhere. I figured I could stand the decorating scheme for a while until I found my own house, but that's because I hadn't counted on the bulldogs.

The bulldogs? Yes. Dorothy Jane is a professional trainer and judge in the rarefied world of dog shows and her specialty breed is bulldogs, which as you probably know is the University of Georgia mascot. The team mantra is *Go Dogs!* (it's pronounced "Dawgs" and don't you forget it!), and I'm told that when the grandstands chant for Uga the mascot (it's pronounced UH-guh), it's truly overpowering.

Okay, so except for the dismal color scheme in the house, none of this was impinging on my personal space until the UGA breeder/owner had to go into rehab and needed someone to dog-sit the three bulldogs who take turns making appearances as the UGA mascot. Dorothy Jane got the nod to dog-sit (it's quite an honor) and proceeded to move the three bulldogs into her finished basement, where they could have privacy and their own cable TV.

Again, this was all right with me except that bulldogs, especially championship purebreds, make a lot of noise. *They need to exercise their vocal cords,* Dorothy Jane would explain, and then she'd turn up the volume on *Animal Planet,* or whatever program the dogs were watching, so they could vocalize with the TV.

Was she doing that passive-aggressive thing, trying to force me out? I didn't know for sure, but I knew I was in a spot. Then I bought a futon and a small fridge and moved them into my office at school so I could work late and stay overnight occasionally, but someone reported me. I suspected the Wiener but couldn't prove it, so I figured I simply had to find my own place to live—soon.

Let's get this show on the road, I thought to myself, *because I am ready to make the final cut.* Then I started laughing. Whoa, I thought, that's funny. Just like Dorothy Jane, I'm ready to pick the best in show.

PORTER'S MAGIC SCHOOL BUS

Suddenly my search for a new domicile had intensified. I needed stability, and I needed a homeplace where Schrödinger would be comfortable when he came back.

Ford was being impossible, continuing to insist that Booker and I get *Proust and His Cookie* ready for publication immediately, no excuses, and, by the way, he wouldn't take me house-hunting again until I'd delivered the book. Monica was at a conference, Bobby and Jules were both out of town, Pandora had to mind her store, and the three Ugas needed every minute of Dorothy Jane's time, so on a whim I asked Porter to go with me while I took a final look at my three top house-possibilities.

Porter said sure, he'd be glad to go with me, so we agreed I'd pick him up the next morning. Which I did, right on time and noticed that when he got in my car he smelled like patchouli oil—pure, uncut, certified organic—which he orders in large quantities from a shop in San Francisco called The Essential Herbarium. It's his only extravagance.

Porter's one of those idealists who never got over the sixties. He's a real sweetheart, just continues trying to teach the world to sing in perfect harmony, and in the meantime keeps himself financially afloat by clerking at Junkman's Daughter, a far-out shop down at Little Five Points. You need purple lace-up platform boots? brass knuckles? Mohawk wax? Porter'll help you find it at Junkman's Daughter.

Porter is Ford's cousin, which is how I met Porter in the first place because Ford rescued Porter and set him up in a co-op in Atlanta. As the story goes, Porter had spent the previous seven years living in a rattletrap school bus that he drove around the country following the Grateful Dead, and he loved being a Deadhead.

He plays a pretty good bass guitar himself. So good, in fact, he'd jam sometimes with the band when they were between gigs. Those were the magical years, Porter says, just one long toke-filled mind-blowin' ride on the freedom-screamin' roller coaster of the soul. Which is why Ford had to rescue him. The "mind-blowing" part, I mean.

I picked Porter up at his place because he doesn't drive. Nope, he says, he already made enough of a carbon footprint driving his school bus for those seven years, so now he walks or takes mass transit. It wasn't that I valued Porter's opinion as a potential homebuyer or anything, more that I wanted company while I looked again at the three houses because the realtors were getting kind of pushy. They're all women (two Muffies and a Peggy Sue), and I figured Porter would distract them a little. He's good-looking in a scruffy kind of way, sort of like Viggo Mortenson in *The Lord of the Rings* movies while he's still a Ranger called Aragorn, before he has to get cleaned up and be crowned as the long-lost King of Gondor.

Well, my distract-the-realtors plan worked just fine, yet after we'd toured the three houses, I was more confused than ever. I was trying to picture myself in one of those new spaces, but none of the mind-pictures worked. I told Porter I'd treat for dinner so we could sit talk about the day, and he said that would be fine.

After we got a table at my favorite little Mexican place, I started talking. *So Porter,* I said, *what do you think about the houses?* Porter said he was sorry, but he couldn't be much help because the houses all looked the same to him: beautiful, elegant, expensive, claustrophobic. *It's the Rooms-to-Go aesthetic,* he said. *The one-size-fits-all mindset, except it doesn't.*

Then he asked me if I remembered a song called "Little Boxes" that got famous in the sixties when Pete Seeger recorded it. Malvina Reynolds wrote it, he said, and it's a shame Malvina didn't get more credit for the song because she was some kind of kickass lady.

You knew Malvina Reynolds? I asked. (I was impressed.)

Sure did, Porter said. *Couple of years there, while I had my bus, me and Malvina and Bud would go hang out, and sometimes Pete would stop by.*

Pete? You knew PETE SEEGER? (I was super-impressed.)

Not as well as Bud and Malvina but yeah, Pete was an okay guy. It's just that he shouldn't have gotten all the credit for "Little Boxes."

Porter was full of stories about Jerry Garcia and The Dead, and he told one legendary story about Jerry that hit me between the eyes like a spitball. As the story goes, Jerry and some hell-raising teenage friends were carousing in a car, traveling ninety miles an hour when it skidded round a curve, hit a guard rail, and started rolling. Everyone was injured, some more than others, and one kid died.

That accident, Garcia said, was "the slingshot for the rest of my life." Before the accident he hadn't known whether he wanted to be a musician or an artist or anything at all. After the accident, he said, when he realized he'd gotten a second chance, he got serious. Porter said he knew Jerry "after the slingshot," and that's why the band was worth following because by that time they were serious about their music. Jerry could improvise endlessly, Porter said, and they were all such superb musicians that the band never played a song the same way twice.

Porter did admit, though, his school bus looked pretty bad there at the end. And he (Porter) was always one rail away from being a train wreck. *But you know, Mags*, he said, *that old bus was magical to me. Jerry even wrote a song about it, called it "Porter's Magic School Bus." I'll never forget those years, and I'll never forget my bus.*

That's when I told Porter about my Amazing Technicolor Dreamcar, how it was magical to me just like his bus was to him. And I told him about Scary Mary, Reenie's purple motorcycle. Scary Mary "liberated" her, is what Reenie used to say. I hadn't thought about Reenie for a long time, but I didn't think about her in a sad way. She lived the way she wanted to, and I always believed she, like Porter, found her own magic.

I was so involved in Porter's stories that I temporarily forgot about the houses we'd looked at, and while we were chatting, I asked him if he'd ever met B.J. Smithfield. He said no, he was just a kid when BJ died, but he loved her last song, the one called "Wolf." Said it still sends chills down his spine. And that's when he said it was a shame about B.J., dying in that plane crash when she was just starting to hit the charts. *And you know, Mags*, he said, *stories and songs don't come out of nowhere, so I figure there must've been some real bad dude lurking in B.J.'s past, provoking her to write that song.*

I know, I said. *I've suspected something about the real bad dude for a long time, myself.*

Finally I was ready to get back to business, meaning I was ready to talk about the houses we'd seen, and that's when Porter referred again to the song "Little Boxes." Do you remember it? So plain, so simple it sounds like a children's song: *There's a green one and a pink one and a blue one and a yellow one.* Supposedly Malvina and Bud were driving along a hillside development when she felt a song coming on, and that's when she wrote it. Just started singing *Little boxes made of ticky tacky and they all look just the same . . .*

The song goes on in the same simple sing-along style for four or five verses about the people who live in the little boxes, and that's when you realize that the song isn't about houses at all. The point of the song is, you have to be courageous enough to be your own person. And *that* means making your own box instead of living in one that's mass-produced and mass-approved—the one-size-fits-all-box, except it doesn't.

I dropped Porter off at his place, no farther along in my residential planning than I'd been six weeks ago. Damnation, I said to myself. Boxes again. Seems like I'm thinking all the time about boxes, like my new Commonplace Box. I still can't believe Pandora called it a piece of crap. Well, a vintage Wonder Woman tin lunchbox might look like a piece of crap to Pandora because it's a little rusty and bent, but I love it.

It's like the Velveteen Rabbit: well-used and loved. And it's the same with Porter's school bus. He filled that bus with enough music and stories to last him for the rest of his life, and that's why it was magic. That's why it didn't matter that everyone else thought his bus was a piece of crap.

Mags, I said to myself, you have to keep looking for the magic.

AND WALLY MOVED TO FLORIDA

It's funny the way things happen, isn't it? In my family Wally was always the world traveler, taking off every summer to dig around in old catacombs and buried cities, looking for the missing piece of the puzzle so he could finish his dissertation on Saint Julian and become world-famous. But after one of his summertime "digs" he always left time for travel, staying in chateaus and villas while overdosing on opera and wine and *haute cuisine.*

Sigh. Not that I was jealous or anything. Well okay, maybe I was a *little* jealous. I mean, my travels have been mainly at the Holiday-Inn-Express-level, forget about flying first class or having a "driver" ready to ferry me wherever I wanted to go.

So you can understand why it floored me when Wally called to tell me he'd moved to some acreage in West Volusia County, Florida. He didn't explain why, just said he was building a house on the St. Johns River near Blue Spring State Park. Wally? *Really?* That puts him smack in the middle of The Boonies, for sure. No chateaus, villas, or *haute cuisine,* in other words.

After my phone talk with Wally, I couldn't get him off my mind. So my brilliant, multi-lingual, scholarly cousin had moved to Florida, of all places? Thinking back over our phone conversation I remembered his plan to build his house in sections. "Pods," he called them. He said the first is was a geodesic dome, and the second—still under construction—will be a trapezoid partly on stilts.

I also asked him about transportation, because I knew he didn't drive his beloved BMWs (the last time I checked, he owned three). What? Why doesn't he drive his cars? Good question. He knows the history of every vehicle he owns, keeps them in tip-top shape, and loves riding in them so he can admire the engineering. I guess it just never occurred to him to get a driver's license.

Anyway, he never learned to drive, and I knew he'd be pretty isolated out there by the St. Johns River, but Wally had a transportation plan also. He said it was no problem because our friend Christopher would drive him wherever he needed to go. I hadn't known that Christopher, too, was in Florida, so Wally explained that Christopher was beginning a three-year appointment at Stetson University in DeLand as Resident Composer. And since Christopher loves driving BMWs, Wally told me excitedly, he'll be happy to drive Wally all over creation.

In addition to such interesting concepts as building his residence in pod-sections and owning expensive vehicles he can't drive, Wally told me he was planning a Japanese garden of the *Karesansui* type. What he said precisely was this:

> *Karesansui, Mags, is a garden style unique to Japan, which appeared in the Muromachi period. Using neither ponds nor streams, it makes symbolic representations of natural landscapes using white sand, stone arrangements, moss, and pruned trees.*

Then he finished up by saying he'd construct his *Karesansui* garden in the open space under his trapezoid-pod: *My trapezoid-pod backs up to a hill,* he said, *and the open space beneath will be perfect for my Karesansui garden and all my model trains!*

I felt better, then, about Wally.

Mags, I assured myself, *it's okay. Florida might be weird, but you know what? I think Wally will be okay there. Yep, I think he'll fit right in.*

SEND ME A SIGN

I've been noticing lately that college students seem so *young.* I notice this at the beginning of a semester when I'm standing in front of a classroom full of new faces. Or now, when I'm in an airplane full of pulsatingly hormonal young persons with electronic devices sprouting from their heads and multi-colored wires trailing into backpacks.

It's spring break—an important concept for those of us involved in higher education. So am I going on a spring break vacation? Not exactly, no, but you could say I've had one of those Jerry Garcia "slingshot" moments.

It all started when Wally heard about my condo fire and called to tell me about a loft apartment in Daytona Beach that's owned by an old friend of our family from Pittsburgh. Well, not an old *friend,* exactly, more like a guy who's related to Big Tony DiCicco through Ralphie Marbles Junior who's divorced from Wally's best friend. Anyway, Wally said the friend's name is Geno, and he has a great loft apartment for rent so why don't I fly down during spring break and look at it?

When Wally called I was not keen on the idea of the trip because I had my spring break all planned, what with looking again at the three houses I really liked, plus Ford was driving me crazy about *Proust and His Cookie,* so I knew Booker and I needed to finish the damn book. But most important of all, I planned to camp out every afternoon in my neighbor's yard (her name's Mrs. McGillicuddy) so I'd be there when Schrödy made an appearance.

Then I got some really bad news.

At that point in time The Little Weiner and I managed to ignore each other even though he'd moved into the office next to mine on the third floor. Then Monica came in my office one day, closed the door behind her, and sat down.

Uh oh. What's this about? *Mags, I'm leaving. I've turned in my resignation. I'll be leaving Georgia Tech, effective after the commencement ceremony in May, when the new Provost will be named.*

The new Provost? I thought you were in the running for provost.

I was in the running, but I didn't win the race. Got tromped on, actually. Arsenault J. Springer will take office on May 31st, and may God help the university.

Was this a signal from above? A message from the stars? A cosmic slingshot? Mags, I said to myself, if this is a sign, you'd better pay attention to it.

Here's why. The Provost of a college is the Chief Academic Officer, the official where the buck stops when such faculty issues as pay raises and promotions and release-time are involved. The point being, if you're a faculty member you want to make sure the Provost likes you. But Arsenault J. Springer— the Provost-designate—is also known to me as *The Little Weiner*, and it's a safe bet he definitely does not like me. *Ipso facto*, it is reasonable to anticipate that when he is Provost he will not be nice to me when I am up for a pay raise or a promotion or release-time. Or anything else that would work in my favor.

Not only that.

Monica stayed for a while and filled me in on the whole story, which was pretty grim because The Weiner'd been toadying up to the Trustees. Everyone knew the current President was practically dead on his feet, and the Trustees were looking for a replacement and—

Oh no! I said. *Monica, surely it isn't possible?*

I wouldn't take bets it won't happen, is what she said.

Okay, I thought, if Arsenault J. Springer becomes the next president of Georgia Tech, I won't just be at the bottom of the pecking order eating dirt. I'll be *under* the dirt. Assaulted by nightmarish visions of my new office in the sub-basement next to the boiler room and my teaching schedule filled with sections of Remedial Composition, I decided to call Wally.

Wally and Christopher met me at the Daytona Beach International Airport. Have you flown in there lately? You should, because it's a hoot—a first class facility planned for lots of major airline traffic. *If you build it, they will come.* Right?

Wrong. The major airline traffic never materialized, meaning if you're flying into Daytona it's a real treat to de-plane as scheduled (no circling overhead, stacked up and waiting for an empty runway). Then you wander through the mostly-empty terminal (no line at the loo), pick up your luggage without hassle (only one baggage carousel is operational), and meet your driver or shuttle right there at the door (no standing outside in rain or diesel fumes or 100-degree heat or all of the above, waiting for your ride).

I was having serious flashes of déjà vu while we drove downtown to meet Geno at his store. After all, this was my old stomping ground, first when I rode my bike all over creation and later when my Amazing Technicolor Dreamcar took me and my girlfriends around town. Yes, things had changed and growth had happened, but I was still having serious flashbacks.

Geno's building is on a downtown corner, where Beach Street meets Magnolia Avenue. On the first floor Geno has a store called Toyz 'n Trainz, along with a coffee shop. The second floor 's devoted to Geno's wholesale business called Middle Man, and he was developing the third floor into a loft apartment for himself until his cousin Ralphie intervened.

Ralphie had just inherited Big Tony's beachside hotel and made Geno an offer he couldn't refuse, to-wit: Geno would move into the luxurious Godfather Suite in the hotel, which Ralphie was vacating because he already bought the penthouse in the high-rise next door. All of which meant Geno was left with the half-finished loft that Wally called to tell me about.

I liked Geno right away. He's loud, funny, talks like Sylvester Stallone in *Rocky*. And he's just as good-hearted and unaffected as the Italians I knew in Pittsburgh. While we were walking upstairs, he apologized the whole time because the loft wasn't finished—no kitchen yet, no carpeting, no dropped ceiling to hide pipes and beams.

The bathroom was plumbed, and the bedroom drywall was up, though. The rest was just open space—one huge airy sunlit open space with redbrick walls, distressed hardwood floors, ceiling beams that looked like they'd been salvaged from a nineteenth century schooner, and banks of windows on three sides: facing east, south, and west.

I was intrigued enough to ask Geno if he'd hold up on the renovations for twenty-four hours until I got back to him with some drawings and ideas, and he said sure, no problem. *And before I forget*, he said, *Old Sonny wants to say hi.*

Old Sonny?

Yeah, he says he remembers you from Pittsburgh, although he might disremember you at the particular time you're talkin' to him. Old Sonny goes in and out, if you know what I mean. Geno tapped his head, shrugged. *Sometimes when you're talkin' to Sonny you realize that he stayed too long at the Fair and he ain't made it back yet.*

Then Geno said the magic words: *And by the way, let's go look at the fire escape. My cousin Frankie Moose designed it. Frankie, he's an artist and he did us proud.*

Can you picture a copper-colored spiral staircase three stories high?

A stairway to the stars with steps continuing up to the rooftop?

A monumental sculpture ending in a filigree-like gazebo on the rooftop, giving you a bird's eye view of the city stretching below and beyond in all directions?

I couldn't either until I saw it with my own eyes. That is, I couldn't picture it until I stepped out of the loft's back door onto the fire escape's third-floor landing, then climbed with Geno up to that filigree rooftop gazebo and stood there, enraptured.

Wally and Christopher are blasé about the fire escape because they've gotten used to it, and they were so oblivious to its symbolic significance to me that neither one even mentioned it while we were heading downtown. We hadn't seen it from a distance, either, because we drove to Geno's building along the river, heading south on Beach Street. So I didn't know anything at all about the fire escape, much less that it's a local landmark and bona fide tourist attraction, until I stepped onto that landing and climbed with Geno up to the rooftop gazebo.

I mean, think about my state of mind at that moment when I stood with Geno above the cityscape on a fire escape so gorgeous, it qualifies as art.

Oh yes, I thought, *this is magical.*

I was waiting for a Sign, and now I have one.

THE YELLOW BRICK ROAD BECKONS

Commencement was over, and it was time to get Agatha packed up for the drive to Florida (Agatha's my ancient Volvo and how she keeps on going is a mystery). What little I had to pack, that is—a few things salvaged from the fire-site (including, ironically, my mom's and dad's ashes), my Commonplace Box, clothes and shoes I'd purchased since the fire, all the books from my office at Georgia Tech.

And Schrödy's box, of course.

Mrs. McGillicuddy's sure she sees Schrödy all the time because the little dickens is so recognizable—a tuxedo Manx, all black except for white feet and a white chest that goes way up over his nose, creating a black "Lone Ranger" mask over his eyes. Oh, and his eyes are green but sometimes you'd swear they're turquoise. Mrs. McGillicuddy and I agree there's no way anyone could mistake him for another cat.

Here's our plan: Mrs. McGillicuddy will put out some half n' half and a little dark meat from a Publix rotisserie chicken every day by her back door. Once Schrödinger gets used to having his all-time favorite dinner every day like clockwork, he'll deign to peek in Mrs. McGillicuddy's kitchen. Then the minute he's inside her house, she'll pick up the phone and call me in Florida. That's when I'll jump in Agatha and head for Atlanta with Schrödy's box.

After all, I figure, I'll be self-employed then. Since I won't be on anybody's time clock but my own, I can be ready in a heartbeat to drive to Atlanta, bring Schrödy back to Daytona Beach, and introduce him to our new digs. I worried a little that our skybox-apartment in Geno's building will be a bit of an adjustment for him, being as he can't just go in and out as he pleases.

But we'll have a fabulous balcony overlooking the river and the park, and the two of us can climb up to the roof any time we want to, and we can walk across Beach Street to Riverside Park where he can run around and chase squirrels. And ducks. I bet Schrödy will love chasing ducks.

So all in all, I think he'll be happy in Florida. In fact, I'm sure of it.

Finally it was my last night in Atlanta.

I'd said goodbye to everyone else, but I was meeting Dorothy Jane at the Fox Theater on Peachtree Street for an Elton John concert. The theater's known as "The Fabulous Fox," for at least a hundred good reasons including the fact that it looks like an authentic Moorish temple, inside and out, with balustrades and porticoes and an enormous Kremlin-style dome.

Mostly, though, I identify with the Fox because of its history, so much like my family's history. Like us, the Fox started out with big dreams in the twenties, got bankrupted by the Depression, was shunned for years as a poor relation (*Gone with the Wind* premiered at Loew's, not the Fox, which was the snub of the century), made a comeback in the forties but declined again for decades before recovering, even suffered enormous damage by a fast-moving fire in 1996. Somehow through all of this, the Fox Theater survived.

As did my family. And as did I.

Dorothy Jane was waiting for me at the box office, but she seemed distracted. *Every second of every minute of every day,* she said, *I know that the world is white but I'm black.* When I asked her what happened, she said she stopped at a convenience store and when she was checking out, the salesclerk *dropped* the change into her palm. *He didn't want his white hand to touch my black hand,* she explained matter-of-factly. Dorothy Jane's used to this sort of thing, I know, but I still find it difficult to fathom. While she hunted in her purse for our concert tickets, I was tripping down Memory Lane . . .

In memory I recalled an earlier Dorothy, standing on the front porch of the Lyndhurst Hotel to welcome the new owners. *Dorothy comes with the hotel,* my dad said. *She's been the maid at the Lyndhurst for three years.* We'd arrived that morning on the plane from Pittsburgh—Mom, Muti, and me—pilgrims on the yellow brick road of my dad's dreams.

Walking through the airport lobby, following him to the car outside, we passed drinking fountains with signs that said *White* and *Colored.* Stopping for lunch at the Volusia Diner, we saw a black family eating their lunch out back, on the hood of their car. Turning onto Second Avenue on the way to the hotel, we saw two lines of people outside the Justice of the Peace office: whites at the front door, blacks at the back.

Jim Crow was alive and well in Florida but, trying desperately to deal with my own moving-to-Florida anxieties, I hardly noticed. Then we drove up in front of the hotel, and I was transfixed by the sight of Dorothy. Hands down, she was the most beautiful woman I'd ever seen, but how she looked was part and parcel of how she *was*—straight-backed, self-contained, the essence of dignity. Like Aïda, Princess of Nubia, plucked from her royal home and set down in an alien land.

But that wasn't the Lyndhurst Dorothy's story. Dorothy Willis was born on a farm in Georgia and left on her own. She was *on the run,* she told me, but she never told me who or what she was running from.

My mom got the call on Christmas morning that Dorothy died the night before, on Christmas Eve. Later I heard overheard talk about a mysterious illness that killed Dorothy, but I didn't believe it. I knew *IT* got her, the unnamed horror that chased her from Georgia.

In my mind's eye, I pictured Dorothy's terrifying flight through swamps and woods while owls and bats came hooting and shrieking—riding the wind that bit her, coiled around her, tore her clothes. I could see the Yellow Brick Road, so friendly in daylight, glowing bilious green in the light of the full moon. And I saw Dorothy running, running, running in that unearthly light.

We would've had to fire Dorothy anyway because we didn't have money to pay a maid. We never got another one. That's when Mom and Muti and I took over the work in the hotel. But I never forgot *our* Dorothy. I never stopped hoping, somehow, that she made it to the Emerald City.

Back to my last night in Atlanta.

Dorothy Jane purchased our Fox Theater tickets as soon as the concert was announced because she knew it would be a sellout, and that's exactly what it was. Sir Elton doesn't perform often in his adopted hometown, so when he does, it's standing room only.

For Dorothy Jane and me, the evening was a nostalgia-trip, a journey back to an era when we were optimistic about justice and progress and integrity. Elton John performed a medley from his hit show *Aida,* and when he played and sang "Goodbye, Yellow Brick Road" as an encore the crowd went crazy, swaying to the music, clapping and screaming.

Just like everyone else, Dorothy Jane and I sang along when we got to the last chorus and those haunting final words:

> *So goodbye yellow brick road*
> *Where the dogs of society howl . . . .*
> *Oh, I've finally decided my future lies*
> *Beyond the yellow brick road.*

After I got back to my hotel room, I couldn't get the Yellow Brick Road out of my head. It was dawning on me, I think, that I didn't *want* to say goodbye to the Yellow Brick Road. And that's because I didn't want to give up on stories. *Yes of course,* I said to myself, *the Yellow Brick Road's a paradox. After all, it ends at the Emerald City, and guess what—the Emerald City's a false promise and the so-called "Wizard" is a fake.*

But here's that thing again about stories: they end. Some have happy endings; some don't. But one way or another, stories come to a close. And that's where life is different from a story. In life you have to keep on going, accepting the reality that no one's guaranteed a happy ending. Why? Because human nature doesn't change. There will always be con artists who pretend they're wizards. There will always be cowardly people and heartless people and stupid people. And yes, there will always be white convenience-store clerks who intentionally *drop* the change into a black person's hand.

Yet even in the elegiac message of Elton John's lyrics, the potency of that amazing symbol, the Yellow Brick Road, remains. Somehow through the phenomenal process of creative imagination, L. Frank Baum encapsulated in one striking image—one magnificent metaphor— the oldest story of all: the story of the journey, the story of the quest.

That's what a writer can do, I thought to myself. *That's what I'm going to do.*

I knew then that I'd write my own version of Oz into existence, a fantastic world with magical beings and corrupted minions and fabulous, scary places. And I knew my story would be about a journey and a quest.

Because that's what life is all about.

It's all about the journey.

So there I was the next morning, leaving Atlanta on the first day of the rest of my life with my few remaining earthly possessions packed in my ancient Volvo. In my mind's eye the Yellow Brick Road gleamed seductively, and I knew I'd follow it, wherever it might lead.

Did I anticipate the otherworldly adventure that lay ahead of me?

Did I believe, even for a second, that what lay waiting for me in Florida was a fantastic-yet-real world with magical beings and corrupted minions and fabulous, scary places?

Of course not. How could I? After all, such things only exist in fiction.

Or do they?

PART TWO
NOW: IT BEGINS WITH A HOUSE

This is the way the world ends
This is the way the world ends
This is the way the world ends
Not with a bang but a whimper.
                    T. S. Eliot
                    ***

yet say this to the Possum:
a bang, not a whimper,
with a bang not with a whimper
            Ezra Pound

BACK TO DAYTONA BEACH

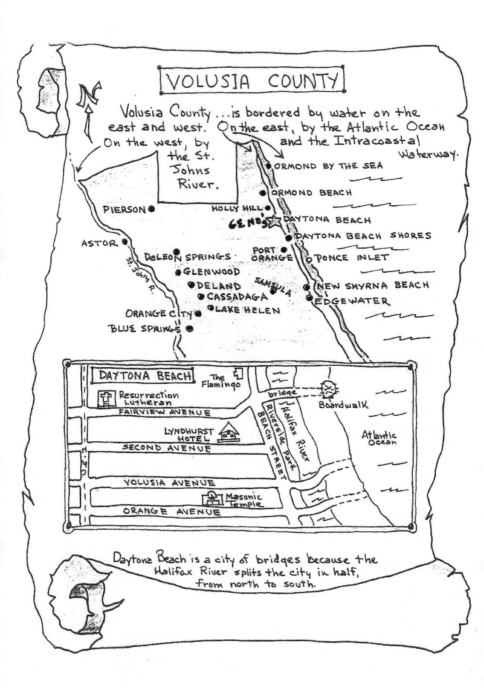

VOLUSIA COUNTY

Volusia County ... is bordered by water on the east and west. On the east, by the Atlantic Ocean and the Intracoastal Waterway. On the west, by the St. Johns River.

ORMOND BY THE SEA

ORMOND BEACH

PIERSON · HOLLY HILL · GENO'S ☆ DAYTONA BEACH

ASTOR · DAYTONA BEACH SHORES

DeLEON SPRINGS · PORT ORANGE · PONCE INLET

GLENWOOD

DELAND · SAMSULA · NEW SMYRNA BEACH

CASSADAGA · EDGEWATER

ORANGE CITY · LAKE HELEN

BLUE SPRINGS ·

St. Johns R.

DAYTONA BEACH

The Flamingo

Resurrection Lutheran

FAIRVIEW AVENUE

bridge

Halifax River

Riverside Park

BEACH STREET

Boardwalk

Atlantic Ocean

LYNDHURST HOTEL

SECOND AVENUE

VOLUSIA AVENUE

Masonic Temple

ORANGE AVENUE

Daytona Beach is a city of bridges because the Halifax River splits the city in half, from north to south.

PIGEON POOP

Coo! Coo!

Must've rained last night, balcony's slimy . . . yuck! Careful, don't slip, fall on my butt. Probably get bird flu anyway from all this guano . . .

POW! WHAP! KAPOOEY!

"Oh shut up, you expensive piece of trash! *You have one job! One! Scaring pigeons! And you can't even do that! You're worthless!*"

Coo! Coo!

"*Shoo!* Fly away, you disgusting poopers! I'll whap you with my broom—"

BOOM! CRAA-A-CK! . . . THUD THUD THUD thud-d-d . . .

"What the *hell?*"

"*SUMMA-beech! STOW-puh! STOW-puh!*"

WHIM WHAM! *BOP!*

"*No HEET! No HEET! Ban DOOSH-ko!*"

"STOP IT, MAGS! DON'T HIT 'EM AGAIN! THEY'RE FRIENDS!"

Just another day in Paradise.

There I was, sweeping pigeon poop off my balcony and cursing the pigeons when BLAMMO! two thugs with scruffy beards and black turtlenecks come crashing through my front door, screaming in Bad English and riding on a refrigerator. Naturally I assumed a Ninja-posture and defended myself. Wouldn't you? Of course you would. You'd defend yourself, I mean, if the Russian Mafia crash-landed in your living room accompanied by a massive kitchen appliance.

Which is why, when Geno came rushing in and hollered for me to cease and desist, he was greeted with a standoff: the Brothers Karamazov hunched in fetal positions, protecting their private parts while I hovered over them, brandishing my broom.

"Geno, what the hell's going on?"

"Mags, I *told* you the Bandushkos were coming to rectify your AC. Don't you remember? This here's Dmitri on the floor, and that's Grigory in the corner."

"So why'd they bust through my front door?"

"It was on accident. They were helpin' me move refrigerators when one of the dollies skidded off the freight elevator, right into your door."

"Right *through* my door, you mean. Holy crap, Geno! I can't live here without a front door—"

Mee-N'AH zah-VOOT Ban DOOSH-kos! FEEX! FEEX!

"What? What'd they say?"

"They said Bandushkos are stand-up guys, they'll fix your front door pronto."

I wasn't confident that the Bandushkos were "stand-up guys." Nor was I going to suggest that long-sleeved black turtleneck sweaters were a questionable fashion choice, given Florida's heat and humidity. No, those were not my problems. My problem was to get Geno's attention by hitting him where it hurts.

"As of this moment, Geno, I am on a rent strike until my front door's replaced *and* my apartment's so frigid you could hang meat *and* my balcony door stays shut."

"Mags, your front door—"

"Has a hole the size of the Holland Tunnel. And I want the door *replaced,* not patched with plywood!"

"Okay, *okay!* The Bandushkos'll put in a new door. Right, boys?"

Vigorous nodding from the floor and the corner.

"And we're addressin' the problems with your AC, a priceless vintage machine —"

"Vintage my ass, it's *ancient!* If I die of heatstroke it's on your head!"

"All right, already! But your balcony door—"

"Blows open with every gust of wind off the river, permitting inquisitive pigeons to enter my domicile and poop. You promised the balcony door would be fixed before I moved in!"

"Yes I did, and—"

"And NOTHING! I moved here three months ago, and I'm still waiting. Jesus, Geno! It's bad enough the pigeons shat all over my balcony! Which I was sweeping with my heavy-duty broom, by the way, when your buddies Raskolnikov and Razumikhin came crashing in—"

"What? *Who?*"

"Never mind, it's a joke about Crime and Punishment."

"Which I do not joke about and you know it! So chill, already."

"You should be so lucky. *And as I was saying about a rent strike—*"

POW! WHAP! KAPOOEY!

"Holy cannolis, Mags! *Look!* Batman just landed on your balcony!"

"Batman didn't <u>*just*</u> land there, Geno, he's been there the whole time. He's a motion-sensitive pigeon-chaser for which I paid an outrageous sum at Universal Studios in Orlando. You'll also notice that he swivels his head while he hollers *POW! WHAP! KAPOOEY!* Unfortunately he doesn't scare the pigeons, *which is why I need you to fix my balcony door so the damn pigeons don't come inside and poop in my apartment.*"

"Mags, pigeons are problematical for owners of commercial buildings such as myself—"

"Which is not the issue at hand. I'm demanding that you fix my balcony door, not the pigeons. And I *don't* mean a temporary fix with duct tape."

Geno was paying attention, and I was on a roll.

"And now," I said, "because I'm sweating like a wart hog, I need to shower and change before I attend an evening performance in Riverside Park. Thusly, I will take my clothes and toiletries to your cute little efficiency apartment. You know, the one you keep for your so-called 'bookkeeper' when she wants to work all night?"

"Mags, you know I don't appreciate—"

"And furthermore, I will treat myself to dinner at your coffeeshop *on the house* before I depart for the performance!"

This exchange between Geno and me wasn't as unpleasant as you might think, being as we both enjoy a bit of drama once in a while. That's why I didn't let on that I saw him grin and wink at his Bandushko buddies while I was leaving in a huff through the hole in my front door.

Just for fun and because I was feeling puckish, I decided to walk down to Geno's efficiency apartment by way of his *secret staircase*. It's old and narrow and rickety, but I don't care because I love that I discovered it. Geno thinks I don't know about it, but *au contraire*. I've seen "the bookkeeper" sneaking in and out that way more than once.

After showering and changing in the blessedly cool efficiency (it's behind Geno's office, on the mezzanine), I headed downstairs to the ground floor of our building, to his coffeeshop in a front corner overlooking Beach Street. I'd been salivating like crazy, anticipating one of Geno's come-to-Jesus muffuletta sandwiches accompanied by a chilled glass of chianti classico. Finally, after scarfing a slab of his justly famous tiramisu, I was ready to experience Opera in the Park.

OPERA IN THE PARK

As you can imagine, opera's not easy to pull off, especially a local production on an outdoor stage. That evening's performance, though, was sheer magic. Shoot, I said to myself more than once during the show, I wish I'd asked a friend to come with me. Geno claims he loves opera so maybe I should've asked him . . . naw, Geno loves those Verdi and Puccini warhorses, so I don't think he'd like this one. Probably would've gotten pissy about the fairies and the enchanted forest. *Too artsy fartsy,* he'd say.

One thing for sure, though, next time I have a hair appointment with Christine I'll compliment her on the makeup and wigs. I mean, you see wigs everywhere these days, but most of them are fakey, not like these.

And the video backdrops have Wally's signature all over them. I wonder where he . . . there he is, his computer console's behind that curtain! Jeez, he looks just like the Wizard of Oz: pudgy, glasses falling off his nose, joysticks jiggling. Those backdrops are brilliant, though. No surprise there except . . .

Whoa! There the fairies go again, hovering above the stage, and they look so *real.* Can't see any wires hooked on them, but they're flying all over the place. And omigod, those poor singers in the mushroom costumes must be sweating bullets. How did they sing through those masks? For that matter, who designed the masks? The artist who created those masks belongs in New York or Hollywood, not Daytona Beach.

I was truly flummoxed, trying to figure how in the world a local opera company could stage such a world-class performance. It wasn't just the costumes or Wally's spectacular backdrops, not even those flying fairies. It was the whole production. Set changes flowed from one to the next like chiffon in a breeze, and somehow the stage lights followed the music: pulsating, brightening, then diminishing as if on cue. And when the lights and music swelled together, I tingled all over. Oh, yes, I said to myself, something extraordinary was happening onstage tonight. Something uncanny.

Leaving the park after talking with my friend Casey and his girlfriend, I was thinking so hard about the performance I walked right into Christopher, probably would've knocked him over if he weren't so tall. Uh oh, and I bet I scuffed his shoe when I stepped on his foot. "Sorry, Christopher, sorry, I was distracted."

"Dammit, Mags, can't you ever watch where you're going?"

"Hey, I apologized, didn't I? Anyway, why're you here? Are you Wally's transportation, driving him and his BMW back to Orange City?"

"You got it. Now I have to wait around while he packs up his computer gear. You know how anal he is about protecting his precious stuff."

And I know how anal you are about YOUR stuff! That's what I was thinking, but of course I didn't say it out loud. Instead I just said, "Cool. Let's get a drink at Three Graces Café and talk about our opera."

To clue you in: Christopher and I started talking about writing an opera when he landed in one of my courses at Georgia Tech.

Even though we lost touch while he was in grad schools and con-servatories, he got the gig of Composer-in-Residence at Stetson University in DeLand around the time I retired from Georgia Tech and moved back to Daytona, and that's when we got serious about it. We got serious about collaborating on an opera, I mean.

The thing is, though, an opera's never finished. We've won prizes and grants, had partial performances at festivals, but we never hit it big time with a production at a major opera com-pany. Which is why we keep on working. And revising. And rewriting. I guess you could say this opera for us has become a quest. We might eventually be successful, or we might not. But as I've said before, you can't win if you don't play. And how sad would it be to give up?

We stayed long enough at Three Graces for Christopher to fill up napkin after napkin with music, and it was almost mid-night when Wally called to say he was packed up and ready to go. Wouldn't you know it, though, Christopher had to get in a parting shot while we were saying goodbye: "Say hi to your imaginary cat for me."

"Christopher, I resent your implication!"

"What implication? I didn't *imply* anything."

"Oh yes you did, you implied I'm a crazy cat lady. *I told you* Schrödinger's in absentia right now, but he'll be back. You would've run away too if your house was burning down around you, the way my condo burned down around him! He'll be back when he's good and ready, and he'll love living in Florida!"

"Sure he will, Mags, sure he will. Ciao!"

I walked home in a sour mood, naturally, and my mood didn't improve when I found my front door boarded up with plywood and duct tape. Geno and the Bandushkos were long gone, of course, so I patiently (not!) rode the freight elevator back down to the ground floor, went out to the alley, and climbed up the fire escape to my back door.

It takes a while to unlock the cage at each landing, then bolt it behind me, so by the time I reached the third-floor landing I'd calmed down and decided to climb up to the rooftop gazebo where I could look at the stars. First, though, I went in my apartment and got a soft fuzzy throw so I could get comfy while I stargazed.

When I reached the gazebo and got settled on a bench, I was still thinking about Schrödy, laughing to myself about the way he'd cock his head and look at me, as if to say *Settle down, Mags!* and *It's time to get your head on straight.* Then I reminisced about the many conversations I'd had with Schrödy, marveling that memory can bring to life the loved ones who aren't with us any longer. Remembering, reminiscing, I tucked my fuzzy throw around me and let the stars carry me away to dreamtime.

SCHRÖDY'S BACK—EXCEPT HE'S NOT

There we were in my dream, Schrödy and I, back together again.

I was still enraptured by the performance I'd seen at Opera in the Park, and I wanted to talk about it with Schrödy like we always used to after I got home from an evening at the Fox Theater. We'd do our version of a "good cop, bad cop" critique wherein I'd praise everything, and he'd be his usual snarky cat-self. Accordingly, I started:

"Schrödy, the opera was stunning. And the costumes were out of this world, especially for the dream sequence in the Enchanted Forest. If I hadn't known they were actors in costume,

I'd have sworn they were real—flying fairies, an orange dwarf with a beard down to his knees, a couple of singing mushrooms, and a shaggy white bear with a voice like Placido Domingo."

"Sounds more like Disney than Shakespeare."

"Well, *I* think it was quintessential Shakespeare, and the singers were Met-quality."

"All of them?"

"Almost all. The coloratura who sang Tytania was a little weak, and the guy playing Bottom was pretty bad. He was movie star handsome, though, until he got the ass head. Oh, and there was an interruption right before the finale when a geezer in the audience flashed the crowd. The old dude's wife was there with him, so she hustled him home."

"Anything else unusual happen?"

"Only that Casey's girlfriend stole the show. I *knew* I recognized her. Turns out she was one of the Maypole dancers at Midsummer, that Celtic Festival in Ormond Beach. I told you about the Festival, remember? How I got weirded out when they started the big bonfire?"

"I remember that you went to the Festival without me."

"Dammit, you weren't here, so how could I take you?"

"Don't swear, Mags. It's not becoming." (Sniffs from the cat.)

This was part of the game we played, of course, so when Schrödinger got snarky I'd start talking to myself instead. I call self-talking *going walkabout*, and in my dream I was starting a lively walkabout-conversation with my own self when he piped back up. "Sorry I got pissy, Mags. I really want to hear about Casey's girlfriend."

"Good, because we're already friends. Her name's Sterling, and she's gorgeous, a Snow-White-lookalike with stunning turquoise eyes. I kid you not, her eyes are brilliant blue-green. She's super talented too, plays the flute and has an amazing singing voice, really deep and resonant. Casey introduced me to her after the performance, and we talked a long time. *A Midsummer Night's Dream* is her favorite Shakespeare, just like me, and we love Britten's opera because it foregrounds romance and magic. No *angst*, in other words."

"Sounds like two English majors being nerdy together."

"Very funny."

"Yeah, I thought so."

"And I thought *you* were over being pissy."

Apologetic sniffs from the cat.

"Anyway, Schrödy, you know what? I don't miss Atlanta, and neither will you. You'll love our apartment and Riverside Park across the street and seeing Wally and Christopher whenever we want to. And I have a premonition . . ."

"Mags! A premonition about *what*? You're doing that walk-about thing again, where you stop talking right in the middle of a sentence."

"Sorry, sorry. I was thinking about transformations. That's what life in a new place is all about, and I have a premonition that the future will be just like Shakespeare's play—rife with transformations."

"So-o-o, is that a good thing?"

"Well, transformation means change, and change can be good, can't it?"

"I guess it depends on the play."

"Excuse me?"

"Duh, Mags, you love that dream sequence in *A Midsummer Night's Dream*. But what if the opera'd been *Romeo and Juliet*? Would you be just as excited about Romeo's dream?"

"What? *Whose* dream?"

"Romeo's dream, Mags. It's a *premonition*! Shakespeare's plays are full of premonitions, and they're all warnings because that's exactly what a premonition is—it's a warning, not an invitation to a tea party. I'm surprised you don't remember."

"I *do* remember, dammit! And I'll thank you not to lecture me about Shakespeare!"

"Hey, I'm just sayin' you can't have it both ways. Sometimes it's better to keep the cat in the box, so to speak. That way, you can dwell in possibility."

"Well guess what, *Miss Emily*! You can keep your little Manx butt in the box forever, if that's what you want to do. I, on the other hand, prefer to be excited about this new life. And I'm holding onto my premonition! AND FURTHERMORE—".
. . uh oh. I was hollering so loud in my dream I woke myself up.

Mags, I said to myself out loud, *you have to get a grip!*

I know, I answered. Again out loud.

Then I sat there for a while in Geno's gazebo, pondering my situation. It was true, what I said about not missing Atlanta. Sure, I missed Schrödy terribly, but I knew in my heart I'd see him again someday. I didn't know, of course, how long I'd have to live without my feline roommate. But I decided it didn't matter because I could go on talking with him, just as I did in my strangely prescient gazebo-dream.

Finally, comforted by my decision to go on talking with Schrödy as if he were really here, I climbed down from the roof and went back to my apartment, laughing about my "imaginary cat" the whole time.

The next morning Sterling met me for coffee downstairs at Geno's, and then we walked over to the park. I was still thinking about my conversation with her after the opera when Casey introduced us, and I was intrigued by our similar interests.

What was it that Schrody said in my gazebo-dream? I know, he said Sterling and I are like "two English majors being nerdy together," and that's it precisely. We're practically each other's *alter ego* in that we both love books and music and poetry and we're both writers. Shoot, she could be a younger version of me except . . . Reality check, Mags. She's beautiful, she's already a published poet, and she's under contract to write a screenplay. Not exactly a description of me at any age.

Not that the screenplay she's writing sounds like much of a concept, though. Something about Superheroes coming out of hiding to save the world from Snake-people and getting help from engineers called Archies.

When I heard that, I had to protest. "Sterling," I said, "can't you find a better name for your worker-bees than *Archies*? Sounds like they belong in the Sunday funnies."

Sterling was looking at me like I'd started talking in Polish.

"The Sunday funnies," I said. "Comic strips in the Sunday newspaper, in full color."

Silence. "Okay, how about comic books? Don't you remember *Archie & Friends*?"

No response, just a quizzical look. "Sorry," I said, "it must be a generational thing. I was only wondering if audiences will take characters called *Archies* seriously."

"No problem, Mags. I have a reason for the name, and it'll work in context. Trust me on that."

"Okay, if you say so. *Archies*, they are."

"Thanks, because the name's important."

"Got it. But you said the Archies are complicated?"

"Right, because in the screenplay I'm writing they're supposed to align themselves with the Forces of Good, but some of them go AWOL and side with the Forces of Evil."

"Sounds like the way of the world."

"Exactly."

Remembering that conversation, I have to wonder how many more Superhero movies we need. And you can forget about me paying good money to watch snake-people on a giant screen. Snake-people? *Seriously?* I mean, I get it that Sterling's screenplay has a dead-serious message about looming environmental disaster. It's important to get that message out, and I admire it, but the Superhero concept's still not my cup of tea.

I didn't say any of that to her, of course, because it'd be rude. And after all, who am I to cast stones? Sterling's barely out of college, and she already has *a movie contract?* Get outta' town! And me? To be honest, I figured once I got comfortably resettled I'd start working on my novel. Part memoir, part fiction—basically the story of my life with a few romantic embellishments. Actually a few romantic *accomplishments*, or whatever you call it when you get lucky in love.

I'd forgotten a couple of things, though. Writer's Block for one (I call it my "funk" and it always blindsides me). But more importantly, I forgot that no one pays you while you're writing your blockbuster first novel. A typical scenario, in fact, is you write your heart out for years on end and hope you get published before you die. Not that I mean to be to be cynical or anything, just that while you're writing your heart out you have to pay the rent. That's where my Kitchen Table Books come in.

KITCHEN TABLE BOOKS REDUX

I told you about inventing Kitchen Table Books when I was a professor in Atlanta, right? And I mentioned pitching the idea to my friend Booker? Well, I'm reporting to you now that Booker and I hit the jackpot with *Proust and His Cookie*, which I also told you about earlier. (Yes we finished it, and it's a hoot! Also a big seller.)

You'll probably also remember that our publisher's in Atlanta and so's our editor, Ford. I mention this now because Ford's bugging me to do a new book, so I started thinking about one with an Irish theme after I fell in love with syllabub and rhubarb bread at that Celtic Festival in Ormond Beach. Rhubarb bread because it's heavenly-sweet and crunchy—not bitter like Groosma's stewed rhubarb, thank the powers that be! And syllabub because—have you ever tried it? Think heavy cream, sugar, lemons, and a whole bottle of sherry or brandy. Whisk until blended, chill in tall glasses, sprinkle with nutmeg, and enjoy with crunchy squares of rhubarb bread. Yum!

After discovering these delightful confections, I knew the next Kitchen Table Book would have an Irish-Celtic theme, and the literary part would focus on Oscar Wilde. I was already creating a paste-up in my mind: the new book would have spectacular photos of the Emerald Isle, a short quirky bio of Wilde, some Irish recipes, of course, and I'd give it a catchy title, something like *The Importance of Being Hungry* or *The Porridge of Dorian Gray*.

And the great thing about Wilde is that he was so witty. Every page, I figured, would feature one of his epigrams at the top or bottom. Pithy sayings like *One should always play fairly when one has the winning cards*, and *Be yourself, all the others are taken*.

My favorite Wilde epigram of all, though, is the mantra I intone every time I settle down to write: *If you want to tell people the truth, make them laugh. Otherwise they'll kill you.*

So I had this fabulous notion for the new book all set in my mind, but I'd neglected to factor-in Ford, who is notoriously small-minded. "Mags, has your brain turned into friggin' mush?"

"No, Ford," I said. "My brain is just fine, so you need to calm down and think rationally about this concept I'm describing to you."

"You call this a *concept?* This is not a concept; this is a nightmare. Do you recall that our target audience for Kitchen Table Books is Mrs. Middle America?"

"Of course I haven't forgotten our target audience. I'm told, in fact, that the Ladies Who Lunch, as well as the Blue-haired Tearoom Dears, just adore Oscar Wilde's witticisms."

"Well, forgive me for choking on my crappucino, Miz Dostoyevsky. So you're telling me Sweet Aunt Lucille and Dear Granny Mobley will *love* a book that quotes the Queer of the Century on every page? Or did you forget that teeny detail about Oscar Wilde's peccadillos?"

Ford was on a roll, I could tell, and there was no stopping him. "Jesus Q. Christ, Mags, we'll be boycotted by every Hallmark store in the country! Why don't you just start a series called *Flaming Fags in the Kitchen* and—"

Sigh. I hung up on Ford, then turned off my phone. This kind of heated exchange between Ford and me isn't unusual, just part of the game we play. Nevertheless, Ford's tirades always make me mad. I knew I'd get nothing accomplished if I stayed home and fretted, so I decided to call my friend Slim and set up a racquetball game.

"Sure," Slim said, "I'll meet you at the gym in an hour."

STERLING SILVER BUCK

Racquetball's the only sport I really love. If it's indoor racquetball, that is, meaning you play in an enclosed climate-controlled court with four walls and a ceiling—all of which are fair
game as targets when you're slamming the ball with your racquet. My racquets (I have two) are an E-Force Terminator V-6
(makes me feel like Linda Hamilton in *Terminator*, buffed-up
and deadly), and a Wilson Big Stick BLX (speak softly but
carry a big one, is what I always say).

I'm basically a C level player, but I love the reactive aesthetic of the game. You never know how the ball will bounce
so you exhaust yourself chasing it, and in an hour's time you
work every single muscle in your body. And I do have an ace-
in-the-hole: my kill shot. Slim easily beats the pants off me, but
I salvage a little self-respect when I manage to set up my kill
shot. BLAMMO! Slim knows it's coming, she gets ready, but
she's never yet returned it.

After we played for a while (we don't keep score, just trade
serves and run around a lot), we were cooling off on a bench
when we noticed noise coming from the far court at the other
end of the gym. "Wow," Slim said. "Sounds like a couple of gut
busters are dookin' it out down there. Let's go watch." But when
we walked over to the far court we saw that only one person
was playing, and lo and behold, that one person was Sterling
(all the courts at our gym have a glass wall, so spectators can
watch from outside the court).

Sterling didn't see us because she was totally focused,
whaling the spit out of two balls that she was keeping in play.

I'd never even heard of keeping two balls in play at one time, much less seen it, so I was fascinated. Slim was bowled over too, so we plopped ourselves down on a bench outside the court and watched. After ten minutes or so Sterling started winding down, and that's when she saw us.

"Sterling?" I said. "You didn't tell me you're into racquetball."

"You didn't ask, Mags," she said. "You never told me you're into it either." Chitchat ensued until Slim said she had to get on the road because she was pulling the night shift at the sheriff's department (Slim's a deputy).

After packing up our gear and waving goodbye to Slim while she drove away, Sterling and I agreed we were both starving, so we headed next door to Sergio's Spaghetteria & Organic Delicatessen. It's a genius marketing strategy—a spaghetteria combined with a health-food-type deli. Healthy eaters like Sterling can get their fill of wheat straw shakes and unblanched almonds, while carb enthusiasts like me can dine on triple-cheese pasta and spumoni. As you probably guessed, I hang out at Sergio's a lot.

"So tell me," I said to Sterling when we settled into a booth with our victuals, "how long have you been playing racquetball? I've *never* seen one player keep two balls going. Never. Where'd you learn to do that?"

"Oh, I taught myself. You can have a lot of fun playing racquetball all by yourself, just hitting a ball around and whacking the crap out of it. At some point it seemed natural that I try to keep two balls going at one time. It forces me to really, really concentrate. Especially if I'm pissed off."

"So you're pissed off now? At what? Anything in particular?" No answer.

"Sterling, what's wrong? Why're you pissed off?"

"Mags, I hate whiners. I don't want to sound like a whiner."

"You won't sound like a whiner to me. Everyone needs to vent once in a while, so go ahead and vent."

Which Sterling was glad to do. Over a meatball stromboli (me) and a hummus wrap (Sterling), I got filled in about Sterling's family. One reason she needed to vent, she said, was because she was sick and tired of being the one in charge. "In charge of your brothers, you mean?"

"Exactly. They're both head-cases. Michael blasts his music so loud we have to scream over it to get his attention, and Red doesn't want to do anything but fly."

"Red's a pilot?"

"No, he's a jumper, spends all his time at Skydive DeLand. Anyway, I gave up on getting help from them, and it still pisses me off."

"You mean like help with cooking and laundry? Maybe you could hire someone . . . ." Strange hesitation from Sterling. She wasn't paying attention to her hummus wrap, either, just looking past me with those gorgeous turquoise eyes unfocused, like she was trying to think how to answer but couldn't. Uncomfortable silences bother me, which probably explains my tendency to barge back into a conversation when I should quietly wait for the other person to speak. "Well anyway," I said, "I know what you mean about the boys because it's all about expectations, isn't it?"

"Expectations?"

"Uh huh. It's like, somebody has to be in charge or else things fall apart. But once you're in charge it's hard to stop because you've set yourself up in other people's expectations. I remember a story my friend Reenie used to tell about a homeless guy she shared her lunch with every day. Things were going great, she felt good about helping him, yada yada, but before long he wanted ham sandwiches instead of baloney and, by the way, where's the kosher pickle?"

Sterling got a laugh out of the Reenie story but got serious again when she asked me if Reenie was a nickname. "More than a nickname," I said. "She told me she hated her real name so she made up *Reenie* and wouldn't answer to anything else."

"Wow, I'm jealous."

"Why?"

"Because that's what I wanted to do."

"How so?"

"Because I hate my name. The backstory here is that my dad's name is Ben Bulben, and my mom's name is Mary Buck, and they're both *very* attached to their surnames: Bulben and Buck. So when it came time to name us kids, Dad wouldn't give up Bulben and Mom wouldn't give up Buck. Their genius solution was to flip a silver dollar and whoever won the coin toss got to name the child. Dad won twice and got to name the boys: Michael Robartes Bulben and Red Hanrahan Bulben."

Which are pretty far-out names, I was thinking. But I didn't say anything, just nodded and looked interested. "And," Sterling continued, "Mom won the coin toss once, so she got to name me."

I had to admit that Sterling had a point. I mean, what's more important than your name? I'm not wild about my own real name, which is why I insist on "Mags." But there are lots of names worse than Sterling. Hippie-names like Rainbow and Prairie and trendy place-names like Brooklyn and Nebraska. I even had a student once whose name was Guantanamo, which I figured should be considered a form of child abuse. I mean, what are parents *thinking*?

I decided it was my job to comfort Sterling, so that's what I tried to do. "Sterling's a beautiful name," I said. "Really."

"It may be beautiful by itself, but you know as well as I do—it's the combination that matters."

"The combination?"

"Mags, my name is *Sterling Silver Buck*. It's as bad as those stupid joke-names people make up, like Rick O'Shea and Willy Leak and Sally Forth."

"Oh, wow, I had no idea. It's like those prank calls Bart Simpson makes to Moe's bar. Bart says he has a message for *Seymour Butz,* or he asks to speak to *Hugh Jass.* So Moe gets caught off guard and hollers the name over the intercom. Then, when he realizes he's been snookered, he freaks out on the phone."

"Well, it might be a great schtick on TV," Sterling said, "but it's not so funny in real life. Try to imagine how many guys holler *heads or tails!* when they see me coming, and then describe in disgusting detail how they'll 'flip' Sterling Silver Buck."

"Yep, I can totally imagine that. Have you considered a legal name change?"

"Yes, but Mom wouldn't help me, and I was underage so I couldn't do it on my own. I threw a tantrum, told her I hated my name *and* her, and I'll always regret it. It was just a few days later when her plane went down."

"Sterling, I'm so sorry. I didn't mean to hit a sore spot."

"No worries, Mags. Talking helps. It's hard to believe Mom and Dad have been gone more than three years, though."

BEN AND MARY

Sterling had already told me about the family tragedy one day when we met for lunch at Three Graces, including the "story" she and her brothers concocted about it. "Dad was a passenger in Mom's plane when it went down near Bimini,"

Sterling said, "but no one knows that. After the Coast Guard gave up the search, we had a family meeting and decided to pretend Dad was still here, that Mom was flying solo when her Tomahawk disappeared."

"Jeez, Sterling, how'd you manage to front a fiction like that?"

"You do what you have to do," Sterling said, "and we had to come up with a plan because we were afraid do-gooders might start meddling. Our extended family's unusual, to say the least, and we didn't want strangers poking around, upsetting everyone—"

"Oh wait, I remember. You told me your aunt and uncle from Ireland live with you, and you also have some Roomers? And when you moved here you were home-schooled, so your dad renovated some outbuildings for your Tutors?"

"Right."

"Sorry to interrupt your story. Go on."

"So we had a family meeting and decided to pretend Dad was still around, starting with a notice on our family website that we'd appreciate privacy. We're lucky about funds because the Bulben Family Trust makes monthly deposits electronically, and as long as people think Dad's still here, we have access. The major part of the plan, though, is that Michael puts on Dad's clothes and a pony tail wig, then shows up at the campus in DeLand at odd hours."

"Isn't that chancy? Even at odd hours?"

"Not really. Dad was never much for being sociable. Michael opens his faculty office, strews stuff around, maybe leaves a half-cup of coffee on the desk. Then he locks the office and drives away, being sure to wave absent-mindedly at someone who looks official."

"That's quite a plan."

"It was clear to all of us," Sterling said, "that Michael had to be the one to impersonate our dad because Michael looks like Dad and Red doesn't. Red's a little guy with a headful of long wavy red hair, whereas Michael's tall and skinny with long dark hair. Just like Dad."

Also, according to Sterling, Michael's a quiet type, a brooder like their dad, while Red's hugely dramatic and has one of those VOG theater-type voices. I'd never heard of "VOG" so I asked her to explain, and she said VOG stands for "Voice of God"—the disembodied voice that comes out of the sound system before a performance, warning folks to turn off their phones. "With that voice," Sterling laughed, "Red could start an avalanche from a mountaintop."

"Or part the seas, like Charlton Heston."

"What? *Who?*"

Sigh. "Never mind, it's another generational thing."

Sterling got back to her story then and said it should be easy for Michael to pull off the dad-impersonation because Ben's demeanor was so shambling and absent-minded. "All Michael has to do," she said, "is wander around talking to himself, forgetting people's names—stuff like that. But no, he had to go fall in love. Now we literally have to pry him away from his inamorata for an afternoon so he can do his dad-lookalike thing at the college."

Thinking about Sterling's situation later, I realized it wouldn't have been easy to pull off the Michael-impersonation if one factor hadn't worked in the kids' favor—when Ben and Mary disappeared, Ben had just started an open-ended leave of absence at Stetson. This meant he didn't have to teach classes or go to meetings, so the fact that he didn't interact with anyone at Stetson on a daily basis wasn't considered strange, certainly not suspicious.

I was intrigued by Sterling's parents and wanted to know more, so the next time I was in DeLand I stopped by my friend Talisman's office (she's a professor at Stetson) and asked her about Ben and Mary. "I didn't know Mary at all," Talisman said, "except by reputation. She taught math at Embry-Riddle and was a superb mathematician. And everyone says she was a crackerjack pilot, which is why it makes no sense that her plane went down. They never found a trace, from what I hear."

"And what about Professor Bulben? Do you know him?"

"I don't think *anyone* knows Ben Bulben," Talisman said with a laugh. "He's one of those creative geniuses who can do anything except relate to other people. Has the social graces of a hermit crab, basically. Most folks think he's just another absent-minded professor. But I figure he's a trickster, a devil in disguise."

"That's what you think? Why?"

"For one thing, because of his artworks. Have you noticed the oversized campus statuary? The Bronze Brobdingnagians?"

"Sure, can't miss them, actually. And I really like the one in front of the Lynn Center, the old guy playing a violin. But what's 'sly' or 'devilish' about it?"

"Nothing, until you recognize the irony of *The Fiddler of Dooney* perched on the lawn of a Business School. Part of Ben's schtick is a wicked sense of humor."

"Okay, so Ben was having fun with *The Fiddler* statue, I get that. But how about the statue in front of the Chapel? The one on the steps? Looks like a clergyman talking with a supplicant, nothing outrageous."

"You think so? *Crazy Jane and the Bishop*? Talking on the Chapel steps of a college affiliated with the Southern Baptist Convention?"

"Omigod, you're right. That's wicked funny. So . . . am I sensing a pattern here?"

"Only if you trust the jaded eye of this beholder. Speaking of which, how about the statue in Folley Fountain?"

"*The big pink bird*? The statue that looks like Dolly Parton naked, riding sidesaddle on a flamingo? That's Ben's too?"

"It's his, all right. The Trustees approved a huge commission for that one because Ben proposed a sculptural homage to Leonardo's lost masterpiece *Leda and the Swan*. Naturally the Trustees assumed it'd be a perfect centerpiece for the campus—classical, elegant. By the time they realized they'd been hoodwinked, it was too late."

"But if the bird's supposed to be a swan, why's it pink?"

"Because the students can't leave it alone. Maintenance cleans it in the daytime; students paint it again at night. The word is, our local Ace Hardware makes a killing on fluorescent-pink spray paint."

"Wow, I bet the administration's distressed."

"That's for sure, but it must not bother Ben. After he installed *Leda* in the middle of the fountain, he moved his artistic endeavors off-campus. I haven't seen his current magnum opus, but I hear it's a doozy: a faux-Byzantine architectural monstrosity at the Boardwalk in Daytona, replete with a hundred-foot-dome and classical-statue-knock-offs."

"You mean the bowling-center-*cum*-arcade they call Byzantium? Did Ben Bulben design the buildings?"

"No, but he painted the murals, interior and exterior, including a Sistine-Chapel-travesty in the dome. He's still finishing it, I hear. Meanwhile the word from our Art Department is that Ben's codifying a unique decorative style he calls *whorehouse rococo.*"

Before I left DeLand that day Talisman and I talked again over dinner, and when we got back on the topic of Ben Bulben, I got an earful. "What'd you mean," I asked, "when you said Ben's a devil in disguise?"

"I mean Ben's a cipher, an enigma. The official story is that he came to Stetson from the University of Dublin, but every time I try to search, I get stonewalled and have to give up."

"That doesn't sound like you, Talisman. You never give up— just keep on, keepin' on. It's the secret to your success."

"Well, all I know is, I've met my match in Ben Bulben. And while we're talking about mysteries, what's with that big old house on the beach?"

"You mean the Genius House? The old mansion in Ponce Inlet? Looks like a castle?"

"That's the one."

"I didn't know it's still standing, much less that people live in it. So Ben Bulben bought it and moved his family there?"

"Sure did. Every realtor in the state wanted to list that house, but they all gave up because the public records are mysteriously opaque. Then zip! Ben Bulben shows up, acting like Lord of the Manor and moves in. Who is he and how'd he get the house? Nobody knows."

"Is it still famous for being haunted? The house, I mean."

"Depends on your definition of haunted. Folks can conjure all kinds of haunts out of squeaky squirrels and swamp gas. Then before long they've convinced themselves that Ghosts are real, and Fairies live among us."

I drove back to Daytona on autopilot that night, remembering my midnight adventure at the Genius House many years ago with my high school friends. I thought, too, about my conversation with Geno and Ralphie one day not long ago at the coffeeshop when they told me they'd had big plans for buying the whole beachfront property.

"Me and Ralphie," Geno said, "we had a genius plan. You got a big old house that looks like a castle, with a tower plus mom n' pop cottages and gazebos—all on the beach. It could a' been a franchise all by itself. We figured we'd do an Italian theme like Bucca di Beppo, fancy it up with authenticated antique knock-offs, pictures of Popes, spiritous touches like that."

"For sure," Ralphie chimed in. "Me n' Geno were set to do it real classy. You rent out the castle for parties, retrofit a serious Italian kitchen, put fountains in the gazebos and lights along the dune walks. And you pipe in some Dean Martin. You know, *When the moon hits your eye / Like a big-a pizza pie / That's amorr-rayy . . .* " Ralphie should not sing in public, but I bit my tongue so I wouldn't laugh. "And you run a cable car from the house to the tower," he continued, "which we would call the Leaning Tower of Pizza."

"Yeah," Geno enthused, "we was even gonna turn the cottages into a stable, get a couple horses for Godfather types which want to ride on the beach."

"So why didn't you buy it?"

"We tried, drew up a couple contracts, but they kept blowing us off."

"Who's *they*?"

"Suits n' ties, big shot lawyers. Then those professors came outta' nowhere and moved in. They were authenticated geniuses which fit the house, I guess, but they were *woo woo*. Like after they moved in, they'd party with their Mensa friends, go around chanting and ringing bells, making drum circles down on the beach. Weird stuff like that."

I was still laughing to myself when I turned in the parking area behind Geno's store and practically ran him over. "Whoa, Mags! Take it easy!"

"Sorry, Geno, I got distracted because I was thinking."

"Is that so? Thinking so hard you forgot which pedal's the brake?"

You gotta love a guy who makes a joke out of it after you just missed slamming into him with your vehicle, right? Besides that, I was feeling friendly because I love my new front door. "Geno," I said, "your Bandushko buddies did good work, but that door must've cost you a fortune. I mean, why? A solid-wood door with steel casing and double deadbolts?"

"Just bein' careful, is all."

"What do you mean, 'being careful'? Careful about what?"

"Just that there's a suspicious dude hangin' around Riverside Park lately. Sammy the Sabrett Guy told me about him, so me and Old Sonny, we're payin' attention."

"A suspicious dude? You mean Diff, the old guy with a drum and a pet ferret?"

"Naw, not him. This dude's a scary type dressed all in black with shades and bling, has a shitload of hardware hangin' off him and—"

"Hardware?"

"Yeah, keys and chains. Big thick chains like those butt-crack dudes wear. You know, the dudes which exhibit their butt-crack because their extra-large pants are fallin' off?"

"Okay, yeah, I know what you mean, but he's probably just a punk flaunting his *gangsta'* style. Or maybe he's a Goth. Those types love black clothes and chains, but it's all about being different, about standing out in a crowd. I had lots of students like that. The way they dress doesn't make them dangerous."

"I hear you, Mags, but lemme' tell you, I know what I know."

"Which is?"

"Which is *The nutcase will always surprise you.* That's why me and Old Sonny, we're on the lookout. And that's how come you got a kickass front door."

LUNCH AT THE GENIUS HOUSE

I'd been excited all week, ever since Sterling called and invited me to Sunday lunch at her house. I mean, I'd been thinking practically non-stop about that mysterious old house, starting with my teenage adventure when I got spooked by mysterious lights. And everything I'd heard since then about the house and its secrets whetted my appetite.

Not only that. When Sterling called to invite me she said, "Every Sunday we make a special lunch for Uncle Billy, one of his favorite Irish recipes." And when I asked her if she did the cooking, she said "No, his wife George makes his favorite dishes, and she's an awesome cook, authentically Irish." Well, this fit right in with my idea for an Irish Kitchen Table Book, the one I was already referring to in my head as *The Porridge of Dorian Gray.*

So at noon on Sunday, Sterling was waiting for me on a park bench and came running when I pulled Agatha up to the curb and honked. I'd told Sterling I didn't need an escort to her house, but she said no, it'd be best if she arrived there with me, just in case. "Just in case of what?" I'd asked, but when she didn't answer, I dropped it.

"Okay," I said when we were driving, "I'll recognize your brothers because I was at the opera and they were in it. You told me, remember? You said Red was Puck and Michael was Oberon, and you said your aunt and uncle from Ireland were in the audience. Did I see them too? Your aunt and uncle, I mean."

Sterling hesitated, then told me the flasher dude in the audience was Uncle Billy while the white-haired lady who hustled him out was his wife George. "Omigod, Sterling, I had no idea," I said, "but don't be embarrassed about your uncle. Every family has a ditwad or two."

"Mags! I'm not embarrassed, okay? Well, maybe a little embarrassed. But we all know that each peculiar family is peculiar in its own way, right?"

"To paraphrase Tolstoy?"

"Precisely. Anyway, Mags, I *want* you to meet my family, including Uncle Billy and George, and I also want you to meet my Tutors."

"Oh, right, your Tutors. You said they were in the opera, but I wouldn't remember them because they were in costume?"

"They were in costume, sort of. In a manner of speaking, that is. A few of our Roomers were in the opera as well. Also in costume."

"So I'll meet them at lunch? The Tutors and the Roomers?"

"No, lunch is just with the family. I'll introduce you to the Tutors after lunch, and you'll meet the Roomers some other time."

"Fine, whatever. I'm excited about an authentic Irish meal and like I said, it's perfect timing because I'm writing a book about Irish cooking—" I cut myself off because we'd arrived at the Genius House. "Pull in over there, Mags," Sterling said, "by that closed gate."

"Gate? I don't see a gate, but I see an old naked guy by the fence. Omigod! Wait, wait, don't tell me! That's Uncle Billy, right? The old guy holding a broomstick?"

"Shit!"

"Uh oh. That's not a broomstick, is it?"

Sterling jumped out, slammed the car door, and took off running, yelling "Michael, god*dammit*, where are you? And where the hell's George?" Then, "Mags, park over there on the other side of the house, okay? And go around to the front door. I'll be there in a minute."

While I was backing and turning, I heard snatches of heated conversation, mostly coming from Sterling. Things like "Holy crap, Michael! I *told* you we were on our way. Why couldn't you keep tabs on Uncle Billy?" The rest was murmurs, interspersed with a few cackles. I took my time going around to the front door, giving Sterling plenty of time to get the situation in hand. Oops . . . not a good metaphor. Not a good metaphor at all.

By the time I knocked on the front door, Uncle Billy was nowhere in sight. But except for Sterling, neither was anyone else. Sterling apologized, said there'd obviously been a miscommunication because Michael had to go to New Smyrna Beach to practice with his new girl band, and Red was at Skydive DeLand. "Sterling, it's okay. I'll be happy to hang out with you for a while, and maybe we can walk on the beach?"

"Perfect. George says she needs another half hour to finish up in the kitchen, so I'd love to walk on the beach. Let's do it!"

Sterling told me more about the boys while we walked, and I had to admit (only to myself, of course) that I didn't envy her life with them one bit. Michael, for example, is a musical prodigy. "Salsa, bluegrass, Celtic, jazz. You name it, Michael can hum it," Sterling said. "Oh, and don't forget Mozart."

"Wow, I am truly impressed."

"Well, you get over being impressed when he's practicing because it's so loud, the house practically shakes off its foundations. *And he's always practicing.*"

"Okay, I get that, and I agree. I like my music loud but only when I'm in the mood for it and it's my choice, not someone else's. But how about Red? Didn't you tell me Red ran away once with the circus?"

"He sure did. Ran off with the Cole Brothers Circus, the one that winters over in West Volusia County. Red was like, twelve years old, and he conned one of the clowns into believing he was a midget. That big voice in his little body, you know. If you couldn't see him, just heard him talk, you'd think he was thirty years old. Even way back then."

"But why the circus? What was the appeal?"

"He said it was the closest he could get to real flying—flying through the air. He figured he'd sign on with the circus as an aerialist so they'd teach him how to fly and fall into those huge nets. He was back home within a week."

"The plan didn't work, obviously?"

"Nope. They wanted him in a clown act—which was okay, he said, kind of fun. But then they told him he had to muck out the elephant pens and trailers to earn his keep. Said he'd never seen so much shit in his whole life." Sterling laughed, then went on. "I'll never forget the look on his face when he described his first encounter with a three-hundred-pound mound of elephant dung. *You could have climbed on top of it and seen Mount Kilimanjaro,* is what he said. He left the circus after a show in Jacksonville, hitched back home, and decided he'd take up a career as a sky diver. He got his learner's permit as soon as he was old enough to qualify, and he was ecstatic after his first jump."

Sterling laughed again, remembering. "I'd never heard Red talk exactly like that before. He said you're like a god when you're up there. You feel like you could fall into the sun if you wanted to. You could flame out like shining from shook foil, be a fireball, fill the sky like Halley's comet and live forever."

Sterling's mood had obviously taken an upswing, and while we headed back, she talked enthusiastically about Sotto Vochay, the chorus she organized at the college in DeLand. "I needed an outlet, Mags. When you played for me at your apartment, you probably noticed that my singing voice is unusual?"

"You're kidding, right?"

"Why would I be kidding?"

"Sterling, your voice isn't just unusual, it's phenomenal. You have, what? Four octaves? And D below middle C without straining?"

"Right, and that low D is why I can anchor our women when we perform Christopher's *Upside Down Obbligato*. I mean, I love his creativity, but that piece is a killer." Big smile from Sterling while she continued: "Anyway, our ladies call me 'our baritone' and I love that they mean it affectionately. Unlike those jerks who want to 'flip' Sterling Silver Buck!"

We were in sight of the Genius House when she started telling me about Uncle Billy. "Uncle Billy never got over being disappointed that he missed out on Viagra, Cialis, all those erectile enhancers," Sterling said. "He wanted to come back *an' get some good fookin'*, is what he says. The way George tells it, he nagged her to death until—"

George had appeared on the back porch and called to us. "Ladies, lunch is ready. We're having a Dublin Coddle, Billy's favorite."

"Perfect!" Sterling called back. "We'll be right there, George."

That's odd, I thought, while we hurried along the dune walks to the house. What does Sterling mean, that Uncle Billy wanted to come back? Come back from where?

The Genius House has two dining rooms on the ground floor: a big formal one on the front side of the house and a smaller informal one on the back side with a pass-through to the kitchen. "I much prefer the smaller dining room," Sterling said. "It's nice to look out at the dunes and the beach through the big windows." Which is what we did while we ate. We looked out at the dunes, I mean, just the two us, because we were the only ones at the table. The boys stayed gone and George excused herself, saying she hoped we wouldn't mind if she took Billy's *sassige n' stout* to him upstairs in the Library.

Sterling seemed lost in thought and the Dublin Coddle was scrumptious, so I was content to concentrate on my food and contemplate the beach scene outside. Before long George came back, brought coffee to the table, and roused Sterling from her reverie. "Sterling, you seem bemused," George said.

"My dad volunteered to be Uncle Billy's sponsor, didn't he?"

"He did," George said. "Your dad was proud of his family and felt he should take responsibility for Billy. When Ben asked your mom about it, Mary Buck said sure, so we made the arrangements and . . . what's that noise?"

George and Sterling started looking for the noise, so I did too. "Up there," I said, "through the window and on that side balcony. See him? There's a naked dude dancing around, jerky-like. I think he's beating on a tambourine, and that's what we hear."

George and Sterling looked up. George laughed, but Sterling swore under her breath. "No, that's not a tambourine," Sterling said. "It's his Celtic drum, a bodhran. We told Uncle Billy if he didn't stop running around in the nude we'd hide it. Sometimes I wish he'd been sent to Reykjavik. It's so cold there he'd *have* to wear clothes." Sterling ran out then, leaving George and me alone at the table.

"You realize I'm confused, don't you?" I said to George.

"Of course I do, Mags. Being a writer, though, you know that people and their stories are complicated."

"That's for sure."

"So, Mags," George continued, "if you have questions for me, I'll try to answer them."

"Okay, Sterling said she wished Uncle Billy *had been sent* to Reykjavik. What does that mean? Who sent him here, instead?"

"As you can imagine, Mags, it's complicated. I'll need to refer to Celtic mythology, wherein a race of legendary Celts called the Danaans—"

"Omigod, of course!" I said, interrupting. "Celtic mythology! I have an old book, my only memento from my grandfather— my dad's dad. It's all about Irish Fairies and those legendary Celts called the *Tuatha dé Danaan*. They're a race apart. And they live in the legends and stories of Tara, the Irish equivalent of Camelot."

"That's exactly right, Mags, and it's a beautiful book you have, one of the classics."

"What? How do you know about my book?"

"Oh no. No, no, I was just assuming. Old books like that are priceless. Go on."

"Okay, so in Celtic mythology the *Danaan* are not exactly Fairies. More like part-human, part-fairy. They're beautiful and long-lived but not immortal. Like Aragorn in *The Lord of the*

Rings." George was nodding her head and smiling. "Oh, yes," she said, "Ronald drew on Celtic mythology for his creation of Aragorn. You see, Ronald was a scholar like Billy, and they loved talking about the Celtic legends. In addition, they were—"

Wait a minute. George knew J.R.R. Tolkien? *Ronald?*

George was still talking. "—good friends, compatriots. Ronald and Billy were unusual among scholars because they were both Mythmakers, as well." George smiled and paused for a moment, obviously enjoying a memory, then went on. "In case you're wondering, Mags, we need Mythmakers, now more than ever. It's why Billy got another chance. A Second Coming, so to speak." *Uh oh*, I thought. *What's going on here?* Nevertheless, I decided to play along. "Uh huh," I said, "so Uncle Billy got a Second Coming?"

"Yes, and he never expected to end up in the States, much less in Florida of all places. He wanted to go to Monaco."

"Monaco?"

"Yes. He said he wished he'd spent less time trying to decipher the messages of cranky disembodied spirits. He asked the *Danaan* to send him to Monaco so he could do some gamblin', along with all the *fookin'* that goes on there." George laughed out loud, remembering. "He's such a complicated man," George said, "there's nothing I can do but forgive him his foibles."

Sterling came back then, carrying Uncle Billy's bodhran. "Mags," Sterling said, "I'm sorry about this. It's not the way we planned for you to meet the family. How about making a fresh pot of coffee while George and I clean up the kitchen? Then you and I can take our coffee out on the porch."

I agreed, of course, but before I headed out to the porch with the coffee tray, I thanked George for the Coddle recipe she'd written for me on a sheet from one of Uncle Billy's notepads. "Any time, Mags," she said. "I have a head full of Billy's favorite recipes." Then she put a small decanter of Irish whiskey on the coffee tray for Sterling and me. "We call it fairy juice," she said.

Outside, the air was heavy, weighty with immanence. Or imminence. Or both. Okay, the air felt turgid and swollen, but it threatened, as well. Something was going to happen, but what? *Calm down, Mags,* I said to myself. *You're reacting to a jigger of Irish whiskey in your coffee.*

You're right, I said back to myself, *and I could get used to this, especially if I'm ensconced in a comfy padded porch rocker and enjoying an ocean breeze...* "Um, Sterling? Look there, near those funny-looking buildings, up toward the road. Is that a cow?"

"Where? I don't see anything."

"It's outside ... wait, there it goes. It's a big brown cow, and it just went in the door. Actually, I think it just *opened* the door."

"Mags, we don't have cows."

"But I know what I saw. It was big and brown and looked like a cow." Sterling shrugged. "Dunno, Mags. Maybe one of our Tutors was pushing a cart or carrying a box or something."

"One of your Tutors? Is that where they live?"

"Uh huh. Those are the outbuildings I told you about. When Dad and Mom moved here they talked to the Tutors and reno-vated the outbuildings to their specifications: classrooms, a con-ference room, a lab, music and art studios, and a private cottage for each tutor. Anyway, Mags, I said you'd meet the Tutors after lunch, so let's go."

We started walking toward the jumble of low coquina struc-tures north of the Genius House, and in a few minutes we'd reached the biggest one. Sterling told me we'd meet in the conference room and because she called ahead, the Tutors were expecting us. Which seemed strange to me because I hadn't seen her use a phone.

Just as we arrived, the big front door swung open and we went in.

MEET THE TUTORS

We all just stood there, looking at each other.

No one spoke. No one moved.

"Sterling," I whispered, "you didn't tell me. You didn't even *hint*."

"Yes, I did, Mags," Sterling whispered back. "I hinted as hard as I could, but you didn't get it. And I couldn't tell you straight out because you would've blown me off."

Sterling was right. If she'd told me straight out, I would've thought she was delusional. Possibly dangerous. "No matter what I said, Mags," she continued, "you wouldn't have believed me. And by the way, you don't have to whisper. They can read your mind."

Yes, I could feel it. They were in my head, all three of them. It was like brain tickles. Weird little brain tickles. There was music, too, and bright colors. And one of them was laughing. "Mags," Sterling said, "I'd like you to meet my Tutors—Datta, Jengu, and Kells." Then Sterling motioned toward a table with chairs around it, and the five of us sat down.

Damnation, I thought, this is one for the record books. Here I am with my normal young friend Sterling, exchanging stares with three . . . three *whats?* The tall furry one looks like a white Wookiee, the short one with the skanky beard looks like a bald Hobbit, and the third one with enormous eyes looks like an Alien. An iridescent Alien.

What was it Sterling said? *You don't have to whisper, Mags. They can read your mind.*

Fabulous. So these so-called Tutors already rummaged around in my defenseless brain and downloaded my life history? My issues with body image and relationships? My pitiful fantasies regarding romantic escapades with Johnny Depp and Jeremy Irons? Even my real name, which I've never told *anyone*?

For the rest of the afternoon, I listened while the three of them talked:

- Datta (the white Wookiee)
- Jengu (the bald Hobbit with the skanky beard)
- Kells (the iridescent big-eyed Alien)

I say they all "talked," but that's not exactly what it was. It was more like they were singing. A round, maybe. No, not a round. This was more like a fugue, a vocal fugue—where you hear all three voices, and they're in counterpoint sometimes, in harmony other times, occasionally in unison. Each voice has its own range, its own timbre, its own solo parts. And each carries certain motifs, certain themes, until the final resolution.

As if that wasn't mind-blowing enough, when they sang their story they sang in color. I heard ruby red that shimmered and glowed, midnight blue that thundered and surged, yellow and orange and purple that bounced and jiggled. It was music like I'd never heard—sorry, never seen—before.

If I hadn't been so snockered, I would've jumped up, started running, and never looked back. But that's not what I did. I stayed glued to my chair and listened while their voices painted a story-pageant so vivid, so detailed, so *real*, I seemed to be sitting in a front-row seat, watching a technicolor movie—What? I know, I *know*, technicolor's old hat. It's one of those generational things again, okay?

What I meant to say is I seemed to be immersed in high-definition digital surround-sound cinematography. And while they sang in my mind, they pulled me into the diorama their voices painted. While I stayed glued to my chair, in other words, they went inside my head and opened my mind's eye so I saw ... no, in some way I can't explain, I *lived* the fantastic story they told. Were we sharing a dream? Journeying together in virtual reality? I didn't know. All I knew for sure was that we, all five of us, were communicating in a language beyond words.

I can't begin to replicate the textural fabric of their story-singing, much less the interplay of sound and color. The best I can do is re-cast what they told me as a simple story, a fantastic-but-true story that begins roughly 100,000 years ago on Planet Earth.

The main point of the story is that we're all cousins—the Wookie, the Hobbit, the Alien, and us. Countless millennia ago we were simply four tribes of early people, four branches on the same evolutionary tree. Or as we call them now, four hominin species: *homo Neanderthalensis, homo Floresiensis, homo Boskopis, and homo Sapiens.* For simplicity we'll call the four tribes Neanders, Floreans, Boskops, and Sapiens. As I'm sure you realize, the tribe we'll call Sapiens—i.e., *homo Sapiens*—is us.

It's important to remember that way back then we all tended to resemble each other and that, when you get right down to it, life was relatively simple. You knew your neighbor and your neighbor's business but that was all right because you didn't see your neighbor very often. And *that* was because (unlike today) there were very few people on the planet and a gazillion square miles of undeveloped land.

Folks from different tribes got together mainly once a year when the Four Tribes Council held a meeting to talk stuff over, make decrees, and elect a new leader. This yearly council meeting was a moveable feast, depending on who held the leadership. That is, the place and time were determined by the current leader's tribe, so the event would generally be held on that tribe's favorite holiday at one of their sacred places.

Freeze frame: 100,000 years ago.

The way Sterling's Tutors were telling the story—sorry, singing it—the world was a nicer, gentler place precisely because people had enough space to live the way they chose. Every tribe had its nomads and its nesters, all free to form alliances and follow their chosen life plans. I guess we'd say now that some were naturally hunter-gatherers who moved with the seasons, some adopted semi-nomadic lifestyles as herders, while others preferred to live settled lives in small agricultural communities. And that's not counting the Loners.

The only problem that cropped up occasionally was when a member of one tribe and a member of a different tribe fell in love. Then there'd be compromises to make about where the couple would live and whose church they'd attend and whether the kids would go to public school or not. Those kinds of things.

Sometimes if compromise didn't work, they had to bring in a mediator, and if that didn't work, it could be a Hatfield-and-McCoy situation all over again. Not to mention that once in a while, when a controversial issue like same-sex unions reared its contentious head, the couple might just decide to hell with it and leave town for a place where people were open-minded.

Wow, I thought when they got to this part of the story. Even way back then, eons ago, folks got their knickers in a twist if someone in the family broke tradition and brought a stranger—someone different—home for dinner.

I possibly got a little distracted at that point, thinking about all the family-feud stories I knew, because that's when the Tutors' mind-music shifted from a major key to a minor key. Then they got back into harmony, so to speak, and that's when they started in on the part about the snake in the garden. Oh, boy, I thought. Isn't there *always* a snake in the garden?

To back up for a minute, things were going along pretty well until about 85,000 years ago, give or take a few millennia. You see, three of the tribes practiced safe sex and family planning, and they assumed that the fourth tribe, the Sapients, had been doing the same. *Au contraire.* Those promiscuous Sapients had been breeding like rabbits. The more they bred, the more space and food and consumer goods they needed.

Had the Sapients been long-range thinkers and equal-opportunity planners, they might have averted the disaster to come. But no, not the Sapients. Their Haves were embracing unrestrained consumerism, caring not one whit about all their Have-nots. It was a volatile situation, and it didn't augur well that the Sapients' teen-age phalligers (their word for young male persons) were out of control. Wherever you went you'd see them in packs, just hanging around playing rock-paper-scissors and comparing the length of their spears. Looking for trouble, basically.

Their teenage vuvulas weren't much better, either (vuvula was their word for young female persons). Instead of focusing on getting themselves educated so they could embark on careers and be responsible contributors to society (like teenage females of the other three tribes), all the Sapient vuvulas wanted to do was get fake nails and shop for ridiculous shoes.

The situation went from bad to worse. Sapients became more contentious, more aggressive. Pretty soon someone decided it was easier to take a hut than to build one, easier to grab someone else's mate than to romance your own, easier to steal food than to hunt it or grow it. Sapient phalligers got all puffed up and their vuvulas unprotestingly tagged along, setting up a genderfied power dynamic that would persist through millennia. It was like a mob flash-dance: some of it choreographed, some of it spontaneous.

And it grew.

Nomads attacked nesters, and nesters responded by fortifying their nests. Along the way someone invented the wheel (Sapients are always re-inventing the wheel), someone else figured out how to start fires on cue, a few cowboy types decided horses were good for raids and fast getaways, and a stone-age ancestor of Alfred Nobel figured out how to blow stuff up. Eventually the furor came to the attention of the Four Tribes Council, which met that year at Uluru, a sacred mountain in what we now call the Australian Outback.

The meeting started quietly enough, but there was a disturbing harbinger of impending disharmony, to-wit: when the Sapient representatives filed in they declined to mingle, even though inter-tribal mingling had always been part of the ritual. Instead, Sapients insisted that during this meeting they would sit together in their own caucus throughout the Council's deliberations—*for protection*.

Uh oh. The best way to mount an offense, as they say, is to claim it's a defense.

Almost as soon as the meeting began, it was over. The entire Sapient contingent stormed out in an act of defiant secession from the Council, claiming duress and announcing they would protect their campfires and herds and hearths (CHHs) from unprovoked attacks by weapons of mass destruction (WMDs). Which they had proof of, by the way.

Before the seceding Sapients faded into the distance, the remaining council members re-formed into a tripartite council and held a pow-wow long into the night. What can we do about this? they asked. Do we want to spend our lives on the defensive? No, they agreed, and that means we have but one course of action open to us. In a nutshell, Neanders, Floreans, and Boskops (NEFBOs, for short) decided if they didn't want to spend all their time circling the wagons, it was time to get the hell out of Dodge.

We'll fake our extinctions and make it look as though we're all gone, some said. *Yes!* everyone agreed. *If we retreat to faraway places, we can live in peace.*

The vote to leave was unanimous. Neanders, claiming mountains and forests as their territory, would leave first. Floreans, claiming the seas as their bailiwick, would leave next. And Boskops, claiming the subterranean sectors of Planet Earth as their domain, would be the last to embark on their diaspora.

Sapients will forget about us because they'll think our tribes have died out, they exulted, *and, in the meantime, we will live long and prosper.*

As planned, Neanders left first, some 35,000 years ago. After preparing a number of staged burial sites, most famously (for us) in the Neander Valley near Düsseldorf, the tribe folk started their arduous trek north and west, into the mountains of what's now Eastern Europe and even farther—into the coldest, most inhospitable habitats on earth.

Floreans stuck around quite a bit longer, partly because it was easier for them to stay out of sight. Floreans, you see, were as comfortable in water as on land, and there were a lot of archipelagos with small habitable islands where bands of roamers could settle and thrive undisturbed. Even so, Floreans eventually got squeezed. Bowing to the inevitable some 13,000 years ago, Floreans staged their fake burial sites in caves on the island of Flores and a few others in the Indonesian Archipelago, afterward dispersing to the remote oceanic waters of the world.

Boskops stayed longest of all. But finally, about 10,000 years ago, Boskops staged their extinction in several forested areas of South Africa near the east coast: Boskop (near Potchefstroom) for one, Fish Hoek for another. Unlike Neanders and Floreans, though, Boskops decided to observe from a distance and keep records.

Which they did, assiduously, while Sapients went forth and multiplied—again, and again, and again. Sapient civilizations rose and fell, empires waxed and waned, dynasties flourished and withered. Through it all, Boskops observed and recorded and extrapolated, roughly until the Sapients' Industrial Revolution in the West was well underway.

That's when the three still-hidden NEFBO tribes met in an emergency meeting to discuss the fate of Planet Earth—specifically its biosphere, upon which all living creatures depend for survival. Why did they call an emergency meeting? Because Boskops had done the math, to-wit: the exponential growth of Sapient population, combined with their (our) compulsion to savage the planet and each other, was a recipe for disaster. Soon.

In other words, the Writing on the Wall stated clearly that it was time for the three supposedly extinct tribes to emerge from their self-imposed isolation and stage an Intervention.

End of story.

Exhausted and overwhelmed, I sat there while Sterling's Tutors sang-talked their way to a final atonal chord, then fixed their combined gaze on me and waited. I didn't know what they wanted from me, and I didn't want to know. I knew what *I* wanted, though. More than anything else at that moment, I wanted to run away from the Genius House as fast as I could possibly run.

Oh sure, Sterling and I had a good time talking about the so-called "screenplay" she was writing. Remember that? All about Superheroes coming out of hiding so they could save the planet, yada yada? Right. That was amusing and entertaining like a comic book, fun to think about. But this was different. This was real.

I don't remember saying goodbye to Sterling and the Tutors, getting in my car, driving home, climbing my fire escape, going in the back door of my apartment, slumping on my sofa. I must've done all those things on autopilot.

"Mags, you've been slumped on the sofa for over an hour."

"Mags? *Mags!* What's wrong with you?"

So I told Schrödy everything. About Uncle Billy and George, meeting the Tutors, getting bowled over by the story about un-extinct hominins who are people like us except they don't look like us. And why they decided to fake being extinct. And why they've had to come back.

"Schrödy," I said, "I couldn't protest, I couldn't argue. I mean, I was in a room with the Tutors and they were real. They weren't holograms, they weren't 'virtual' anythings. I need to do some major mental gymnastics to get my head around this."

Schrödinger was unsympathetic. "Mags," he said, "get over it. Haven't you ever heard of Pandora's Box?"

"Well, of course I've heard of Pandora's Box. What does Pandora's Box have to do with this?"

"Duh, Mags. You never know what will happen when you open the box, right?"

"Right, but I still don't see how that's relevant."

"Because Pandora's Box is a metaphor for life. If you go around opening boxes, you have to accept what's inside when you open one. You never thought that Greek story was about a real Pandora opening a real box, did you?"

"No, of course not."

"Okay, then, act accordingly. You're the one who wanted to see what was in the box, metaphorically, that is. And now you know. Metaphorically."

Advice about metaphors from a cat was not what I wanted at the moment, so I decided to go up on the roof and commune with the stars. By myself.

KELLS

The next day I was still in a daze, so I walked across the street to the park, hoping to clear my head. Sitting on the seawall and looking out at the river, I was lost in my own thoughts and had no idea Sterling was sitting beside me until she started talking. "Mags, I know you're bummed but I won't let you shut me out."

"What the *hell*, Sterling? You scared me! How long have you been here?"

"Not long. I called a dozen times but your phone's off."

"I didn't want to talk."

"Mags, we *need* to talk. You need to understand that the Tutors are real people just like us. They don't look like us anymore because the three tribes evolved in isolation, away from us and away from each other."

"Right, like blue-footed boobies in the Galápagos."

"Actually, that's not a bad analogy because—"

"Sterling, stop! Can you imagine how freaked out I'm feeling? Ignoring for a moment the unsettling issue of Uncle Billy and George, I was up all night researching Neanderthals and those little hominins in Indonesia called Hobbits. Even the big-brained Boskop skulls in South Africa. It's all in the fossil record."

"I know."

"So everything the Tutors said . . . sang . . . shit! It's all possible."

Silence. Sterling was doing that thing where you stay quiet and let your friend vent.

"So," I said, "all that bull puckey about the so-called 'screenplay' you're writing? Superheroes coming out of hiding to save the planet? That's the *hint* you referred to? Your way of getting me ready to meet the Tutors? And come to think of it, *why me*?"

"Because you're part of this."

"How so?"

"It's complicated. For now, let's just accept that you have a part to play."

"You're saying I have no choice? What if I decline to be involved?"

"Mags, look at it this way. Life's an adventure, right?"

"I guess."

"So where would you rather be while you're adventuring? In Kansas or in Oz?"

"I've never been wild about Kansas."

"I didn't think so."

Sterling stayed quiet, just looked at me with those dazzling turquoise eyes and let me mull until the silence got so loud I couldn't stand it. "All *right*, already! I give up. What if we say—*hypothetically*—that I might be interested in being part of whatever this is. Where do we go from here?"

"You get acquainted with the Tutors, especially Kells. She's at home right now, waiting for us to come talk."

"She wants to *talk*? Will she sing to me? Or tickle my brain while she downloads all my secrets?"

"Mags, when I said we'll 'talk,' that's exactly what I meant. The Tutors' minds were attuned to your mind yesterday in the conference room because they had to be sure about you."

"They had to be 'sure' about me? What the hell does that mean?"

"I don't know the whole backstory, Mags, just that you're part of it, and Kells knows how and why."

Sterling had me, and she knew it. Try as I might to stay pissed off (not to mention terrified), I could hardly say *Gee, Sterling, I don't think I'm interested.* I mean, *seriously?* How could anyone with a functioning intellect and half a gram of curiosity elect to be uninterested in what was going on at the Genius House? It wasn't possible. "Okay," I said, "you've got me, but I'm warning you. If even *one* flying monkey shows up, I will be outta' there so fast you'll choke on my dust."

Sterling waited for me in the park while I went back to my apartment and told Schrödinger I'd be gone for a while, then headed down my fire escape to the garage behind Geno's store to get Agatha. Backing out of the garage, I thought I bumped something. But how could I? There was nothing behind my car when I got in it, no trash can or anything. Then—

"Diff! You scared me!" Diff was looking in at me from the passenger-side window. "Sorry, Miz Mags. Phyllo got chased by a cat, and I'm trying to find him. Poor little guy gets all nervous without me."

"Fine, Diff, but next time please don't just *appear* like that. Announce yourself somehow. You could get hurt. You're lucky *I'm* not a nervous type. If I were, I might've stepped on the gas instead of the brake and run you over."

After I picked up Sterling and started driving across the bridge, I saw Diff on a bench in the park with a couple of the street performers, Cassandra and Harlequin. They were all talking, and Phyllo the ferret was perched on Diff's shoulder just like always. *That's funny,* I thought to myself, *how'd Diff get to the park so quickly? And how'd he find Phyllo? I thought he told me Phyllo had gone missing.*

Yeah, right, I thought. *Nothing nervous about me, no reason to be suspicious. But I will be vigilant about those flying monkeys.*

After we drove in at the Genius House and parked, we headed toward Kells's cottage. The inside was a surprise, although I'm not sure what I expected. Floating furniture, maybe, like in *The Jetsons*. But it was all ordinary. Very nice, as if the Ethan Allen delivery van had just unloaded a houseful of furniture. But still ordinary.

I thought I heard music, but it was practically inaudible. It was pleasant, though, almost white noise but not quite. More like mother-of-pearl noise, opalescent, like the diffused light that was coming through the high windows. Or for that matter, like Kells herself, who seemed to glow. When I met Kells yesterday, I thought she was iridescent. But "iridescent" wasn't the right word, and anyway she stopped. She stopped being iridescent, I mean, and I forgot about it until now. But now—I could've sworn she had an aura.

Okay, Mags, I said to myself, settle down and . . . wait. The aura around Kells is coming from that big ring she wears. I noticed the ring yesterday when the Tutors were singing their story. Couldn't *not* notice it, actually. It's gold and silver, with a crest that looks like one of those "spinner" wheel covers you see on juked-up cars. The crest's the size of a quarter, and when it spins, the light in the room changes. Just like now . . .

"Mags? Are you with us? Can we talk?" While I zoned back in, I noticed Kells had stopped glowing. "I'm here, Kells," I said, "and I'm ready for *you* to talk."

Which she did, exhaustively, starting with a rehash of yesterday's song-saga in the Conference Room. This time, though, she talked in regular language. No brain tickles or mind movies or colored music, in other words, while she bluntly reviewed the reasons why we—Sapients—are Planet Earth's most invasive species. Eventually we got to a pregnant pause while Kells looked me in the eyes without talking, which is very disconcerting when you consider that her eyes are three times as big as mine. Gulp.

Finally Kells continued: "Simply put, Sapients are too many, too greedy, too arrogant. Assuming you don't manage in the meantime to blow up the planet and yourselves along with it, the current projection is that Sapient population could reach ten billion by 2050. Absent a drastic Intervention—"

"Mags," Sterling cut in, "when we talk about over-population, we're using analogies. We talk about people *breeding like rabbits* and *spreading like kudzu* because the analogies make sense, right?"

"Sure, absolutely."

"Okay, so now it's time to consider another analogy—flour beetles."

"*Bugs?* First we're like rabbits, then kudzu, now bugs?"

"Exactly, and this is how the analogy goes: Throw a handful of flour beetles into a fresh bin of clean sifted flour, then put a screen on top of the bin. The beetles eat and reproduce like crazy until the flour's stripped of nutrients, at which time the madding crowd goes berserk and starts consuming the only food left: each other."

"Sounds like science fiction, *Soylent Green* for the 21st century." Me, of course, attempting to inject a note of levity into a downright dismal discussion.

Kells took over then. "Mags, it's not only Sapient survival that's threatened, it's survival of the planet. Planetary death has happened before and, without an Intervention, it can happen to this world as well, meaning all of us—Neanders, Floreans, Boskops *and* Sapients—face extinction. For real. None of us can survive on a dead planet."

As you can imagine, Kells's comment was a conversation-stopper. While Sterling went to check something-or-other, I excused myself for a much-needed potty break and a chance to clear my mind. Extinction? *Seriously?* I mean, I'm no climate-change denier, and I'm environmentally aware, but are we Sapients are looking at the possibility—no, the *probability*—of going extinct as a species? Gulp. When I arrived back in Kells's parlor, she was ready to keep talking, but I stopped her. "Kells, I have a question. You said 'planetary death' happened before?"

"Yes, many times in distant universes. Closer to home, though, it happened in our solar system eons ago, to the Red Planet."

"You mean . . . *Mars*? There really was life on Mars? Sentient life?"

"Who do you think built those fabled canals? You of all people, Mags, ought to have paid attention to your great prophetic writers . . ."

Kells continued talking but I hardly noticed because my imagination had gone into overdrive, carrying me back to all those wonderful stories I'd read through the years: *Omigod, so there really might have been a Barsoom or a Shambleau? Naw, Burroughs and Moore were pulp writers but others like Asimov and Lem were geniuses. And LeGuin and Delaney and Butler, going as far back as Plato. And Bradbury . . . no, wait. Bradbury's Martian stories are about Sapients who abandon Planet Earth because they're killing it. Holy crap, it's the same old story.*

"Mags? *Mags!*" Kells was looking at me, boring right into me with those enormous eyes.

"I'm back, I'm back. Sorry Kells, sorry. Um, you were in my head, weren't you? So you know what I was thinking?"

"Yes, you were remembering stories you read a long time ago, wondering if fiction's a lie or if it contains a peculiar kind of truth. You were wondering, basically, about reality itself— what's real and what's not."

"So stories might be real?"

"What do *you* think?"

"Well, stories are real to me when I'm living them. When I'm there, the Land of Oz is as real to me as Ponce Inlet. And when I'm with them on the Yellow Brick Road, Dorothy and Toto are as real to me as my cat Schrödinger. Uh, maybe that's not such a good example . . ."

"No Mags, your cat *is* a good example, and that's because the genius of Sapients is to imagine, to envision, to see beyond. Your greatest thinkers have pondered the nature of reality, and they continue to do so." Sterling arrived back in the parlor then and cut in, impatiently. "Kells, could we cool it with Philosophy 101? We agreed to get Mags up-to-speed on the Intervention today. *And* convince her to help us."

"Sterling, I'm sorry," I said. "*I* distracted Kells, not vice versa. Anyway, this 'Intervention' you both keep referring to, it's already in the works? I mean, you already have a plan?"

"We have a plan that's been 'in the works,' as you put it, for over a century," Kells said. "And you, Mags, are a crucial part of it."

"That's what Sterling said, too, that I have a part to play. But when I asked her to explain, she said she doesn't know the whole story."

"Sterling's right, Mags. It's a long story, and it's extremely complicated."

"But it's not fair to keep me in the dark! Tell me *something* about why I'm here today. Why me, and not someone else?"

"Mags," Kells said, "I promise you'll get the whole story as we go along. For now, though, the short answer is that you're part of this because of your DNA, specifically through your paternal grandfather, Michael O'Duinn Magee."

Oh. My. God. I never knew him, he died before my dad was even born. All I have from him is the old book about Irish Fairies, and there's one photo of him with Groosma. Just that one photo. I always wondered .... Kells and Sterling stayed quiet, letting me talk out loud to myself. Finally I focused on Kells again. "And you know this about me—how?"

"Because as we told you yesterday during our meeting in the conference room, Boskops have been observing Sapients and keeping records. Don't you remember?"

"Um, not exactly. I mean, there's no way I could forget our meeting, but I don't recall that particular detail."

"Don't worry about not remembering specific details," Sterling said. "This is a lot of information to process, and we don't mean to dump it all on you at one time."

"That's exactly right," Kells said, "so let's take a break and then talk a little more. I have several talking points to cover, then Sterling wants to make you an offer. After that we'll be done here for today."

George bustled in then with a coffee tray, and I was happy to see a basket of cinnamon buns on it. Could have used some fairy juice too, but oh well. Caffeine and sugar would take the edge off while I tried not to panic. Kells has talking points to cover? And Sterling wants to make me an offer? I had that distinctly uncomfortable feeling you get when you're trapped at a car dealership, and they're putting the squeeze on you. George even patted me on the shoulder conspiratorially before she bustled out.

Finally Sterling and Kells came back, ready to talk. Kells started off by summing up (again!) how abysmally we Sapients have failed as Stewards of Planet Earth. "The bottom line," Kells said, "is that Sapients are out of control, and this 'global village' you like to talk about is a joke. You're nothing but a planetary hodgepodge of warrior states. What you need is a charismatic leader who can forge a consensus. A messianic guide who can pull you together—*all of you*—into a real global village."

"Kells," I said, "I get it. Believe me, *I get it*. I can't imagine a global consensus about any issue whatsoever, so it makes sense that we need a messiah-type to turn things around. Is that part of the Intervention? Will you be the charismatic leader?"

"Look at me, Mags, and tell me what you see."

"Umm . . . well, uh . . . I see . . ."

Kells cut me off. "It's okay, I'm not trying to badger you, just making a point. So let me tell you what you *don't* see. You don't see a person, a human being."

"Yes, but umm . . . yes. That's right."

"Now picture this scenario: Someone who looks like me—or like Jengu or even Datta—announces a New World Order, effective immediately. A total transfer of power. New laws, new rules, new sovereigns and sovereignties. Can you picture the global reaction?"

"Ahh, yeah. It wouldn't be pretty."

"Exactly. The end result would be Armageddon. So in answer to your question about who'll lead the Intervention, the charismatic leader has to be a Sapient."

"Okay, I get that, but who—"

Sterling cut in. "It's me, Mags. I have to be the messianic guide who'll be known as the Piper. Michael and Red are supposed to be my team, my helpers. It's why I'm pissed off at them right now because I can't depend on them for squat."

Silence. No one was talking, but I could hear voices. No, not voices. Music. It was that mother-of-pearl noise again, soft and opalescent. Except it was mind-music, delicate and soothing. The light was back, too, and I felt strangely comforted . . .

"Mags? Are you okay?"

"What . . . oh, sure. I was listening to the music. And watching it. It's beautiful."

"I'm glad you can see it and hear it, Mags." Sterling said. "Not everyone can, you know, just some of us. So-o-o, are you ready for my offer?"

I have no idea why I started laughing, but I did. Maybe because I've been escaping into fantastical adventure stories all my life, and now Blammo! at this late date I'm living one. "You bet I'm ready," I said. "And I won't even flinch if those flying monkeys show up."

EVERY MOVEMENT NEEDS A MANIFESTO

So there we sat in Kells's cottage, the four of us—what? Sorry, I forgot to mention that George came back with a fresh pot of coffee and stayed. Then while George and Kells listened, Sterling pitched her "offer" to me. Basically, she needed a Scribe on her team to write a "foundational text," and she wanted the Scribe to be me. "Every movement needs a manifesto, Mags," Sterling said. "When we're ready to launch the Intervention, we'll need *The Book*. Somebody has to write it, and I want that Somebody to be you because—"

"Wait, slow down. You'll need this 'book' when you launch the Intervention? But that means it has to be already written when you launch."

"Right."

"Sterling, you *know* you can't write a book overnight. Or in a week, or a month. For crying out loud, it takes a long time to write a freaking book!"

"Exactly. Which means you'll need to start working on it right away, collecting stories and piecing them together. Start with—"

The enormity of Sterling's "offer" hit me like a punch in the gut. While I was picking myself up off the floor (metaphorically, of course), Sterling kept right on talking: "—today's meeting here, then reconstruct yesterday's confab with the Tutors. You're perfect for this, Mags. Keep a journal, record conversations, write the narrative any way you want. Write poems, a few songs, keep it lively. People need magic and ritual and fantastic stories in a sacred text they can debate endlessly, so we'll give it to them . . . sorry, *you'll* give it to them. Set it up in frame-tales, epic sequences with interleaves, strings of sutras, any genre-combination at all."

"So . . . I'm hearing you say this Book will be a sacred composite? That's what holy books are, or at least it's what I call them. But omigod, it's so much work . . . and it could be dangerous! Look what happened to Salman Rushdie with *The Satanic Verses*! I've never been a big fan of fatwas, and this Book of yours would put me right out there in fatwa-territory . . . it might never be over for me, just like it's still not over for Rushdie. No no, I just don't think I—"

"MAGS, *STOP!*"

Whoa. I already knew about Sterling's prodigious vocal range, but I didn't know she can erupt with jackhammer decibels. She caught Kells and George by surprise, too, because they looked as startled as I was when she hollered.

"Now that I have your undivided attention, Mags" (Sterling, back in her everyday voice), "think of this as the opportunity you've been waiting for all your life—the chance to write a bestseller, a blockbuster that'll go down in history. The fact is, Mags, the Intervention's coming whether you're part of it or not. Do you really want to be left behind? Or do you want to lead the charge? Humanity's at a crossroads, and we have to help them—help *us*—forge a new path."

Talk about being hot-boxed.

Damn it all! I thought, while the voice of My Cautious Self started clamoring for attention in my head: *Be careful, Mags!* and *Don't fall for this!* and *You're too old to get involved in saving the world!*

Then the voice of My Adventurous Self started up: *What are you, Mags, a wuss?* and *You're the one who always says you can't win if you don't play!* and *You know you're already bored with this retirement thing, so show some gumption!*

On and on and on. It's like good cop bad cop, once the voices get started.

In case you're wondering, My Adventurous Self usually wins. It's how I've ended up in one pickle after another, and I could hear that voice doing it again: *Think about it, Mags. This might be your last chance to write an important book. The Epic of a lifetime. Do you want Kitchen Table Books to be your only claim to fame? Think how pathetic that would be . . .*

"Well," I ventured out loud, "we live our lives through stories. Shoot, our lives *are* stories . . . and this story promises to be a humdinger. And it'd be cool to write a really significant book, something epic like *The Odyssey* or *Beowulf . . .* even a new-age quest like *The Lord of the Rings.* Except starring a Woman Quest-Hero for a change . . ."

Then I started laughing, thinking about the stories I'd stumbled into so far: how Sterling and her siblings got their names by flipping a coin, and how the Tutors sang their saga into my mind, and omigod! the story of Uncle Billy and George, which I don't even know yet. But it promises to be another humdinger . . .

Silence from my three companions, except they all knew what I was thinking, even George (those weird little brain tickles again). Accordingly, they started back in.

"When we launch the Intervention, *The Book* has to be ready," Kells said.

"It sure does," Sterling laughed, "and remember, it begins with a house. In fact—"

"What? Sorry for interrupting but—what'd you say?"

"I said the story begins with a house—the Genius House, and actually that's not a bad title: *The Genius House*." Sterling was still talking, but I was thinking a mile a minute, missing something, but I didn't know what it was . . .

"Yes indeed," George chirped, "that's an excellent title for *The Book*, and we're all available to answer questions . . . well, maybe not Billy. Or at least, not right away."

Three earnest faces, all staring at me and waiting.

"Okay," I said finally, "but you need to be straight with me. I have a sneaking suspicion there's a lot I don't know yet. Correct?" With Kells and Sterling nodding in agreement, George sealed the deal. "You're absolutely right, Mags, and we promise not to hold anything back." George patted my shoulder again and headed back to the house while I retrieved my shoulder bag and got ready to leave.

Actually I was *dying* to leave because I wanted to get home and find my old book about Irish Fairies, my grandfather's book. Even though there'd been nothing more said about my DNA and how it got me into this, I thought the book might hold a clue. Before I could get away, though, Kells and Sterling asked me to meet them on Thursday at a local pub where Uncle Billy would do a poetry reading.

"Excuse me? You just co-opted me . . . no, you just *coerced* me into being part of your fantastical plan based on a doom-and-gloom scenario that makes me feel like I should apologize for having been born. And now you cap off our conversation by suggesting I accompany you to a *poetry reading?*"

"Please, Mags?" Sterling said. "Uncle Billy's going stir-crazy, and we need to give George a break, so we checked out bistros that have live music and open-mic nights where locals can get up and read their poetry. Uncle Billy loves an audience, so—"

"I know a great place for Uncle Billy to read," I said. "The Cafe da Vinci in DeLand."

"Too far," Sterling said. "We want a place close to home in case we have to hustle Uncle Billy out in a hurry. Michael says he can persuade his friend Prax to come along, and I figure having two great-looking guys in our group will help—"

"I know another place!" I said, interrupting. "Sopotnik's Cabbage Patch in Samsula. It's practically a straight shot from Port Orange, out along State Road 44."

"You're kidding, right?"

"Why would I be kidding?"

"Mags, the Cabbage Patch is a redneck biker bar, so—"

"I know, but rednecks and bikers are nice people. They'd be totally polite to Uncle Billy, probably adopt him as a mascot or something."

"Mags, I'm trying to tell you we already found a place."

"You did? Why didn't you say so?"

"We *did*, Mags. We *did*."

Once I stopped interrupting and started listening, I realized they'd done their homework. They checked out a couple beachside venues but decided Uncle Billy would be distracted by a club full of hot chicks wearing next-to-nothing. Finally they found a copacetic place in Downtown Daytona: Pigs Will Fly, a long-established pub under new ownership (it used to be called The Black Pig).

"We figure we'll start off this week at Pigs Will Fly," Sterling said. "It's small and relatively low-key. The proprietor's a creep who looks like Harrison Ford and thinks he's Indiana Jones." Sterling made a face but went on, "He's full of himself, fancies he's a lady-killer, but he agreed to give Uncle Billy the prime spot on the program."

Sigh. "Okay, I give up. I'll meet you at Pigs Will Fly on Thursday. What time?"

PIGS WILL FLY

"Mags, what's wrong with you? You've had your nose buried in that old book for two whole days." *. . . it isn't just old, it's ancient . . . handwritten, like someone's diary . . . it's easy to read, though, beautiful swooping script . . .*

"Mags! I'm talking to you!" *. . . stories of the Faeries are so real . . . the old leather cover disintegrated, just a piece of it left, with the signature 'Michael O'Duinn Magee' . . . glad I kept it . . . pressed it like a flower in a plastic sleeve . . .*

"MAGS!"

"What?"

"You're ignoring me. It's bad enough when you go walkabout, but this is different. You look weird, like you're in another world."

"Sorry Schrödy, sorry. It's my book about Irish Fairies, the book that didn't get burned up in my condo fire because it was in my Commonplace Box. It's the only thing I have from my dad's father . . . and you're right about weird. He's my connection to all the Genius House stuff, like why they want me to write *The Book* for the Intervention. I told you about the Intervention, didn't I?"

"Only a hundred times."

"Cut it out. You know I don't appreciate sarcasm." Schrödy went on talking, but I wasn't listening because I couldn't stop thinking. *Kells said Boskops kept records and that's how they know about my DNA. Did they know my grandfather too? Mick Magee? Is that even possible? And not only that . . .*

"Oh shoot, Schrödy! I have to be at the pub in an hour. If you'd asked me a month ago I'd have said pigs will fly before I get involved in anyone's crusade. But that's what Sterling and Kells are on, isn't it? A crusade to save the planet? And here I am, involved up to my ears."

Silence, not even a sniff from the cat.

"Schrödy, I apologize for ignoring you, okay?"

Barely audible sniff.

"Come on, Schrödy, please don't be mad. I'll tell you all about it when I get home. Sterling said she and Kells are getting dressed up for Uncle Billy's poetry reading, so I'd better make myself look decent."

Pigs Will Fly is on the second floor of a downtown building that used to be Kress Five and Dime many years ago. Since then the Kress building had been home to one failed venture after another, and the word around town is it almost became a Dollar General Store. Then a group of investors from DeLand bought it and leased the second floor to the pub which relocated from Seabreeze Boulevard when the original one burned down.

The pub also got a new name when it relocated (it used to be The Black Pig, but now it's Pigs Will Fly). No one knows why the owner changed the name, except it had something to do with insurance and an ongoing investigation into the fire that destroyed the old pub.

Kells and Sterling said they'd meet me outside, and we'd go up to the pub together, so I didn't want to be late. Besides that, I was dying to see their outfits because I knew the two of them make a game of it when they want to go out on the town. First they rifle Mary Buck's closet for vintage clothes and accessories, then they each pick out one of Christine's famous wigs from Sterling's collection . . . you don't remember Christine? Sure you do. She did costumes and wigs for Opera in the Park. Also a donkey head for the character Bottom.

Anyway, Kells needs a wig because she doesn't have any head hair, and Sterling has a whole collection of wigs because she loves dressing up like classic film stars. So while they're playing their "game," the two of them get all gussied up. Then, like celebrities going on the prowl incognito, they can go out and mingle with the natives.

Even though I knew all that, I was bowled over when I saw Lauren Bacall and Joan Crawford waiting for me on the sidewalk outside Pigs Will Fly. Lauren (Kells) was stunning in a black trench coat and red stiletto pumps, a pageboy-style blonde wig, and smoke-tinted glasses to hide her big eyes. Joan (Sterling) vamped in black-and-white herringbone gabardine with exaggerated shoulder pads, bright red lipstick, fluffy hair tucked in a glossy *chignon-net*, and platform wedges.

"You two are crazy!" I enthused, but I was glad I'd done a little gussying-up myself. Nothing age-inappropriate, of course, just my fabulous new Jimmy Choo ankle boots in a vivid color called Veitchberry Violet and a matching shoulder bag with studs and fringe.

I was feeling really good about myself while we headed upstairs then BLAMMO! déjù vu slapped me right in the face. *What's happening? Why am I flummoxed?* Omigod, it's because I'm in the Kress building!

Climbing that old dark staircase to the second floor, I'd moved back in time. There I was again, going with my mom to the creepy loan shark's office—so tiny there was no place for me to sit except on the floor. The loan shark was long gone, but memory made palpable the shame and helplessness I'd felt, sitting there on the hard floor under his dirty window . . .

The present reasserted itself when we met our group upstairs in the pub, and while we were getting our tables Sterling laughed about Uncle Billy being super-excited. "He says *destiny's* involved tonight."

"I don't get it," I said. "What does destiny have to do with a poetry reading?"

"I'm not sure I understand, either," Sterling said, "except it's something about the Valley of the Black Pig in Ireland, back in Celtic times. When Uncle Billy found out this pub used to be called The Black Pig, he figured destiny's calling him."

Hmm, I thought, looking around, I wouldn't recognize destiny if it came knocking at my door, but when you've seen one "authentic" theme-pub, you've seen them all. The only distinctive touch in this one was an enormous neon sign hanging above the bar and proclaiming in bilious green letters: *PIGGLES BLACK MALT—IT'S WORLD FAMOUS.*

Sterling stuck close to Uncle Billy, getting him and George settled with her at a table for four along with Jengu who was dressed conservatively in jeans and a denim jacket. He'd also stuffed his inordinately large feet in high heeled black boots (I was sure the boots had lifts as well as stacked heels) and brushed his long beard so it didn't look skanky. And since it was dark in the pub, Jengu's vivid red-gold coloring just looked like a serious suntan.

Kells introduced me to Michael as "Sterling's friend" and together the three of us claimed an adjacent table, with a chair saved for Red who was running late and another chair for Michael's friend Prax in case he showed up. While we sat down, I noticed that Uncle Billy was carrying a notepad and a small beat-up wooden box.

While Michael went to order our drinks, Jengu leaned over from his table and pointed out the owner of the pub who truly was a dead ringer for Harrison Ford. "Really? He owns the pub?" I asked. "Sure does," Jengu said, a huge grin splitting his face. "His real name's Max Finkelstein, but he calls himself Indiana Jones, owns a chain of Pig Pubs that're famous for Piggles Black Malt, just like the sign says. They brew it from a secret recipe that's a big fuggin' deal. The secret ingredient's supposedly an exotic strain of barley malt that's grown on one of the islands. Bimini, I think."

The next time I looked toward the bar I didn't see Max, but a table of three in a far corner caught my attention: two grim-looking older men in suits and one much-younger woman. One of the men looked vaguely familiar—fiftyish, a mustache and small beard, round black-rimmed Harry Potter glasses, and a bad hairpiece. The other man resembled a cadaver—tall and skinny with stick-out ears and a bony face, rimless spectacles, a few wisps of whitish hair. The woman, probably in her early thirties, was definitely a "type"—bleached hair with dark roots, too much makeup, a size fourteen squeezed into a size ten. As we used to say about Bouncy Miss Babs at Vacation Bible School, *Her cups runneth over.*

In contrast to most of the crowd who were talking, laughing, high-fiving each other, the mysterious trio stayed silent. The cadaverous one sat rigidly straight in his chair, sipping a cup of coffee. The other man, more relaxed than the cadaver, had a glass of red wine in front of him, and the woman was already working on her second Margarita.

Hmm, I thought, why do they seem suspicious? Well for starters, if I wanted to sit in the darkest spot in the room, that would be it. So are they trying to be inconspicuous? Because if they are, it's not working. No, I know why they look suspicious. It's because they're Bogos—a bogus group, people who don't belong together. They look like three people who can't stand each other, so why would they want to hang out together at a pub? I decided to keep an eye on them, but they needed names.

Okay, the two men are easy. Bad Hairpiece in brown tweed with elbow patches, looking down his nose at the crowd as if offended by their body odor, is *The Professor*. And Monsignor Cadaver in the white linen suit, who looks like he gets his jollies running the Inquisition, is *The Confessor*. The woman's a little harder, though, because . . . whoa. Is that her third Margarita? Sure is, and she's a perfect *Rita*.

The Professor, the Confessor, and Rita. Note to Self: Put them in a story sometime; with a title like that, I can't miss. "Michael," I said, "who're the Bogos in the back? Two men and a woman. They don't belong together, but there they are."

"Oh, them. They're just some Archies," Michael said, "Sterling's friends." Omigod, I thought to myself. Archies are *real?* I figured Sterling made them up while she was pitching her so-called screenplay to me. "Michael," I said, "why are they called Archies?"

"Dunno, Mags. I never asked." I was getting ready to ask Kells about the Archies when Red arrived at our table (can't mistake that big voice and long wavy red hair) and pulled his chair out to sit down, so I decided to save my questions for later.

In the meantime, our mugs of black malt had arrived, which we duly lifted in a toast. All of us except Sterling, that is, because instead of Piggles in a mug, she got water and a lemon wedge in a Mason jar. Damn, I said to myself, why can't Sterling relax her healthy standards just this one time and join us in a drink? I mean, she'll self-destruct if she doesn't chill out once in a while. Won't she?

"*Sláinte agus Beannachtai!*" Uncle Billy led the toast, after which we all followed suit, including Sterling with her Mason jar. "Sláinte! Sláinte! Sláinte!"

"Damnation, this beer's as black as coal," I said when I got a good look at what was in my mug. "That's why they call it black malt," Michael answered. "It's a special brewing process that burns the barley malt to the point of carbonizing it. Different brewers use different proportions of the carbonized malt. It adds color to the brew, is what they say."

"Another reason they call it black malt," Red chimed in, "is if you have sensitive taste buds, you think you're drinking liquefied burnt toast." Sipping his beer and making a face, Red continued, "This *might* be the worst black malt I've ever tasted, hands down." Sterling raised her eyebrows and looked down her nose at Red, as if to say *I told you so,* but Jengu laughed and high-fived. "Copy that, Bro," Jengu said. "Makes you wonder why Piggles is so frakkin' famous."

I thought Jengu and Red exchanged a *look* at that point, but before I could ask what was going on, the show got started: Max postured and told innumerable lame jokes, a girl band called Gooseberry Fool performed a few Celtic pieces, and an interminable contingent of local poets read their work. Finally it was Uncle Billy's turn. After two off-color jokes and more posturing, Max winked suggestively at Sterling and crooned into the microphone, "And now, Chits and Chieftans—"

"Oh God," Sterling groaned, "please tell me he didn't just say *Chits and Chieftans.*"

"—we have a new talent here tonight. They tell me he's sensational, and he brought his entourage with him, too." More winks at Sterling. I motioned to Sterling in a panic. "What?" I whispered. "Uncle Billy's *entourage*? We don't have to get up there and do anything, do we?"

"No, Mags, we don't have to perform," she whispered back. "Just settle down and enjoy." While Uncle Billy got up from his chair and walked to the stage, carrying the notepad and the box, Max intoned, "And now, please welcome *Uncle Billy's Magic & Poetry Show*."

The crowd sat enthralled while Uncle Billy stood at the mic and read. Except it seemed to me he didn't actually do much "reading" except for his signature poems, the ones we all know because they're anthologized to death. Those poems he read very deliberately, perching his glasses on his nose and looking down at pages on his notepad.

The rest of the time, though, he seemed to be making it up as he went along. The familiar themes were there, to be sure, but at least half the poems he read that night were unknown to me. Not that I was ever an authority on his poetry, yet I was familiar with his body of work (I *was* an English professor, after all!). And I found his extemporizing that evening strangely disquieting.

I was surprised at the strength of his voice, though, especially its resonance, and I wondered if the sound system was re-mastering his voice as he talked. Naw, I thought, this pub wouldn't have such sophisticated electronics, so maybe Uncle Billy's fairy friends are providing an otherworldly amplification?

Yep, I decided. That must be it, and I was right because the box he carried when he went up on the stage held a few of the Genius House Fairies who came along to help him with backup: pipes and drums, a fiddle, some *a cappella* vocalizations and harmonies. They also flitted decoratively around the stage and flashed fairy lights when it was appropriate to do so. As you can imagine, that night's performance was ...

What? You don't believe fairies are real? Well guess what, you're wrong. Different cultures call their fey creatures by different names, of course, but in the end it gets down to whether you believe in a spirit world or whether you don't.

"Uncle Billy knows all the genealogies," Sterling told me when I asked her about the Genius House Fairies. "Our Fairies are Irish, of course, and Uncle Billy can reel off all the tribes and clans and rivalries. It's so freakin' complicated, though, I just call the good ones shiners and the bad ones snarks."

For sure he knows all the genealogies, I thought to myself, recalling what he wrote in one of his early prose collections: *No matter what one doubts, one never doubts the faeries.*

When Uncle Billy started in on his final poem, "The Stolen Child," the Fairies gathered around him and joined in the refrain at the end of each stanza:

> *Come away, O human child!*
> *To the waters and the wild*
> *With a faery, hand in hand,*
> *For the world's more full of weeping than you can*
> *understand.*

Silence. There wasn't a dry eye in the house, and you could have heard a pin drop. Then, while Fairies flitted and the Fiddler fiddled, folks jumped up to applaud and cheer until everyone was standing, clapping and hooting to beat the band. Our group was joining in enthusiastically, even Michael and Red who'd started a staccato boot-stomp on the hardwood floor. Aww, I thought, how sweet that they're so supportive of Uncle Billy.

When I turned around to look at Sterling's table-group to see if they were stomping too, though, I was stunned. There stood Sterling, bathed in light. Light swirled around her, enveloping her in a shimmering gauzy cocoon that flung diamonds in all directions, like shards of light flashing from a revolving disco ball. In my astonishment I looked for confirmation from my table-mates, then frantically from one table to another, but everyone seemed oblivious to the flashing light-show that surrounded Sterling. *How can they not see it?* I screamed in my head. *It's so bright! It's blinding! It's too bright, blinding me . . .*

"Mags? Are you okay? " Sterling was holding my arm, looking concerned.

"What? Uh . . . sorry, sorry, I'm fine now. Whew, every once in a while I see flashers."

"Flashers?"

"That's what my optometrist calls them. Had them since I was a kid when some boys shone a bright flashlight in my eyes. Something about too much light for blue eyes."

"Your eyes are certainly an unusual color."

"Yes, but my eyes are weak, very sensitive to light. Anyway, flashers are nothing to worry about, just annoying."

Sterling said something noncommittal about optical illusions being all about light, I eagerly agreed, and chatter ensued while the crowd made ready to disperse, everyone congratulating Uncle Billy and saying this was the best open mic night ever, and when was he coming back?

But I knew something wasn't right, something important. Making my way toward the exit with our group, I looked for a disco ball. *Please please PLEASE!* I was thinking. *Please let there be a disco ball!* I didn't see one, though, not hanging above the stage or the bar or anywhere else. Then I looked for the three Archies, but they, too, were nowhere to be seen.

ARCHIES & PATHICS

I was working on *The Porridge of Dorian Gray* when Casey knocked on my door. He'd just deposited Wally downstairs at Geno's model train depot and said he was curious to see my apartment because Geno told him about it. "Wow, Mags," he enthused when he walked in. "What a great space!"

"It is, isn't it? Geno'd barely begun the renovations when I flew down here during spring break to look at the apartment. At that point he'd just gutted the interior and stubbed in the bathroom and closets. I fell in love with it, asked him if he'd do the buildout to my specifications, and he said sure, why not."

Casey was walking around, looking out of the windows at my vistas, taking it all in. "Um, Mags? Where's the kitchen?"

"See those French doors over there, on the west wall?"

"Uh huh."

"Open them. That's right. Now pull down that countertop."

"Dang, Mags, this is cool!"

"See? It's like a Murphy bed except it's a kitchen. It has everything I need to live luxuriously: coffee service, microwave, a mini-fridge and icemaker and wine cooler."

Casey was looking around again, obviously puzzled. "So . . . do you have a bedroom?"

"Sure do. It's over there on the south wall. It *is* a Murphy bed."

Casey said he'd stay for coffee so I made some while we talked. "Okay," he said, "explain to me why you designed the space this way. I mean, you're not exactly cramped for square footage. You must have, what, a couple thousand square feet, and yet you fold up your kitchen on one wall and your bedroom on another?"

"I know, the design seems odd to most people, but I love the idea of a big open airy space. I didn't want to break it up into rooms except for the bathroom and two closets: one for clothes, one for brooms and laundry."

Casey continued to look around while I was talking, nodding his head. "I get it, Mags, I get it. Up high like this, perched at the top of the building with windows all around, this could be a tower room in a castle. And I love the distressed wood floors and exposed ceiling beams."

"Exactly. It's like living in a Johnny Depp movie. Any minute now I expect Don Juan DeMarco to land on my balcony and invite himself in."

Casey explained that Wally would be downstairs until dark, working on Geno's model train setup. In the meantime, he (Casey) and Sterling would play racquetball at the gym and get dinner at Sergio's. Then Casey would come back to get Wally and drive him to DeLand.

It amuses me no end that Wally doesn't drive his BMWs, just admires the engineering. Also that he has drivers for his BMW vehicles whenever he wants them. Especially Casey who doesn't own a car, just a motorcycle. And Christopher, too, who's as besotted with BMW engineering as Wally is.

After Casey left I started back in on *The Porridge of Dorian Gray* and thought about Oscar Wilde. He was one of the greatest wits who ever lived, yet he ended up disgraced, exiled, and broke. Just like me. Well okay, I'm not disgraced, just disgraceful sometimes. And I wasn't exactly "exiled" being that I chose to leave Atlanta, even though I had a whopper of a reason. I sure will be broke, though, if I don't hurry up and finish the Irish book.

Dammit, I said to myself, I can't focus on what I need to do because I stay so distracted by this Genius House stuff. Which is not exactly paying my rent, by the way. And oh shoot, I need to ask Sterling about—

"Mags? You're talking to yourself again." Schrödy, of course. "Mags, I worry about you when you talk to yourself. If you need someone to talk to, talk to me. I'm listening."

"You're all heart, Schrödy, but I need to call Sterling anyway so that's what I'll do. You can go back to sleep."

Except I couldn't get through to Sterling because of static on the phone line. It's exasperating how phones work at the Genius House—sometimes but not other times. And when they're not working, the static's so screechy it gives you a headache.

Sterling says the static comes from the Tower where her dad installed complicated electronics. *There's a lot of synaptical energy,* is how she explained it, *and when the synaptical energy spikes, it knocks out the phones.* That made no sense to me whatsoever, but I decided not to worry about it, just like I decided to take a chance that Sterling would be home if I drove down there and showed up unexpectedly.

George opened the kitchen door when I knocked, said she'd let Sterling know I'd arrived so I should make myself comfortable on the porch. Which I was doing when I saw Michael in the distance, halfway between the House and the Tower, involved in an intense arm-waving conversation with the Professor and

Rita. *What?* Michael blew me off when I asked about the Bogos at the pub, said dismissively they were "just some Archies." So why does it look like Michael's browbeating the Professor and Rita while they holler back at him?

I was so mad I wanted to spit. I mean, what the hell was going on and why hadn't anyone clued me in about it? I was ready to hightail it down the path to confront them when I stopped dead in my tracks and gawked at Sterling—who'd appeared in the Tower's open doorway with the Confessor (couldn't mistake Monsignor Cadaver in his white suit). Whatever Sterling called to the group on the path made them pay attention because they hustled back to the Tower, went inside with the Confessor, and closed the big door behind them. Sterling stood outside until the door to the Tower was closed, then started walking toward the House and waving to me.

The following exchange encapsulates the dynamic of the ensuing conversation between Sterling, and me, and George:

"Mags, please stop interrupting and calm down so I can explain!" (Sterling)

"I can't calm down because I'm totally pissed off!" (Me)

"Mags, Dear, have another rhubarb square? And more syllabub?" (George)

I settled down eventually, giving Sterling and George a chance to explain that the Professor and the Confessor and Rita are 'Noids. That is, they're humanoid robots engineered by Boskop technology a long time ago. Many millennia ago, actually. "It was after Boskop roboticists climbed out of the Uncanny Valley—"

"The what?"

"Mags," Sterling said, "the Uncanny Valley's a Sapient concept, an AI term referencing robots that creep people out because they look human—but not quite. *They're uncanny,* people say, so they refuse to accept them. They—we—refuse to accept robots that are human-ish, that is. It's why our Sapient roboticists create machine-looking robots. To keep people happy."

"Oh, yes," George chimed in. "It'll be a long time before Sapient scientists can climb out of the Uncanny Valley, but Boskops mastered biological robotics long ago. And after our Gardeners decided—"

"*Biological* robotics? Sorry about interrupting, George, but—biological robotics? Are you serious?"

"Never mind about interrupting, Mags," George said. "And I shouldn't have said anything yet about our Gardeners getting involved in the Intervention—"

"What? Who? Are you telling me you belong to a Garden Club?" This time Sterling cut both George and me off on purpose, and she shot George a withering look. *What's going on?* I wondered, but there was no stopping Sterling.

"As I understand it, Mags, Boskop roboticists opted for carbon-based machines, not silicon. It was a risky decision because it meant their machines would learn and evolve. Their Boskop makers wouldn't be able to control them, in other words. Boskops halted production, in fact, until it became clear that helper 'Noids—crafted to look like Sapients—would be needed for the Intervention. That's when Boskop roboticists created the biobots called *Archies.* Archies are just like us Sapients except for two major differences—"

It was my turn to interrupt, and I had a good reason. "And you already told me what one of the differences is," I said to Sterling. "Remember? You said all the Archies are engineers. I still don't understand why you call the biobots 'Archies,' though."

"Excuse me? *Engineers?* What do you mean, all the Archies are engineers?"

"It's in that piece-of-crap screenplay you concocted when you were setting me up to meet the Tutors. That's when you said Archies are engineers." Sterling started laughing, and that pissed me off bigtime. "What's so freaking funny? That's what you said, they're engineers."

"I didn't say Archies are engineers, Mags, I said they're *engineered.* Boskop roboticists engineered Archies to be Archetypal. That's why we call them Archies. Get it? They're Archetypal, so we call them Archies."

Just in time, George passed me the plate of rhubarb bread and insisted she top off my syllabub. Of course I "got it," but I didn't appreciate being the butt of a joke. I was willing to be placated by sugary food and drink, however, so once again I settled down to listen. "Think about Archetypes," Sterling said, "in relation to the 'Noids you saw on the path to the Tower—"

Whoa, I thought to myself. I really do get it about the Professor and the Confessor and Rita being "types." I mean, that's why it was so easy to name them ...

Sterling was still talking. "—and there are others. The police officers who patrol downtown Daytona Beach, for example, and the street performers."

"Um, the street performers? Like Harlequin and ... oh no, don't tell me, not Cassandra the Cyclist. *Please* tell me she's not an Archie."

"Sorry, Mags, but Cassandra's an Archie too. And funny old Diff with his drum. He's a Different Drummer, of course."

Looking back, I realize that Sterling and George fully intended to continue our conversation after we took a much-needed break for sustenance. Before George headed for the kitchen, she invited me to stay for lunch because her special Shepherd's Pie was baking in the oven. And before Sterling excused herself to go check on the Roomers, she suggested I clear my head before lunch by going for a walk on the beach.

That's not what I did, though. I jumped in Agatha, got on the road, and drove home where I could be normal and ordinary, living my dull boring life with my malapropish landlord and my genius-nerdy cousin and my friends . . . my friends . . . some of whom, I now knew, were biobots.

Having reached the safety of my apartment, I looked out my big window and saw Cassamdra balanced on her unicycle, playing her flute for tourists in the park. I couldn't hear what she was playing, but I figured it was probably her signature song "White Coral Bells." Remember it? When I was a kid we used to sing it at Girl Scouts, around the campfire:

> *White coral bells upon a slender stalk—*
> *Lilies of the valley line my garden walk.*
> *Oh how I wish that I could hear them ring;*
> *That will happen only when the Fairies sing.*

Watching Cassandra through my window, remembering the talks she and I shared, I knew my world had tilted. So my friend's a biological robot? A biobot? What the hell does *that* mean? Is she really my friend? Or just a highly advanced cousin of my GPS? Mags, I told myself, get serious. Cassandra hasn't changed, and your relationship with her hasn't changed. It's all about perspective, which is exactly what Sterling said when I was bummed about the Tutors—that I should adjust my perspective.

Adjust your perspective. It's simple, right? Wrong. There's no telling how long I would've stayed stuck in "Tilt" mode if Talisman hadn't called and asked me to go with her to the last night of a classic film fest in DeLand because Slim would be getting an award for her work in community theater, and our friend Deirdre would make the presentation. Then after the awards ceremony Talisman was hosting a party at her house, and I was welcome to stay overnight. "Schrödy, we're going to DeLand for a getaway," I hollered.

Then I got busy in my closet, deciding which fabulous outfits I'd wear: one for the ceremony, one for the party at Talisman's house. In less than an hour I'd packed up my suitcase, Schrödy's traveling box, and a supply of MoonPies, and we were on our way.

The film fest awards ceremony that night was over-the-top. Slim was spectacular as Marlene Dietrich's *Morocco* twin: black satin tails and top hat, blonde wig, one of those e-cigarettes that look realer than real. (Slim loves dressing up like classic film stars just like Sterling does, and Christine outdid herself again with costuming,) Deirdre didn't assume a persona other than her ordinary gorgeous self. (She's a natural redhead with flawless creamy skin, looks like a twenty-year-old Julianne Moore.) Still, she was stunning in a floor-length green satin sheath and dangly emerald earrings as long as her wavy auburn hair.

Watching them up on the stage, I couldn't help pondering the so-called "burden" of being beautiful. Some *burden*, right? As burdens go, I can think of tons I'd rate higher. I mean, I love my friends dearly, but it's undeniable that some of us were at the back of the line when beauty-chops were handed out.

I was home by noon the next day, humming while I unpacked, when Sterling called. "Mags, we didn't finish our talk when you were here yesterday—"

"I know, Sterling, but I had to leave because—"

"*Mags*! Listen to me and don't interrupt."

"Okay, okay. Sorry."

"You ran away, Mags, you didn't even say goodbye. George and I looked all over creation for you. I know you're bummed about the Archies, but you can't back out on us now. George and I are free on Sunday and so is Kells, so let's continue our talk. Do you want to come to the house? Or should we come to your apartment?"

"I'll come to your house. Is noon-ish okay?"

"Fine."

Sterling met me at the kitchen door on Sunday at noon, and George was waiting inside, in the small dining room. "George and I will take up our discussion where we left off," Sterling said, "and Kells will join us soon."

"Fine with me," I said, following my plan of being eminently agreeable. "I am ready for the Apocalypse. Or the Rapture, depending on what's in the cards for today." Good. Sterling was laughing, and George was all smiles while she started us off. "So you've adjusted to the idea of Archies, Mags? And you're clear that Archies are here to help us?"

"Right, I understand that Archies are inconspicuous because they look just like us Sapients, and that means they can be out and about without attracting undue attention. Unlike Datta or Jengu or Kells."

"Exactly."

"Okay, I get that, but *why* do they go 'out and about'? What's the point? I mean, take the three Archies at the pub when Uncle Billy was reading his poems. Why were they there? Who or what were they looking for?" George nodded for Sterling to answer: "Archies are always on the lookout for Pathics because—"

"Omigod, Sterling. Wait! You had Pathics in your screenplay-setup, too. You said they're snake-people. *Please* don't tell me snake-people are real!"

"Pathics aren't exactly snake-people, Mags . . . well, in a way they are, but—"

"Holy shit, Sterling! I'm terrified of snakes! I'm a herpetophobe! Did I tell you about the time a student showed up outside my office with a huge snake draped around her shoulders? Talk about putting a whole new slant on *accessorizing with a boa*! And there was another time—"

"*Mags*! Calm down, okay, and let me explain? Pathics don't look like snakes, and they're not snake-handlers. They're a hominin sub-species, specifically a sub-species of *homo Sapiens*."

"So they look like us?"

"Pretty much but—"

"Then why'd you call them snake-people?"

Big sigh from Sterling. "Mags, you're not helping. Stop interrupting and listen?"

"Okay okay, I'm listening."

"Remember this term: *synergetic species*. You'll hear more about it as we go along because it's an important accident of evolution—what our Sapient scientists would call 'deep homology.' It means, basically, that hominin species have long depended on other species for assistance, communication, even friendship. In the case of—"

"You mean like us? With dogs and cats? Except cats can be very uncooperative—"

"Mags, *please!*"

"I'm zipping my lip. Promise."

"So in the case of the other three tribes—the ones who hid out so they could get away from Sapients—each tribe befriended another species to the extent of forming a synergy. That is, while those tribes evolved in response to new environments, they befriended other species who helped them adapt. At the same time . . ." Sterling stopped talking but not because I interrupted, more like she was rehearsing her next line in her head.

Eventually she started off again. "At the same time, Sapients were also befriending another species, but sometimes they—we—took it to the next level . . ." What's going on? I wondered. Sterling stopped talking again, until finally George jumped in. "What Sterling's trying to say, Mags, is a few Sapients formed a synergetic relationship with snakes—so close a synergy, there was some interbreeding. Not much, but a little."

Talk about dropping a bomb in a conversation! *Interbreeding with snakes?* Fortunately, I didn't have to react with chitchat because George left to make coffee, and Sterling said she'd be back after checking on the Roomers.

So there I sat, just me and my bemusement, thinking disjointed thoughts and staring out the window at the beach. George brought our coffee tray then, and I was glad to see a plate of scones. Sure could have used some Irish whiskey to liven up my coffee, but oh well. Then when Sterling came back, she started talking where we left off.

"Mags, we can't *not* deal with Pathics. They've been trouble-makers ever since Sapients started co-evolving with them. The process is called bio-cultural co-evolution, specifically HGT— also known as Horizontal Gene Transference, or 'jumping genes.' It's about patterns of behavior being passed on to descendants."

"Wow."

"Unfortunately, wow's an understatement. Although Pathics account for roughly one percent of our Sapient population— basically one in every hundred—that's actually a lot of people, and their capacity for stirring up trouble is huge." George broke in then. "Oh my, yes. They can be cold, predatory, totally emo-tionless. Because they're incapable of shame or guilt or empathy, they're free to do despicable things simply because they crave excitement."

"I get it," I said. "They're sociopaths and that's why you call them Pathics."

"Sorry to say, but there's another reason we call them Pathics," Sterling said. "They're also telepaths."

"Uh oh."

"Exactly. Pathics have mastered the skill of implanting vir-ulent memes in unsuspecting minds. Toxic memes, like venom. Lies, rumors that take on lives of their own. Ideas that can turn a friendly crowd into a vicious mob in no time."

"Wow again. And you said Pathics look like us?"

"Exactly like us, except for the eyes," Sterling said. "If you meet the gaze of a Pathic, you might see nothing unusual—." Sterling stopped, as if she wasn't quite sure how to continue. "Or," George said, finishing for her, "if the Pathic's in full reptilian mode and not careful to conceal it, you might see snake eyes."

George left us then, saying she had some gardening to do. Gardens again? There's no sign of a garden at the Genius House. No flowers, no vegetables, just acres of sea oats and ice plants. Oh well, I figured. No sense worrying about George's invisible garden when I have to come to terms with Archies and Pathics. And heaven only knows what else. Sterling watched George leave, then turned toward me. "Mags, you're bummed again, aren't you?"

"I'll get over it, Sterling. Right now I just need to go home, climb up to my rooftop gazebo with a Rob Roy, and chill."

Geno was working the counter at the coffeeshop and high-five'd me when I walked in. "Yo, Mags. You still hangin' with weirdos?"

"Geno," I said, "you wouldn't believe me if I told you."

"Yeah, probably not. Myself, I have never been one to hobnob with the intelligentry. Takin' care of family is enough sociability for me."

Geno's good-hearted under all that bravura, and he makes me laugh, so I wasn't reluctant to postpone my Rob Roy when he said we needed to talk. In short order we were tucked into a booth: I with a bearclaw and mug of coffee, Geno with a worried look on his face. "Mags, it's not like I'm sayin' *I told you so* excepting you should know the police are looking for Mister Butt Crack."

"No joke! What for?"

"Breaking and entering, is what the cops told me. It's like I always say—"

Uh oh. Geno didn't know what *I* knew about our downtown cops. Some of them are Archies, remember? Not exactly something I could spring on Geno, so I had to fake it. "Geno, I get it about nutcases, and I promise you I am paying attention, so finish telling me about the robbery."

"Yeah, so specifically some loser dudes lock-picked the Chocolate Factory after hours and scarfed down enough chocolate to constipate an elephant."

"Seriously?"

"Okay, maybe I'm hypothecating a little for comedic relief. But the owner, he ain't laughing one bit. Says those jerkoffs made a mess in the store while they tromped back and forth through the kitchen to load his whole inventory of boxed chocolates in their truck."

"They had a truck? Where? In the alley?"

"Yeah. Old Sonny, he was out back emptying trash and saw the getaway, said the truck tore off in a cloud of gold candy wrappers. Left a trail all up and down the alley."

"Sonny recognized him? Them? The robbers?"

"Naw. It was gettin' dark and Sonny, he don't see so good any more. But he's sure there were two pipsqueaks and one super-size robber, dressed all in black with lots of bling. Anyway, that's what he told the cops."

"Did the crooks steal anything else? Other than chocolates, I mean?"

"Not that I heard."

"That's totally weird."

"You got it, Mags, which is what I've been telling you, it ain't smart to hang with weirdos because you gotta' watch them. Today they steal your chocolates, tomorrow they frost your nuts. It's like I always say—"

Just then six sunburned tourists in white socks and sandals came in the coffee shop and sat down. "Mags, I gotta go," Geno said. "Next time we talk, you can tell me about your friends at the Genius House. Wouldn't ya' know it, I had to miss my last Mensa meeting. Ruined my whole week."

Like I said, Geno makes me laugh. I was still smiling when I got out of the freight elevator at my front door, upstairs.

THE MOUND CREATURE
AND THE NASCAR BALLOON

It was a quiet day at Ponce Inlet. Sterling, Kells, and I were taking a break, sitting in one of the dune-walk gazebos, and enjoying a pitcher of George's fresh-squeezed lemonade. I'd been going walkabout, gazing aimlessly across the dunes, when something caught my eye down at the shore. It was a giant mound with tentacles, and it was moving. "Holy crap! Sterling! Kells! Look over there! What the hell is it? It's alive, and it's coming toward us!"

In my mind's eye I saw myself jumping up gracefully and running like the wind over the wooden dune walk toward the big house. But that didn't happen. What happened was this: when I jumped up and tried to push off, I jammed the pointy toe of my boot in a space between two deck boards and fell flat on my face.

Kells helped me get up, and Sterling dislodged my boot toe while I tried to decide between stunned and terrified. For the moment, I chose stunned. "Dammit, I think my ankle's broken." Then I looked around behind me toward the beach, and terrified took over. "*And the Mound Creature's almost here!*"

"Jengu, stop right there!" Kells hollered. The mound stopped moving, and two heads popped up. Both heads were bald but one of them, rather alarmingly, was multi-colored. I recognized one of the heads—the plain bald orangey one—as Jengu's. "What's wrong?" Jengu called. "We're just gathering kelp."

"I know," Kells said, "but Mags hasn't acclimated to all of us yet, so go home around the back way, all right?" The mound stopped talking and began moving toward the outbuildings.

Sterling went to the house and came back with a couple of towels and a wide bucket filled with ice. "Mags," Sterling said, "if your ankle isn't broken, it's sprained. Can you drive your car to get back home? Maybe you should go to an emergency room and get an X-ray."

"You know what?" I said. "Any ER will be packed, meaning I could be there until the wee hours of the morning, breathing innumerable infectious air- and spittle-borne pathogens. If it's okay with you two, let's sit here for a little while. Whether my ankle's broken or sprained, the ice will retard swelling. Then I'll drive back to my apartment."

"What about stairs?" Kells asked. "Sterling told me about your apartment, that you have an amazing fire escape you like to use. And you're on the third floor, right? How will you negotiate all those stairs?"

"Don't have to. I also have my choice of two elevators: a big freight elevator inside the building, plus a small personal elevator that opens onto the alley out back. One of my elevators will zip me right up."

"Okay, then," Kells said, "I guess that's a plan."

"And," Sterling added, "I can lend you a pair of crutches, just in case. Michael got them last year during auditions for his new girl band when he tripped over a microphone, but he doesn't need them anymore."

I appreciated that both of them were willing to sit there with me, especially since it was stupid of me to wear high-heeled pointy-toe boots when I knew I might be walking on the beach or the wooden dune walks. I'm usually more sensible than that, but today I simply hadn't felt like donning industri-al-grade footwear. Not a good decision, for sure.

I knew Kells and Sterling were talking to each other in their minds, but I couldn't hear them. The only thing I heard was the whisper of the surf, the *twee twee* of gulls. Oh, well. It was a beautiful time to be still, looking out at the beach and the ocean, looking up at the sky. Leaning back on the bench I watched a hot air balloon drift slowly above us, heading south. I knew what it was because I'd see it before: a NASCAR hot air balloon shaped like a racecar. I wondered why it was this far south, though, because you usually see it above the Speedway in Daytona.

"Sterling? Why would the NASCAR balloon be flying down here?"

"No idea, Mags, maybe it's—"

SKRACKK! WHOOSH! *BLAMMO!* One minute the balloon was placidly drifting; the next minute it was a fireball. *And the fireball was falling out of the sky toward us.*

"Shit!" Sterling hollered. "Mags, run! Kells, RUN!" With Kells holding me up on one side and Sterling on the other, I managed to hobble-run along the decking to the back porch and into the kitchen. Sterling slammed the door behind us while we watched through the big windows as the fireball slammed into the gazebo where we'd been sitting just minutes ago.

Thick black smoke was all we could see at first, then pieces of balloon debris that floated in the smoke. As the smoke began to clear, we could see that the passenger basket landed smack in the middle of the gazebo. And what? Omigod, we could see a body . . . no, *two* bodies. One was half-in, half-out of the passenger basket, and the other was sprawled on the decking, nearer the house.

For the next thirty minutes, pandemonium reigned. Michael came running toward the house from the Tower while Kells took off along the path to the cottages, and Sterling talked on her phone to Slim at the Sheriff's Office. It seemed like an eternity, although it was less than ten minutes, until we heard sirens and watched Slim barrel into the driveway in her squad car. Me? I sat on a kitchen chair and wondered how in the world I'd managed to fall down that dadgum rabbit hole. Again.

Soon more deputies arrived along with Doc Kumagai, the Coroner. While Michael paced outside, talking to the deputies, Sterling and Slim talked in the kitchen. "Sterling," Slim said, "Leon's watching on a satellite feed." (Leon heads the Florida Department of Law Enforcement in Tallahassee—FDLE— and he's Slim's good friend.) "He says we need to take a look inside the outbuildings and the Tower." Uh oh, I thought. Is this when the Tutors have to come out of hiding from their cottages? And what about all those electronics in the Tower, the ones that cause static? "No problem, Slim," Sterling said. "Send your people in."

Within twenty minutes, the deputies were back and reporting to Slim. "No one in the outbuildings. Looks like they're ready to be rented, all cleaned up and stuff, but no sign of current occupancy." What? I couldn't believe what I was hearing. How'd the Tutors hide themselves in the cottages? And where'd the Mound Creature go? I didn't ask out loud, of course, just in my head.

"Nuthin' in the Tower, neither," claimed the deputy called Trooper. "Mainly lots of rocks, dirty old coquina. Shore does make you dizzy, though, climbin' that big stone staircase that winds all the way up to the top of the Tower. An' once you get there, there's nuthin' up top, neither. Just a long walk down."

Excuse me? What about the electronics, the equipment that causes "synaptic spikes"? Sterling also told me the Tower's important because it's a greenhouse, said she'd take me there soon and explain what's going on. So how come Trooper didn't see anything but rocks? "My dadgum phone stopped working, too." Trooper hadn't quit talking. "I couldn't get nuthin' but static the whole time I was in the Tower. Oh, okay. It's back on now."

Slim recorded my statement about the balloon blowup, but when she asked if there was anything else, I said no. I mean, Sterling hadn't mentioned the Mound Creature, and Slim assumed I'd hurt my ankle running to the house, so I didn't think it was up to me to elaborate.

"Go home, Mags," Slim said, "and take care of yourself."

Finally I was ready to go, so I packed myself in Agatha and got on the road, but it wasn't easy. First I drove *very* slowly, crawling north on A1A in first gear. (I told you Agatha's an old lady, but I might not've mentioned she's a stick shifter. Given my injured ankle, there was no way I could manipulate three foot-pedals).

Then, over the bridge and back in Daytona, I found the parking lot behind Geno's store so crammed full, I had to park down the block. Gimping my way gingerly to the alley, I discovered that both my backup-elevator *and* the freight elevator weren't working. No way could I climb my fire escape on crutches, so I went inside to the coffeeshop to find a strong back to help me up the stairs—but the store was deserted because the Downtown Seafood Festival was in full swing. Sigh. I should've remembered the festival because Deirdre talked about it non-stop at Talisman's party, said she and some buddies from Bimini were sponsoring a booth. She told me about it at least a dozen times, but I forgot. And that's why there was no sign of Geno or Old Sonny or *anyone* who could help me up the stairs.

The final blow came thirty exhausting stair-climbing minutes later after I collapsed (literally collapsed!) on the landing outside my apartment and saw Geno's un-dated note stuck on my front door with duct tape: *Mags, the stairs are temporary until next month.*

"Schrödy," I announced when I limped inside, "life's given me lemons, but I'm going to make lemonade. I will pamper my ankle, take it easy, and use the period of my recuperation to get back to writing. Which is my chosen career, after all."

I'd forgotten something, though, to-wit: pain is not helpful when a person's trying to work. I'd get settled at my desk, ready to start, when my ankle would throb. Then I'd need a cup of coffee or a MoonPie to distract me from my throbbing ankle. Then when I got back to my desk, I'd realize I left my glasses by the coffee pot or my pen had dried up because I forgot to put the cap back on. Every time I got back up, I'd have to hobble on Michael's crutches to my destination, hobble painfully back to my desk, and start over.

I was getting nowhere, and I knew it. "Mags," Schrödy sniffed, "the next time life hands you lemons, maybe you should just take the lemons."

Great, I thought. My cat's a comedian. And anyway, what does that mean? *Just take the lemons?* I couldn't help laughing, though, because I knew he had a point—that I was fighting the situation. To distract myself I walked over to my big window and, looking out at the park, noticed Cassandra and Harlequin in a gazebo with another person. *Whoa*, I thought, *are they with a real person? or an Archie? Does it matter? I wish I could see . . .*

That's when I put my computer to sleep, neatened up my desk, and retired to my comfy sofa to ponder how my supposedly quiet retirement had spiraled out of control.

DATTA AND MERCEDES

It'd been four days since I gimped home after injuring my ankle at the Genius House, and I was itching to ditch those blasted crutches so I could don fashionable shoes. Thusly, and as I'm sure you can imagine, I was so-o-o careful not to trip or slip or otherwise misstep because I was determined to rejoin the ranks of the stylishly shod. *However* . . . that was before I had a morning encounter with pigeon poop.

You remember that I've been battling pigeon poop ever since I moved into this apartment? Right. It's the reason my balcony's now *triply* festooned with motion-sensitive pigeon-chasers: an Owl, an Eagle, and the life-size polystyrene Batman I purchased at Universal Studios shortly after I moved to Florida. The Owl hoots while her eyes light up, the Eagle flaps his wings, and Batman shouts "POW! WHAP! KAPOOEY!" while he swivels his head.

Nothing. Scares. The pigeons.

This morning was the last straw. A light rain had fallen during the night, just enough to turn poop-pellets into sludge. Even though I cautiously trod onto my balcony, that slippery-slimy poop-sludge did me in. I fell flat on my butt, but not until I'd flailed my way through an aerial arabesque—dislodging the Owl from her perch and inspiring the Eagle to flap his wings while Batman swiveled and shouted POW! WHAP! KAPOOEY!

Over and over and over again.

Okay, Mags, I said to myself. Calm down. Grind some coffee beans, inhale that delicious aroma while your coffee's brewing, and think happy thoughts. Then I remembered that my coffee grinder died two days ago, and I hadn't bought a new one. I know, I know, a defunct coffee grinder isn't the end of the world, but for me it was the last lick on the lollipop. I'd just decided to go with Geno to the City Commission meeting so I could complain about the pigeons (Geno prides himself on being a "god-fly" and crashing the meetings) when Sterling called. "Mags, how's your ankle?"

"Better until I reinjured it this morning."

"How?"

"I got tangled up with the wildlife on my balcony."

"Excuse me?"

"It's a long story."

"No doubt. Anyway, the reason I'm calling is to ask you to drive down here today. Kells wants you to get better acquainted with Datta, and the best place is Datta's cottage because he's so comfortable there."

"Can you have a fresh pot of coffee ready when I get there?"

"Sure, why not. Oh, and Kells also wants you to meet Mercedes."

"Mercedes?"

"Datta's special friend. Interesting in her own right."

"Got it. I can be there in an hour. Um, I'd better not return Michael's crutches yet, though."

"Not a problem."

I arrived on time, as promised, and Sterling was waiting for me at the kitchen door, holding winter-type clothes for both of us. "Sterling, you've got to be kidding. It's ninety-five degrees in the shade today, and there's no shade, so why do we need Eskimo duds?"

"Because it's cold in Datta's cottage. He and Mercedes can't stand the heat, so they keep the AC down really, really low. Here, carry yours (handing me a coat, scarf, and gloves). You'll need them when we go inside, so we'll bundle up when we get there."

While we walked, Sterling vented about Michael who refuses to go in Datta's cottage. "He went inside once and says he almost died of hypothermia before he could get out. Sterling made a face and went on. "Anyway, we seldom have meetings in the cottages, so it probably doesn't matter."

"But if you don't often meet in their cottages, why are meeting at Datta's today? And how come I had that first talk with Kells at *her* cottage?"

"Because you're an exception, Mags. It's like I told you, once the Tutors knew you'd been sent to us—"

"*What?* Hold on a minute! I wasn't *sent* here by anyone!"

"Sorry, Mags. Poor choice of words. Anyway, here we are, so button up."

Datta was in a grumpy mood, which I gather is his normal disposition. It's hard to blame him, though, for feeling resentful about being outposted to Florida. I'm not a big fan of heat and humidity, myself, and I remember how miserable I was when my dad moved us from Pittsburgh to Daytona Beach. It has to be a hundred times harder for Datta, coming to Florida from the Himalayas where his tribe of Neanders have been evolving for thirty-some thousand years in ice and snow.

He was talking to Kells when Sterling opened the door, and we went in. "It's *simple* for you," Datta was saying to Kells. "You just click your brain switch and go *bleep*—and you're where you want to be. Mercy and I have to gear up, and it's not easy. We practically have to meditate our brains out, and once we're ready to come back, there's no guarantee where we'll land."

Come back from where? What's he talking about? I whispered to Sterling, who whispered *Later* and shushed me. Kells was looking annoyed, and Datta wasn't finished. "Did I tell you about the time we landed in Las Vegas, smack in the middle of the fountain at the Excalibur?"

"*Honk honk, mugga.*" Mercedes had interrupted Datta, obviously addressing a comment to him. "What, Mercy?" Datta said. He listened intently for a minute, nodding his head up and down. "Yes, well, the Las Vegas blipple had its compensatory factors, didn't it?" Datta smiled then (I *think* he smiled; it's hard to see facial expressions under all that white fur) and went on talking to Mercedes. "Cirque du Soleil loved us, didn't they? Promised us superstar billing, the presidential penthouse—"

"*Honk! honkhonkhonk muggamug—*"

"—wish we'd taken them up on their offer—"

Kells broke in at that point. "Oh, for heaven's sake, Datta! Quit complaining! We have a mission to accomplish. I was at the meeting when we pledged our support for the Intervention, and you were there, too. I saw you. You raised your hand and pledged, just like the rest of us."

Kells, in case I didn't make it clear before now, is the manager of the Tutors. Sterling says Kells rarely loses her cool, but maybe that day she was trying to handle one problem too many being as Jengu was having a nervous breakdown because his girlfriend had gone missing again. That's another story, though, so getting back to this one: Kells was all worked up and reading the riot act to Datta. "You know perfectly well that we Boskops can jump ship whenever we please. It'd be a damn sight easier than trying to save the planet from Sapients, with their oil spills and deforestations and stupid, stupid wars."

"Mmmff, nnngugwa," Datta said, sounding like the noises Mercedes makes when she talks. Then he segued into people-speak. "Kells, I was just venting. You know I need to vent once in a while. I can't help it that I have issues."

"Issues!" Kells was really worked up. "I'll give you issues! I ought to leave all of you here on this melting planet with the Sapients. I give them fifty years—no more—to finish fucking everything up." Silence. Nobody moved or said a thing. "Then you'll be here to see how it all ends," she said in a voice like shrapnel. "With a whimper or a bang. If I were taking bets, I'd bet on that bang." *SLAM!*

After delivering her *coup de grace*, Kells stormed out and slammed the door behind her. Which is no mean feat, considering the door to Datta's cottage, like the walls, is six inches thick.

So there we were, the four of us: Sterling, myself, a white-furred Wookiee look-alike, and a Musk Ox. Sitting around a conference table in a fortress-quality cottage where the thermometer read fifty-five degrees Fahrenheit.

The Wookiee and the Musk Ox were sweating.

Oh, I didn't tell you Mercedes is a Musk Ox? Actually, she's a *Takin*, the Himalayan version of a Musk Ox. Most people have never heard of a takin, though, so Mercy agrees it's okay to call her a musk ox. You'll recall that I thought I saw a brown cow going in one of the cottages? During my first visit to the Genius House, right before I met the Tutors? Well, it wasn't a cow; it was Mercedes the musk ox. At that point Sterling didn't know how to explain Mercedes, so she didn't try.

It takes a while for the idea to sink in that a musk ox can communicate like a person, but Kells says that's because Sapients suffer from an extreme case of speciesism. She's generally kind and tries not to criticize, but I know she's disappointed in us Sapients. I was thinking about that and the sorry fact that no one was offering me pastry to go with my coffee, when the door to Datta's cottage opened and Kells came back in.

"Sorry, friends," she said. "When we signed on for this mission, we knew it wouldn't be easy. I apologize for losing my temper, and I won't let it happen again. Not today, anyway." Nods all around, accompanied by a collective sigh of relief. While Kells busied herself at a holo-board, Datta and Mercedes settled down in two overlarge chairs, and I rummaged vainly through my shoulder bag for an errant MoonPie or Andes mint. Finally Kells started talking, and our meeting was underway. "For simplicity's sake," she said, "let's use acronyms to refer to the four hominin species."

"Fine," I said. "I'm all for simplicity."

"Good. We'll refer collectively to the three clans—Datta's Neanders, Jengu's Floreans, and my Boskops—as NEFBOs."

"Yep. Heard that before and it makes sense," I agreed.

"And, Mags, we'll refer to your Sapients as SAPs." Sterling was examining her fingernails, studiously avoiding eye contact with me. It was obviously my turn to say something, and I'm pleased to report that I swallowed my pride and rose to the occasion. "SAPs it is," I said. "Now let's get on with the history lesson."

Two hours later (still no pastry, just coffee) I'd gotten filled in about the Neanders' Songnet and their amazing facility for long-distance voice throwing—an adaptive strategy they developed during their diaspora so the clan could stay connected over vast distances and steeply divergent elevations. I have to admit I was impressed, picturing those tough clannish Neanders spending tens of thousands of years while they worked their way into this planet's highest, coldest, most inaccessible regions. Along the way their adaptation was profound, and it was touching to hear how they and the musk ox became co-survivalists, evolving on parallel planes.

Finally it was time to leave Datta's cottage and walk back to the big house. Sterling and Kells accommodated my gimpiness by walking slowly, and George brought us lemonade when we got settled on the back porch. "All that facial fur," I said, half to myself. "Datta has a natural-grown ski mask that protects his mouth, nose, eyes, and ears from frostbite, doesn't he?"

"Exactly."

"Okay, but even with fur on it, his face looks flat where his nose should be. His nose is squashy, like the nose of a Pekingese, or one of those little pug dogs."

"Once again," said Kells, "you're seeing the magic of bio-adaptation. In a pitiless subzero climate, a fleshy protuberant nose invites instant frostbite. Over time, Neanders developed snub noses like the monkeys in China's Qin Ling Mountains. They're called Golden Snub Noses, I think."

"Poor Datta," Sterling laughed. "That's why he sneezes all the time, what with all the water in the air in Florida. If it isn't humid, it's raining, so Datta's always getting water in his little snub nose, and he has to sneeze it out."

Meanwhile my thoughts were racing every which way, one feedback loop connecting with another and another ad infinitum. "I think I understand," I said. "All those stories and legends about the *Yeti*—the Abominable Snowman. And Sasquatch and Bigfoot. They've been Neander-sightings?"

"A lot of them, for sure."

"Okay, but those stories and sightings come from lots of places, not just Europe and Asia and the Himalayas, *and* the Bigfoot and Sasquatch stories are about dark-haired creatures, not white-hairs like Datta."

"It seems confusing," Kells said, "but that's partly because your paleontologists don't have a fossil record yet for all of Datta's cousins."

"His cousins?"

"Neander clan members whose diasporas took them in different directions, away from Datta's people. Some of them evolved differently, in response to different environments. And the crucial point is that for thousands upon thousands of years, it wasn't hard for adventurous individuals to stay hidden while they roamed and explored."

"But that changed?"

"Drastically. The upsurge in Sapient population made Neander sightings inevitable, and those sightings fed the legends. They still do." Sterling cut in then. "Kells, you're being politically correct, as usual. We all know the woods are full of Bubbas with video cameras, even here in Florida where our legendary creature's called *The Swamp Ape*."

"And that puts us back again at the bottom line, doesn't it?" I asked. "Too many people—sorry, too many SAPs—crowded onto Planet Earth. And that's why Datta and Mercedes, who would obviously rather be back home than here, are willing to help with the mission?"

"Yes."

"Okay, I get it and don't worry, I'm not taking any of this as a personal criticism. But I do have one more question before I head for home."

"Fine, what is it?"

"I understand that musk oxen helped Neanders, protecting them from the cold until Neanders grew their own protective hides and pelts."

"Correct."

"Okay, but what did the Neander do for the musk ox? You said they were synergetic species, right? So that means they helped each other out, that it wasn't a one-way relationship."

"They certainly did help each other," Kells said, while Sterling and Kells exchanged *a look*. "Neanders," Kells continued, "taught musk oxen to sing."

BRIGADIER'S BULLPUCKEY STORY

Sterling called a few days later, sounding edgy and ragged out. "I need to talk, Mags. How about meeting me in the park in an hour?"

"Perfect, because I'm hungry for one of Sammy's footlongs. You want to try one too?"

"No, I just want to talk." I knew there wasn't the chance of a snowball in hell that Sterling would chow down on a weenie, so I went on over to the park and enjoyed one of Sammy's deluxe footlongs (sauerkraut, cheese, chili, sesame seeds because you want to eat healthy, and a personal-size bottle of ketchup on the side). I'd just finished wiping sauerkraut and ketchup off my shirtfront when Sterling showed up, so I was ready to talk. "Okay, Sterling, what's up?"

"Only that I have a bad feeling ..." Eventually Sterling looked up, smiled, and said, "Sorry, Mags, about going heavy-duty on you. It's just, sometimes I wonder why trolls and freaks won't leave us alone. Michael says I'm being paranoid because they're not dangerous. But it still creeps me out that so many nutcases hate me and my family."

"Hmm, it's interesting that Michael says nutcases aren't dangerous, exactly the opposite of what Geno says."

"Geno? Your landlord?"

"Un huh. Geno's all het up about 'suspicious characters' lurking around, and his mantra lately is *The nutcase will always surprise you.*" What I didn't say to Sterling, of course, is that Geno includes "those Genius House weirdos" among the nutcases. I mean, Sterling's aware that her family has a reputation for being eccentric, so why rub it in? Mainly I wanted to help out my friend, so I encouraged her to talk. "Tell me about your local nutcases," I said, "the ones Michael says are harmless."

"Glad to. The creepiest one calls himself *Brigadier,* as in 'Brigadier General.' He passes himself off as a war hero, holds court at the local VFW hangout. If he *is* making trouble for us, he could be in cahoots with a teenage thug called Beebo. And that's because—"

What? A guy called "Brigadier"? That sounds familiar . . .

"—other prime suspect's a neighbor, unfortunately. Her name's Lily Amaryllis, and she lives—"

Shoot, I still can't place "Brigadier" but I know I've seen him . . .

"—all hang out at the Temple with Preacher, who's another wingnut —"

I had to interrupt at that point because I remembered Brigadier. "Sterling, wait. Now I remember. Brigadier was at Uncle Billy's poetry reading at the pub. At Pigs Will Fly. He was duded up in desert camou, and I remember because you pointed him out to me."

"Yep, that was Brigadier."

"And he was there with his followers. Michael called them *Brigadier's GD Gang*, which I thought was shorthand for Brigadier's Goddam Gang. But Michael said no, 'GD' stands for Geezers & Delinquents. And you think Brigadier was there because he's stalking you?"

"Could be. Any of us at the Genius House are fair game for Brigadier ever since Mom exposed his bullshit story."

"Brigadier's *bullshit story*? Sterling, you can't stop now. Tell me!" Which Sterling was glad to do because it helped her vent, and I was glad to listen appreciatively because trust me, it's a doozy.

It all got started when Brigadier gave a VFW presentation at Embry-Riddle Aeronautical University where Mary Buck was a math professor and legendary stunt pilot. After his lecture Brigadier was chatting her up about his exploits as a fighter pilot, said he was injured in an air fight which is how he lost his right hand, yada yada. It didn't take long, however, for Mary Buck to figure out he was a fraud. She wanted to laugh in his face, actually, because she could tell he didn't know zip about flying.

That's when she set him up, told him she'd be honored to take him up in her Tomahawk so he could enjoy a leisurely sightseeing flight over the city. Once they were in the air, though, she flew out over the Atlantic and did some tricks: a few stalls, a couple of barrel rolls, and her signature stunt that's sometimes called a suicide spiral.

Brigadier freaked and begged God to save him, actually got born-again right then and there, up in the sky. And while he was confessing his sins to God about pretending to be a hero,

Mary Buck was listening (and pulling her Tomahawk out of the suicide spiral). By the time they landed and Brigadier stumbled out of the plane into a crowd of Embry-Riddle faculty and test pilots, he'd barfed all over his bomber jacket and peed himself soaking wet. Needless to say, he's been a joke at Embry-Riddle ever since.

That could've been the end of it, but Mary Buck wouldn't let go of Brig's phony schtick. It made her so mad, in fact, she did some records searches and found out he's not a general, much less an officer, never even went overseas. Nope, his highest rank was PFC in the Quartermaster Corps at an air force base in North Carolina, until he got busted for running a black market in supplies.

"Sterling, that's incredible," I said. "But what about his hand? How'd he lose it?"

"He didn't. He idolizes George C. Scott's character in the *Dr. Strangelove* movie. You know, the unhinged air force general who wants to bomb Russia?"

"Yeah, I remember. General Turgidson, right? But it's not Turgidson who lost a hand and wears one black glove; it's the mad scientist himself, Dr. Strangelove."

"You're absolutely right, Mags," Sterling laughed, "but Brigadier got the characters confused."

"That's for sure. So Brigadier's a fake fighter pilot, a fake war hero, a fake general, and he wears one black glove to hide his fake missing hand? How's he get away with all that?"

"He wouldn't get away with it if Mom hadn't disappeared. She was totally ready to expose his sorry charade, but then she and Dad went missing. That's when we agreed at our family meeting not to pursue it because we need to lie low, not make trouble for ourselves."

I woke Schrödy up when I got home and told him all about Brigadier. "Oh, shoot, Schrödy," I said, "I got so interested in Brigadier's crazy scam, I interrupted Sterling when she was ready to tell me about another troublemaker. A neighbor. Now I'm dying to know about the other one, a nutcase named Lily Amaryllis."

"So call Sterling and ask."

"You're right, I will. But I interrupted her again when she was going to tell me more about a teenage thug called Beebo, so I need to ask her about him, too. About why he's in cahoots with Brigadier, I mean."

"Mags?"

"Yes?"

"You might want to spend more time listening and less time interrupting because—"

"*What?* I resent that! I'll have you know I'm a good listener, and . . . umm . . . I just interrupted you, didn't I?" No answer, just a sniff. "Okay, Schrödy, I get it. I'll call Sterling, and this time I won't interrupt while she's talking." Except Sterling called me first, but she was in a hurry and didn't want to chitchat. "We'll have plenty of time later to talk about Lily Amaryllis, Mags. She's probably harmless, like Michael says."

"Okay, you can tell me her nutcase story some other time, but I'll reserve judgment. I'm not sure someone named Lily can be harmless. You can't trust a Lily, not like you can trust a Rose."

"What? How do you know about Rose?"

"Who's Rose? I'm talking about *names* like Lily and Rose. You and I agreed names are important, right? So when Cassandra and I talked about her signature song, you know, *White Coral Bells*? That's when she and I agreed you can eat rose petals but you sure better not eat a lily because—"

"Mags, you're not making sense, and I don't have time for this right now. I called to ask for a favor. I need you to go with me to Byzantium tonight because Uncle Billy's going to read his poetry."

"*Excuse* me? You got pissy when I suggested that Uncle Billy read his poetry at a redneck biker bar, and now you're saying you set him up to read at a *bowling alley?*"

"It's not as crazy as it sounds," Sterling said. "If Uncle Billy thought destiny was calling him to read at a pub because it used to be called The Black Pig, can you imagine how ecstatic he is about reading at a place called Byzantium?"

"Okay, I get your point."

"And," Sterling continued, "this event at Byzantium is hugely important to Michael because it's Prax's debut as a cultural entrepreneur. You remember Prax, right? In Opera in the Park, he was the character Bottom."

"Oh sure, I remember. Couldn't sing worth a crap but he was movie-star handsome. Until he got the ass-head, that is." Sterling started laughing. "Mags, you nailed it. Prax is a total asshole who had the good fortune to be born beautiful. Greek God beautiful, in fact."

"Geno told me a little about him, too. But why are we talking about him now?"

"Two reasons. First because, like I already said, this event at Byzantium is Prax's debut as a producer. And second, because Michael's in love with Prax. Head over heels in love."

"*What?*"

"I told you about Michael being in love, remember?"

"Well yeah, but you didn't mention the teeny detail that his so-called *inamorata* is a guy."

"So? My point was that Michael's love affair distracts him from his dad-lookalike duties at the college. And it's been worse than ever since Prax came up with the idea of producing a show at Byzantium and asked him—Michael—to be his aide-de-camp. I keep telling my blockhead brother to get real, that Prax is using him, but Michael won't listen. He and Prax have been stuck together like glue for weeks."

"Gosh, Sterling," I said, "I'm sorry but I can't help you out tonight."

"Please, Mags? I'm really in a bind. Kells is at a garden club meeting and—"

"Kells is at a *garden club* meeting?"

"She has some friends who call themselves Gardeners. They get together every once in a while, and—"

First George, now Kells. Who knew? Apparently you can be actively involved in garden clubbing without ever gardening. Kind of like belonging to a bridge club where they don't play cards, and . . . Sterling was noticing I'd zoned out, so I zoned back in. "—and Jengu's trolling the Intracoastal Waterway for Jitsu."

"Jitsu?"

"His teenybopper girlfriend. I told you about her, remember?"

"You told me about her, but I didn't know her name's Jitsu."

"Well that's her name, and after she went AWOL a couple of weeks ago, Jengu's determined to find her. I'm so tired of these soap operas I could scream."

"Sterling, I'd love to help you out, but I can't do it. I'm meeting some friends for dinner. We do this a couple times a year, and I can't back out."

"Okay," Sterling said tiredly. "I'll tell George she has to go with Uncle Billy and me to Byzantium tonight."

Later, over my second mug of coffee at Geno's, I was feeling guilty for lying to Sterling. I didn't really have a dinner engagement, but Amateur Night at a bowling alley? I didn't think so. Nevertheless, that little voice inside my head wouldn't quit: *You're not much of a friend, are you, Mags? Sterling sounded exhausted, so why can't you help her out? It isn't like you have a hot date or anything. Not that you* ever *have a hot date—*

"Oh, shut up!" I said to the voice.

"Mags? Who you talking to?"

"Sorry, Geno, just thinking out loud."

"You wanna tell me about it?"

"Naw, it's nothing important. I'm invited to Byzantium at the Boardwalk tonight, but I don't want to go."

"Don't blame you for that. Me, I'd rather spend time at a reptile show."

"Excuse me? I didn't know you're a fan of reptiles."

"Naw, 'course I'm not. I was just indulgin' in one of those tropiaries. Like you're always talking about."

"You mean tropes? Figures of speech?"

"Yeah, one'a those."

Geno hurried off in a rush, something about being late for a business meeting at Ralphie's hotel. Which surprised me because who schedules a business meeting on Saturday? I decided not to worry about the arcane details of Ralphie's business model, though, because I was amusing myself by remembering Geno's stories about long-running disputes with Pan Papanicolaou, the owner-developer of the Boardwalk bowling center.

According to Geno, Byzantium's a cash bonanza because Pan built it on the cheap, not to mention greasing a lot of palms along the way. Also, according to Geno, though, Byzantium would be just another cheesy bowling alley without Pan's brother Petros. "You gotta' hand it to Petros," Geno told me, "because he got the genius idea to cash in on bowling balls."

"Bowling balls are a cash crop?"

"These are. They're personalized, one of a kind." At that point in his story Geno started laughing so hard, he wheezed and snorted. As per usual, though, the punch line was worth waiting for. "The bowling balls are such a gold mine, Pan even gave Petros credit for them at first. Pan would say *Petros is a genius. In addition to making us rich, we now got designer balls.* This would get a laugh, naturally, so Pan, who's funny as a heart attack, started takin' all the credit himself for their 'designer balls.' Last I heard, Petros was pissed off and wanted out of the family business. but Pan lawyered up, and Petros is stuck."

Casey had told me a little about the Papanicolaou family, too, mostly about Prax. "He sees himself as The Unappreciated Artist," Casey said, laughing. "What?" I said. "Prax is an artist?"

"Frak no, but he thinks he is because he spent Pan's money to commission some Sistine-Chapel-ish murals for the dome in Byzantium's rotunda. The classical statues at Bozarts Bumper Cars were Prax's genius idea as well."

"Wait. Murals at Byzantium? And statues at Bozarts Bumper Cars? Ben Bulben created those, right? The murals and the statues?"

"Sure did," Casey said. "Have you seen them?"

"No, but I heard about them."

"Well, check 'em out sometime when you're bored and need a pick-me-up, especially the statues. When you crash into the *Venus de Milo* with your bumper-car, her arms fall off. And when you rear-end your bumper-car into the *David's* legs, his fig leaf pops off."

So there I was at Geno's, thinking about Byzantium and realizing it's actually a pretty interesting place. Figuring I'd check out those break-apart statues sometime (I've *always* loved bumper cars!), I headed upstairs to my apartment.

A MIDNIGHT VISIT

Four hours later I'd crumpled countless sheets of paper (yes, I often resort to pen and paper when I'm stuck for ideas) while thinking dejectedly that whoever said "Be careful what you wish for" was a genius. I mean, back when I was a professor I *couldn't wait* to retire from teaching and be a full-time Writer—self-employed, working when I felt like it, not working when I didn't. I even pictured myself writing leisurely on a beach in Florida, sipping a Rob Roy while I finished yet one more novel that my readers awaited with bated breath.

Yeah, right. Now here I am, contemplating the book project from hell—a surefire bestseller about the end of civilization as we know it.

To say my thought processes were dismal while I surveyed the crumpled paper surrounding me is a serious understatement, so I was glad for the distraction of a phone call from Sterling. "Mags, Kells and I are downstairs on Beach Street outside Geno's store. How about buzzing us in so we can come up on the freight elevator?"

Kells hadn't seen my apartment before. so she wanted to walk around and peer out the windows, taking it all in. I told her about my fantasy, that it's like living in a Johnny Depp movie. But since she didn't know who Johnny Depp was, I figured I wouldn't bother mentioning Don Juan DeMarco. Sterling was in a bad mood about the evening's events at Byzantium, so to distract her I asked her to tell me what happened at Prax's so-called *Cabaret*.

"Well, for starters, Brigadier was there with Preacher and Fat Guy—"

"Preacher and *Fat Guy?*"

"One of Preacher's cronies. I've seen them together before, but I don't know who Fat Guy is. Sometimes he dresses in black but other times he wears a white monk's robe, so maybe he's from the monastery in Orange City. Anyway, Brigadier and Fat Guy hang out with Preacher at the Holistic Temple."

"The Holistic Temple?"

"Yeah, it's near our house."

"Near your house? There's nothing near you except the Lighthouse."

"I *wish* there was nothing near us except the Lighthouse. The Holistic Temple's a joke the State of Florida sees fit to protect. It's Preacher's eccentric wet dream on a spit of high ground that's mainly scrub pine and palmetto, south of our property line."

"So, did you talk to them? Preacher and Fat Guy, I mean."

"No, we were trying to keep Uncle Billy away from the Harem Girl—"

"Who?"

"—some bimbo in a harem outfit, and Red kept trying to get Deirdre alone—"

"Deirdre? Why was *she* there?"

"—she's in love with Michael, but he was stuck like glue to Prax all night, but it didn't matter because the audience freaked when Uncle Billy's Irish Fairies popped out of their box and that's when the Vineyard went up in flames."

"The fairies set fire to a vineyard?"

"Valerian's Vineyard. It's the wine cellar at Byzantium, but the fairies didn't start the fire. A patron knocked an oil lamp off a table. Now Michael's despondent because the oil lamps were his idea, and Pan Papanicolaou's pissed at Prax, threatening to disinherit him. That's when we got the hell out."

Kells was still looking around, so I encouraged Sterling to tell me the stories of the star-crossed lovers: Michael and Prax, Red and Deirdre. Again, as with Brigadier's 'bullshit' story, Sterling was glad to talk.

Both stories, she said, started at a beach party down near the Lighthouse. Red saw Deirdre from a distance across the dunes, told his friends she looked like a Celtic goddess (she does), and fell in love. Immediately he jumped up on a dune buggy and struck a pose, proclaiming that as the incarnation of his avatar, the Celtic warrior Caoilte, he would go up in flames rather than renounce his devotion to the beautiful *Deirdre of the Sorrows*. (As Sterling often says about Red, he's nothing if not dramatic.)

While Red was becoming infatuated with Deirdre from afar, Deirdre was dancing with Michael and falling madly in love with *him*. Sterling says it was no surprise because Michael always did that to girls: captivated them with his great looks, cool dance moves, and willingness to stare long and deep into their eyes while thinking about something else.

Then fate stepped in. Prax jumped up on a picnic table to announce a toast (picture Michaelangeo's *David* wearing a black Speedo), whereupon Michael unceremoniously dumped

Deirdre on a cabana chair and proceeded to ignore her. "You can imagine it, I'm sure," Sterling said, "Michael got blindsided by Prax, right then and there."

"Wow," I said, "so it was a triangle. No, a quadrangle: Red was in love with Deirdre who was in love with Michael who was in love with Prax."

"Except Michael hit a snag because Prax was digesting an ultimatum from Pan that he'd be disinherited and shunned by the Greek community if he didn't soon get a serious girlfriend. *Not* another boyfriend."

"And?"

"And the 'serious girlfriend' candidate was at the beach party that day in the person of Galatea Gallimachos. We found out later that Galatea's mother Gigi paid bookoo bucks to a matchmaker in Corfu to insure that her only daughter would marry Praxiteles Papanicolaou. Who, by the way, is known to all the Greek mothers in Volusia County as *The Catch of the Century.*"

"Too funny!"

"Exactly. Anyway, ever since she made a deal with the matchmaker, Gigi's been stalking Prax. She annotates Galatea's calendar with Prax's whereabouts so she can personally deliver Galatea to the vicinity of said whereabouts. I noticed Galatea and Gigi at Byzantium tonight. Gigi was in the back, talking to Pan, but Galatea was at a front table with her eyes glued to Prax the whole time."

Kells got our attention at that point. She was standing by my gas fireplace and peering into the tall antique mirror that hangs next to it. "Mags," she said, "where did you get this mirror?"

"A long-ago friend in Pittsburgh gave it to me, an old gypsy woman. She lived in the woods near my cousin Wally's house. Wally and I called her Aunt Sasa, and we loved her, but she scared people, and they ran her out of town."

"Go on, Mags. Keep talking."

"Well, when the vigilantes came for Aunt Sasa my family had already moved to Florida, but Wally told me about it. He was home from college for the summer and visiting Aunt Sasa at her house. She knew the mob was coming soon, so she asked Wally to take her big mirror that I loved, told him to keep it safe and make sure I got it." Kells peered into the mirror while I continued talking. "Wally kept it in storage for me all these years," I said, "and when I moved in here, he surprised me with it."

"I'm glad you have this, Mags," Kells said. "Your cousin . . . what's his name, again?"

"Wally."

"Yes, Wally." Kells was quiet for a minute or two, looking into the mirror and tapping it with her finger. Then she said, "Mags, your cousin Wally did us a big favor by keeping this safe for you." I wanted to ask Kells what she meant by doing "us" a big favor. Who's *us*? I wondered. I didn't push it, though, because Sterling was obviously ready to leave.

"George is waiting for us back at the house," Sterling said. "She wants to let Uncle Billy talk about the evening and brag a little. I mean, until the fire started, he had the crowd in the palm of his hand."

"But don't you think the fire freaked him out?"

"Uncle Billy? Naw, he figures he's invincible. Says he has a *fire in his head* just like his hero Aengus."

"Aengus? As in the god of love? One of the beautiful Tuatha dé Danaan?"

"That's him," Sterling said. "Uncle Billy says he talks to Aengus through his poems. If I've heard him recite 'The Song of Wandering Aengus' once, I've heard it a hundred times, especially that haunting conclusion:

We'll pluck till time and times are done,
The silver apples of the moon,
The golden apples of the sun.

"I always loved that poem because it's so magical," I said, "but it never occurred to me it's a conversation."

Kells hadn't seen my fire escape, so I suggested she and Sterling leave by way of my back door. "What about a car?" I asked. "How'll you get home?"

"Not to worry," Sterling said. "Michael will meet us."

"Mags, this is spectacular," Kells said when we exited my back door and stood on the third floor landing, looking out at the city stretched below us. "Oh, yes, and I see why you love your fire escape. It's a work of art, truly a monumental sculpture."

"It's my landlord's pride and joy," I said. "His cousin Frankie designed it, and it was hugely expensive, but Geno doesn't care because it's one of Daytona's famous landmarks, like the boardwalk and the bandshell."

"I agree that it's spectacular," Sterling said. "Walking down the spiral's like descending into the chambers of the nautilus. And it's stunning in the daytime, when sunlight turns the staircase into copper fire."

After we got to the bottom and stepped off, we chatted for a few minutes more because I was interested in Brigadier and his friends. Like why they were at Byzantium tonight, because Sterling said they didn't fit in with the rest of the crowd, actually stood out like sore thumbs. "I figure Brigadier was on the lookout for perverts," Sterling said. "Remember, Mags, how he got born-again? While Mom was flying him around and doing stunts?"

"Of course I remember. How could I forget?"

"Well, he got born-again with a purpose, because he's convinced God saved him so he—Brigadier—can rescue the world from perversion and debauchery. Being as he's always on the lookout for sin, doesn't it make sense that a cabaret-type performance with music and poetry is exactly where you'd expect to find it? And omigod, he kept his eyes glued to Semi Sweet Charity the whole time."

"Who?"

"A spectacular drag queen."

"Well that's typical, isn't it," I said, laughing. "The Brigadiers of the world are predictable. They're fascinated by what they denounce."

"Exactly, but I wish he'd find another target and leave us alone. He has a Tree-stand in one of the Holistic Temple's pine trees where he sits with his binoculars, spying on us. And sometimes Michael sees him at night on our property, hiding in his Foxhole with night goggles."

"He has a *foxhole*?"

"Yep, Michael knows where it is, says it's in the center of that big expanse of ice plant north of the house, the area that stretches from the beach to the highway. He figures Brigadier's buddies have foxholes staked out too, probably along the perimeter."

Kells chimed in then, "Sterling, that's funny but it's also sad. And that's humanity, isn't it? Funny, but also sad."

I was watching them walk to the corner when I got a creepy feeling. Something's not right, I thought, but what is it? Then I saw a shadow. Someone was standing out of sight around the corner, maybe in the front doorway of Geno's building. Wait, the shadow's following Sterling and Kells, walking behind them. Now they're crossing the street and ... where'd they go? They said Michael was picking them up, but I would've seen the Suburban because Beach Street's deserted. The shadow's gone too and ... Damn! there goes the streetlight! I'll tell Geno about it because—

Suddenly everything went black. I was in a blanket, a thick black blanket that wrapped itself around me. I couldn't see but I could hear—thuds and muffled cries and a high-pitched keening. *Omigod*, I thought. *It's a Banshee! I'm dying and the Banshee's keening for me!* I was suffocating, gasping for breath and choking in the blanket that was wrapped around me tight, like a straitjacket. An eternity went by ... until ... the blanket was unwinding, falling off my head, away from my face. Light was coming back, and I could feel the blanket slipping down, off my shoulders ...

"Miz Mags, are you okay?"

"What? *DIFF!* What the hell's going on?" I looked for the blanket on the sidewalk, but it wasn't there. "Where's the blanket, Diff? Goddammit, where's the blanket?"

"Miz Mags, the police are coming. You'll be fine."

Yes, I could hear the siren. It was wailing, screaming, coming closer. "The damn streetlight just blew and ... oh okay, it's back on, must've been a power surge. But why're you out here so late, Diff?"

"Bye, Miz Mags."

"No, wait! Why are you—" Diff disappeared into the night while a police cruiser pulled up at the sidewalk and two officers got out, explaining they were patrolling downtown because there were reports of suspicious characters. After they walked me to my fire escape and waited, I unlocked the cage enclosure door at street level, bolted it from inside, and climbed to the third floor landing where I waved goodbye and went in the back door to my apartment.

"Schrödy, wake up!" I hollered. "Something weird just happened." So I told Schrödy everything: how a shadow followed Sterling and Kells, and the streetlight blew, and someone started screaming, and I was suffocating in a hot black blanket when Diff appeared and pulled the blanket off me, but he left when two cops showed up.

"Mags?"

"What?"

"Get real."

"What do you mean, get real? I *am* being real. Don't you believe what I'm telling you?"

"Here's the thing, Mags. It takes you ten minutes just to walk down the fire escape while you're unlocking the landing-doors, then another ten minutes to walk back up again while you're bolting everything behind you."

"So?"

"So you weren't even gone ten minutes. How'd you have time to schmooze with your friends *and* squeeze in an encounter with an Attack Blanket?"

I was in no mood to argue with a non-commiserative cat, so I told Schrödy to get over himself and go back to sleep. Sleep was out of the question for me, though, because I couldn't stop thinking. Okay, I walked with Kells and Sterling down my fire escape. Then they were crossing the street when I saw the shadow. Was it Diff's shadow? Must've been. Then everything went black when the streetlight blew, and someone—no, some*thing*— started howling like a Banshee, and I was suffocating in a . . .

Uh oh. Did I have a mini-stroke? Not that I'm old enough to have a stroke, of course, but I do have an overactive imagination sometimes and that must be what happened—I blacked out for a few seconds and then my brain concocted a story to make sense of it all. But I know I heard screaming because . . . Oh, the police siren. Maybe it was the police siren I heard because the two cops were patrolling downtown anyway. Then they waited while l locked the fire escape cage from inside so I could climb back up to my apartment.

Okay, I said to myself, the commonsense explanation is that I had a brain fart just when Diff happened by, and then my imagination kicked in.

And yet. And yet . . . I knew it was real. All of it. Someone following Kells and Sterling, then howling in frustration when they got away, then coming for me instead, then Diff appearing in the nick of time. It was just like Sterling said when she told me about Archies—they're here to help us. That's why Diff showed up, because he was on the lookout.

But on the lookout for what? I didn't know . . .

THE HOLISTIC TEMPLE

"No sleep last night, Mags? You look like something the cat drug in. Not my favorite metaphor, of course, but you have to admit—"

"It's *dragged,* not *drug,* which you know very well except you're trying to annoy me. And *of course* I didn't get any sleep, how could I after I was attacked down on the sidewalk? Sometimes I feel like I've wandered into a Woody Allen movie. *Shadows and Fog* or *Midnight in Paris.* Remember those?"

"Vaguely. I prefer *The Wizard of Oz.*"

"*Dammit, that's not the point!*"

"Okay okay! Calm down. You sure do get grouchy when you're sleep-deprived."

Sigh. "I know, Schrödy, and I apologize. Let's start over?"

"Good idea, here goes: *No sleep last night, Mags? You look like something the cat drug in. Not my favorite metaphor, of course—*"In spite of myself I started laughing, and it felt really really good. Schrödy was laughing, too, I think (it's hard to tell with cats).

Anyway, by the time I settled down I realized I desperately needed a change of scene, and I knew exactly what would do the trick. "Schrödy, I think that attack last night was a message—actually a Sign—so I will act accordingly by changing my agenda."

"Uh oh."

"What? *Now* what's wrong?"

"Just that you always get in trouble when you think you've been given *a Sign*. Like the time you got snookered into that scam in Cassadaga? And how about that other time—"

"Stop it! How about wishing me luck instead of being negative? After all, I paid attention to *a Sign* when I moved back to Florida, didn't I? And that was definitely a good decision. Today I'll put on my private-investigator-hat like I do when I'm working with Talisman on one of her cases, and I'll go check out the Holistic Temple. There's no way I can get snookered, and I'll be back by 5:00 so we can go to the park. Deal?"

Sniff. "It's okay, Mags, you won't have to hurry back. It's not fun for me in the park any more since the squirrels went AWOL. There aren't many birds around lately, either."

Stopping by the coffee shop on my way out of the building, I found Geno and Ralphie sitting in a booth with a stack of invoices on the table between them. Sliding in next to Ralphie, I laughed because Geno was making cash register noises. "*Ka-CHING! Ka-CHING!*"

"Okay, you guys," I said. "Business is obviously good, so tell me about it." Which they were happy to do while I sampled a new breakfast pastry. It's called *cornetto alla crema,* and it's so delicious, you should eat more than one. A happy thought which I acted on while Ralphie started in about "those freaks at Tooterville."

"Tooterville?" I asked. "Where's Tooterville?"

"Down at the Inlet," Geno cut in. "You got a goof-ball calls himself Preacher, runs a tax-dodge called the Holistic Temple, has a big model train which he rides all around his property line. It has three two-seater cars, an engine, and a caboose. Calls it *Mystery Train,* says one of these days, it'll take him home to Glory."

"Whoa, that's creepy."

"You got that right, Mags," Ralphie said, "but me and Geno will decline to enlighten him. He just ordered another two-seater car, and you wanna' know the punch line?"

"Can't wait."

"He says he'll run new tracks into the Temple and use the train as the front row of seats."

Wow. Talk about timely information. There I was, ready to go on the prowl and scope out the Holistic Temple when Geno and Ralphie started filling me in about it. "Me and Ralphie," Geno said, "when we went the first time to lay train tracks, we couldn't believe it. Preacher'd been there ten, twelve years already, so the Temple was mostly finished, and the Bottle Wall was already built."

"The Bottle Wall?"

"The wall around his property line, where we laid the train tracks. It's coquina with beer bottles mortared in. Looks kinda' like low-rent stained glass, and it has a pass-through on the back line that he calls his Glory Hole."

"His *Glory Hole*?"

"You got it. Me and Ralphie, we figure he uses it to spy on the Genius House. Which I wouldn't blame him because weirdos are hangin' out—"

"Geno, stop! I know you think there's *woo woo* stuff going on at the Genius House but believe me, nothing matches the Temple setup. That sounds *really* bizarre."

"Be-zarr-o for sure," Ralphie said. "And the Temple's humongous, like that famous Spinx in Egypt."

"You mean the Sphinx?"

"Yeah whatever." Ralphie was frowning. "Mags, there's something about Tooterville we don't understand. Me and Geno don't understand it, I mean. Preacher's a little guy with a real bad limp and a gimpy arm. His wife's a lot younger than him, but she doesn't move good. and she's blind as a bat. So who built the temple and the wall? Who moved those ginormous coquina rocks? Who piled them up and cemented them?"

"Maybe he hired work crews from around town?"

"Not that we heard of—"

Geno got an emergency call from a client, and Ralphie said he had to go meet a trucker, so I poured my coffee in a to-go cup, got in Agatha, and headed over the bridge to the beachside.

While I was driving, I went over my agenda in my head. As in, what did I hope to accomplish by scoping out the Temple? As per usual, Schrödy provided yet another reality check while

I was getting ready for my outing. "Mags, aren't you supposed to be *writing*? I haven't heard you moaning about writer's block lately. Haven't heard anything about royalty checks arriving in the mail, either."

"Bulletin to Schrödinger: sometimes you're very annoying."

"Is that so? Well, all I know is, every time you start thinking you're Nancy Drew, you find trouble."

"What? For your information, Schrödy, I gave up on Nancy Drew years ago. She's a teenager, for crying out loud, and she's unbearably privileged. My investigator-role-model is Kinsey Milhone, a mature down-to-earth P.I. with whom I share many proclivities."

"That's for sure. Enviable proclivities like dead-end relationships and an addiction to junk food. And by the way, you look like you're going on a bear hunt. Where'd you get the leather jacket and hiking boots? Did you forget we live in Florida?"

"Schrody, can you give me a break here? I need to cover up so I won't get mosquito-bit, and I need heavy boots in case I have a snake encounter. You *know* I'm terrified of snakes."

I was upset with Schrödy for giving me grief about following my Sign, but I knew he had a point. I mean, *of course* I don't consider myself a real P.I., not even an investigative journalist. Mainly I tag along with Talisman when she's helping her friend the FDLE Director on a case, then I write it up.

Besides that, Signs are important, and I was sure I'd gotten one. Why else would I be embarking on a death-defying romp around the Temple property?

Two snake encounters later (I didn't see them, but I'm *sure* I heard them) I'd high-tailed it back to Agatha and gotten on the road. Okay, so maybe my tromp around the Temple property wasn't "death-defying" exactly, but it was no picnic, either. Which you'd realize if you ever trudged on foot through Florida's palmetto scrub. You haven't? Well trust me, you don't want to. Palmetto fronds are pure evil—flexible shards that give you nasty cuts wherever you brush against them, and every time you disturb a palmetto, you piss off the stinging insects that build their nests in them. *And* if you're so unlucky that the nest you disturb belongs to guinea wasps, run like hell because they will chase you for miles.

While I was tromping and snooping, I'd been ready to go into Kinsey-Milhone-mode if I encountered anyone (Kinsey's great at concocting stories and alibis), but the whole place was deserted. An old silver Airstream RV was parked in some scrub pine, and there's an outdoor kitchen area with brick ovens and rusty grills under a weathered canvas tent. But no people. By that time I'd finished my walk-around and heard those suspicious snakey noises in the underbrush, so I decided to beat a hasty retreat.

Hiking back to Agatha, I was in complete agreement with Ralphie that the whole setup is "be-zarr-o." As it would turn out, too, I was correct about my *Sign* pointing me in the right direction.

Flushed with the success of my adventure, I decided to stop at a great little seafood place near the Inlet for lunch. Decompressing over a plate of yummy shrimp scampi and a chilled glass of chardonnay, thinking back about my journey around the Temple grounds, I realized Geno and Ralphie hadn't exaggerated. The Temple itself is huge (not as big as "the Spinx,"

but pretty dang big). The Bottle Wall (it really looks like "low rent stained glass") is eight feet high in most places. And the large-scale train's a hoot: big enough to transport Snow White and all Seven Dwarfs around "Tooterville."

I'd finished my scampi and started in on my lemon gelato when I noticed four people at a table outside on the deck: two old guys, one punk, and one sexpot-type blonde. I could see them, but they couldn't see me because of glare on the window glass (I was inside, looking out) so I could stare all I wanted. Which I did right away because I recognized two of them for sure: the little geezer in a black suit and dog collar had to be Preacher, and the fat guy in dark glasses, with a beard and pony-tail, was his friend. Sterling said she'd seen the two of them together before, but she didn't know who Fat Guy was. What else did she say? I know, she said he might be a monk, because sometimes he wears a white monk's robe.

I had a nagging feeling I was missing something but couldn't figure out what it was, so I focused on the other two at the table on the deck outside. The punk, a Sid Vicious type, had his hair slicked up in spikes and sported a muscle shirt that showed off his scrawny arms and TATTs. And omigod! Look at the butt-crack pants and "shitload of hardware" on him! He's exactly the way Geno described Mr. Butt Crack.

The blonde sexpot looked familiar, but I couldn't place her. Shoot, I thought, I know I've seen her before, but where? She's a "type" also, but nothing like Sid Vicious. More of a young Jayne Mansfield, flaunting a skintight red dress cut so low in front, it defies gravity.

Okay, I thought, why are the punk and the sexpot here with Preacher? Especially the sexpot, because no way can she be Lily Amaryllis. Geno said Preacher's wife is a lot younger than he is, but she wouldn't be *that* young. And Sterling said Lily

Amaryllis is legally blind (in Geno's colorful terminology she's *blind as a bat*), but the sexpot wasn't wearing glasses. I still had my nagging feeling, but I wasn't getting anywhere. No epiphanies, in other words.

That's when it happened.

A bee or a horsefly or *something* started buzzing around Jayne Mansfield, whereupon Sid Vicious stood up and tried to swat it away but knocked it toward Fat Guy, whereupon it buzzed noisily around Fat Guy's head while he yelled and swatted and fell over backward, whereupon it got stuck in his beard, whereupon he pulled it off.

Fat Guy pulled off his beard, I mean.

I paid my bill and called Sterling as soon as I got out the door. Please please please, I was begging, no static! Sterling, please answer your phone! Which she did. "Mags, what's going on? Slow down!"

"Sterling, I'll be at your house in ten minutes. I have something important to tell you!"

"Okay, okay, I'm here. I'll meet you and we'll go sit on the porch."

So I told Sterling about Lily Amaryllis. How she dresses up like a man, pulls her long hair into a low ponytail like a guy would wear, and puts on a fake beard. "But why?" I asked. "Why in the world does she do that?"

"Mags, I have no idea why. I'm embarrassed that I've seen her before when she was in disguise, yet I didn't recognize her. I mean, she's always been partial to muumuu-type clothes. But when I saw her in that white monkish getup, which looks exactly like a muumuu, surely I should have suspected something."

"Well, don't beat yourself up about it. Now you know, and she doesn't *know* you know. So from here on out, you'll have the edge."

"You're right, Mags. That's the way I'll look at it."

"Okay, one last thing while you're walking me to my car. Do you have any idea who the other two are? Sid Vicious and Jayne Mansfield? The ones I told you about?" Sterling laughed and said, "Sure do. They're Preacher and Lily Amaryllis's kids. Sid Vicious is Beebo, and—"

"Whoa. So that's Beebo. The punk who hangs out with Brigadier?"

"Right. And the sexpot, the one you dubbed Jayne Mansfield, is Rose."

"Omigod, Rose? As in Lily and Rose, the flower names I told you about on the phone? And you thought I was talking about *this* Rose, but I never met her before . . . except I swear she looked familiar, but I couldn't place her. Still can't."

Sterling made a face but went on, "Rose is my former best friend, Mags. Emphasis on 'former.' Rose and I go way back—"

"Umm, Sterling? Sorry to interrupt, but look there, near the front sidewalk."

"Oh. My. God. It's a body. The body of a naked woman. A big dead naked woman . . ."

Uncharacteristically, I had nothing cogent to volunteer.

"Mags, stay here while I call Slim, okay? Don't leave yet?" Sterling turned away while she talked to Slim. "Slim, where are you? Well, pack it in and come to the house, pronto! *Please!*" Pause on Sterling's end. "Holy shit, Slim, please hurry. What? No, just you and whatzisname. You know, the fruitcake pathologist. Thanks!"

"Crap," Sterling said, as much to herself as to me, "just what we need. A Crime Scene ribbon and TV reporters again!"

Slim pulled up in no time with Doc Kumagai, but Sterling and I had already discovered that the naked woman wasn't a dead body at all. It was a blow-up doll. Amazingly lifelike, but still just a blow-up doll.

Doc Kumagai was mad about it at first. "This is your idea of a *joke*?" he said to anyone and no one. Then he got interested. "Hot chiles, this is no cheap toy. This is one EXPENSIVE toy. Oh boy, oh boy," Doc muttered, "this is better than the dummies we had in med school. Look here," he said to Slim. "See the mouth? Teeth, tongue, everything. It's deep throated, too, and look at the uvula. Boy oh boy, somebody paid big bucks for this baby!"

Doc poked it, stroked it. "And oh yeah, oh yeah. Holy Christ, look down here at—"

"Doc? *Doc!* THAT'S ENOUGH, ALL RIGHT?" This was Slim. "Pack the goddam thing up in a body bag, and let's get it back to the lab. I'm guessing we can get DNA from it?"

"Oh yeah, yeah. It's been used for sure. Recently."

Sterling was in no mood to chat after Slim pulled out with Doc and "the body," and I was glad to drive home where I could ditch my bug- and snake-repellent items of clothing, then chill out. I hadn't been home more than five minutes, though, when Geno started pounding on my front door, hollering to let him in.

"Hold your horses, Geno!" I hollered back, then opened the door. "What?"

"Mags, it's your weirdo Genius friends again. Last night over at the Boardwalk they had a Jamboree and—"

"It wasn't a Jamboree, it was a Cabaret. Spelled C-a-b-a-r-e-t, and it's French."

"Which is no surprise because they procurated a Drag Queen—"

"It was a *variety show,* Geno, and it was completely tasteful."

"Sure it was, and while the Jamboree was going on they set the bowling alley on fire, which practically gave the Bowling Magnet a heart attack—"

"You mean the Bowling *Magnate?*"

"That's what I said, Pan Pappadiculous, the Donald Trump of Bowling. And as if that wasn't bad enough—"

"Geno, I heard what happened at the bowling alley last night because I talked to my *weirdo friends* about it, and I'm telling you they had nothing to do with the fire . . . well, maybe just a little."

"Oh, yeah? Just a little? Like I started to say before you kept on interruptin' me, the fire at the bowling alley last night was bad enough, but today's even worse at the Genius House. The place is crawling with cops and TV, and it's nuts because a tipster called in a dead body in the front yard! A dead naked woman! And it musta' been out there all day in the heat because it's swole up and puffy!"

A TRIP TO BLUE SPRING

"Good game, Mags."

"Slim, you're full of it. I played a lousy game, and you know it. It was fun, though, great exercise, so thanks for coming on short notice."

"No problem. I like getting a morning workout; it sets me up for the day. So-o-o, Mags, what's on your mind?" Slim was looking down her nose at me and raising her eyebrows. And laughing, so I started laughing too. "Okay, you got me. I'm dying for updates on the NASCAR balloon explosion and the blow-up doll. I mean, I was right there at the scene for both of them, but Sterling's been in a mood lately and won't talk."

"I know what you mean about Sterling and her moods," Slim agreed. "She seems to have a lot on her mind."

"That's for sure. So 'fess up, Slim. What's happening?"

"Sorry to say, but not much on either front. We're stalled on the blow-up doll because Doc Kumagai's lab assistant misplaced the evidence. Doc says it's no big deal, claims the sample got temporarily misplaced because they're reorganizing the lab. But we all know what's going on."

"We do? What?"

"He's balling the assistant, of course. Gets a new 'girl' every year, more incompetent than the one before. Doc has friends in high places, though, so no one blows the whistle on him."

"That sucks."

"Sure does, but it's the way of the world."

"Okay, how about the NASCAR balloon?"

"Funny you should ask."

"Why? There's something funny going on with the balloon crash?"

"Not hilarious-funny, but Leon says mum's the word."

Did I mention before that Leon's the Director of FDLE in Tallahassee? Right, I thought I did, but I might not have mentioned Slim's hotline to FDLE because she and Leon were Talisman's student assistants some time ago, just like Casey is now. I knew they all "talk shop" about current cases, and I wanted to be included in the loop.

"Come on, Slim," I said, "you know I'm tight with Leon, so spill the beans." (I knew she was dying to tell me, just needed a little persuasion.)

"Well to start with, someone shot down the NASCAR balloon. There's no suspect yet but they're sure about the gun. It was a high-powered rifle, Leon says, not your garden variety shotgun. And the balloon exploded because the shooter hit a bomb that was stashed in the basket, which means the shooter knew about it. Knew about the bomb, I mean. Not to mention that whoever did this was a crack shot."

"Wow. How about the dead guys?"

"That's a mystery because they were already dead, didn't die in the crash. Forensics identified them through fingerprints, though. Two drug dealers from Bimini."

"Holy cow, that was quite a plan. Hijack the balloon, send it up with a bomb and two bodies, then shoot it down?"

"Yep. Don't know who, don't know why. Leon says they're baffled. And by the way, Mags . . ." Slim was looking down her nose at me again.

"What? *By the way* what?"

"The next time you want an update, just call me. You don't need to set up a racquetball game as an excuse. Unless you can't resist demonstrating your kill shot, that is. Which is flat-out devastating."

Back home and pumped after my morning workout, I was super-excited, planning to get all dressed up and enjoy a long leisurely lunch. My longtime friend Monica, an expert on French wines, had arranged a wine-tasting-plus-luncheon at Three Graces.

You might remember Monica, my dean at Georgia Tech? We both left GT at the same time, me to be a writer and Monica to be a dean again at Embry-Riddle Aeronautical Institute. As she likes to say about dean-ing a Liberal Arts Department at a technical college, "Sometimes you have to scratch and claw your way to the bottom."

Anyway, Monica's luncheon would be very elegant, totally *trés chic,* and I was perusing my clothes closet, imagining how smashingly sophisticated I'd look, when my phone started squawking (my ringtone's a singing parrot—it's a long story). It was Talisman calling from DeLand, and she sounded weird. "Mags, I have a message for you—*Find the river of crystal and pour it forth.*" Then she hung up.

Crap, I thought. Here we go again with Talisman's horoscopic mandates.

Here's the thing about Talisman: even though she denies it, folks say she's psychic. That's how she got started consulting for law enforcement way back when Leon and Slim were her student assistants, and she's kept it up. Not long ago, in fact, she sussed out a hugely complicated murder at the college in DeLand. Casey was her student assistant, so she got him involved, and together with Slim and Leon, they solved the case. I was basically just an observer, but I had so much fun, I decided to write it up like Watson does for Holmes.

So there I was in my apartment, in a pickle because my friend The Delphic Oracle had gotten astrologically inspired. As per usual I wanted to pay attention, but I didn't know how. *Find the river of crystal and pour it forth?* What the hell does that mean? Surely she doesn't mean "Crystal River" because it's way the heck on the other side of Florida.

Just then my phone squawked again, and this time it was Sterling. "Mags? Please please *please* say you'll come with us to Blue Spring."

"Who's *us?*"

"Jengu and me. We're all packed up in the Suburban, and we'll be waiting at the bottom of your fire escape in ten minutes."

Uh oh. Do I feel goosebumps? Talisman says this is my day to answer a water-mandate, and now I'm invited to go hang out at a spring? Okay, I thought, it's a spring, not a river, and even if I find a river, I'm not sure how I'll pour it forth. But at least I'll be aligned with the stars. Or the cards. Or something.

After Sterling hung up I called Monica and told her I felt the flu coming on. Why did I lie? Because Monica gets pissy if you're a no-show at one of her soireés, which means you might never get asked again. Also, if I told her I was ditching her party because of a horoscopic warning she'd think I've gone around the bend. I did ask her to save me a bottle of wine, but when she said *You should be so lucky* or something like that, I decided not to push it.

Then I packed up my casual-trip necessities for a day at the spring (sunscreen, snorkel gear and floatie, and a brand-new box of MoonPies in a waterproof canister), told Schrödinger I'd be back by dinnertime, and walked down my fire escape just as the black Suburban from the Genius House pulled up at the curb.

Blue Spring is southwest of Daytona Beach, about thirty minutes by car. It's pretty famous, part of the watershed of the St. Johns River and the place where manatees cluster to stay warm during the winter months. When the manatees are around (starting in mid-November and ending in March), the spring itself and the "run" are closed to swimmers and divers. This was just the beginning of October, though, so we could swim to our heart's content.

And dive? Me? Surely you jest. I enjoy snorkeling in the springs occasionally but snorkeling's all about staying on top of the water, not going down where it's dark and spooky and oxygen deficient. As soon as I climbed in the Suburban and saw wetsuits and masks and tanks in the back, I declared my intention to stay on the surface. "No problem, Mags," Sterling said. "In fact, if you're on top of the water while we're diving, you can take some video of us below." I agreed enthusiastically, said I'd love to video their diving exploits, adding as a caveat, of course, that I would film from the surface while hanging onto my floatie with my snorkel-goggled face in the water.

Jengu chattered like a magpie while we were in the Suburban, displaying a wealth of information about Florida's freshwater springs. I hadn't realized, for example, that there are more freshwater springs in Florida than anywhere else in the whole world. Oh, yes, he said, and he loves being outposted to Florida because of the opportunities for cave diving in the springs.

At that point we arrived at the entrance to the state park, drove in, and parked the Suburban. While the two of them got into their wetsuits I figured out how to use the video camera. Then we divided up the gear (I carried the camera, my floatie, and my backpack) and headed for the dive site. With Jengu leading the way, Sterling and I got a chance to talk while we were walking. "Thanks so much for coming," Sterling said. "I've been trying to get Jengu out of a funk about his stupid girlfriend going AWOL, so it's nice to have someone different for him to talk at."

"I'm glad to help out with Jengu, Sterling, and he's really knowledgeable about the Florida aquifer. He's like a poet when he talks about it—'water like crystal gushing through limestone, pooling with frothy bubbles by banks of ferns that drop their tears'—really, I love to hear him talk when he's inspired."

"I'm glad you do, and so does George. I wasn't keen about going to Blue Spring today, but George insisted we make the trip. Wouldn't leave it alone until I gave in."

"Seriously? That's weird, because Talisman called this morning with a horoscopic mandate, insisting today's a water day for me and I should pay attention."

While the two of them were registering to dive, I sat on the swim platform at the head of the run, dunking my toes and trying to remember why I agreed to forego a wine-tasting (French wines, no less) and a real lunch (*trés chic* and elegant). For one thing, I'd forgotten about the springs being very very *very* cold, which you know if you've ever jumped or dived into DeLeon Springs or Gemini Springs or any other Florida spring including this one. The water's so cold, when you hit it you expel every bit of breath in your lungs. WHOOSH, gasp . . .

Then you sink like a rock.

How could I have forgotten? For me, swimming in the springs is a sinister prick of déjà vu from when I fell through black ice on that lake in Pittsburgh. The ice didn't *look* black, of course, because it was covered with new snow, a sparkling shiny-white blanket that enticed me to slip and slide on it, zipping back and forth.

I almost drowned in that lake, and black ice remains a potent symbol to me of the precariousness of life. One minute you're skimming along. The next you're looking up at that dark ceiling of ice, seeing the cracks in it, knowing you've fallen through.

It's the exact same feeling I get any time I take the plunge into a Florida spring. WHOOSH, gasp . . .

Pretty soon they were back from registering, so we walked to the dive site. It's a good thing Jengu's wearing a wetsuit, I thought. If he were wearing baggies, that red-gold hide of his would be attention-getting. With the wetsuit covering him from neck to knees, though, his other oddities (huge hands and feet, bald head, long beard that looks like seaweed) just made you think he was one more weird tourist visiting Florida from God Knows Where.

For the next half-hour they scuba'd and posed while I paddled my floatie on the surface and video'd. Nobody else was diving that day, just them, so I got some cool video. We'd agreed that while they were diving the cave and out of sight I'd wait for them at a ramp, so that's what I did. Sterling surfaced soon, saying she only went as far as the warning sign about sixty feet down. "Jengu's going deeper because he's a pro," she said. "There's a strong current around 100 feet down, and Jengu loves riding it."

"Riding an underwater current? Is it like riding a wave? or a boogie board?"

Sterling laughed and said, "Riding the current's something Squiggs taught Jengu."

"Squiggs?" I asked. "Who's Squiggs?"

"Uh, he's Jengu's best friend. Squiggs promised to teach me too, sometime, but he couldn't come with us today. It's why I wanted to get a video." Then Sterling cut me off when I tried to ask more about Squiggs. "Mags," she said, "if you'll stay here with the tanks and equipment, I'll change out of my wetsuit, then drive back to get you and Jengu."

"Sure, no problem. I'll just have a MoonPie while I'm waiting and—*oh damn!* I put my MoonPie canister in the water so the cookies wouldn't melt in the sun, but the waterproof canister wasn't. It wasn't waterproof, I mean. My MoonPies are mush. Look, they're pathetic."

Disconsolate is a good word for how I felt. I'd brought a brand new special-edition box of MoonPies (the Neapolitan Assortment: vanilla, chocolate, and strawberry) in a collectible tin canister, and now they were schmucky. They looked like deflated jellyfish when I dumped them out on the ramp, especially the strawberry ones. I was devastated. "Mags," Sterling laughed, "I'll pick up some energy bars at the snack stand for you and be back in thirty minutes or less."

"Okay, fine," I said, trying to be brave. It wasn't anyone's fault that my canister leaked but guess what. An energy bar is no substitute for a MoonPie. You can trust me on that. Oh, well, I thought. I might as well organize the gear while Sterling's gone. It'll give me something to think about besides how I will never get steamrolled by Talisman's horoscopic predictions again . . . what? Wait a minute.

There are two tanks here. And there's a mask here, too. I wonder if Jengu surfaced when I wasn't looking? I put on my snorkeling goggles and stuck my face in the water. No sign of Jengu. I thought I saw a light down at the mouth of the cave, though. Could that be him? I wondered. Naw, that'd be one heck of a free dive. And besides, he said he didn't bring a light.

Someone was running, coming toward me. "Mags! Mags!" It was Sterling, running back along the path. "Have you seen my ring? I can't find it! I *never* take off my ring!" Suddenly Jengu was there too, pulling himself up on the platform from the water.

The next twenty minutes were chaotic. We looked everywhere for the ring— a chunky gold ring with three turquoise stones, is how Sterling described it. She said Mary and Ben gave it to her for her thirteenth birthday, and she never ever took it off, even wears it when she's surfing at the beach. Jengu and Sterling went free-diving, retracing their dive paths, but they found nothing. Meanwhile I looked through every pack, every piece of equipment, every case and cover, but I came up empty-handed too.

To say that Sterling was distraught is an understatement. She got droopier and droopier, finally just sat down on the dive ramp, hopeless. Even though she's a tall woman and incredibly strong, she looked so tiny there, hugging herself—a beautiful forlorn nymph who'd just lost everything in the world that mattered to her.

We stayed at the spring for another hour while we backtracked along the trails.

Nothing.

Finally Sterling left notes at the snack stands and ranger stations, saying there'd be a substantial reward for anyone who found her ring. There wasn't anything else we could do then, so we got ready to leave. Jengu said he'd be glad to drive so Sterling climbed into the front passenger seat of the Suburban, leaving me to climb in the back. "Oh, wait," I said. "I know it's dumb, but I want to get my MoonPie canister. I'll be just a minute. I left it over by the swim platform."

I spotted my canister right where I'd left it, and when I bent down to pick it up, something caught my eye. It was tiny, just a glint on the bottom, right below the platform where the water's less than two feet deep. The spring water's crystal clear, but the spring bed itself is mottled: whitish, greenish, bluish. The ring was on a greenish patch, making it difficult to see. But at the very moment when I bent down, a ray of sunlight hit the ring and lit it up, enough for me to notice a gleam, a shine, a sparkle.

In a flash I scooped it up with my canister and went running back to the van, faster than I knew I could run. "I've got it! I've got it! I found the ring!"

Sterling tumbled out of the car and held out her hands while I upended the canister and we all watched the ring settle itself in her cupped palms, gleaming to beat the band while the crystal clear spring water washed over it.

Sterling and Jengu chattered happily during the drive back to Daytona, but I couldn't stop thinking. I was elated about finding Sterling's ring, but I had so many questions. Did Jengu really dive without a tank? And why's Sterling's ring so important? And if Squiggs is such a good friend, why didn't he come with us to the spring? Also, wasn't it weird that George insisted they make the trip to Blue Spring? Even weirder, why was Talisman reading my horoscope this morning? I certainly didn't ask for a reading. In fact, I have *never* asked Talisman for a reading.

But a spring's not a river. Or is it? After Talisman said *pour forth the river* and Sterling called, I'd thought immediately of the St. Johns River because Blue Spring feeds the St. Johns. So is that the same thing? Naw, that would be stretching it . . . wait. What was it Jengu said about the springs? Yes, I remember. He said Florida's freshwater springs are part of the Florida aquifer, which is an underground river.

Okay, so I guess we were at a river, after all. Just one that runs under the ground. And what else did Jengu say? I know—the underground river breaks through the limestone substrata, and when that happens the limestone cleans and filters the gushing river water, polishing it to the clarity of crystal.

Find the river of crystal and pour it forth? Bingo! Talisman, I said to myself, I don't know how you do it, but you're still batting a thousand.

When we got back to Daytona, I watched from my rooftop gazebo while the black Suburban with its passengers headed over the bridge. My gazebo's usually a perfect place to muse and mull, so that's what I tried to do. The more I thought about the day, though, the more my brain felt scrambled.

Screw this! I thought. Geno's always good for a laugh and a laugh's exactly what I need right now. A chilled glass of Chianti wouldn't hurt either, especially with a plate of Geno's scrumptious antipasto . . . which I proceeded to anticipate until I stepped off the freight elevator downstairs and heard RonJon shouting.

RonJon, Geno's elderly surfer friend, talks LOUD. ALWAYS. But that's not his only distinguishing characteristic. In fact, you only have to meet RonJon once, and you'll never forget him: long white ponytail, tattoos on every bit of exposed skin including his face. He and Geno go way back, and they have a sweetheart deal: stale food for gossip.

"It's a win-win," Geno says. "I can't sell expirational food so RonJon takes what he wants, gives away the rest, then clues me in on the locals so's I can inventory-up for bikers, beach rats, spring breakers. All the touristy riff raff."

Well, Geno's win-win deal notwithstanding, RonJon was obviously not in a hurry to leave, and I couldn't stand the decibel level, so I paid for my Chianti and antipasto and headed upstairs. Back in my apartment and dejected, I tried three times to call Sterling because I wanted to talk about the day, but no luck. I got that infuriating static every time.

Dammit! I thought. *I'm done calling. I spent my whole day with them, so they owe me. I'll drive on down to the Genius House and demand that Sterling makes time to talk with me.*

MEET THE ROOMERS

By the time I got there it was after dark, and the whole place was lit up like a Christmas tree. Nobody came to the door when I rang the bell and knocked, so I decided to go inside and find someone.

The downstairs was empty, and I have to admit I had one of those creepy déjà vu feelings again, remembering my midnight adventure at the Genius House when my high school girl-fiends and I escaped just before the Beach Patrol arrived. The more I remembered about that night, the more I got spooked, and I might've left at that point if I hadn't heard voices and laughter coming from upstairs. Also piano music.

What? Piano music? I'd never been invited upstairs to the music room even though Sterling knew my history as a pianist, occasionally dropping by my apartment to practice solos for Sotto Vochay while I accompanied her on my piano. *Damn it all,* I figured, *I'm already here so why shouldn't I join the crowd?*

I made it to the second floor after a few blocked hallways and locked doors, but I couldn't find anyone, so I climbed to the floor above that. Still no one. *Whoa,* I thought, *it's looking old up here.* True, I knew the house was built almost a century ago, but the downstairs parts had been modernized. Here on these upstairs levels, however, it looked ancient. There was a weird smell too, like dirt. The way fresh beets smell while you're scrubbing and peeling them.

Voices got louder as I climbed the next stairway, still a conversational buzz until they started singing, and that's when I heard Sterling's voice. Yep, I said to myself, that's Sterling. Can't miss that full-throated female baritone. I didn't want to interrupt the singing, so I tiptoed toward the open doorway at the end of a long hall. When I reached the doorway I looked in, expecting to see Sterling and her Sotto Vochay chorus friends gathered around the piano.

When they saw me the music stopped abruptly.

And when I saw them, I stopped dead in my tracks.

"Dead in my tracks" is a good description of me at that moment, less metaphoric than you might suspect. I was rooted to the floor and completely unable to move, in other words, while I took in the inhabitants of the room and watched Sterling come walking over to me.

"Mags, you didn't call."

"Yes, I did, but all I got was static."

"And I apologize for that, but since you're here you might as well meet a few of our Roomers. That's Amanita at the piano, Chanterelle and Copeland over there by the window, and the one sitting at the bar is Mrs. Grales."

When Sterling called them by name, four people-size Mushrooms stood up and waved. And smiled, I think. Maybe. Then two of the Mushrooms sat down again while the hefty one called Mrs. Grales (the bright red one with two heads) started toward us. "Sterling, you'll break my arm if you don't let go," I whispered.

"I'm holding on to you because I don't want you to run away," she whispered back. "I told you it's not a good idea to drop by unexpectedly, but since you're here, please be polite."

My sojourn that night with the Roomers is a blur in my memory. It's possible that my brain's protecting me because this was, after all, not your ordinary cocktail party with chit-chat and cheese cubes on toothpicks. Well okay, there was lots of chitchat, and they did have cheese cubes on toothpicks, but you sure couldn't call it ordinary.

When I look back on it, what I *do* remember for sure is being surrounded by intelligence and compassion. The Roomers I met that night, in other words, were smart, kind, and welcoming. Completely non-threatening and non-confrontational.

I remember their voices, too, because they were as varied as their personalities: some spicy, others fruity, still others that were mellow and layered. In terms of human voice types, we might say the sopranos were spicy, the contraltos fruity, the baritones and basses mellow and substantial. And the tenors? As Christopher always says about tenors, they were *the cocks of the walk*. Especially the one named Copeland who slipped as smoothly in and out of falsetto as a knife spreading warm butter.

Somehow, too, the light in the room conspired with their voices while they sang: brightening, dimming, and brightening again. Dimming, it reminded me of the soft opalescent haze in Kells's cottage. Brightening, it reminded me of the flashing light-cocoon that swirled around Sterling at the pub called Pigs Will Fly.

Sterling stayed right with me the whole time, even asked me to accompany them on the piano while they practiced a Sinatra medley: *Strangers in the Night, Summer Wind,* and *That's Life.* And while I accompanied them, I was inspired. An accompanist's job is to follow, to support, to lead without seeming to lead. Over the years I'd accompanied soloists, ensembles, choirs, choruses. But I never played as I played that night.

No wait, that's not exactly right . . . because it wasn't about me, about Mags. It was about all of us, together, communicating through the music. It was like being back in the Conference Room while the Tutors sang-talked their way into my mind. By the time we finished the Sinatra medley I'd calmed down considerably and suggested we add *Fly Me to the Moon* as a coda, but Sterling said no, it was time for the two of us to leave.

After we went downstairs and got settled on the back porch, Sterling called Kells to come join us. She mind-called Kells, that is, because I saw no evidence of a phone.

"I want some of George's fairy juice." (Me)

"No fairy juice. Just coffee." (Sterling)

SQUIFFY STATIC AND FLUKEY FOG

Kells arrived almost immediately. "Mags," she said, "it's not hard to understand. While Sapients dedicated their energies toward dominion over all life, we Boskops dedicated our energies toward co-habitation. And along the way we learned to communicate with other life forms—not just with Fauna, but with Flora as well."

"So you talk to plants? As in synergetic species?"

"Exactly as in synergetic species. But there's more."

"Of course there's more. I'm just not sure I want to hear it." Sterling was looking exasperated. "Mags, you can't have it both ways. You say you need the whole story but when we try to tell you, you back off."

"All right, all right. I'm listening but I feel a little faint. You wouldn't happen to have any more of George's rhubarb bread, would you? To go with the coffee?"

I don't know why I was surprised about the Roomers. They're biobots—'Noids—like the Archies. But instead of humanoid biobots, they're *shroomanoid* biobots. And that's because they want to be. They want to look like mushrooms, I mean, instead of people. "But why," I asked, "do they want to look like mushrooms?"

"Because that's their identity," Kells said. "They're part of a global mycelial network—" I must have been rolling my eyes because Sterling broke in then. "Mags, the mycelium connection's vitally important, but it's not hard to understand. It's as common as dirt. Literally. Mycelium is what mushrooms grow in. Remember when I told you our Tower's a greenhouse?"

"Yes, I remember. So you grow mycelium there?"

"We do. The Roomers tend it, round the clock."

"Then what about all those electronics your dad installed that cause static? You told me that, remember? And I've been wondering why I can't ever get a straight story because—"

"Mags, it's time to do LSS."

"Long Story Short?"

"Exactly. Kells will keep it short, and you won't interrupt. Got it?"

"Got it."

They were as good as their word. Once Kells started talking, it took her less than ten minutes to encapsulate the history of life on Our Blue Gaia (it's what she calls Planet Earth). I'll keep it short, too, so here goes—first the Prequel, then the Sequel.

The Prequel starts around 100,000 years ago when both Flora and Fauna were already well-established on Our Blue

Gaia, the plan being that they'd be partners. Plants would need animals; animals would need plants.

In other words, co-existence was the name of the game, and co-existence meant communication: plants communicated with each other via neural nets that lay underground (root systems), while animals communicated with each other via neural nets in their skulls (brains).

By that point in time, plants and animals co-existed in harmony. Mushrooms, via vast underground neural nets called mycelium, ruled the world of Flora. And Hominins, via self-contained neural nets called brains, ruled the world of Fauna.

Again, though, the most important thing was communication. Plants talked to each other *and* to animals, while animals talked to each other *and* to plants.

The Sequel starts with the exodus of the NEFBOs to their new domains:

— by 35,000 years ago, all the Neanders had gone;

— by 13,000 years ago, all the Floreans had gone;

— by 10,000 years ago, all the Boskops had gone.

While the diasporas of the other three hominin tribes were happening, Sapiens lost their (our) ability to communicate with plants and with other animals. Reproducing like crazy, ruled by hubris and greed, Sapiens cared only about themselves: their clans, their territories, their jealousies and hatreds, their wars.

Eventually *The Tipping Point* arrived when Sapiens created a global network rivalling the communication potentialities of mycelium. Colloquially, we call it the Internet, and it was the tipping point because it allowed Sapients to exercise hubris and greed on a global scale, without restraint.

"Wait!" I said. I knew I wasn't supposed to interrupt Kells, but at that point in her story I couldn't stop myself. "The Internet's a *good* thing, isn't it? I mean, its potential for healing the planet and bringing people together is enormous. Isn't it?"

"You're right, Mags," Kells said. "Global communication via the Internet has enormous potential for good."

"But?"

"But Sapients invented it before they were ready for it. Globalization requires a moral infrastructure, a global consensus about environmental and ethical issues."

"So when you say it always gets back to the whimper or the bang, you're saying again the problem is people, aren't you? But Sapients have good qualities, too, don't we? Some of us?"

"Absolutely, Mags. You're smart, but you're flawed. Sapients' capacity for genius may have inspired the Enlightenment, but it created the Holocaust, as well. And that's why we say the Intervention is 'to buy time.' Given time to set things right for the planet and each other, Sapients may avoid both the whimper *and* the bang."

Kells had to leave then in a hurry, something about getting a "distress call" from Jengu.

Which was fine with me because I'd just been insulted . . . *I know*, I know. Kells wasn't insulting me personally, but how am I supposed to take it when my *species* is insulted? I felt like I'd just failed an IQ test, and I couldn't argue because I know Kells is way smarter than I am, just like Boskops are way smarter than Sapients.

Have I mentioned that Kells's head is too big for her face? It's called paedomorphism, and it's because the Boskop skull is huge. Bigger than ours. Way bigger. That's why the Boskop fossil skulls found in South Africa are said to be fake, because a skull casing so large and commodious implies that Boskops were—are—significantly smarter than we are . . . smarter than Sapiens . . .

"Mags? *Mags?*"

"Sorry, Sterling, sorry. I was distracted, thinking about what Kells just said because . . . um, you know what I was thinking, don't you?"

"I do, and I don't blame you at all for feeling insulted. Come on, I'll walk you to your car. And call me when you're back in your apartment?"

"What if I get static when I call?"

"You won't get static, Mags. I'll make sure of it."

"You can control the static that messes up your phones?"

"Yes, in the sense that we can start it and stop it. I told you the hollow core of the Tower's a greenhouse, and we grow mycelium there, but you interrupted me before I could tell you why we grow it. Mycelium's the growth medium for mushrooms. It's a neural net that works like the neural nets in our own brains. Boskops discovered they could use mycelium as brain material for the Roomers."

"Of course, and it explains why the Roomers want to look like mushrooms. I get that, no problem, but what's the connection between mycelium and static? Are you saying the mycelium you grow in the Tower causes static?"

"Yep. Mycelium causes those 'synaptic spikes' I mentioned, the spikes that knock out our phones."

"So-o-o-o . . . if the neuronal network in *our* brains operates by sending signals across synapses, the same thing must happen in the mycelium? And the signals 'spike' when there's a lot of brain . . . sorry, a lot of *mycelium* activity in the Tower?"

"Right."

"So that's the 'static'? Bursts of brain—mycelium—activity?"

"Right again." While we talked, Sterling and I were walking to my car. "Okay," I said, "I'm sure I won't fathom how you control the static, but why do you *want* to control it? What's the point? It's not that you want to control the Roomers, is it? Because they're independent creatures with minds of their own, like the Archies. That's what you told me."

"Exactly. Brain material for the Roomers was an important discovery, but there's another use for mycelium that's way more important. Remember while you and Kells and I were talking tonight, and I tried to tell you about *a global mycelium network*?"

"Right, I didn't get it then, but now I do. The Tower's a gigantic brain, isn't it? A network that generates electrochemical energy and causes static across various frequencies."

"That's correct, but only as far as it goes. In the context of a 'global mycelium network,' the operative word is *global*."

"Um, meaning there are more greenhouses? Like yours in the Tower?"

"Lots more."

"And all of them disrupt frequencies at will?"

"Yes. We call the disrupt-at-will function *Selective Static*."

"Selective Static?"

"That's what we're calling it for now, anyway. We'll change the name later, after our global mycelium network is up and running. At that point we'll be ready to launch the Intervention, so we'll program the network for randomized disturbances that we'll call *Squiffy Static*. A major strategy of the Intervention will be to disrupt global communication, including the Internet, with Squiffy Static."

"*You'll close down global communication? All at once and for good?*"

"Of course not. Disruptions will be localized, occurring in different places at different times and always random, never targeted. In other words, Squiffy Static will be annoying, not terrifying—geared to slow things down, to cause consternation but not outright panic."

"Right. Consternation instead of panic. Good luck with that. And while I'm being skeptical, who came up with the cutesy name? *Squiffy Static*? Why?"

"Because it's catchy, accessible, something the general public can talk about, complain about, agonize over. Would it be better to call it by its scientific name—Randomized Electrical Spikes Across Mycelial Synapses? And the acronym, RESAMS, is just as bad." Sterling was wearing her sympathetic face. "I know you're rattled, Mags, and I don't blame you. You've had one helluva ride lately, topped off tonight by meeting the Roomers. Tell you what, give yourself some time to think everything over, then let's meet for dinner and I'll finish what we started tonight. I'll explain Flukey Fog."

"Flukey Fog?"

"The scientific name is Adventitious Transpirational Effluence from Myrcorrhizal Mycelium, or ATEMM. It's part of the plan, like Squiffy Static. I didn't mention it because I didn't want to dump too much on you at one time. Let's meet on Thursday at Three Graces. Thursday's my un-birthday, so I'll be ready to celebrate."

ROSE AND LILY

So there we were at a table at Three Graces, celebrating Sterling's un-birthday. I know, I know. An "un-birthday" sounded strange to me, too, until Sterling explained that she and her brothers don't know when their real birthdays were, so they pick different ones each year. Once I got used to the concept, I thought it was totally cool, so I asked Sterling why she picked October 3rd as this year's un-birthday. "October 3rd was an obvious choice," she said, "because it's Virus Appreciation Day."

"And we should appreciate viruses . . . because?"

"Because anyone who's curious about the origins of consciousness ought to be interested in viruses."

Sigh. Where's Wally when you need him? If Wally'd been there he could have made a pithy rejoinder, whereas I at that moment was totally lacking in pith. Sterling just laughed, said it's too complicated for dinnertime chat, so we'd talk about it some other time.

"Fine with me," I said, "because you never finished telling me about Rose. Why'd you say she's your *former* best friend? What happened?"

"I always knew I was different, Mags, but at least I had Rose. We were misfits, spent every spare minute reading, loved to sing and write stories and talk about books. And both of us knew we'd been stolen from our real parents. I told you about being stolen, remember?"

Sterling was still talking but I zoned out because I was remembering her remark, the night we talked at Sergio's after we left the gym. She'd been telling me how she hates her name, Sterling Silver Buck, and how all three Bulben kids were adopted. And that's when she said she remembers "being taken." It was a remark I'd recalled ever since because it bothered me. I mean, just because you're adopted doesn't mean you were *stolen* from your real parents. That only happens in fairy tales and . . . Uh oh. Sterling was giving me *a look*. "Sorry, sorry, where were we?"

"*I was saying*, Mags, that Rose figured she must have been a foundling too, just like Beebo."

"He was a foundling? You mean they 'found' him? Literally?"

"Yep, found him outside the Temple, screaming bloody murder. Rose said he couldn't have been more than a day old when someone dropped him there and left."

"That's awful."

"Sure is. Rose says they didn't want to keep him at first, tried to find out who he belonged to until Preacher decided the foundling was a Penance sent from Above."

"A Penance? For what?"

"Don't know. According to Rose, though, that's when they had a big ceremony, baptized the baby in that old bathtub they keep outside the Temple, and named him Moses."

We stopped talking for a few minutes while the Graces presented Sterling with their signature birthday cocktail: *Salutary Grace*. Sterling laughed, took a swig of her cocktail and grinned, then drank the rest of it—guzzled it, actually—and ordered another. I was stunned. "Sterling? Since when do you drink alcohol?"

"On occasions like this, when the drink itself is special. I've heard you rhapsodize about single malt Scotch, haven't I?"

"Absolutely."

"Okay, then. We all have to name our poison, and I've been known to drink strong men under the table if someone pops a keg of Beamish Black."

"Beamish? A black malt? But you wouldn't touch Piggles when we were at the pub, not even to toast with Uncle Billy."

"Of course not. Piggles is swill. Beamish, on the other hand, is ambrosia, and it's part of the Bulben family legacy. That's another story, though, and it's complicated, so let's save it."

"Got'cha, especially since I want to hear more about Rose. And Lily." Starting in again, Sterling said Lily Amaryllis bad-mouths the Genius House every chance she gets. "She really, really hates us. It's not rational, goes way back to a feud between the Lighthouse and the Genius House that got started years before Preacher took over as keeper."

"Preacher used to be the Lighthouse-keeper? At the Ponce Inlet Lighthouse?"

"Yep, like his father and grandfather before him. They kept it in the family, so to speak."

"Okay, back to the feud. What started this one?"

"The story is that Preacher's grandfather salvaged some treasure from a shipwreck but couldn't remember where he buried it after he brought it ashore. Then he got senile, started babbling about a priest who survived the wreck and cursed the treasure before he disappeared." Sterling stopped to take a swig of her second cocktail, then continued. "Anyway, Preacher's grandfather got progressively crazier, started roaming around at night with a shovel and a shotgun. Said he'd find his buried treasure and shoot the priest, until the family finally had him committed."

"Was there really any treasure? Or a priest who survived the shipwreck?"

"Who knows? Once a story like that gets started, it takes on a life of its own."

"Just like a family feud."

"That's for sure. The feud was still simmering years later when Preacher took over as Lighthouse-keeper. Supposedly he was quite a Casanova at that point, and the parties he threw at the Lighthouse are legendary. He wasn't known as 'Preacher' then, of course, just Stanley Clinkscales. He didn't get religion until later, after he fell down the big spiral staircase in the Lighthouse during a storm."

"That's when he got the gimpy arm and leg?"

"Guess so, but he must have cracked his head too because he didn't just get religious, he went God-crazy. Anyway, the feud blew up bigtime at that point because the Clinkscales family blamed the Genius House for Preacher's tumble. Something about bad karma."

"How could the Genius House make bad karma for the Lighthouse?"

"Dunno, maybe the Fairies got involved. Dad was here then, gutting the cottages. He said there was a big stink about the accident and a scandal that wouldn't wait. Politicians from Tallahassee got involved, Stanley got a land grant and started calling himself Preacher, and when they moved to the Temple property, Lily Amaryllis was appointed Honorary Mayor of Ponce Inlet. In perpetuity."

We stopped talking long enough to start sampling our tapas. (Princess's tapas are luscious, especially her *eggs agraciado*: devil the eggs with homemade aioli sauce, add chopped guindilla peppers and crumbles of fried oyster, top with crispy chorizo bits. Yum!) "Sterling," I enthused, "I am so happy you wanted to have an un-birthday dinner. I'm thinking I'll have an un-birthday dinner every month from now on, so's I can catch up."

"Mags, you're impossible." (Said with a laugh.)

"That's what I always say to Schrödy, too, that he's impossible. I mean it affectionately, of course."

"I mean it affectionately too, Mags. It's important to me that we're friends. I really, really want you to remember that." Uh oh, why does that sound ominous? Like Sterling knows trouble's on the way so she's warning me. She's also giving me a *look* like she knows what I'm thinking, which she probably does but oh well . . .

"I'm glad for our friendship too," I said, "and honestly, I love hearing your stories. So go on telling me about Rose."

"Okay, so Rose was born right after Preacher and Lily Amaryllis moved to the Temple property. To give Lily Amaryllis credit, she adores Rose and wants to be a good mom. But Rose was ashamed of that horrible old silver Airstream they live in—"

"They *live* in that beat-up RV near the Temple? I saw it when I was scoping the place, but it didn't occur to me it's where they live."

"Well, it is. Preacher poured every cent into his crazy Temple and Bottle Wall, and Lily Amaryllis didn't push him to build a house. She doesn't push him to do anything at all, from what I hear. Just puts up with his nonsense and adores him, the same way she adores Rose. And she detested me because she thought I was a bad influence on her *blonde baby angel.*"

"You? A bad influence?"

"Yes, and she wasn't half wrong. I was a wild child, Mags. All of us were wild. Mom would take us flying, drop us off in St. Augustine or Crystal River to fend for ourselves until she came back to get us. Dad would let us sculpt and paint and weld, making god-awful messes while he worked on his art. He even let us climb on his scaffolding while he was painting that dome at Byzantium on the Boardwalk. Lily Amaryllis worried all the time about Rose being gone with us, finally put her foot down and forbade Rose to see me ever again."

"So she didn't? Rose didn't see you anymore, I mean?"

"Not much. She'd sneak when she could, but things got complicated when Michael got involved with Preacher, and we drifted apart.

We'd finished our tapas and cocktails by that time so Sterling was ready to leave, but I said no, let's stay and have dessert. I mean, I was loving Sterling's storytelling so much . . . okay, so maybe I was intrigued by a new dessert on the menu called *Grace Under Fire* (picture Baked Alaska topped with Cherries Jubilee and served *flambé*). In my defense, however, I didn't want to cut off Sterling's story about Michael getting tight with Preacher, so after we ordered dessert Sterling was glad to comply.

"You remember, Mags, that Michael gets obsessive about his current passion?"

"Right, you told me how obsessive he is about music."

"Well, before he got obsessed about music, he was trying out different religions, and a passion for Pentecostalism hit him when he saw Jesus on a pop tart."

"You're serious?"

"Totally. The pop-tart was brown-sugar cinnamon, and after Michael heated it in a toaster oven, the Jesus-face appeared in a pat of melted butter on top. Voila! He was off to the races."

"Sterling, that's way too funny."

"I know it is, but Michael wasn't amused. He framed the damn pop tart, kept it in his bedroom until George trashed it because it drew ants. In the meantime, Michael got so gung-ho about Preacher, he designed a website for the Temple called *Apocalypse Now and Then.*"

"Isn't that a strange website for a church?"

"Is it? For *The Holistic Temple of Apocalyptic Exaltation?*"

"No, I guess not."

"Anyway, Preacher was building his Bottle Wall around that time, so we heard all about it from Michael. Also heard about the Glory Hole. Preacher thinks we don't know he uses it to spy on us, but of course we know."

"I saw the Glory Hole when I scoped out the Temple property. Geno told me to look for it, so I did. It's a pass-through in the Bottle Wall, around back."

"And did you notice the stone? A big block of coquina cut in the shape of a wheel?"

"Yes, now that you mention it. The stone was pushed to the side of the pass-through, leaning up against the wall. So they roll it to block the Glory Hole, and to open it up? And . . . oh no. Are you telling me what I think you're telling me?"

"Afraid so. I never attended any of their so-called 'services' but Rose had to go, couldn't get out of it no matter how hard she tried. She said Preacher started off every sermon with his mantra: *Who among us shall roll away the stone and reveal the treasure?*"

"Glory, hallelujah."

"Amen."

We stopped talking at that point because the three Graces arrived with the extensive paraphernalia necessary for *Grace Under Fire*. Talk about *performance art* and a feast for the eye! I sat spellbound while the confectionary creation in the center of our table took shape.

First Princess unmolded the cake-layer base and ice cream topper for the mountain. Then while Mazie set in place a circular moat around it, Mary Fuller caramelized cherries in a big brass pan (butter chunks, a sugar-cinnamon-vanilla mixture, lemon zest, cherry liqueur). Thus, in a matter of minutes, a miniature Mount Fuji took shape: fluffy meringue swirled to a peak, circled by a moat of cherries in brandy—then the moat and the meringuey mountain itself set aflame.

Mesmerized, I watched the red-orange flames leap high before diminishing, burning to blue, then nothing. *The beginning and the end, fire and ice,* I mused. *I could write the story of my life in fire and ice. They're my nemeses . . . but ice came first, black ice lurking . . . burning like fire . . . a prophetic paradox . . .*

"Earth to Mags! You can come back now, Mags. There's no fire, no ice in our vicinity. Your nemeses are rendered impotent, in other words, while we're in thrall to our dessert. *Which you insisted we order, by the way.*"

"Dammit, Sterling! You went inside my head again!"

"A necessity at the moment because you chose to 'go walkabout,' as you call it, while we're still eating. Look, your Alaska's melting, and your Cherries are cold."

"Oh. Sorry. I must've been distracted."

Walking home that night, I was still thinking about the stories Sterling told during dinner. They were great stories, she was in a storytelling mood, yet something was wrong.

I mean, why isn't she interested in the obvious connections between the Lighthouse and the Genius House? Further, she doesn't seem to know the legends surrounding the Genius House itself while I, on the other hand, am fascinated by the house and its history. Not to mention, of course, that I'm supposedly writing a book about it!

As we all know, legends can have more than one version, but the more I thought about the Genius House, the more I wanted to know the "official" version. That's why, bright and early the next morning, I walked over to the City Island Library where Booker's the Chief Archivist (she's an authority on the history of Volusia County, works with all the county historical societies). Booker was glad to fill me in, and here's a summary of what she told me:

There were only two survivors when a treasure ship sank off Ponce Inlet in the early 1900s: the captain of the ship and a priest who laid a curse on the treasure. The priest was never heard from again, but the captain used his ill-gotten swag to build a huge beachfront house known then as "John's Castle." During the Roaring Twenties, John's Castle was the Playboy Mansion of its time and place. Once the Great Depression hit, however, the captain disappeared, and the empty house fell into disrepair.

Fast-forward to the mid-1960's, when the Town Council of Ponce Inlet hired a psychic to investigate complaints about eerie lights and strange music emanating from a big old house on the beach. The Council fully expected a "don't-be-silly" report from the psychic, who was a dead ringer for Eleanor Roosevelt and projected a no-nonsense persona. Imagine their surprise when, after a full week of on-site habitation and exploration, she reported to the Council that Irish Fairies did indeed inhabit the house and grounds.

Then she disappeared.

The Council members were flummoxed, scared to death that property values would plummet if word got out about the psychic's findings. Finally, a Councilman by the name of Roswell Booty wrote up a fake report claiming "unsubstantiated rumors" about the old house. Because the Council didn't want any mention of fairies in their "official" report, though, Booty opted for genii—which is the plural of genius. Before long, ipso facto, John's Castle became enshrined in the folklore of Volusia County as "The Genius House."

Like I said, this is the "official" version. If you're curious and want to examine any of the old books or records for yourself, just make an appointment with Booker at the City Island Library. She'll be glad to help you out.

BIKETOBERFEST

I was also up bright and early on Saturday because I was looking forward to my monthly hair appointment at Christine's Cottage. I need regular, expert color treatments on my hair because I'm prematurely gray and because—okay, so maybe I'm not *prematurely* gray, exactly, but who's checking? Anyway, I love the ambiance at her little salon—black and white décor, your choice of wine or coffee, catch-ups on local gossip.

After settling back for my haircut and blow-dry, I was ready to chat with Christine. "So," I said, "do you have any special gigs coming up? Any shows or performances?"

"Just a wedding, but it's a monster. We're already practicing with hairstyles, and I *hate* what they're asking me to do."

"Like what?"

"Like threading lilies of the valley in the bridesmaids' hairdos. The flowers are gorgeous when the florist delivers them, but they don't last. I practiced on one of the bridesmaids yesterday, and it was an unqualified disaster. After I worked in a hundred dollars' worth of wilted lily stems, she looked like she had a headful of white bird poo."

"So what do you do, when something like that happens?"

"Try again. One more time, anyway. The bridesmaid will be here in the morning for Session Number Two, along with the bride and her mother, to critique the result. If it turns out to be another disaster, I may resign on the spot."

"Did the bride's mother sit in on Disaster Number One?"

"No, and I'm not looking forward to meeting her tomorrow. Everyone says she's loud and pushy, one of those controlling Greek matriarchs. I think her name's Gigi."

"Gigi? Is the bride's name Galatea, by any chance?"

"It is. Do you know her? Know them?"

"Nope, just heard some stories."

Back in my car and driving, I kept thinking about the wedding. So, I said to myself, Galatea's getting married? Christine said she didn't know the name of the groom-to-be, just that this matchup's a big deal in the Greek community. But surely if Prax is the bridegroom, Sterling would've told me about it. Unless she doesn't know. But that wouldn't make sense because she and Michael are close, aren't they?

When I got home, still thinking about lilies of the valley and "White Coral Bells," I looked out my big east window toward the park to see if Cassandra might be there, performing or just hanging out. She wasn't, but Diff was there with Phyllo on his shoulder as usual. I was still standing by the window when I saw Phyllo leap off Diff's shoulder and go streaking toward the seawall where a hunky young guy was walking a Doberman. How'd that happen? I wondered. Diff keeps Phyllo on a leash, so where's the leash and why didn't it restrain the ferret? Okay, there goes Diff and I think he's calling to Phyllo ...

What? Omigod, that Doberman'll kill Phyllo unless Diff can catch up with Phyllo and grab him. Damn, Diff runs pretty well for an old guy. Yes! C'mon, Diff, you can catch Phyllo. You can ... Oh no, shit! *Shit!* Phyllo's a goner; he's mangled meat for sure except ... except Phyllo won the face off with the Doberman. Scared the Doberman so thoroughly, in fact, the dog slunk away with his tail between his legs while the hunky young guy made an insulting hand signal at Diff.

I was relieved to see Phyllo nestle himself back on Diff's shoulder, but I was puzzled because I remembered that day not long ago when Diff showed up suddenly, peering at me through the passenger-side window of my car. Didn't he say he was looking for Phyllo who'd been chased by a cat? And didn't Diff say the ferret gets nervous when he's scared? I was sure that's what Diff said, but now it didn't make sense. Because a ferret that can dominate a Doberman can sure as hell handle a cat.

Any cat. Not only that. Phyllo went after the Doberman, not vice versa. Which is a pretty gutsy thing to do.

Remembering the way the ferret flew off Diff's shoulder and cornered the dog at the seawall, I was getting pissed off at Diff and wanting to confront him about lying to me. That's when I had an epiphany. Oh my God, I thought. I understand. That day in the alley behind Geno's store, Diff was doing guard duty. He and Phyllo were watching out for me. It's just like Sterling says, Archies are on the lookout. I was all set to go down to the park and give Diff a big hug when Sterling called. "Mags? Are you busy tomorrow?"

"Not really. What's up?"

"I want to go to a bike parade and rally in DeLand, but I don't want to take the Suburban. Could you drive?"

"Sure thing. Agatha needs some highway exercise, and she loves the drive from Daytona to DeLand. So do I, for that matter." I'd noticed all the bikers in town, of course, because you can't *not* notice them when they're roaring up and down the street in front of your apartment. Plus I knew Biketoberfest was getting underway because Geno hired in some extra help at the coffee shop and the model train depot.

By the time I went back to my big east window and looked out, I saw lots of bikers but no Diff and no Phyllo. Oh well, I thought, next time I see Diff, I'll give him that hug.

Geno loves bikers because they spend money at his store, but also because they're nice people. "Mags," he said to me when I stopped in the next morning for coffee, "bikers get a bad rep, and they don't deserve it. All that hoohah about the One Percent might be true, but—"

"The One Percent?"

"Yeah, or maybe they call themselves the One Percenters. Meaning out of thousands of bikers, it's only one percent that cause trouble."

"And I bet they're the ones with scary gang names? Like Hell's Angels and Pagans?"

"Exactly. Those guys are bad news. Wally was tellin' me—"

"Wally? How does Wally know about biker gangs?"

"I dunno. How does Wally know about anything? You're his cousin, you tell me."

"You're right, Geno, sorry I interrupted. So Wally was saying?"

"So Wally said he was at the Cabbage Patch. You know, the biker bar over in Samsula where they have coleslaw wrestling—"

"What? Wally was at the Cabbage Patch to watch *coleslaw wrestling?*"

"Mags, if you keep interruptin' me I'm gonna charge you for all those biscotti you're dunking, because you're scarfing down my inventory."

"Got it. I will zip my lip. And while I'm zipping I'll have just one more *biscotto*, and aren't you impressed that I know the singular term as well as the plural?"

"Yeah, right. I am blown away." Then Geno finished telling me about Wally's sojourn at the Cabbage Patch when Wally and his friend Cedric were out for a ride, exercising their bikes. (Wally doesn't drive his BMW cars, but he loves driving his BMW bike.) It was last year, Geno said, and the locals were concerned because a few Pagans showed up for Bike Week.

So Cedric met up with his posse at the Cabbage Patch (they were there to restore the peace in case trouble erupted), and that's when Wally got friendly with one of the Pagans, the one called Socrates. So friendly, in fact, that Socrates gave Wally a couple of patches for his leather bike jacket. "Yeah,"

Geno explained, "Wally loved the official Pagan patch because it has a fire god on it. Name's Stuart and he's from Up North somewhere."

"A fire god named Stuart from Up North?"

"That's what Wally said. He showed the patch to me, and it definitely had a guy on it with a flaming sword."

"Could the guy's name be *Surtr*? And could he be the *Norse* fire god?"

"Could be. Anyway, Socrates gave Wally two other Pagan patches. One said ARGO and the other one said NUNYA, which lots of Pagans have for tattoos to show they're serious. So Wally was all set to put the patches on his jacket when Cedric said he better not, Socrates was playing a joke on him. But Wally wouldn't listen, got the patches sewn on his jacket right away. And next day at the Cabbage Patch, the Pagans were all set to initiate Wally into the club, kind of like a mascot."

"Initiate him? That sounds ominous."

"Yeah, they were gonna give him ARGO and NUNYA tattoos, until Socrates called a halt to it." Geno started laughing then and choked. After he stopped coughing and sneezing, he said, "Cedric, he busted a gut laughing, said it was the only time he ever knew more about something than Wally did."

"So are you going to tell me?"

"Tell you what?" Geno was giving me *a look* over his glasses, like he knew the punchline, and I didn't, so too bad for me. "Geno! Don't be an asshole. What do ARGO and NUNYA stand for? *Tell* me!"

"Yeah, okay. So ARGO means *Ar Go Fuck Yourself* and NUNYA means *Nun'Ya Fuckin' Business.* I thought Wally'd be pissed off about the patches, but he thinks they're funny. Says he'll keep them on his jacket to show he's a serious biker dude."

Sterling and I laughed all the way to DeLand. First I told her about Wally and Socrates at the Cabbage Patch, then we traded Wally stories back and forth. When we got to town, I found a place to park just off the Boulevard, and we joined the sidewalk crowd to watch the bike parade. "Tell me more about Cedric," Sterling said. "Seems like a strange name for a biker."

"Cedric's grandfather started it. He's a local legend, formed a biker posse to keep the peace and called himself Cedric the Saxon. Then Cedric's dad assumed the mantle, so to speak, and now it's been passed to the third generation."

"So what's Cedric's real name?"

"Ralph Palfer. He's the registrar at Stetson. That's where he and Casey got to be friends, and now they ride together a lot." At that point we knew the bikers were close because we had to yell at each other to be heard. "Look, Mags," Sterling said, "there's Casey now, on his blue bike behind Wally! And there's Talisman, on the yellow three-wheeler!"

"Omigod, it sure is. She told me Casey was designing a motorcycle for her. She rolls into it from the back in her wheelchair and uses state-of-the-art hand controls to drive it." Talisman saw us and pumped her fist. "Yo, Talisman!" I hollered. "You go, girl!"

I poked Sterling then and pointed at a massive silver bike with a sidecar. "There he is. See the guy wearing chain mail and a metal helmet with a spike on top? That's Cedric."

"Who's he with? The woman riding in his sidecar, I mean."

"That's his wife Nancy. She calls herself Lady Sennacherib, and she makes the chain mail duds they're wearing. She crochets chain mail out of wire instead of yarn, then sells whole suits of it on the Internet."

Sterling and I clapped and hooted while our friends passed by, but once they rode away from us down the Boulevard I insisted we head for Twig's Deli. Not that I had a hidden agenda or anything, except Twig's Reuben sandwiches are to die for. Once we got settled at Twig's with the rumble of bikes in the distance, Sterling talked nonstop because she was pissed off at Rose for flirting with Casey. "I can't believe she used to be my best friend," Sterling said, "but that was when she was still Red's girlfriend."

"Rose was *Red's* girlfriend?"

"Yep, they were a couple before Red got infatuated with Deirdre and dumped Rose. Then Rose started stalking Red and pleading with me to put in a good word for her, which was bad enough until it got worse when Uncle Billy scared Rose to death. After that, Rose boycotted us and started plotting to steal Casey from me."

"Wait, back up. You said Uncle Billy scared Rose to death?"

"Sure did. It happened after Red fell in love with Deirdre at that beach party and told Rose to get lost. One afternoon Rose parked Preacher's old junker car up the road and hid in the ice plant, hoping to waylay Red and plead with him to take her back. But she didn't know Uncle Billy was also hiding in the ice plant with a garden rake, pretending he was Manannán mac Lir, the Celtic god of the sea. When he saw Rose—"

"Um Sterling, you're done? Can I have your fries?"

"Help yourself. They're kinda greasy, though."

"Not if you squirt lots of ketchup on them. So Uncle Billy was hiding in the ice plant?"

"Yep, and when he saw Rose burrowing down near him, he figured she was a nymph sent to seduce him. But when an elderly bare-chested Poseidon rose from the dunes, brandishing his trident, Rose freaked. She jumped in Preacher's junker and burned rubber getting out of there. Uncle Billy was so insulted, he ran out in the road, shaking his rake and hollering, *An' where's she goin', like a bean-sidhe flyin' to the Hellmouth Door?* He kept on yelling it, over and over."

"Sterling," I said, "that's hilarious! You should write a book!"

"That's why we have *you*, Mags. Did you forget?"

"Of course not! How could I forget? I have tons of notes, but notes aren't a book. I'm still listening, thinking, planning. So I guess I don't consider that I'm writing our book yet."

"Well, if you include Uncle-Billy-as-Poseidon, make sure you mention the codpiece."

"The *codpiece*?"

"It's Michael's old hairpiece, the party-store wig he bought after he shaved his head but still needed to impersonate Dad at the college."

"Oh, right, you told me the plan, and I still think it's genius, having Michael dress like your dad and show up at the college once in a while. And you told me Christine made Michael a really good wig, but I didn't know Uncle Billy got the old ratty one."

"Well he did, and he loves it. Sometimes he wears it on his head, but other times he makes a codpiece out of it with George's bobby pins. Says it makes him feel like Cúchulain, another one of his heroes. The ancient Celts wore garments made from animal skins, you know, and Michael's old wig does look kind of shaggy, like it came from a goat."

"Whoa, that's *trivia obscurata* for sure, isn't it? That the ancient Celts wore garments made from animal skins, I mean. Especially codpieces."

THE ANSWER'S 42

It was time for me to get the lowdown about Florean evolution from Jengu, the same way I learned about Neanders from Datta—except we were caucusing in the Conference Room instead of Jengu's cottage. When I asked why, Sterling blew me off, said something vague about Jengu "not being much of a housekeeper."

Waiting for Kells to show up with Jengu, Sterling and I were both in foul moods. I was ticked off because my supposedly "rectified" air conditioner was on the fritz, and my apartment was so hot you could fry eggs, and Sterling was clearly not happy but wouldn't say why. "I'll get over it Mags, just give it a rest—" Then she got cut off when an Irish Setter ran in the door of the Conference Room, shook herself all over us and the floor, then bounded back out again.

"Ewww!" Sterling hollered, "I'm all damp and sticky!" while she got a broom and started sweeping sand out the door. "I didn't know you have a dog," I said.

"I don't have a dog," Sterling said. "She's Red's dog."

"What's her name?"

"Her name's Sorrow. It's a long story."

"A dog's name is a long story?"

"Oh, all right. Her name started out as Deirdre. Red got her when he fell in love with the real Deirdre, said she (the dog) is a purebred just like Deirdre of the Sorrows, his beloved Celtic Goddess. But when the real Deirdre made it clear to Red that she was not the least bit interested in becoming romantically involved with him, Red started calling her (the dog) Dumbitch. None of us wanted a dog named Dumbitch, and we were sick and tired of listening to Red moan about the real Deirdre, so we told him either give the dog a decent name, or we'll put her up for adoption. That's when he named her (the dog) Sorrow."

"You're absolutely right," I said. "I'd never guess a dog's name could be such a long story." Sterling finished sweeping, but she stopped for a minute before closing the door. "Look," she said, pointing down toward the beach, "there's Jengu now, with Sorrow. When Red quit paying attention to Sorrow, Jengu adopted her. He plays frisbee with her, takes her for rides on his board if the surf's low, taught her to dig for mole crabs in the wash zone when the tide's going out."

I joined her then at the door, both of us engrossed in a truly arresting vision, as if Jengu and Sorrow were figures in a watercolor beachscape. I assumed that earlier they'd been running, jumping, twirling about, but now they were resting quietly at the juncture of sea and sand. Motionless there, they seemed painted with the same brush: Jengu and Sorrow, the Florean and the Irish Setter—both the vivid red-gold color of a setting sun.

I need to remember this vision, I thought to myself. It could be a frontispiece, maybe one of the color plates in our book.

While Sterling went to put away her broom and wash her hands, I settled myself at the big table in the Conference Room and realized there was no sign of victuals, not even coffee. I decided not to mention my distress to Sterling, though, because I saw no sign that her mood had improved. At that point she joined me at the table while Kells walked in the big door with

Jengu, and I noticed that even though he'd donned a Hawaiian shirt and huaraches, his beard was full of sand. It was obvious, in other words, that he'd been beachin' it until just a few minutes ago.

"Howdy, Mags," he said to me and grinned. "Are you still feeling gnarlacious, being as you're the one who found Sterling's ring?"

"You bet, Jengu," I said, "and by the way, I really appreciate that you educated me about Florida's freshwater springs. I'll never take them for granted again."

"Frabjous," he said. "And you're getting more education today? A lesson called *Who's Jengu and Why Do We Care?* Or something like that?"

"Something like that," I said, laughing, but I was the only one. Kells looked like a thundercloud, and Sterling made a dismissive hand gesture at Jengu. "O-*kay*, then," Jengu said, "I'm outta here. Kells, you and Sterling give Mags the background scoop, and I'll be back in an hour to answer questions."

"Don't forget to come back!" Kells called after him, but Jengu was out the door and gone.

Uncomfortable silence ensued, so I figured it was up to me to start our discussion. "You know what, Ladies? I've come prepared, because I get it about Floreans evolving to live in water as well as on land. After Jengu went cave-diving at Blue Spring without a tank or a light, I figured he must have a swim bladder and gills, plus an ability to bioluminesce. And remember when we three were out on the dune walk and saw the mound-creature coming toward us from the ocean? Two heads popped up when you called to it—sorry, called to *them*. I recognized Jengu as one of the heads, but the other one was multi-colored. So that must've been one of Jengu's Florean buddies, flashing bioluminescence?"

"No," Kells said, "the other head belonged to Squiggs, who isn't a Florean."

"Squiggs? I've been wondering about Squiggs. Sterling told me Squiggs taught Jengu to ride underwater currents, but he's not a Florean?"

"No," Sterling said. "Squiggs is to Jengu as Mercedes is to Datta. Squiggs is a cuttlefish."

Excuse me? Squiggs is a *cuttlefish*? I'm no dummy, I saw that PBS special about cuttlefish, how they have pixels in their skin that change color and how they can shape-shift. Oh, wow. So there they'd be, Jengu frolicking in the depths with his best bud, Squiggs the cuttlefish. Jengu'd be glowing, and Squiggs would be pixellating a technicolor slide show all over his body while he shapeshifted into a thorny coral.

Then I had a horrible thought. A cuttlefish is like a squid, like the fried calamari appetizer at Three Graces. Omigod. How can I ever eat fried calamari again? It'd be like eating barbecued dog paws. Or deep-fried cat tenders . . .

"Mags? *Mags!*" Sterling was trying to get my attention.

"Sorry, sorry, I was trying to get my head around the cuttlefish idea. It's back to synergetic species again? Floreans developed a synergy with cuttlefish?"

"That's exactly right," Sterling said, "but there was an unexpected blip in Florean evolution when they discovered fendelin. Fendelin's a powerful hallucinogen to creatures with gills. That day when you sprained your ankle, Jengu and Squiggs were carrying a pile of kelp back to the cottage because Jengu hoped he'd find some fendelin weed in it."

"Whoa. So Floreans are stoners?"

"No and yes. No, because fendelin's mind-blowing potential enabled Floreans to develop psychic powers, but yes, because they use it as a tranquilizer as well. Especially when they're stressed out, the way Jengu's been since Jitsu went missing."

"Not to change the subject," I said, "but this stuff about the Floreans is just like the Neanders."

"Sorry," Kells said. "I'm not following. What do you mean?"

"I mean all those creature-sightings. If Sasquatch and Bigfoot and the Abominable Snowman were really Neanders, then it must be the same with Mermaids and Mermen, Sirens and Selkies. The myths must have started with Florean-sightings."

"You're not wrong, Mags," Kells answered. "As we Boskops have been saying for ages, biology *is* mythology. And vice versa."

I'd like to report that we had a productive session, but that's not what happened. Sterling's mood got worse instead of better, and Kells stayed pissed off because Jengu bailed on us, so we decided to break while Kells went to find Jengu and chew him out. Sterling was obviously restless. "Too bad we don't have time go to the gym. I could sure wear off some frustration whacking a racquetball around."

"Sterling," I said, "I appreciate that you're willing to play racquetball with me, but I *know* I'm no competition for you. I'm just a duffer, and I get worn out really fast."

"Stop apologizing, Mags. I like the way you play racquetball."

"Thanks, but that's not possible. Comparing the way I play with the way you play is like comparing apples and oranges. Better yet, it's like comparing me walking around the block while you're winning the Boston Marathon."

"I'm not talking about skill or energy, Mags, I'm talking about strategy."

"Strategy? Like when I slam into the wall and try not to fall down? Or when I recover gracefully after hitting myself with my own racquet?'

"No, Mags," Sterling laughed, "I'm talking about the way you envision the game, just trading serves and not keeping score. Enjoying the process but not worrying about winning or losing. What you're doing is genius: taking a finite game and transforming it into an infinite game."

"Well good for me, except I didn't know that's what I do. I mean, I wasn't thinking theoretically in terms of finite versus infinite. Sounds like a course in advanced mathematics."

"Mags, it's a crucial concept. In an infinite game you play as hard as you can because you enjoy playing. You get in the zone; you experience *flow*. You're a Player, in other words, but never a Winner or a Loser. There's no Black Belt, no Olympic Medal, no Superbowl Ring. Just personal satisfaction."

"Oh."

"Think about Tetris. It's the classic example of an infinite game. When you're playing Tetris you just keep on, keeping on."

"Yes, *but*," I said. "Some people are clearly better than others at Tetris. I was watching Christopher play it on my vintage Game Boy, and those blocks were falling like rain. I'll never be as good at Tetris as he is, so doesn't that mean he wins?"

"Mags, don't be dense. It's all about how you play."

"Okay, I'll stop being dense. But is Game Theory really a life-and-death issue?"

"Game Theory's exactly what the Intervention's about and yes, it *will* be a life-and-death issue. The rules will seem brutal because they have to be, but it's the only way to insure that the Game of Life on this planet, for all species including ours, goes on." Sterling wasn't laughing and neither was I. Plus I was getting pissed off because once again, she was talking circles around me. "Sterling," I said, "it's high time you put me on your wave-length. I mean, you talk endlessly about *launching a global plan*. When? Where? How? When do I get The Big Picture?"

"Mags, it's not up to me. Kells has to be the one. When she thinks you're ready for details, she'll tell you. In the meantime, think about what you *do* know. You know we call the Intervention *Pay the Piper*, right?"

"So?"

"So, we didn't just pull it out of thin air. Think about the story."

"The folk tale? *The Pied Piper of Hamelin?*"

"That's it."

"Okay, so the Pied Piper said he could solve the town's rat problem, but he expected to be paid. The Mayor agreed and when the Piper started tootling, the rats joined his parade—all the way to the river where the entire rat brigade drowned."

"And then?"

"The Piper demanded his money, but the Town Council reneged on their deal, so the Piper retaliated. He started tootling and marching again, but this time the township's children followed him and drowned in the river, just like the rats." We were both quiet for a few minutes, until I said out loud what I was thinking. "That story's really brutal."

"Sure is."

"And the Intervention will be just as brutal?"

"In some ways, yes. There's been too much hubris, too much greed. Not enough concern for the planet and for other people and for other species."

"So it's time to pay the Piper."

"Exactly. Once we launch the Intervention, the smartest among us will have incentives to innovate and to put reforms into action. It won't be easy, and it won't be fun. But if we're lucky, if we get a few breaks, we'll gain time to avert disaster—whether environmental or nuclear."

"It always gets back to the whimper or the bang, doesn't it?"

"Absolutely. And don't forget the flour beetles."

"Believe me, there is *no* way I could forget those flour beetles."

"Good. If Pay the Piper succeeds, we can avoid the whimper *and* the bang while we maintain life on Our Blue Gaia as the ultimate infinite game."

Kells finally came back, said she'd dusted Jengu's sorry butt, so where were we? "Well, you were gone for quite a while," I said, "and Sterling told me a lot about Pay the Piper, and I'm wondering how in the world one Piper will manage—"

"Actually, Mags," Sterling broke in, "it's not one Piper, it's 42 Pipers. I'll be one, and there'll be 41 others."

"Excuse me? Why 42?"

"Because 42's the God number. Remember? It answers the Ultimate Question of Life, the Universe, and Everything. The answer's 42."

"Excuse me? You're founding a new world order on *The Hitchhiker's Guide to the Galaxy?*"

"Why not? It's no crazier than the Book of Mormon, lots more fun than the Communist Manifesto, and way less violent than the Bible. And you remember what Kells said about our so-called 'global village,' don't you? Sapients simply can't handle globalism?"

"How could I forget? She said, um . . . ." I hesitated because I rememberd Kells's words only too well, and it seemed to me she'd been brutally blunt and insulting. "I remember what I said, Mags," Kells broke in, "because there's no point in mincing words. I said Sapients are *a planetary hodgepodge of warrior states*, and you didn't disagree."

"No, I didn't disagree, but . . ."

Sterling chimed in then, obviously sensing my discomfort. "Anyway, Mags, the Intervention will dissolve present national boundaries and establish new 'regions': forty-two of them, to be exact. My region—or rather, *our* region—will be Number Thirteen."

If I ever needed to go walkabout, I needed to at that moment. I mean, I've laughed my way through Douglas Adams's novel more than once, but I'm not sure it's a valid blueprint for a new world order . . . Omigod, wait a minute. Early on, when Sterling was talking about our Book, our Manifesto, she said *it begins with a house*. That's the way *The Hitchhiker's Guide* starts. The prologue says *it's the story of a book* and *it begins with a house* . . . I *knew* Sterling was sending me a message when she said that, but I didn't get it.

Uh oh, Kells was talking so it was time for me to zone back in. "—in broad terms Pay the Piper's pretty simple: Buy time for the planet while Pipers sign up worker-Sapients to be environmental activists and political organizers. The way we'll do it is to mobilize the Whimperers (afraid the planet is slowly dying) and the Bangers (afraid we're heading for a nuclear holocaust)."

"The Whimperers and the Bangers," I said admiringly. "I love it."

"At that point," Sterling cut in, "we'll have a global network."

"Like the United Nations?"

"No, it'll be a global *network*, but it won't be a single *body*. Small groups of Whimperers and Bangers will work in different regions."

"But how'll you find them? The Whimperers and the Bangers, I mean."

"They'll hear the Pipers," Kells said. "They'll come to us."

"It sounds like a fairy tale."

"Well, it's not," Sterling said. "It's real, it's deadly serious, and we'll work through the Groupies. I told you about them, didn't I? The Lysistrata Ladies and the Gamer Gurus and the Trader Joes?"

Big sigh from me. "Sterling, you *know* you didn't tell me—"

KNOCK. KNOCK. Sterling got up and opened an inner door, talked to someone I couldn't see, and came back to the table saying it was time to take a break. "Mags," Kells said, standing up and heading for the doorway, "organizing the Groupies isn't at the top of our to-do list. Right now we're concentrating on training 42 Pipers so we can launch the Intervention."

"And *now*," Sterling said again, "it's time for a break."

"I'll be right there," I said. "I just need a minute."

Which was emphatically not true. I needed lots of minutes . . . hundreds of minutes . . . thousands of minutes. Try though they might to convince me, this so-called Intervention of theirs sounded impossible. I get it, I said to myself, that saving the planet's all about power and who has it. But redistributing power on a global scale's easier said than . . .

Wait. That's when I remembered the static. Squiffy Static. Randomized static that knocks out phones, TV, Internet, satellite signals. Static they can turn on and off. I could hear Sterling calling me from an adjoining room, but I couldn't stop thinking. If the Pipers can unleash localized disturbances in the electromagnetic field, they can disrupt global communication and bring the planet's Power Elite to a grinding halt without . . .

"*Mags!*" Sterling was standing in the doorway, glaring at me. "We're waiting for you. Let's take a break."

I was still thinking like crazy but glad to adjourn for afternoon tea, served by an English Butler and a French Maid. I held my tongue until the servers left. Then:

"Okay, you two, what the hell's going on? Are you telling me you engineered a couple of biobots to be *servants*? And you get your jollies by dressing them up in cutesy costumes? All morning long I've heard nothing but doom-and-gloom predictions. *The world's coming to an end! We have to save the planet!* And in the meantime you use your fabulous technology to conjure up a fancy afternoon tea?"

No comment from Kells or Sterling, who were obviously enjoying my outburst. "Hmm." Me, of course, looking at the tea tray. "And by the way, what *is* this? It looks delicious."

"First things first," Sterling said. "You're about to enjoy Irish Lace Cookies with your Gooseberry Fool, and you're right, it's all delicious. *And* they're George's own recipes."

"Wow, I had no idea Gooseberry Fool's a food. I thought it was just a girl band. The one that played at Pigs Will Fly, remember?"

"Of course we remember, Mags," Sterling said. "That's why we thought you'd enjoy this. And the Irish Lace Cookies have a distinctive tang because they're sprinkled with Celtic Sea Salt. George always takes some with her when she and Uncle Billy travel, wouldn't use any other brand."

"Okay, I'm impressed," I said, "but that doesn't explain the Archies. I hope you won't try to claim *English Butler* and *French Maid* are Archetypes."

"Of course not," Kells said, "the butler and the maid are Tricksters—our Boskop engineers' great success story in biological robotics. Tricksters are shapeshifters so they have fluid identities, like professional actors who get to choose their roles."

"It's true, Mags," Sterling cut in. "The Tricksters love to conspire with us. Like now. They get a kick out of the English Butler and French Maid bits. It's a game to them. These two Archies have been with us longer than any of the others, and they'll be with us when we launch the Intervention. The next time you see them, in fact, the Maid may be Eleanor Roosevelt and the Butler may be Captain John. Or vice versa."

At that point I was happy to concentrate on the cookies and Gooseberry Fool (it's a cross between syllabub and ice cream). I did have a question, though, about something that'd been bugging me ever since I got introduced to the Tutors. "Kells," I said, "when I first met you and Datta and Jengu, you talked to me in a language that had music and color. What's the language called? And how come I could understand it?"

"It's called Hummalingus, the protolanguage your paleo-linguists are always agonizing about. It's innate and it's natural. Millennia ago, all hominins were synaesthetes. Not only did we have perfect pitch and perfect rhythm, we could also see music and hear color. It was unfortunate that Sapients got so busy filling their minds with plots and hierarchies and get-rich-quick schemes that their innate linguistic abilities diminished. It happened slowly, but it did happen. You, Mags, are one of the few Sapients who can still comprehend hummalingus."

"And you too, Sterling?"

"I understand it, Mags," Sterling said, "but I can't speak it well. It may be that none of us can regain real fluency. I keep trying, but I'm not good at it. Not yet, anyway."

"So," I said to Kells, "can you say something in Hummalingus for me? Now?" Kells nodded, smiled, and sang-talked a Lyrical

Garden she'd loved long ago, with a patch of red poppies and bright green asparagus fern gleaming in sunlight.

"Do you want another example?" (Kells, talking in English.)

When I nodded yes, Kells smiled again and commenced a Legend of Lost Love, starting with a multi-hued obbligato that soared like snowy white cranes through clouds backlit by the setting sun. Cirrus clouds billowed like layers of silk, pink then peach then orange, then became the gown of a woman who walked toward us through a field of blue grass before pirouetting, turning, running away, disappearing into a vanishing point—one silver point that hung and shimmered like a far-away star in a midnight blue wash.

Gulp. For a few moments, I'd lived inside a Maxfield Parrish painting.

Kells explained that Hummalingus remains the *lingua franca* for all three NEFBO Tribes, even though each Tribe also crafted its own language. "So your Boskop language is different from Datta's Neander language and Jengu's Florean language?"

"Correct."

"How's your Boskop language different?"

"Well, you already know that Boskops appropriated subterranean areas as our post-diaspora domain, so use your imagination. Picture us in the underground. Imagine how we'd have to adapt and how we'd communicate." It was obvious I wasn't getting a picture, so Kells went on. "Mags, while Boskops were exploring the subterranean areas of Our Blue Gaia, we were making friends with bats and rats and crafting a communal language that drew upon the talents of all three species."

At that point I embarrassed myself, but I couldn't help it. "*Ewwww!*" I exploded. "You talk to bats and rats? You're kidding, right?" Wrong. Kells wasn't kidding, and she was annoyed with me for assuming that she was. "Mags," she said, "I'll not even *tell* you what Boskops learned from bats and rats because you're obviously not ready for it. I can tell you one thing, though. Laughter's a crucial element of the Boskop language, *and* it's essential for brain-to-brain communication. So when we were learning our new environment, Boskops taught bats to laugh."

"Sorry, Kells. Really, I'm sorry to be so dense. So, umm, did you . . . um, did your people also teach *rats* to laugh?"

"No, rats already knew how. They've been laughing at us for millennia."

MYSTICAL GEOMETRY

I didn't sleep well that night, probably because my mind kept racing all over creation, and no wonder! Finally, I gave up, got up, made some coffee, and began working on *The Porridge of Dorian Gray*. I fully expected Ford to call and raise holy hell because I hadn't delivered the book yet, and I was right—my phone started squawking just after sunrise. Once more, twice more, three times more. By then I was grinding my teeth because I knew it'd go on squawking at off-kilter 15-minute intervals until I answered.

This is part of the game Ford and I play. He's like Sheldon knocking on Penny's door—just keeps on, keeping on, until it drives you crazy. I've told Ford a million times I hate it, but he does it anyway. Finally, I couldn't stand it anymore. "Ford, god-dammit, what do you want?"

"I want a book, Mags. In case you forgot, you're behind on your contract. And if you insist on writing the Irish Cabbage-and-Potatoes book—which I predict will be a spectacular failure, by the way—can you please do the decent thing and deliver it in time to stock the shelves for St. Patrick's Day? And not only that, what's with the twee title? *The Porridge of Dorian Gray?* Sounds like ad for oatmeal."

"Our 'twee' title, Ford, as you so humorlessly describe it, is a literary allusion. It's also a pun on the title of Oscar Wilde's only novel—from which our well-read target demographic will get quite a giggle because they'll remember that Wilde's novel was scandalous in its time, a real cause célèbre."

"Well ex-*cuse me*, Professor Punster. I will anxiously await such forthcoming classics as *The Adventures of Harry Potroast* and *The Poems of Ezra Poundcake.*"

"Yeah yeah, Ford, you shoulda' been a comedian. Listen, I'm not changing the title, and all I have to do to finish the Wilde book is add one fabulous authentic recipe, but—"

Damn, where's that Dublin Coddle recipe?

"—I'm working on another project right now too, it's—"

There it is, by the coffee maker. I flattened it out to dry after I tumped a mug of coffee all over it.

"—the opera I'm writing with Christopher."

"You're still writing that *opera?*"

"I told you about it, Ford. Remember?"

"Of course I remember, Mags. You asked me what I thought about writing an opera, and I asked how many Kitchen Table Books you can sell during Intermission. Which is relevant because—"

"Ford, hold on a minute, I think Christopher's knocking on my front door."

Christopher wasn't due until late afternoon, but I lied because the conversation with Ford was going nowhere. It wasn't just that, though. I wanted to examine the Coddle recipe because I'd noticed a palimpsest on it—an impression left by earlier writing. I hadn't seen it before but now that the paper was dry, coffee stains made the earlier writing visible.

"Mags? *Mags!*"

Hmm, that's strange. George told me the notepads are Uncle Billy's, but the palimpsest is in George's handwriting, same as the Coddle recipe . . .

"Mags, you better not cut me off!"

Beep.

After I turned off my phone, I tried every-which-way to decipher the ghostly writing, but I couldn't make it out—four lines, mostly illegible because the paper had disintegrated. There were two smudgy looking scribbles, too. Maybe drawings that got blurred? Shoot, I said to myself, I can't make it out. I see *tide* and *lost*, or maybe *loosed*? But what's that word in the third line? *conversion? convention?* No, it's co*nviction.*

Wait a minute . . . *tide, loosed, conviction.* Was George copying lines from "The Second Coming"? Why now and on a notepad? Uncle Billy wrote that poem a long time ago, while George was in a trance, doing automatic writing.

I knew I should forget about George's notepad scribbles, but I couldn't get the idea of automatic writing out of my head. It always fascinated me that George inspired Uncle Billy's *Vision*—with those intersecting, antithetical gyres—while she channelled spectral voices. Did she fake it? Some say yes, some say no, some say only at first. As to what I think, I've always been skeptical about that occultish stuff because—

BANG *CRASH!* "Mmfff! Oh no no no no NO NO!"

Someone was outside my front door, on the landing. "Who's out there?" I hollered. "Identify yourself!"

"OH OH OH-H-H . . . PIFFLE!"

Jeez Loueez, I thought, it's Wally. He's gotta be the only person on the planet who thinks Piffle's a curse word. Sure enough, when I jerked my front door open, I was greeted by the spectacle of Wally sprawled on the landing, smack on top of a tray of Styrofoam takeout containers and to-go coffees. I should probably also mention that he was lying face down on the tray, so when he raised his head to look at me, his glasses were smeared with powdered sugar and chocolate.

"I'm so sorry, Mags. I tripped coming out of the elevator, and now look at this mess!"

"No worries, Wally. Let's get you and the floor cleaned up, then go downstairs and have brunch at the coffeeshop. Too bad about the pastries, though. What are they? Or rather, what *were* they?"

"Pumpkin pasticcios, Geno's new Halloween confection. He says you're his taster, and he wants me to be a taster too."

After we settled ourselves in a booth at the coffeeshop Wally started in on a current passion—the Zen garden he's building at his house. (I told you about it, remember? He calls it his *Karesansui* garden, and it's underneath the trapezoid-pod at his house.) Anyway, I'd already decided I'd be a captive audience until Wally's ride back to DeLand showed up, so I might as well pick his brain about something *I'm* interested in. "Wally, excuse me for interrupting, but I'd love to know what you think about automatic writing."

"Automatic writing?"

"Sure, you know. It was popular in the 1920's when all that occultic stuff was in vogue. Personally, I always figured it was hogwash—"

"I'm shocked at you, Mags. How can you call Hermeticism hogwash?"

"I didn't say *Hermeticism's* hogwash, Wally. I said *automatic writing* is hogwash."

"I heard you correctly, Mags, but you can't pick and choose. Surely you know—"

Good move, Mags, my girl! Wally's good for the duration, so I can concentrate on Geno's yummy pumpkin pasticcios . . .

"—the occult practice of automatic script is subsumed in the Hermetic tradition, with philosophers ranging from St. Augustine to Ralph Waldo Emerson believing Hermes Trismegistus to be the most astute of pagan prophets. And not only philosophers—"

Damn, I should've known better. I mean, where's Wally's ride? For that matter, who drove him here this morning?

"—scientists admire him too. Isaac Newton, for example, believed the *Corpus Hermeticum* held the secret to influencing the forces of nature, and other scientists—"

Christopher's driving him back here this afternoon, something about Wally needing to go home for a break so he can work in his garden . . .

"—admire Hermes Trismegistus as well. I've often wondered, in fact, if Francis Crick's theory of Directed Panspermia was initially inspired by the *Corpus Hermeticum*—"

"Yo Mags! Wassup? Are you ready for Halloween?"

Thank the Stars! Once again I was saved by Wally's disinclination to get a driver's license. "Am I ready for Halloween? You bet, Casey. My Halloween ritual is watching *The Wizard of Oz* with Schrödy, sipping Rob Roys and OD'ing on candy corn."

"O-ka-a-ay. That sounds really . . . um . . . interesting."

Casey wasted no time herding Wally to his car, so after I waved goodbye and watched them drive away through Geno's front window, I headed back to my apartment to work. I couldn't stop laughing, though, about my conversation with Wally. Not that Wally tries to be funny, just that he's so intense. Before I opened the floodgates and made the comment about automatic writing being hogwash, he'd gone on and on about his Zen garden and how he's designing it on the dictates of mystical geometry . . .

Oh shoot, that reminds me: I promised Wally I'd come to his house soon to see his garden. Geno says it's awesome, but I take that with a grain of salt. Wally sets up model trains in his Zen garden, so I figure Geno's just on the lookout to sell more train stuff.

Back in my apartment and waiting for Christopher to arrive I sat at my piano, letting my mind wander back to Opera in the Park. Sterling sang the mezzo role of Hermia, and I started wondering what other roles she could've sung since she has such an amazing vocal range. I remembered Red too, as Puck in the opera, doing some death-defying aerial stunts. The weakest link in the cast, in fact, was the blonde who sang the coloratura role of Tytania. I remembered looking her up in the program; her name was Rose something . . .

Oh. My. God. Of course. The coloratura in the opera was Sterling's Rose, Jayne Mansfield with double-digit cleavage. I *knew* she looked familiar when I saw her at the seafood restaurant, but I couldn't place her. And now Rose is latching onto Casey but . . . oh no . . . Casey wouldn't dump Sterling. Would he? Please, Casey, don't be an idiot. Maybe I can talk some sense into him . . .

Give it up, Mags, you know you can't tell Casey what to do. Surely you remember what Shakespeare said about the course of true love? How it never runs smooth? Which you of all people should understand, being as your love life reads like a dime store tragedy—

"Shut up and leave me alone!" I said to the voice in my head. I couldn't stop thinking about Sterling, though. And worrying about her. How can she be a Piper and have a normal life? It's not possible. And it's no wonder she's in a mood lately, with this Piper thing looming. I mean, *I* have trouble keeping my ordinary life and my Genius House life separate, so how can Sterling do it?

Besides that, she told me Casey doesn't know. He doesn't know about the Tutors or the Intervention. Or anything. "Sterling," I protested, "you have to tell him *some of it* at least. How can you not?"

"I'll tell him, Mags, but not yet. I want to be normal—with Casey—as long as I can." I told her I understood, but I still ask myself: What happens when Casey finds out?

And there's no good answer.

It was almost five o'clock when Christopher arrived at my front door in a huff. "Thanks a bunch, Mags, for setting me up as Wally's driver," he said when I opened the door. "He talked my ear off the whole time we were on the road, wouldn't shut up about the Fibonacci sequence in western music. I told him those theories aren't reputable, but he wouldn't listen, of course. Just kept on yakking."

"Hmm, that's interesting. I talked to Wally earlier today about . . . uh, things . . . "

"What *things*?"

"Oh, nothing much .. things about his Zen garden . . . sort of."

"You're making no sense whatsoever, and we need to get to work. Not to mention, of course, that I'm here *under duress!*"

"C'mon, Christopher, don't be a grouch. Working here today's a win-win for all of us. Wally gets to play with Geno's trains, Geno gets Wally's help finishing up his Halloween Village, you get to drive Wally's BMW, and I don't have to use my valuable time traveling to DeLand and back. See? It's a quadruple win."

The reason I cut myself off, changed course with Christopher in mid-sentence, is because I had to stop myself. The thing is, I remembered only too well what Wally said when he was telling me about his Zen garden in the coffeeshop this morning: *Mags, the Fibonacci Spiral may be the key that unlocks the Secrets of the Universe. That's why I'm using Fibonacci—and the Golden Rectangle—as crucial design elements in my garden.*

And *that* comment started me thinking about the Fibonacci spiral's connection to Uncle Billy's gyres. I mean, the connection between Fibonacci and the gyres is a no-brainer—they're both spirals, and they're both infinite. But try to explain that without mentioning the unsettling information that Uncle Billy himself is an in-the-flesh resident of Ponce Inlet. It's not possible.

And this always happens to me because I have to keep my Genius House life separate from my other life . . .

No, that's not right. I have just the one life, but I can't go public about parts of it. Not yet, anyway.

Christopher had barely sat down at my piano when we heard a godawful BOOM! *CRASH!* followed by silence. Then sirens howling in the distance.

Running out my front door to the landing we saw a big *Out of Order* sign on the freight elevator, so we ran down the stairs. (Okay, Christopher ran down the stairs, and I walked reasonably fast.) When we got outside, Geno, Ralphie, and Old Sonny were already there on the sidewalk along with Wally and a crowd of gawkers.

"Geno," I said, "what the hell's going—oh my God! OH MY GOD!" Two storefronts up from Geno's, a black Suburban was stuck half-in, half-out of The Chocolate Factory's front display window. "That's the Genius House vehicle," I hollered. "I need to see if Sterling's in it. Where's the driver? I don't see anyone in the car!" Christopher helped me push through the crowd to get closer, and that's when I saw Slim.

"Slim! Slim! Over here! Who's in the car? Is anyone hurt?"

Slim looked my way, mouthed *Nobody's hurt. Stay back. Call you later.* Then she got busy with crowd control.

"Mags," Christopher said, "we can't do anything here except get in the way. Wally's already heading back to Geno's train depot, so let's finish work at your apartment."

Later, we talked to Geno and Ralphie at the coffeeshop.

"It was another nutcase plot," Geno said. "The Driver crashed into the store on purpose, jumped out which nobody noticed in the confusion, and ran along the side alley to join his buddies out back which were preparing a getaway."

"Yeah," Ralphie chimed in. "It was nutcase, but it was genius too because the Chocolate Factory closes at five in the p.m. so's the staff can clean the candy machines in the kitchen. Everybody ran to the front showroom when they heard the crash, but meanwhile the crooks came in the back and cleaned out the inventory."

"Also meanwhile," Geno cut in, "the Driver which crashed the Suburban into the front window had time to climb in the getaway truck out back before it roared off, loaded with boxes of chocolates—"

"All they stole was boxes of chocolates? Again?"

"It's like I say with regularity, Mags—"

"I know, Geno, I know. The nutcase will always surprise you."

"You got it. And I hate to tell you, but your weirdo friends are implicational in this. Me and Ralphie heard the cops talkin'. They've been on the lookout for that black Suburban from the Genius House because it's a hot car."

THAT CELTIC THING

I couldn't settle down the next morning because I was in a funk. You don't remember about my funk? Writer's block, some people call it. When my funk moves in, it's like there's a big black cloud hovering overhead, ready to plop down on me. Makes me feel like that character in the Little Abner comic strip, Joe Btfsplk. Remember Joe? Wherever he goes, his drippy dark raincloud goes with him. I recall one story line where Joe was in love and wanted to get rid of his raincloud, so he trapped it in an anti-pollutant jar. Which might work in a comic strip but sure isn't helpful in real life.

My funk hung around all morning. I'd write something, delete it, start over, delete again. Then I'd get panicky about losing what I deleted because maybe it wasn't so bad after all, so I'd go into my trash bin and start sifting. I was getting nowhere, and my funk was getting worse, so I was glad for a diversion when Kells and Sterling surprised me by showing up at my back door.

It would've been nice to go out for lunch, except Kells would have attracted too much attention in her neon-orange wet suit (apparently she wasn't aware that you only wear wet suits at the beach). Adding insult to injury, she'd accessorized by tying a flower-print babushka under her chin (no head hair, remember?) and stepping into a pair of platform jellies. All of which didn't exactly add up to a trendy ensemble. More like a bad Barbie getup put together by a three-year-old.

"You know what, Ladies?" I said. "I'm hungry and ready for a break, but let's eat here. I'll run down to the coffee shop and get some sandwiches while one of you makes coffee. For me it'll be Geno's ham-turkey-bacon club deluxe with double provolone and mayo. And for the two of you, veggie combos but hold the mayo? Also the bread? Got that too and I'll be back in a jiff."

Geno was being chatty while he made the sandwiches. "So, Mags, Old Sonny says he saw a strange-looking person on the fire escape, said she looked like a giant Barbie doll. Freaked him out, actually, 'cause she looked like one of his old boyfriends."

Then he peered over his glasses at me and frowned. "Mags? Could that be one of your weirdo friends from Ponce Inlet, up on the fire escape and coming to visit you? I only ask because I am particulate about keys to the fire escape, which in case you forgot, we agreed we would not have extras made for bestowing upon friends and other non-residents."

"Geno, I am *The Vault at Tiffany's* when it comes to protecting our fire escape keys."

"What?"

"It's a metaphor, Geno. It means that regarding the security of keys to our fire escape, I am burglar-proof, puissant to a fault, one hundred percent secure and inviolable. Also impregnable and completely impervious to solicitation."

"*What*? You need to quit talkin' like a professor being that you declined to be one anymore. But since you mention solicitation, did'ja hear about the party the police busted up in South Daytona? Seems the mayor and a couple commissioners were hangin' out at the Yum Yum Tree—"

"Geno, I gotta go. Put the sandwiches on my tab, okay?"

"Sure thing. Gotta hurry when you're havin' lunch with Big Barbie. You're positive there's nothing you want to tell me?"

"Nothing at all, Geno, but thanks for asking."

Back in my apartment I was starving, ready to plow into my sandwich, but Sterling wanted to talk. "You know, don't you, Mags, that Halloween's tomorrow night?"

"You're kidding, right? How could I not notice skeletons and scarecrows every time I turn around? Plus Geno's been obsessing about Halloween for weeks. He even talked me into collaborating with him on a new Halloween pastry."

"You've been *baking*?"

"Of course not. I've been tasting. It's called pumpkin pasticcio, and it took some serious tasting before he finally got it right. I kept telling him, more chocolate! more chocolate! until he finally paid attention."

"Pumpkin and chocolate?"

"Don't knock it if you haven't tried it. Which we are going to do for dessert, because Geno baked up a fresh batch this morning. And by the way, why're you two so interested in Halloween? You're going trick-or-treating?"

"Not exactly." (Sterling)

"But we're glad you asked." (Kells)

Uh oh. I was sensing a Halloween agenda that included me, so I decided to try a diversionary tactic. "Sterling, didn't you tell me you're researching how Halloween evolved from Samhain? From the Celtic equivalent?"

"I did, Mags," Sterling said. "I want to learn more about the Celtic traditions that are so important to Uncle Billy. It seems like Red's gotten Celtic-inspired lately too. George says he's cooking up something for Samhain, but it's all hush hush."

"Well if Red's serious, it makes sense to get excited about Samhain," Kells said, "It's a high point in the Celtic Wheel of the Year, the time when spirits cross from the Other Side to visit the living."

"I remember now," Sterling said. "Didn't the Celts believe a Veil separates our world from the Other Side?"

"Yes," Kells said, "a Veil protects the living so they won't be haunted by the past. But once every year, when the Wheel turns from the Autumn Equinox to the Winter Solstice, the Veil is thin and can be breached."

Cool, I thought to myself, my diversionary tactic worked, plus this is actually interesting. I didn't say any of that out loud, of course, just smiled encouragingly at Kells and Sterling while focusing on my sandwich.

Kells was still talking. "On that night—Samhain—ancient tribes would gather on hilltops and light huge fires. Then they'd throw the bones of cattle into the fires and the burning bones would crackle—"

"I remember reading about that in the *OED*." Me, of course, forgetting to stay quiet and interrupting Kells. "That's where we get our word *bonfires*. It comes from those *bonefires* the Celts would light on Samhain."

"Exactly," Kells said. "So many customs are ancient beyond belief. The *jack-o-lantern*, for example. You cut off the top for a lid, scoop out the inside, carve a face, put in hot coals from the bonefires, and put back the lid."

"Well, hooray for the Celts," I said, "for giving us the jack-o-lantern. It's one of my all-time favorite things about Halloween. And speaking of pumpkins, pumpkin pie's probably my favorite Halloween treat because—"

"No pumpkins," Kells said, shaking her head. "Pumpkins are part of North American rituals, not Celtic. Celts used turnips. They made jack-o-lanterns from hollowed-out turnips."

Turnips? The Celts used turnips to make jack-o-lanterns? I started laughing and choked, not exactly a good move because it knocked my diversionary conversation-tactic back to square one. "Mags, I need you to do me a favor," Kells said. "You already know I'm taking Datta, Uncle Billy, and George to the Boardwalk for Halloween, right?"

"Uh, no. But I think you're really brave. The Boardwalk will be mobbed on Halloween."

"Well, I'm in a bind. Jengu was supposed to help me, but he's bailing, so I'm asking you to go with us and be our driver. Please?"

"Mags," Sterling chimed in, "that's one more reason Kells is pissed off at Jengu. She counted on him to be their driver on Halloween, but he says he won't."

"And it's not fair to ask Sterling to change her plans," Kells said. "She and Casey planned their weekend over a month ago."

"And that leaves Kells with a mess on her hands, Mags. Can you imagine Kells having to keep tabs on Uncle Billy *and* Datta *and* Datta's brothers—"

"What? Datta has brothers? And they're here? At your house?"

"He has two brothers, and they arrived yesterday," Sterling said. "He was really excited when he heard they were coming to visit, and so was Mercy."

"And now Mercedes wants to come to the Boardwalk party, too," Kells said. "Mags, I need a helper. *Please* say you'll do it."

Sigh. They had me, and they knew it. I told Kells I'd stop by Geno's Halloween Village first, but I could be at the Genius House at 5:30 p.m. to drive her and her groupies to the Boardwalk. While I walked them down my fire escape, Sterling enthused about her Halloween plans with Casey. "Michael's showcasing his new girl band at a concert in New Smyrna, and Casey's borrowing Wally's BMW convertible, so we'll be going in style."

Then she laughed. "I'm *almost* sorry to miss the Boardwalk party. It'll be such a treat for Datta and his brothers because they won't look like freaks, just regular people in costumes. Yesterday morning before the guys got here, Datta gave me a list, and I went shopping for them. Mainly party platters and their favorite movies on DVDs. Oh, and balloons. It's fun for them to have helium balloons floating around while they're levitating."

"While they're *levitating*?"

Sterling laughed again. "Remember, Mags, when we talked about synergetic species? And you wanted to know what Neanders taught musk oxen?"

"How could I forget? You two told me Neanders taught musk oxen to sing."

"Exactly, but you didn't inquire about the opposite trans-action. If you had, we'd have told you that musk oxen taught Neanders to levitate."

At that point we'd reached the sidewalk where we chatted for a few minutes about the Genius House group's costumes for the Boardwalk.

Then I waved goodbye while they headed across Beach Street, and I laughed hysterically while climbing back up my fire escape. They levitate? They *levitate*? I couldn't wait to tell Schrödy.

THE BATMAN DECAPITATION

I didn't get any writing done the next morning because I had to take care of pesky chores like paying bills, purchasing coffee beans and MoonPies, carrying Batman down to the dumpster because his head broke off.

Schrödy blamed the pigeons for Batman's decapitation because they were always out there on the balcony, pestering Batman and making him say POW! WHAP! KAPOOEY! while he swiveled his head. Then they'd giggle and shake all over, the way pigeons do when they laugh. I guessed Schrödy was right about the pigeons pestering Batman, because otherwise I couldn't figure why the Bat Head would swivel off so forcefully, it'd go sailing over our balcony and down to the sidewalk. Which it did.

And landed in the Sammy the Sabrett Guy's ketchup pot.

Geno was falling-down laughing about the Batman decapitation when I stopped in the coffeeshop on my way back from the dumpster, said there were some majorly pissed-off tourists with ketchup spatters all over their clothes, and one geezer totally freaked when Batman's head came plummeting down and landed in the ketchup.

"You couldn't blame the old dude for freakin' out," Geno said. "I saw it happen too and I'm here to tell ya'—a Batman head in ketchup looks just like a certificatable real head with blood all over it. Like it got chopped off in one a' those grillotines."

I figured I'd be persona non grata with Sammy after that, but sometimes you get surprised by the way things happen. In this case it turned out that a passer-by caught the whole thing on video, sent it to Channel 13, and bingo! Sammy, the geezer, and three tourists from Cincinnati got their fifteen minutes of fame.

Then Sammy got inspired, stuck the bat head on a pole, and keeps it bloodied with fresh squirts of ketchup—basically morphing himself into a minor tourist attraction with a built-in photo op. He's thrilled about it, says he never sold so many hot dogs. Geno's happy about it, too, because after the tourists get their pictures taken with Sammy and the bloody Batman head, they come in Geno's store and buy stuff.

After assuring Geno that his Halloween Village was sure to be a hit, I headed upstairs to get myself ready for the Boardwalk party.

HALLOWEEN

Every year Geno ups the ante to attract trick-or-treaters to his store, and he insisted I should experience this year's setup by entering through the front door, just like a customer. "That way," he enthused, "you get the full frontal effect."

"Like a full Monty, you mean?"

"What?"

"Never mind, it's a joke and a movie. Go on."

"So first," Geno said, "you go through the kiddie part which ain't scary, just some historicity with Cedric and Lady in retriculated armorials." (Translation: It's Geno's interactive Playskool medieval village, all gussied up for Halloween including knights in chain mail.)

"Then," Geno continued, "you head to the mind-blowing part at the back of the store, which Wally has outdone himself this year with Vampiricism and Christopher playing his terrapin is total creep-show." (Translation: Wally's Transylvanian model-train diorama features Dracula's Castle on top of a mountain, and Christopher plays a theremin, not a turtle.)

"Like I always say," Geno enthused, "we gotta' keep taking it to the next level so's we can compete with the King of Bowling over at the Boardwalk."

"We? Who's *we*?"

"Me an' the boys: Ralphie, Sonny, Frankie, Wally, and Christopher. And Sammy because the ladies go apeshit over him."

"The ladies?"

"You know, soccer moms and aunties which bring kids for trick-or-treating. We dressed Sammy up in tights last year and he was sensational, looked just like George Clooney in *Braveheart*."

"You mean Mel Gibson?"

"Yeah whoever. All I know is, Sammy's sensational in tights."

It was time to head downstairs. As Geno insisted, I went down my fire escape and around the corner so I could go in the big front doors, and I had to admit I was impressed.

Even though it was early, Geno's costumed cohorts at the medieval village had already attracted a crowd: Squire Samwise (Sammy) handing out popcorn balls; Master Gepetto (Sonny) manning the drawbridge; and Saint Francis of Assisi (Ralphie) distributing chocolate coins.

To top it off as planned, Cedric and Lady were spectacular in head-to-toe chain mail: coif, jacket, hauberk, gloves, spats. It always amazes me when I see them duded up, that you can crochet with wire instead of yarn. You didn't remember that? How Lady Sennacherib crochets their chain mail? It's true, and the chain mail's stunning.

My next stop was the model train depot at the back of the store, where Wally's *Welcome to Transylvania* diorama was breathtaking. I could hear Wally grumbling, but I couldn't see him because he was under the trainscape, fussing with last-minute adjustments.

Christopher, though, was immediately visible. Dressed all in black with a satin cape billowing around him (Geno set up a fan), Christopher stood on the mezzanine balcony—throwing a ten-foot-tall shadow while playing one of his prized rare instruments: a vintage theremin, rebuilt with state-of-the-art electronics. While that gigantic shadow-silhouette loomed like Dracula himself over the castle and trainscape, the theremin filled the store with eerie, demonic wails.

What's a theremin? It's one of the earliest electronic musical instruments ever invented, and the thereminist doesn't touch it. That's right, never. The way you play it is to wave your hands around without ever touching its two antennas: a horizontal loop antenna and an upright rod antenna. Or, as Wally put it when I foolishly asked him how Christopher's theremin works:

It's simple, Mags. A thereminist controls the oscillators for frequency with one hand, while controlling the oscillators for amplitude with the other hand.

Then Wally talked a blue streak about famous theremin music including the soundtrack for our all-time favorite sci-fi movie *The Day the Earth Stood Still.* (When Wally and I were kids in Pittsburgh, our secret password was "Klaatu barada nikto.")

I left Geno's in time to arrive at the Genius House on the dot of 5:30 p.m., as promised. While I was parking Agatha in one of the garage spaces, Michael met me and said the new Suburban had a full tank of gas, so she was ready to rumble. "Thanks," I said. "Why'd you get another black one?"

"When Sterling and I went to the dealership, the two choices were red and black. We figured red would be more attention-getting, and more attention is the last thing we need right now. So we settled on black."

"Makes sense. So you'll be in New Smyrna Beach tonight?"

"Yep, me and my new girl band."

"And what about Red?"

"Exactly. What about Red? Until he gets over his stupid obsession with Deirdre, Red's useless. We ignore him if we can. If not, we tell him to shut up and leave us alone. Which he's glad to do."

It was time to drive to the Boardwalk, so I started the Suburban's engine and honked the horn. Then, while I waited for Kells and company to make an appearance, I recalled what she and Sterling told me about their costumes.

It was Datta's idea to dress up like Star Wars characters for the Boardwalk party, Kells said, so Sterling went shopping for the three brothers: Datta, Dayadhvam, and Damyata. For Datta and Damyata who looked just like full-size Chewbaccas,

Sterling found toy ammo belts and plastic Uzis at Wal-Mart. And for Dayadhvam—the runt of the family who could pass as an Ewok—Sterling scrounged a headscarf from Mary's closet and sharpened a stick she found on the dunes. (Ewoks look a lot like koala bears and carry sharpened sticks as spears.)

Sterling also bought lots of cheap brown hair dye during her Wal-Mart shopping trip because the three Da's agreed it wouldn't be credible for all of them to go *au naturel* as albinos. Damyata won the coin toss to be a white furred Wookiee, but the other two needed dye jobs.

They weren't sure how to outfit Mercedes until Sterling found an R2-D2 costume at Big Lots. Kells said it's just a big plastic tube with a dome-shaped lid, kind of like an oversized trashcan, but it fits Mercy perfectly. And an additional perk is that Mercy says when she's wearing it, it's no problem for her to be in low-levitation mode and glide around just like R2.

Kells regretted that Sterling wouldn't be with us at the Boardwalk because she'd have been a perfect Princess Leia, but when Kells asked *me* to dress up like Princess Leia, I hit the ceiling. "What! You want me to wear a white sheet and glue a bagel on each ear? *Au contraire!* I'll be your driver and party-companion, but no way will I channel Princess Leia. Besides which, it wouldn't be age-appropriate."

"Calm down, Mags, okay?" This was Kells, placating. "You wouldn't have to make a costume. They have two Princess Leia costumes with ready-made wigs at the party store in Port Orange, and I'll be glad to get one for you—." Sterling was laughing, obviously enjoying my discomfiture, but I didn't care. "Forget it, Kells. I've already figured out my costume and trust me, you'll be blown away."

"All right, all right. I didn't mean to upset you."

"I'm not upset, just staking out my territory. So who else is dressing up like Star Wars?"

"George is going as Aunt Beru because it's easy," Kells said. "She can wear something wrinkled and dowdy and she won't have to wear a mask. And she's pleased that Uncle Billy's in a tizzy about dressing up like Obi-Wan Kenobi. He's been practicing for a week with the light-saber she bought him at Target."

"George is more understanding than I'd be," Sterling said. "She knows damn well that Uncle Billy wants to show off for The Harem Girl at Byzantium, but she figures oh, why not? Let him have his fun."

While I chuckled to myself about Uncle Billy as Obi Wan, the back door opened, and the partygoers came walking toward the Suburban. *Bless tú Mags, me Cailín!* Uncle Billy called to me while he and George climbed in the first back seat. Then after Mercy got herself settled in the commodious rear section, the three Da's managed to squeeze themselves into the second back seat.

Wait, where's Kells? Oh of course, here she comes and . . . wow! I'd forgotten about Kells dressing up like Darth Vader. She said it makes sense because Michael had a Darth Vader costume from Halloween a few years ago. The helmet-head's very lightweight, she said, so she wouldn't have to wear a wig under it, and the black cloak's a great coverup. "It'll be perfect," she told Sterling and me. "I won't have to talk because nobody expects Darth Vader to engage in chitchat, and I can keep an eye on our group. That way I can troubleshoot if I have to."

Kells also said if she could find them, she planned to "borrow" Jengu's big high-heeled black boots with lifts in them. Apparently she found the boots because, as she climbed in the Suburban all dressed up including boots and helmet, she was well over six feet tall.

As we pulled out of the driveway, we waved to Casey who was arriving in Wally's BMW convertible, ready to pick up Sterling and head for the concert in New Smyrna Beach.

As soon as everyone left the Genius House, Red got busy on the final countdown for his own Halloween scenario. *Hindsight's always 20/20*, we said later. And *Shouldn't one of us have suspected what Red was up to?* And, *Maybe we should've talked to the Fairies. Surely they knew something was brewing.*

Well, none of us suspected Red would get so crazy and, as we'd find out later, the Fairies had plans of their own. So, while everyone else headed for their Halloween destinations, Red was at the Genius House reviewing *his* plan for Halloween. Sorry, for Samhain. He'd hatched his plan weeks earlier when he realized the Genius House would be empty on Halloween night. That's when he faked Michael's handwriting and sent Deirdre a party invitation. It's hard to imagine that he thought the evening would go well once Deirdre arrived and realized Michael wasn't there, but apparently Red had no doubts.

In thrall to his delusion, Red pictured himself greeting his beloved Deirdre at the front gate and escorting her to the top of the Tower, from whence he would summon the Spirits to burst through the Veil while he torched the sacred bonefire. Then, while his fire lines to the perimeter ignited in an apocalyptic flaming spiral through the dunes, Deirdre would accept her destiny: she and Red would forever be entwined like the Thistle and the Rose. Just like the legend, *Deirdre of the Sorrows.*

Sterling said later she'd heard Red talk about Naoise and Deirdre, the Irish Romeo and Juliet, until she wanted to vomit.

But who would've suspected, she said, that Red would get nutso about it? That he'd try to make the story *real*?

Meanwhile at the Holistic Temple, Preacher and Lily Amaryllis were prepping for *their* Halloween extravaganza—the All Souls Barbecue beginning at sundown in the Commons, followed by the Feast of All Saints at sunrise in the Temple itself. As you probably noticed, Preacher got the "All Saints" and "All Souls" festivals mixed up (All Saints happens *before* All Souls). No attendee had ever cared to point this out, however, because food and drink at both events were free of charge to all comers.

Preacher'd had a windfall just that morning when he went to Chokke's Butcher Shop to purchase pig cheeks and chump chops for the Barbecue. God was watching over him, Preacher figured, because out of the blue, Chokke gave him fifty pounds of free top-of-the-line pork—tenderloin and rib chops, no less. Chokke said he'd butchered four pigs for that redhaired asshole at the big house, and then the idiot didn't want the meat, just the bones. Preacher was jubilant, asking Chokke to pray with him right then and there. But Chokke said he was busy so just take the meat.

Back home from Chokke's, Preacher loaded the Temple's smokers and grills with pork. Then, while Lily Amaryllis carried pans of just-baked brownies to cool on outdoor tables and iced bottles of Piggles Black Malt in their old bathtub-*cum*-baptismal font, Preacher lovingly brushed his windfall pig meat with the barbecue sauce that Brigadier had obligingly lifted from the VFW kitchen.

And for the Feast at sunrise, Lily Amaryllis set out huge trays of chocolates on altar cloths while Preacher conducted test runs of *Mystery Train* into the Temple and out again—making sure those new train tracks were laid just right. (You'll recall, I'm sure, Geno and Ralphie's hilarity over "Tooterville," where Preacher's upgraded train would double as the Temple's front row of seats.)

Meanwhile across town at his pub called Pigs Will Fly, Maxie Finklestein gazed approvingly at his costumed image in a cracked mirror over the lavatory in the pub's single bathroom. (Max was living at the pub *temporarily* while he got his finances straightened out.)

Turning this way and that, he grinned at the handsome dude in the mirror: leather boots and hat, tight-fitting pants with a silk tie rolled up and stuffed in the crotch (up front where it makes an impressive bulge), camp shirt half-way unbuttoned (good thing he pays Christine to dye that chest hair), and a real bullwhip. "Yes *indeed*," he chortled at his reflection, "*Indiana Jones* will nail it tonight!"

Max, you see, was up to his ears in debt and needed an infusion of cash to keep his floundering chain of pig-themed pubs out of Chapter Eleven. Not to mention those Russian assholes who screwed him bigtime on the Bimini deal. He'd settle the score with them, but first things first: right now he needed cash, and Gigi Gallimachos was ready to invest.

To that end Max had been courting Gigi over a year, figuring she'd love being squired around by a handsome debonair young guy, making all her old-lady friends jealous. (Max would never see forty-something again, but who was checking?) So when Gigi proposed they dress up for Halloween and go to the big Boardwalk party, Max didn't dare say no.

It was almost a deal-breaker for Max, though, when he found out Gigi and Galatea would be outfitted as mother-daughter look-alikes. Nevertheless, Max was committed, and he certainly didn't want to wear an airy-fairy costume, so he persuaded the owner of The Little Foxes, his favorite local strip club, to get him suited up for the Boardwalk. ("Furries" costume parties were a big part of the club's success, so Max was in good hands, so to speak.)

Back at the Genius House, the Fairies agreed they were mad as hell and not going to take it anymore! First they nearly drowned in that shipwreck. They're not *merrows*, they told Uncle Billy, so it was a rotten idea to stuff them in a boat and send them across the ocean. And to *Florida*, for Lugh's sake, where there's not a decent dry cave or real hardwood forest! For months on end they hid out, wet and sandy, miserable and pissed off, while the Captain took his sweet time building his "castle."

The Fairies agreed it wasn't so bad once the Captain was gone and the house stayed empty. They'd had some good years, actually, until those professors moved in and started renovating, and once again the Fairies got squeezed. To make matters worse, that trashy Lighthouse family never quit nosing around and causing trouble.

Things came to a head one dark and stormy night while the Fairies were making powerful magic in the Tower. Of all the stupid times to challenge the Fairies, the idiot Lighthouse keeper proposed a duel: the Lighthouse versus the Tower.

There he was, showing off to his bigwig political friends and unhooking the lightning rod from the top of the Lighthouse, like it was a real magic wand. How pathetic! Thunder rumbled, lightning flashed, and there went the keeper, tumbling down the Lighthouse staircase with his ridiculous "wand" burned into his hand.

That's when the Wiccan coven in St. Augustine sent an emissary to the Genius House Fairies with a proposition, to-wit: If they'd relocate to St. Augustine, the Wiccans would make sure the Fairies were accorded the respect and admiration they deserved. The Fairies held out for a long time. After all, moving's a real bitch, and you don't want to do it on a whim, do you? The Wiccans were very persuasive, however, and finally the Fairies decided to go.

Thus on the morning of the fateful day in question, pleased at the prospect of respect and admiration and some witchin' parties, the Fairies from the Genius House packed up and set out for St. Augustine.

Red stayed so focused on putting his plan into action, he didn't notice the Fairies were gone. And giving the devil his due, Red's plan was genius: First he'd encircled the Genius House property with small fire sites, all connected by a long fuse line; then he continued the fuse line through the dunes and the ice plant groundcover, around and around in an ever-tighter spiral until it ended in a huge bonefire site at the base of the Tower.

Red hit a snag at Chokke's butcher shop that morning, though. When he arrived to pick up the cow bones he'd ordered, he realized Chokke had sacks of *pig* bones ready for pickup. After Chokke declined to slaughter a few cows on the spot, Red had no choice but to take the pig bones and depart for home. Then, while everyone else was busy inside the house, Red distributed his pig bones at the smaller fire sites and heaped the major cache at the hub—the central bonefire near the Tower.

Delirious with anticipation, Red pictured himself high on the Tower with Deirdre, summoning the Fairies. Then, when the Fairies breached the Veil, he as the Lord of Misrule would set the gigantic bonefire alight, igniting in turn the smaller bonefires through the ice plant and around the perimeter—*boom boom boom boom boom*—rivalling the Milky Way in an earthbound spiral nebula.

Meanwhile at the Boardwalk, Byzantium had been mobbed by tourists ever since the arrival of the drag queen known as Semi Sweet Charity (in head-to-toe sequins) and a very large Tweetie Bird. While Semi Sweet and Tweetie racked up points at the lanes, excited fans hooted and hollered and tweeted the folks back home in Kalamazoo that they were partying with Lady Gaga and Sir Elton John.

The Great Rotunda attracted a similarly eclectic crowd, including two Marilyn Monroes and a plethora of Batmen (two Classic Batmen, three Marvel Comics Batmen with fake abs, and one Decapitated Batman accompanied by a blonde Robin-ette).

Oh, and lest I forget, the costume parade included Yours Truly, miraculously transformed into a mature, yet fetchingly mysterious, Red Riding Hood—having effected my metamorphosis with a voluminous Dolly-Parton-style blonde wig (borrowed from Christine), a long red hoodie-cape (purchased at

Super-Target), and fabulous silver-heeled Louboutin platform boots (from the Daring Divas consignment shop).

The big hit for Halloween dress up this year, though, was Star Wars costumes, and the Genius House group's were clearly outstanding. To refresh your memory, our contingent from Ponce Inlet numbered two seven-foot-tall Chewbaccas (one white, one brown with highlights); one Ewok (also brown with highlights); Obi Wan Kenobi (Uncle Billy), who was doggedly stalked by dowdy Aunt Beru (George); Darth Vader (Kells); and a somewhat oversized R2-D2 (Mercedes).

When we arrived at the Boardwalk, our Star Wars ranks were swelled by no fewer than three Luke Skywalkers (rednecks from Samsula, all equipped with light sabers) and two Princess Leias (Gigi and Galatea in the mother-daughter look-alike costumes). And wouldn't you just know it? A starry-eyed young woman who'd forgotten to wear her contact lenses (The Harem Girl) persisted in mis-identifying Max Finkelstein as Han Solo.

Max was supposed to be Indiana Jones, not Han Solo, remember? But then again, since Harrison Ford played both Han Solo *and* Indiana Jones in the movies, perhaps The Harem Girl shouldn't be blamed for being confused. And she had, after all, forgotten those contact lenses.

And oh yes, there was one additional Darth Vader—Prax, who'd been commanded by Pan to disguise himself and walk around Byzantium on the lookout for troublemakers. *Don't fuck this up*, Pan warned his son. *If we have any trouble, it's on your head. And don't let NOBODY near the Master Control Room!*

I was standing by Kells when we both spied the other Darth Vader. Kells immediately removed one of her long black gloves so she could take off the big spinner-ring she always wore and put it back on *over* the glove. That way, she whispered to me, no one in our group would get confused about which Darth Vader was which.

She needn't have worried, though, as we both realized right away.

Almost as soon as the other Darth Vader (Prax) saw Kells-as-Darth-Vader across the room, the other one (Prax) seized the moment, walked out a side exit, and disappeared.

Everyone, it seemed, wanted souvenir portraits with the *Star Wars* crowd. Pan Papanicolaou, ever alert for entrepreneurial opportunity, set up an improvised Photo Op Gazebo in Byzantium's Rotunda. For ten dollars a pop you could snap a souvenir photo of your group, along with your choice of *dramatis personae*.

Datta's Chewie (brown fur with highlights) was a popular photo-op choice. As were Galatea's Princess Leia (annoying Gigi, who didn't see why *she* didn't get picked sometime) and one of the Lukes (the three rednecks took turns). And Mercy's chubby R2-D2 was the hit of the photo ops, especially after she and Datta brought down the house with an impromptu rendition of the Sonny and Cher classic *I Got You, Babe*.

It was a little disconcerting to Kells, though, that Galatea stuck to her like glue because she (Galatea) thought Darth Vader (Kells) was her-fiancé-Prax-in-disguise. After all, that's the plan that Pan had confided to Gigi, i.e., Prax dressing up like Darth Vader and patrolling the Palace. So how was Galatea supposed to know any different?

Meanwhile Max had his eye on those two Marilyn Monroes, but to no avail because The Harem Girl (she'd had a crush on

Han Solo since she was six years old) kept hanging on Max and getting in the way.

All of which upset Uncle-Billy-as-Obi-Wan. He'd been showing off with his light saber, hoping to shag The Harem Girl in a dark corner somewhere. But there she was, always slobbering over the *feckin' eejit* in the leather hat and boots and bullwhip. It was disgusting.

More and more people crowded into the Rotunda because it was cooler inside than outside. True, it was almost November but trust me, sticky hot weather on Halloween in Florida is not unusual.

Before long, Datta and his brothers were sweating bullets. Datta's brown hair dye had started to run, leaving dark puddles wherever he walked. Fearing heatstroke, Dayadhvam (the Ewok) disappeared into the ladies' room where he could sit undisturbed in a stall directly under an AC vent. And all three Da's were sneezing uncontrollably.

That's when Datta decided something must be done. Given that Pan was engrossed in squeezing every last dime out of tourists who thronged the Photo Op Gazebo in the Rotunda, Datta walked unnoticed and undisturbed through a door that said *Employees Only: Keep Out.* There he found the central AC control and turned the thermostat down to 55 degrees, which you'll recall is where Datta keeps the temp in his cottage.

Most AC units do not function well at such a low temperature, however. Especially not the Byzantium AC unit which Pan picked up cheap because it was a discontinued model that fell off a truck. *A few dents and scratches won't matter*, Pan figured, *especially if we keep the thermostat set at 80 degrees.* Uh Oh. An extra-large but questionable AC unit is called upon to spew the equivalent of arctic air in a crowded Rotunda with a massive dome? Datta should have known better.

Less than twenty minutes after Datta adjusted the Master Control Room's thermostat, things went awry. Onlookers were startled when a frantic tourist from New Jersey came hurtling out of the ladies' room, screaming *There's a bear in the terlit, takin' a shit!* That's when the crowd in the Rotunda heard a hissing, then a rumbling, then BLAM! as the overworked AC unit blew, taking every electrical circuit and the backup generator with it.

Panic ensued, especially among those patrons who recalled the fire at Prax's Cabaret just a few weeks earlier. Without waiting around to see how Byzantium handled the situation, and even though no one had intended to leave quite so early in the evening, a crowd of people including our Genius House group decided it was time to call it a day. Or a night.

Pan verged on apoplexy, standing at the big front doors and watching hordes of customers pour out onto the Boardwalk proper, taking their wallets with them. *Where the hell's Petros?* he roared. *And where's Prax?* Nothing.

In point of fact, Petros was enjoying pizza and ice cream at the Bandshell with a rowdy girl scout troop and their pneumatically buxom leader. Prax was enjoying himself also, having ditched the Darth Vader costume and gone to an invitation-only party at the Yum Yum Tree in South Daytona—where he met up with Michael who'd not gone to New Smyrna Beach after all. As pre-arranged.

Meanwhile Pan stumbled around in the hot humid darkness of Byzantium's Master Control Room, trying to find emergency switches that would reanimate Byzantium and stop the flow of cash-customers who were leaving in droves.

While all this was happening, Mercedes, who'd slipped into the wine cellar a little earlier to cool off, exited through the back door when the power conked out. Very quickly she glided to the parking lot, looking for Datta and the rest of us. She arrived a little ahead of us, though, and that's when she noticed the wine cart. Which had followed her out of the building.

This sort of thing had happened to Mercy before. That is, metal things had become magnetized and gotten themselves stuck to her when she was levitating. The explanation is that sustained levitation disrupts the electromagnetic field, and Mercy knew it was nothing to worry about, just annoying. For the ride home there'd be plenty of room in the Suburban for everyone plus the wine cart. And once she was back at the Genius House, Mercy knew she could deal with the situation.

Traffic was a mess because hordes of people, like us, decided to leave the Boardwalk before something blew up. Which it did, later. But that was after our group was long gone.

In the meantime I maneuvered the Suburban out of bumper-to-bumper gridlock, and before long we were on our way down A1A at a reasonable clip—followed by a convoy comprised of a white Lexus sedan, a red Mazda Miata, and a silver F-150 off-road pickup. In the Lexus were Gigi and Galatea, with Max driving. (When Galatea saw Darth Vader in the front passenger seat of the Suburban and figured it was Prax, she and Gigi prevailed upon Max to follow us.)

But when The Harem Girl saw Han Solo (Max) climbing into a Lexus with two Princess Leias, she was consumed with outrage. "It's not fair," she said to her girlfriends (the two Marilyn Monroes). Squeezing her friends and herself into her tiny Mazda Miata, then driving enthusiastically but erratically (she really should have worn her contacts), The Harem Girl followed the Lexus.

Meanwhile Obi Wan Kenobi (Uncle Billy) spotted the Miata behind the Lexus. Believing that The Harem Girl was driving crazy because she was finally *coming on* to him (and before George could stop him), Uncle Billy stood up on his seat in the Suburban. Head and shoulders through the open moonroof, he swooshed his light saber around enticingly.

That's when the three Luke Skywalkers in their F-150 pickup pulled out of a side street and saw Obi Wan flashing his light saber. "The old dude says he has a stash, so let's go to *his* party," one Luke said to the others while they burned rubber, made a U-turn, and joined the convoy. "That Boardwalk scene was freakin' dullsville, anyway," the Luke Skywalkers agreed.

Long before we reached the Genius House, Kells was anxious. "Drive Mags, Drive!" she insisted. As I pulled into the driveway with our convoy right behind us, Kells jumped out of the Suburban and started running, leaving everyone else to disembark as best they could. It was dark, pitch dark, which didn't bother Kells but disoriented the rest of us while we stumbled out of vehicles, searching for flashlights and asking each other what the hell was going on.

Running toward the Tower, Kells saw Red and Deirdre, struggling near the base. Deirdre appeared to faint, at which point Red started dragging her, and the two of them disappeared into the Tower through the big main door. Kells was running like the wind, but just as she reached the Tower she heard the *click!* of the master lock and knew it was beyond her power to open it. Beyond her power, that is, *as she was.* Without further hesitation, Kells started her ring spinning, tore off the Darth Vader costume, and got to work.

The three Da's and Mercy, meanwhile, had made a run for Datta's cottage. They came back out bearing torches and lanterns for everyone and passed them around, then went back inside where it was cool.

While George pulled Uncle Billy into the house, where lights had started appearing in the windows, Gigi and Galatea walked around aimlessly, looking for Prax.

Max, who'd sat down on the back patio in disgust, cheered up considerably when the three Lukes appeared with the wine cart (*R2-D2 says knock ourselves out!* they said gleefully), followed by The Harem Girl and her two hot young friends.

That, as they say, was when things fell apart.

Suddenly light blazed from the top of the Tower, pouring through its panoramic windows and lighting up the nighttime sky. Attired fantastically in a shaggy cloak and antlers while declaiming in a voice like a bullhorn, Red appeared on the Tower's high catwalk with Deirdre.

While Red proclaimed that he was the Lord of Misrule—the Heir of Caoilte who would summon the Fairies—the crowd below, transfixed by the drama that was unfolding high above, stood motionless.

Except for Yours Truly, that is. I'd started running toward Sterling when I saw her standing near the base of the Tower, looking up at Red. I'd already changed out of my boots when I had to drive the Suburban, but it was still hard to run because I kept tripping on my long red cape, so I pulled it off and tossed it, and when I did, the curly blonde wig went with it.

I was out of breath when I got to Sterling, who was standing stock still. "Sterling, why are you here? Didn't you go to the concert in New Smyrna?"

"Yes."

"Then why are you back here now?"

"I got a message, Mags. I heard Cassandra's song, I heard *White Coral Bells*."

"What? You heard Cassandra singing?"

"No, Cassandra wasn't singing. The Fairies were singing because Red was in danger. They'd already left the Genius House, but they were singing that I needed to help him."

Up on the Tower's catwalk, Red and Deirdre were struggling. Slowly Red was pushed back as if by an invisible force, away from Deirdre. Then, while the crowd below watched, Red tore off his furry cloak and antlers, tossed them to the ground, and climbed up up up—from the catwalk to the pinnacle above. Teetering on the parapet, Red called in a voice like thunder:

Behold! With the Flaming Sword, I call the Spirits to breach the sacred Veil!

While Red looked from side to side and back again, waiting, the crowd assembled below were spellbound. Well, *almost* all of them were spellbound. "Is that thang in his hand really a sword?" one Luke said to the others in hushed tones. "Dude, it shore does look like a sword," the second Luke whispered back.

Whatever it was, everyone watched while Red brandished it back and forth in big swooping strokes. Then he reached up, set it ablaze, and stood holding it high. Sharp intakes of breath, as the crowd watched, aghast. "Shit fire, Man," the third Luke squealed to the other two, "you cain't set fire to a sword! It must be a palmetter frond!"

Still teetering on the Tower's parapet, Red scanned the crowd below and the darkness beyond, back and forth, back and forth.

Behold! he announced.

Silence.

The Host is riding! he called.

Nothing.

Even stronger than before, Red's voice rumbled like thunder in the night:

> *The host is rushing 'twixt night and day,*
> *And where is there hope or deed as fair?*
> *Caoilte tossing his burning hair,*
> *And Niamh calling—Away, come away . . .*

Again he scanned the darkness.

Again nothing.

Finally it appeared that Red and the flaming brand became one. With a cry that sounded like triumph to some, despair to others, Red propelled himself up and out in a swooping arc that seemed to the stunned onlookers to be in slow motion. Slow—slow—slowly he flew, his long red hair aflame like the tail of a comet, trailing behind him.

In a time of tumult, it is not possible for observers to agree about events in which they have become enmeshed. Some that night said Red disappeared in mid-flight, others that he dove to the ground, slamming into the pile of bones and fire logs at the base of the Tower. Some even said he never flew at all, that he went up in smoke from the Tower's dome.

It is undisputed among observers, however, that whatever the cause, the pyre at the base of the Tower burst into fire with a crack like lightning. Then, while flames leaped high and pig bones crackled, Red's fire lines hissed and snaked like living things as they journeyed through the ice plant and sea oats on the dunes, finally igniting the perimeter fires. Before long, with sirens screaming in the distance, the night came alive with shrieks and howls and wails.

Red! Oh my God, no! Red! This from Sterling—who was standing with me near the Tower when the bonfire erupted.

Darth Vader's dead! Darth Vader went and melted like the Wicked Witch! This from the three Lukes in unison—while they gingerly poked their light sabers at a bedraggled black cape and helmet and gloves and empty black boots, all lying in a heap on the ground near the Tower.

It's not Darth Vader, it's Prax! Oh Sweet Jesus, Prax is dead! This from Galatea—collapsing against Gigi and dumping them both into a large pot of aloe plants by the patio.

Make way! Make way! This from an EVAC crew—pushing a stretcher and heading for Deirdre who had by then appeared at ground level near the Tower, protesting vigorously that she didn't need help.

Watch it! Roll those hoses! This from the Fire Chief—directing his crew through the dunes to the perimeter fires, all the while cursing the crazy fuckwit who set himself on fire and dove into the big pile of tinder.

And folks, this is NOT your typical Halloween celebration! This from Reporter Kalley Drum with the lead mini-cam from Channel 13—obviously thrilled to have something more sensational than kiddies with trick-or-treat bags to report on, for a change.

At the Holistic Temple grounds nearby, where the All Souls Barbecue was in full swing, Preacher had been startled by a blazing beacon of light from on high (Red, lighting the high windows in the Tower).

"Look, look!" Preacher said excitedly to Brigadier. "Truly this is a Sign to us."

A sign, my ass! Brigadier thought. *It's those crazy fucks at the Genius House again, turning the light on themselves while they fornicate and sodomize. And hear that crowd? Must be hundreds of 'em. They're like the Romans with their filthy games.*

Brigadier didn't say any of this out loud to Preacher, of course, out of respect for all the freebies at the barbecue. Instead he just nodded and let Preacher talk while both men girded themselves for surveillance duty.

Preacher slid the heavy chain of his Pectoral Cross over his head and climbed in the engineer's seat on Mystery Train, started her up, and began chugging away from the Temple, along the Bottle Wall. At the same time Brigadier pulled on his black leather glove and, with high-powered night goggles on a leather strap around his neck, headed for his Foxhole in the ice plant on the Genius House property.

While Brigadier was getting set up in his Foxhole, Preacher was chug-chugging along the Bottle Wall in Mystery Train, heading to his Glory Hole behind the Genius House Tower. He wasn't feeling well, though, not well at all. It was those chest pains again, plus he probably ate too much barbecued pork (they'd *never* had so much pork at the All Souls Barbecue!).

Which is probably why Preacher didn't notice that he had a passenger—his son Beebo, who jumped on the caboose when he saw Mystery Train chugging out of the Temple. Beebo had his brand new air rifle with him, and he was itching to use it.

When Preacher stopped Mystery Train at his Glory Hole, he realized he was way too tired to roll the stone away, much less to climb through the wall and investigate the seditious goings-on at the Genius House. That's when Beebo announced himself and told Preacher he'd help him. Beebo rolled the stone away, steadied Preacher while he climbed through Glory, and held the old man's arm while they started walking in the direction of the Tower.

Preacher was too tired to walk very far, though, so they looked for a place where he could rest. Noticing a gigantic woodpile near the base of the Tower, Beebo guided Preacher to the near side of the woodpile. After lowering him to the ground and making sure he was sitting comfortably with his back against the woodpile, Beebo told Preacher he'd be back shortly.

While Beebo was helping Preacher, Brigadier was directing his buddies to strategic positions in the ice plant groundcover around the perimeter of the Genius House property. Brigadier himself occupied the command position, of course, in his capacious Foxhole. The damn static was annoying because it messed up their walkie-talkies, but they had bullhorns in case they needed to signal each other.

Adjusting his night goggles, Brigadier had just gotten himself comfy when—WHOMM! WHOMM! *WHOMM WHOMM WHOMM*! Bullhorns emitted raucous bloops and blongs one after the other, while fuse-controlled fire sites ignited like shotgun blasts in the dunes and around the perimeter. Abandoning their positions and each other, Brigadier's buddies wasted no time in getting the hell out of there. Which was easy for them because they were on the edges of the Genius House property, meaning they could simply hightail it into the palmetto scrub.

Brigadier, though, was right in the middle of things, so to speak. When Red's fire lines started popping all around him, he was trapped. First his camo windbreak caught fire, then errant fire lines started snapping at him like flaming snakes, singeing his flak jacket while hot embers landed on him from every direction.

Naturally Brigadier panicked, started screaming and flailing around like a crazy person. That's when a roving posse of Roomers swooped in to save him. They dragged him out of his Foxhole, beating out the flames, then carried him across the dunes and dumped him on the ground, hollering for one of the EVAC teams to come get him.

The EVAC crew were efficient as always, but Brigadier couldn't stop acting crazy. The whole time he was being strapped onto a stretcher, he babbled about flying fire snakes and giant mushrooms. Naturally the EVAC people figured he was hallucinating, so they ferried him to the ER to get his stomach pumped.

Two days later, when he was still talking crazy about the red two-headed mushroom that picked him up and carried him through the ice plant, the hospital staff had no alternative but to commit him to the psychiatric ward.

Beebo swore in his statement at the Sheriff's office that he never meant to fire his rifle. He was carrying it "for protection," he said, because it was Halloween *plus* a full moon, so you had to be ready to protect yourself against Loonies. (Beebo was wrong about the full moon, which seldom coincides with Halloween. That factual error did not invalidate his Statement, however.) Anyway, after he left Preacher at the woodpile, Beebo headed toward the Big House to scope out the crowd of people he could see in the distance. He hadn't gotten far, though, when he stopped to look up at the Tower.

Here's the relevant part of Beebo's statement, *verbatim*, because you really want to appreciate his inimitable way with words:

Yo, so I'm watching this jerkoff on top of the Tower, holding a ginormous fuckin' torch, and he must of had a microphone up there too, 'cause you could of heard him talkin' a mile away.

Yo, so the dickhead on the Tower gets louder, starts wavin' his torch around like it's a fuckin' flag and people in Halloween costumes are yelling and screaming and running around, and a dog's howling like it's been set on fire, and that's when something slams into me from behind and makes me accidentally discharge my rifle.

Yo, so everything goes crackhead, sirens and bullhorns and the whole world's on fire, and the freak on the Tower does a dive, and I'm chokin' on my spit because fuckin' Bigfoot's sittin' on my head . . .

What really happened is Sorrow and Datta saved the day, and here's how it went down:

Sorrow had been wandering around the property as she did most nights after dark. She was doing her usual doggy thing, just snuffling and salivating, when she heard Red declaiming from the pinnacle of the Tower. Immediately she went bounding at warp speed toward Red's voice, yowling piteously while she ran.

When she saw Red light his flaming brand and swoosh it around, she knew she couldn't help Red, but when she saw Beebo with his air rifle, Sorrow leaped at him from behind. Sinking her teeth into the seat of Beebo's pants (which possibly did cause Beebo to "accidentally" fire his rifle), Sorrow held on tight. Meanwhile Datta (who'd hurtled out of his cottage when he sensed Red was in trouble) ran to Sorrow, thanked her, and sat on Beebo until Slim's deputies could cuff him.

Before the deputies stuffed Beebo into Slim's patrol car, though, the one called Trooper was overheard thanking Datta and saying, "Dang, Feller, that's some costume! I'd think you was Bigfoot if'n I didn't know it's just a bear suit."

Meanwhile back in town, Geno and his crew were pumped because trick-or-treaters had shown up in droves to wander through Geno's Halloween Village and stare at his costumed denizens: Sammy, Ralphie, Cedric and Lady, Old Sonny, even Wally (dressed proudly in his Biker duds). Christopher, though, as black-clad Dracula, was the evening's sensation. His ten-foot-tall shadow-persona, accompanied by those *Inner Sanctum*

theremin-wails, set the tone throughout the store and beyond—across the street in the park where Geno had set up a theater-size screen.

With just a few latecomers still in the store, Geno's exhausted crew—still in costume—were packing up when Geno started yelling from the mezzanine. "*Holy Mother of Christ!*"

"What? Geno, what's going on?"

"Mags's weirdo friends are in a shitload of trouble! It's huge! First they blew up the bowling alley at the Boardwalk, then they went back down to Ponce Inlet and set the whole fuckin' beach on fire!"

"No shit!

"It's true, I'm tellin' you! Channel 13 can't talk about nothing excepting Mags's friends and their incendiary inspirations. And the Fire Chief says to top it all off, a crazy fuckwit dove off the Lighthouse into a bonfire! They bleeped the *fuckwit* out on TV, but that's what he said. You couldn't miss it."

Geno was still exclaiming while Christopher grabbed his theremin (he's *very* protective of his special instruments) and started running. "Wally, come on!" he hollered. "We've gotta help Mags! Come on, Wally, HUSTLE!"

"I'm comin' too," Ralphie yelled. "Make room for me!"

"Okay, but hurry! And get my amp!" Christopher was gunning the engine of Wally's BMW when Wally and Ralphie got tangled up, trying to exit the front door of Geno's store at the same time. Finally Wally popped through, followed by Ralphie with Christopher's amp.

Christopher pulled Wally into the front passenger seat, Ralphie jumped in the back seat, and away they went—the BMW flying over the bridge with Cedric and Lady Sennacherib right behind on their silver Harley Hog.

By the time the BMW and the bike pulled into the driveway at the Genius House, things had quieted down. Slim's deputy Trooper was stationed by the bonefire site at the base of the Tower while he waited for Slim to return with Doc Kumagai. The fire trucks were long gone, and the last EVAC wagon was just pulling out, followed by Gigi's white Lexus sedan.

When my friends arrived I was standing in the driveway, bemused by the sight of them as they emerged from the gloom: Saint Francis with a tinfoil halo, black-caped Dracula, and two Knights in silver armor. Oh, and a chubby Biker Dude in studs and patches.

"Mags," Christopher said, "what the hell happened here tonight? Geno says it's all over the news that your—quote, unquote—*weirdo friends* blew up the Boardwalk, then came back here and set the beach on fire."

Sigh. None of that was true, of course, so I started in on a bowdlerized version of events. "Okay, first about the Boardwalk. If it exploded, we didn't know it because we'd already left, along with lots of others who split when the power blew at Byzantium."

"Well, something obviously happened after you left, Mags," Cedric said, "because the bowling alley's destroyed. It's all over the Internet and TV. And when that big dome on the Rotunda collapsed, it looked like someone bombed St. Peter's in Rome."

"Holy cow, really? We haven't been connected because the damn static's going crazy. I'm not even sure how the media got wind of this mess down here because we couldn't call out and nobody could call in. Locals could see and hear the melee, though, so they've been hanging around, rubbernecking and generally getting in the way. Slim left a few minutes ago to deliver a troublemaker to jail, then go find Doc Kumagai. He's stuck near the Boardwalk, where he crashed into a pelican."

"A pelican?"

"I know, it sounds crazy but after all this *is* Halloween."

"Right," Cedric said, laughing. "It's also Florida."

"Okay," Christopher said to me, "back to what happened here tonight."

So I told them about Red and Deirdre on the Tower, the fires along the perimeter of the property, plus the big bonfire. "I was right here watching," I said, "yet it's hard to remember exactly what happened. Everyone else is like that too. We all agree that Red climbed up to the dome above the Tower's cat-walk, that he stood there calling the Spirits, and when they didn't show up, Red set fire to a branch or something and called again, and when they still didn't show, he set himself on fire too and dove off the Tower . . . I think. Maybe."

"What do you mean, *you think maybe?*"

"I mean it all happened so fast, and I'm not sure what I saw. Dammit! I think I'm crying. Sterling was crying, too, and Sorrow wouldn't stop yowling—"

"Sorrow?"

"Red's dog. At that point Sterling's aunt took the dog and Sterling's uncle in the house."

As you're probably noticing, I couldn't tell them everything. Not about Uncle Billy and George, the Fairies, Kells, Datta and his brothers, Mercedes. *Certainly* not Mercedes, and certainly not the Roomers, who'd come streaming out of the house in droves when light first blazed from the Tower's high windows. After we settled in chairs on the back patio, I filled them in about the aftermath.

"Channel 13 closed up shop just before you got here," I said, "and a young woman we call The Harem Girl screeched out a few minutes later, taking Max Finkelstein to the ER because she'd backed into him in her Miata."

"Max Finkelstein?"

"A creep who owns a downtown pub. The Harem Girl thought Max was Han Solo in the flesh. She hung on him at the Boardwalk and followed him here, but she snapped when Max ignored her and started hitting on her two girlfriends. When she backed into Max with her Miata he was on the patio, opening a bottle of wine. The bottle broke in his hands, cutting him pretty badly. That's when The Harem Girl volunteered to take Max to the ER, because the EVAC crew were busy with some local guy who was acting crazy."

"And the crazy guy is who?"

"Don't know, probably some nimrod who came to check out the commotion, then freaked when all the fires started."

"Mags, how about a glass of wine?" Cedric said, noticing the wine cart still on the patio. "Looks like a nice Shiraz here. Also a Malbec."

"Awesome, Cedric. Let's try the Malbec. I could use a little fairy juice right now."

"Fairy juice?"

"It's how we refer to spiritous libations."

"Gotcha. So back to the story?"

"So after The Harem Girl drove off with Max, her two friends would've been stranded—except they were happy to go with the three Lukes to a party at the Cabbage Patch."

"It's my favorite place!" Wally cut in. "The biker bar in Samsula where I'm an Honorary Brother. They call me *Easy Rider*. Right, Cedric?"

"You got it, Bro," Cedric said, while Wally tried a fist bump but missed.

Christopher was looking astonished. "You might not be aware," Cedric said to him, "that our very own Wally has been *patched* by the Pagans. Show him your patches, Wally."

Which Wally was glad to do while we talked for a little while longer. They all agreed this was the best Halloween ever and after they left here they'd head for the Boardwalk to check it out. Everyone agreed, that is, except Ralphie. Ralphie just looked sad.

"This coulda' been a classy resort," Ralphie said, gesturing toward the House and the Tower. "Like me and Geno wanted to do. Remember, Mags? How we'd do an Italian theme, pipe in some Dean Martin for atmosphere—" I had to cut Ralphie off because I remembered their theme-park idea only too well, including Ralphie channeling Dean Martin. "Ralphie," I said, "sometimes genius has to be its own reward."

"Maybe so," Ralphie agreed reluctantly.

Then the five of them got lanterns and headed for the Tower to look around.

While they were gone, I sat back in my porch chair and must've dozed off. It wasn't a restful doze, though, because my mind was on fire. First I saw Red on the Tower, brandishing a flaming sword; then Red flying up and out, his long hair trailing behind him in flames; then Sterling crying for Red, staring hopelessly at the blazing bonfire. In one fiery image after another, flames leaped and crackled and burned, threatening to engulf me.

When the flames started wailing, though—an eerie howl like the keening of a Banshee—I sat bolt upright in my chair.

Silence.

Damn it all, Mags, I said to myself, calm down. What happened here tonight isn't about you. It's about Sterling and Red and Kells and . . . Oh. My. God. This *is* about me as well. What've I gotten myself into?

There was no sign of my friends coming back from the Tower, so I sat quietly. And sipped my wine. And waited.

The Fab Five weren't gone more than twenty minutes, and when they got back it was obvious they'd been having a high old time. They were talking a mile a minute and falling-down laughing while they interrupted each other, and none of it was making any sense to me. "Okay, you guys," I said. "What'd you do while you were gone, and what's so freaking funny?"

"Mags," Cedric said, "we know tonight was tragic, but—"

"—pitch dark at the Tower—"

"—started when Wally tripped and fell on Frankie's lamp—"

"—told Ralphie to grab my *amp*, not the lamp—"

"—yelled *What the fuck? Douse it, douse it!* but—"

"—volume stuck on *high*—"

"—Dracula ten feet tall on the Tower—"

"—scared the shit outta' Trooper—"

"—freaked out, says he saw a ghost with horns—"

"STOP!" This was me. "Dammit, slow down! You're not making any sense!"

"You're right, Mags, and we apologize," Cedric said. "How about finding more chairs so we can all get comfortable, and we'll tell you about it. And we'll open that bottle of Shiraz?"

Which we did. We settled down on the porch and sipped Shiraz, that is, and it was a relief for me to let them talk. Cedric started off by reminding me that by the time their group arrived here tonight, the excitement was basically over.

"You filled us in, Mags," Cedric said, "about the guy on the Tower with a girl and how everything went apocalyptic, so we wanted to go check out that big fire site by the Tower. We knew it was pitch dark over there, so we scrounged around for flashlights, torches, anything we could find, and that's when Wally grabbed Frankie's magic lantern and—"

"Wait," I said, "Wally grabbed *what*?"

"Mags," Christopher cut in, "the magic lantern was part of Geno's Transylvania setup at the store. You were there; you saw the video projection on the wall behind Wally's diorama, remember? Me all in black, playing my theramin?"

"Of course I remember. If you ever need a day job you can rent yourself out as a Dracula Impersonator."

"I'm not sure that's a compliment but I'll let it pass. Anyway, it was Frankie's magic lantern that made the video projection possible."

"Right, I remember now. Frankie always designs Geno's Halloween Village because, as Geno's told me a hundred times, *Frankie, he does it up real artsy.* But I still don't understand how the magic lantern showed up here tonight."

"Because we left Geno's store in a mad rush," Christopher said, "and when we did, I hollered to Ralphie to grab the *amp* for my theramin. But Ralphie thought I said *lamp*, so he grabbed Frankie's magic lantern and jumped into Wally's BMW with it."

"Okay, so back to what happened at the Tower?"

"So when we got to the Tower," Cedric said, "there wasn't much to see. We talked to Trooper for a few minutes and would have headed back at that point, except Wally wanted to examine those fire lines that spiraled out toward the beach. We said fine, just don't take forever, and that's when things got freaking spectacular."

"Spectacular is right," Lady laughed. "When Wally tripped over a dead fire line and fell on Frankie's lantern, the video of Christopher playing his theremin got stuck at 'ON' and projected onto the Tower. *At full volume.* The theremin-video only played for a few minutes, but it was wild."

"Totally wild," Cedric agreed, laughing. "The Christopher-image on that Tower was ten feet tall."

"Trooper wet himself," Christopher said, grinning.

"No wonder," Cedric said. "I'd have pissed myself, too, if I thought I'd seen Satan in person, ten feet tall and calling me home. But to give him credit, Trooper caught the punk who shot his rifle at the pile of fire logs and started the big bonfire. Trooper arrested him, didn't he?"

"Yeah," Christopher said, "but only after a tall guy in a bear costume tackled the punk kid first and sat on him, holding him down. That's what Trooper said, anyway."

"Maybe Trooper was temporarily blinded, like Ralphie," Wally said. "Ralphie says he saw a big white ghost. It must have been an after-image, though, because—"

"No way!" Ralphie hollered. "That wasn't no freakin' after-image! I saw a ghost, I'm tellin' you, a ghost with horns!"

After we all got a good laugh out of their story, they said they'd be on their way to the Boardwalk. "Just to check it out," Cedric said, "to see if things got as nutso there as they did here."

Ralphie seemed disgruntled, definitely out-of-sorts. "Nutso is right," he groused. "Like me and Geno have remiterated, the Genius House is no place for normal people like us." (I noticed while he was talking that his tinfoil halo had slipped over one ear, and he'd donned black socks and wingtips on his formerly bare feet.)

At first I thought Wally was discomfited, too, by his sojourn at the Tower. But when I heard him muttering to himself about *self-sustained exothermic chemical feedback loops* and *Fibonacci fire-line spiral*, I realized he was fine. Just still intrigued by Red's networked fire sites and fuse lines.

Back at the Temple, Lily Amaryllis was mad and sad and worried. All at the same time.

She was mad because Preacher's so-called "friends" left the Barbecue early. Brigadier did a bunk when it got dark, and everyone else cleared out when the pork and beer and brownies were gone. *They're all freeloaders!* she said to herself. She couldn't be mad at Preacher for inviting them, though, because he loved hosting the Barbecue and the Feast. It was like the old days when he gave parties and had lots of friends.

Preacher had been so sad, though, since they ran out of money, and that made Lily Amaryllis sad too. Thank goodness for Moses! He worked at that Halfway House called . . . what was it? The Little Foxes, that's right, and he even sold squirrel pelts and bird feathers on the Internet, but it still wasn't enough.

And it was hard on a kid to be working all the time. No wonder he stole that big black car and went joy riding with his friends. Lily Amaryllis had to admit, though, the car came in handy when they had to rob that candy store again.

Well, she couldn't help being mad at the freeloaders and sad because Moses had to work so hard, but most of all she was worried about Preacher because he hadn't come back after he chugged away on Mystery Train when all the noise started over at the big house. She wasn't scared of tromping through the scrub after dark, though, and she knew she could find Preacher if she followed the train tracks. So that's what she decided to do.

First she changed into her best white ceremonial robe so Preacher would be sure to recognize her when she called to him, and then she started walking. She found the train, all right, but there was no sign of Preacher. The stone was still rolled away, though, so she knew he went through Glory. What to do, what to do? Should she follow him?

Normally Lily Amaryllis wouldn't have ventured onto the Genius House property because she despised those people. This was not a normal situation, however, so she steeled herself to be strong. Slowly, carefully, she hefted her considerable girth through the opening in the Bottle Wall, stopped for a minute to catch her breath, and started walking toward the Tower.

At the base of the Tower she found Preacher, obviously at peace with his Maker. She was saddened, naturally, but glad someone had been kind enough to cover him with what looked like a blanket. In that all-pervasive gloom she couldn't see color, just shades of gray, so she didn't know at first that the "blanket" was red. As fate would have it, though, a reluctant gibbous moon popped from behind a cloud long enough to illuminate the scene. *It's a scarlet shroud!* she cried out in horror. *They covered him with a scarlet shroud!*

Looking closely, she saw that the shroud was blotched with soot, stained just as Lily Amaryllis knew herself to be. *Oh, Daddy, Daddy*, she cried piteously to the lifeless lump on the ground. *Has our sin come upon us?*

While the moon slid back behind its cloud, Lily Amaryllis sank heavily onto the blackened pyre where Preacher lay. Immersed in darkness and assaulted by memories, she re-lived those years after Mommy died: the parties with Daddy and his

Friends and Pretty Ladies, but then Daddy fell and hurt his head and couldn't remember . . . couldn't remember . .

The truth is, Lily Amaryllis was never much of a thinker. It's also possible that too many "special" brownies at the Barbecue had fuddled her brain. Whatever the reason, she became unstuck in time while reels of memory played through her mind like a slideshow going backward, then forward, then backward again:

> . . . *sweet Daddy said I'm pretty, gave me Rose . . .*
> *my sister and my daughter, my blonde baby angel . . .*
> *Daddy's so smart, found Great Grampaw's treasure .*
> *. . has to teach those bad Fairies a lesson . . . fell so far,*
> *down the staircase, burned his hand . . . God said*
> *build a Temple . . . nice surfer boys help Daddy build*
> *the Temple . . . go through Glory, find the treasure .*
> *. . surfer boys so nice to me, so grateful . . . don't tell*
> *Daddy about them . . . or about Brigadier . . . it was*
> *wrong, it was sinful . . . Daddy claimed the baby,*
> *didn't know . . . sweet baby boy, named him Moses .*
> *. . Daddy fell so far, hurt his head . . . buried Great*
> *Grampaw's treasure . . . can't remember where it's*
> *buried . . . Daddy's friends got mad, took Pretty*
> *Ladies away . . . mean reporters . . . flashbulbs hurt*
> *my eyes . . . Friends went away too . . . shouldn't be*
> *mad at Daddy . . . gave me Rose . . .*

Suddenly the night came alive with an unearthly moaning.

Shifting her gaze toward the Tower, Lily Amaryllis felt a chill hand clutch her heart. While lights flashed and circled erratically, making her blink and squint, she saw The Black Lord himself—Satan—beckoning to her from the Tower. Ten feet tall and glowering while a demented chorus of damned souls moaned in anguish, Satan waved his arms wildly in her direction, motioning that she should bring Preacher to him.

No! No! she cried to the apparition, *YOU CAN'T HAVE HIM!*

She had to get Preacher back to the Temple, away from Satan, but how to carry him? Groping frantically on the ground for something, anything, she felt a heavenly softness, like a cloud. Could it be a cloak? Yes, a cloak! It's a royal cloak! And on it lay something that felt hard, with sharp points. A crown? Yes! It must be a crown!

In that moment Lily Amaryllis knew she'd been given a Sign. Tossing the nasty blanket aside (no way would she wrap him in a scarlet shroud!), Lily Amaryllis rolled Preacher onto the cloud-soft cloak and bundled it around him. Before she picked him up, however, she put the crown on her own head because that way, it would be easier to carry.

As she gazed one last time toward the Tower in defiance of Satan, two Angels appeared—shining, shimmering, clothed in silver so bright and dazzling. It was as if the Light of Heaven itself shone from their garments. Like Saul of Tarsus on the Damascus Road, Lily Amaryllis experienced the Divine Presence in a miraculous Vision:

> *While the Angels banished Satan from the Tower,*
> *Saint Francis of Assisi himself appeared and wafted*
> *a blessing toward her and Preacher.*

The Vision lasted only a few minutes before the Angels beckoned for Saint Francis to come with them, and the threesome faded into the darkness.

Those visionary few minutes were enough, however. Picking up the precious bundle and cradling it in her arms, Lily

Amaryllis headed for home, blissful in the knowledge that The Call had come to her, and that she would answer it.

After assuring Christopher I'd retrieve his amp from Geno's store and take it upstairs with me to my apartment for safe-keeping, I stood in the driveway and waved while the BMW and the Harley drove away.

I was getting ready to drive Agatha home when I heard someone calling to me from the porch. "Sterling, is that you? Where've you been? You were at the Tower and then you dis-appeared. Are you okay?"

"Mostly tired. And mad. Mad at Red for being stupid, for having no respect."

"What do you mean? No respect for what?"

"For the Celtic traditions he makes such a big deal about. Masquerading as the Lord of Misrule was pathetic, starting with that ridiculous getup. He ordered the faux-sheepskin cloak from Land's End, and he got the antlers from Dunn's Attic in Ormond Beach." Sterling looked sad, really sad. "Not only that," she said, "the horned god Cernunnos is Wiccan, not Celtic, and the flaming sword's a Buddhist icon. Red bought the one he torched from a store in Cassadaga."

"So even if the Fairies had been here, they wouldn't have come when Red called them?"

"Hardly." Sterling made a disgusted face, then looked sad again. "It was terrible for George because she's worried sick about Uncle Billy. He's devastated that the Fairies left, keeps saying *That was never supposed to happen,* over and over."

Sorrow came running then, barking and snuffling. "Hey, old girl," Sterling said, hunching down and hugging the Irish Setter. "It's okay. We'll get Red back, I promise."

We'll get Red back? How? I wondered, but I didn't ask out loud, of course.

Finally I said I was blitzed and needed to go home, and Sterling agreed it was time to call it a night.

Agatha was happy to leave the Genius House and get on the road, but I worried all the way home about Red and his obsession with that beautiful old Irish legend *Deirdre of the Sorrows*. I mean, ever since George and Sterling explained Pathics to me, I just assumed that Sterling and her brothers were exempt from those so-called *virulent memes*. But now I wondered.

What was it Sterling said? That Red was trying to make the Celtic Romeo and Juliet story *real*? Well, isn't that the definition of a virulent meme? You find a story so compelling, you want to emulate it? You're so attracted to a story, you want it to be *your* story?

Yes yes, I know, that's also how a role model works—by grafting your life-script onto a story you admire.

But Red's Deirdre-delusion seems crazier, more virulent than a romantic fantasy.

And that's why I couldn't stop worrying.

BANGS AND WHIMPERS

THWAACK! "Dammit, the ball skipped again."

"Crouch, Mags, bend your knees."

"I'm trying, I'm trying . . . *UHH!* Oh-h-h, that hurt."

"Get up!. Okay, now stay low. Keep it low! And when I return your kill shot, *dive* for it!"

"Sterling, I can't play the way you play! I'll hurt myself!"

"Focus, Mags, focus! One more kill shot, one more dive, then we'll go get breakfast."

Groan. "Okay, tell me again why we had to be here at five o'clock in the a.m., especially after our Halloween-from-Hell last night? And how come my kill shot's so freaking important?"

"Just one more killer, Mags. Come on, I'll help you set it up."

Sigh. I'd barely gotten to sleep when Sterling called, said she'd pick me up so we could get to the gym when it opens because I need to practice my kill shot. Which made no sense to me whatsoever, but she wouldn't take no for an answer.

"Just one more and then we quit? And get breakfast? Promise?"

"Absolutely. I know you can get a roll-out this time. Let's do it."

To refresh your memory, I've been completely honest about being a little over-the-hill to play indoor racquetball. Nevertheless, it's the only sport I really love, and I enjoy playing it my doofus way—not keeping score, just running around until I'm pleasantly sweaty, then chowing down on some serious carbs. However, even if I've been conned into playing a "real" game and keeping score while losing miserably, I can salvage a modicum of self-respect by managing— occasionally— to execute a kill shot.

The great thing about a kill shot in racquetball is that your opponent can't return it, so you get a bit of a rest. Unless your opponent is Sterling Silver Buck, of course, which is why I was not a happy camper that morning at the gym.

Anyway, the best kill shot for me is a straight frontcourt kill, the one I'd been practicing with Sterling. To make this shot you get positioned in frontcourt with your opponent behind you, and you slam the ball so hard and low against the front wall that your opponent can't reach it to return it. And if you're *really* on fire you slam the ball into the front wall so low, it can't bounce back up from the floor, just rolls back. Hence, a roll-out.

Sterling kept her promise about one more kill shot and then we'd be done, but it took me twenty exhausting minutes to get it set it up and delivered.

(It was *not* a roll-out.)

I was grumpy when we arrived at Gram's Kitchen for breakfast but cheered up considerably when I noticed chocolate-drizzled bearclaws on a pastry tray. After we got ourselves settled in a front window booth (Gram's coffee isn't as good as Geno's, but it's adequate), Sterling started in on her omelet with a side order of sprouts, and I was ready to talk.

"Okay, Sterling, do you mind explaining why we had to get athletically inspired so early this morning? I mean, I love your theory about making racquetball an infinite game, but what's so important about my kill shot?"

"I needed a workout this morning, Mags, and I know you still have questions about Pay the Piper. So I figured this way, we kill two birds: I get some exercise, and you get filled in about Flukey Fog. I meant for us to talk about it before now, like we talked about Squiffy Static."

"Right, those cutesy names again. I can't believe you say them with a straight face."

"I explained the names, Mags. They're catchy, and they're non-threatening."

"I know, I know. Okay, fill me in about Flukey Fog."

"Let's start," Sterling said, "by defining *Intervention*. You know that's how we refer to Pay the Piper, so define 'intervention.' What does it mean to you?"

"Well, *to intervene* means to meddle, to interfere, to mediate—with the intent of fixing a problem. An intervention's a necessary disruption, a drastic means to a good end. But that's the purpose of the Static, right? To disrupt global communication, thus distracting Sapients from plots and coups and warmongering? So why do you need Fog, too?"

"Because the Fog's different. The Fog will obliterate current national boundaries and set new ones: 42 new ones, to be exact. Right now there are approximately 190 nations on this planet, and they're always at each other's throats. But once Flukey Fog rolls in, 190 old *Nations* will be gone, and 42 new *Regions* will take their places . . . each with its own Piper."

Sterling seemed unaware that I was flustered. "Sterling," I said, "Stop! I truly cannot comprehend what you just said. You'll change the map of the world? And you'll do it with *fog*?"

"Believe me, Mags, I understand why you're confused. The Intervention's as complicated as all get out, and no wonder. After all, Boskops started working with the Gardeners over a century ago—"

"Wait. *Gardeners*? Who the hell are the Gardeners?"

"Not important right now because—"

"Dammit, Sterling! It's important to *me*! You keep on dropping bombs in the middle of so-called explanations that leave me with more questions . . . " Uh oh. The whole restaurant except us had gotten quiet, people in other booths were staring, and Sterling was giving me one of her *looks*. Time to get off my high horse because what good does it do me, anyway?

"Sterling I'm sorry, please go on."

"No more protests?"

"Scout's honor."

"Okay, let's come at this from another angle. The ultimate purpose of the Intervention is to re-direct Sapient evolution. Remember your 'lessons' about Datta and Jengu? How their tribes of Neanders and Floreans evolved in isolation?"

"Sure. It's like Darwin finding blue-footed boobies in the Galapagos Islands. The boobies and a whole bunch of odd creatures proved that any population will evolve uniquely if it's isolated from other populations for a long enough time."

"That's right, as far as it goes. But we Sapients need time to evolve further—into a species that's hardwired for empathy. At that point we'll be able to communicate mind-to-mind."

"We'll be able to mind-talk? Really?"

"That's our hope, but mind-talking's not easy. Mind-to-mind talking requires trust and compassion, an empathetic awareness of The Other so complete that we not only picture ourselves in another's shoes, we also imagine ourselves *walking and living* in those shoes. It requires, in other words, that we be able to adjust our perspective so totally that we literally *become* The Other."

"So we have to *evolve* into empathy? But that could be a long time, couldn't it? Human evolution's measured in generations and a generation's at least 30 years."

"I admit it's a longshot, but that's what Pay the Piper's all about: setting Sapients on a different evolutionary road."

"As I said before, I think this all sounds like a fairy tale."

"And as *I* said before, it's not. Our Intervention will separate humanity into 42 populations, isolate each group into its own Region (using the Fog), and see what happens. We believe—we hope—that *emergent behavior* in some of these groups will skew toward cooperation rather than conflict."

"So you'll launch 42 self-contained experiments in social engineering?"

"Yep."

"But some will fail?"

"Afraid so."

"Then what?"

"Flour beetles."

"Wow. I HATE those flour beetles!"

"I hate them too, Mags, but it's a useful analogy."

"Well I'm trying, but I simply can't picture fog as a barrier that keeps some people in and others out. I mean, it's one thing to build walls. We all understand walls. But you'll just roll in some fog and establish these Regions? I don't get it."

"Okay, consider this: the Fog's mushroom-based just like the Static. But instead of electrical energy that spikes, the fog's an effluence. It's like a ghost—ephemeral, but real."

"Well, getting back to emergent behaviors, let's hope Sapients are smart enough to emulate the self-organizing behavior of bees in a hive. I learned about *emergence* years ago with a great science teacher I had in high school. Her name was Miss Fortunato, and she was really prescient, way ahead of her time."

"Yes, you're right. Alice—Alli—was way ahead of her time."

"What? How d'you know her name? *Dammit, are you in my head again?*"

"Naw, you must've told me about her. Anyhoo, if bees and birds and fish can self-organize, we're hoping Sapients in some of the 42 Regions will do it too."

There's nothing like the possibility of apocalypse to whet one's appetite. While I started on another bearclaw and a second mug of Gram's adequate coffee, Sterling topped off her omelet and sprouts with a dish of stewed prunes before going right back to the topic of Flukey Fog.

"Remember, Mags, about Mycelium, the growth medium for mushrooms?"

"Sure, I remember. Mycelium's a vast underground neural net that encircles the globe, even underlying the ocean beds. And it's attuned to all planetary Flora and Fauna including us. Whoa, wait a minute . . . are you saying the Fog's empathetic?"

Sterling nodded yes. "Omigod, so that means it's *sentient?*"

Sterling nodded yes again. "I know it's a tough concept to get your head around, Mags, but it's true. And once we launch the Intervention—globally, all 42 Regions at once—the Fog will emit its miasmic effluence, in effect beckoning Sapients to join like-minded populations."

"So there'll be some movement of people from Region to Region?"

"A little movement, not a lot. But yes, there will be some re-locating."

"But how will we . . . they . . . find each other? Especially if they start out in different Regions on different continents, miles apart?"

"They'll hear the Pipers and—" Cutting herself off in mid-sentence, Sterling looked out the window by our booth and abruptly stood up. "Mags, I gotta go. These are the keys to the Suburban. Drive it back to Daytona, park it in front of Geno's store, lock the keys inside, and I'll pick it up later."

"Okay, but what—"

"Thanks, Mags. Bye!"

I watched through Gram's window while Sterling ran out the door and jumped in a black Suburban that had apparently been idling in the parking lot. *Damn,* I said to myself while I scooted close to the window.

Trying to get a better look, I bumped my coffee mug with my elbow and tumped it over, sending it careening across the table and crashing to the floor. By the time I'd apologized for the mess and left a big tip, the Suburban with Sterling and an unknown driver was long gone.

At that point there was nothing I could do but head for home, so while I drove I thought bemusedly about our conversation at Gram's about the Fog. *It's a real barrier, Mags,* Sterling said, *like the Veil of the Celts. Or a force field. And since it's organic, maybe it's even like our Sapient blood-brain barrier. That'd make sense, in fact, because our blood-brain barrier is defined as 'highly selective as to permeability'* . . .

That's when I zoned out. Zoned out purposely, I mean, because at some point *my* brain becomes "selective as to permeability" and says stop! No more! We're done here!

Then I amused myself by wondering what Kurt Vonnegut would think about all this, were he here. Flukey Fog? It's no more fantastic than Ice-nine. And the cool thing about Vonnegut is that down deep, he was just like us: unwilling to give up on the human race.

It's like Sterling said, and Kells too, *There's as much good in Sapients as bad. We just want to buy some time with the Intervention, to give Sapients a chance to grow up.*

After I parked the Suburban in front of Geno's store and got back to my apartment, it hit me that Sterling "played" me this morning, and not just on the racquetball court. Mags, I said to myself, laughing, you were out-maneuvered. Every time I asked why it was so freaking important for me to practice my kill shot, Sterling came up with a non-answer and changed the subject. And I never even noticed, until now.

Okay then, I said back to myself, she won that game but I'm not giving up. One way or another I'll find out what that 5 a.m. meetup with me and my kill shot was all about.

I was still laughing while I got comfy on my big cushy sofa and woke up hours later, having rolled off onto my living room floor—exhausted, depleted, and in dire need of caffeine and sugar.

When Geno saw me plop my poor pathetic self in a booth at the coffeeshop, he came to my rescue with pastries and superbold coffee. "Thanks, Geno. I had a helluva night, followed by an exhausting early-morning workout. I'm blitzed."

"Oh, yeah? Well I'm blitzed too because that Greek asshole huffed in here this morning, sayin' I was to blame because Byzantium got blown up last night! You were at the Boardwalk, right? You wanna' tell me what happened?"

"Sorry, all I know about the Boardwalk is what your Village People told me."

"My Village People?"

"The crew from your Halloween Village—Christopher, Ralphie, and Wally, plus Cedric and Lady. They showed up at the Genius House late last night and told me the dome on the Rotunda at Byzantium imploded after my Genius House group and I were long gone. Anyway, how could *you* be responsible for the dome collapsing?"

"Because Pan Pappadiculous wanted to install AC as cheap as possible when he was building the place, so I made him a deal. And now it's *my* fault the dome came crashing down? Gimme a break!"

"So what'd you say to him when he showed up here this morning?"

"*So sue me!* I said to him. And you know what he said back to me? He said *You'll be hearing from my cousins in Corfu.* And you know what I said back to him? I said *Fuck your cousins in Corfu! And get outta' my establishment before I call MY cousins and sic 'em on your sorry ass!* And then he said—"

"Whoa, Geno, hold on a minute! Your cousins? You mean Ralphie Marbles and Old Sonny and Frankie Moose?"

"Yeah."

"Um, not to be disrespectful, but those guys are not exactly Killing Machines."

"Maybe, but the King of Bowling don't know that. And while I was usherin' him out, I administrated a kick in the ass. Metaphoric like you're always talkin' about, also French."

"You mean a *coup de grâce?*"

"Yeah, one a' those." Geno grinned, pushed his glasses up on his nose, and winked at me. "I told him off good," he continued. "I told him my friend Mags is writing a book about all this and if he doesn't back off, she'll say in the book he has a tiny pecker to match his tiny brain."

Geno and I continued to share Halloween stories while I finished my coffee, but as I was leaving he blew me away when he said that after closing his "Village" on Halloween night and driving back to the beachside, he saw Indiana Jones riding *shotgun* in a red Miata."

"You're sure you saw Indiana Jones?"

"Oh yeah, positively. I got outta' the way pronto when this red Miata with Indiana Jones in the passenger seat comes barrelling north on A1A, running red lights and changin' lanes spasmodically."

"You mean *erratically*?"

"Yeah, like I said. Somebody shoulda clapped a citizen's arrest on that driver, but it wasn't up to me. The girl was drivin' crazy and the guy had a big bull whip, so I let it go. Like I always say, it doesn't pay to mess with nutcases."

"What'd the driver look like?"

"Just a kid, looked like she was wearin' a bikini."

"Could it have been a harem outfit?"

"A what?"

"A harem outfit, like Scheherazade would wear."

"*Who?*"

"Never mind, I'll check it out later."

MORE WHIMPERS

As the post-holiday week went on and I gathered stories about Halloween's fallout, I realized that Geno's encounter with Pan Pappanicolau was the tip of the iceberg. All during the days that followed, in fact, I stayed busy capturing the cacophony of voices that clamored for attention, starting with a surprise early-morning visit from Leon.

To say I was "surprised" when Leon knocked on my front door, though, doesn't totally capture my situation. Why? Because I have to add "mortified" to the mix. I mean, there he stood in all his official gorgeousness (he's known to numerous female admirers as "Hot Buns," so I'm sure you get the picture). Meanwhile I— attired in ratty pj's and tube socks—peered up at him through smudgy trifocals. Not my best moment, for sure.

Fortunately, he'd brought pastries from downstairs, and I always have coffee, so after we settled down to talk, he told me about his Halloween raid at a strip club called The Little Foxes where local politicians were suited up like big hairy animals and "the girls" flaunted fluffy foxtails but little else. "Leon, that's hilarious, but I don't get it. You came all the way from Tallahassee to bust some city commissioners outfitted like Big Bad Wolves?"

"Of course not. We wanted the Bandushko brothers, planned to catch them red-handed with drugs so we could hold them while we suss out their Bimini connectives. They were supposed to be at the strip club after they docked their boat on Halloween, but they never showed. And we still need the big guy, Max Finkelstein."

"Why? He's a doofus, isn't he? Strictly small-time?"

"He might be a doofus, but we think he's the key to a bigtime internet operation."

"You mean statewide?"

"Way bigger than that, maybe global."

"You're telling me Maxie runs a bigtime Cartel? *Maxie?*"

"As far as we know he doesn't *run* anything. If he's really the key, he's an unwitting key. Just a dupe. There's no center to this thing, Mags. No dictator, no command post. It's a conglomerate of virulent memes, and they spread—"

Leon was still talking but I zoned out. A conglomerate of *virulent memes?*

"—the way a virus spreads, inexorably. I picture nests of snakes—"

"Whoa, Leon! *Stop!* Sorry, it's that vivid imagination of mine. It's too early in the morning for me to be picturing nests of snakes."

"Hey sorry, I didn't mean to freak you out. I gotta go anyway, figured I'd stop by and get a hug before I fly back to Tallahassee."

Before he left, though, Leon told me the Bandushko brothers (Dmitri and Grigory) "had it in" for Maxie Finkelstein. When I asked why, he said Max murdered their cousins Ivan and Igor (the two dead guys who ended up in the NASCAR balloon's basket).

"So Dmitri and Grigory were eye-witnesses?"

"No, but they crew with a dude who *was* an eye-witness, and he told the brothers he saw Max murder their cousins execution-style in Bimini."

Leon also mentioned he was puzzled about something that happened on Halloween night when the Bandushkos were anchored off Ponce Inlet with their friend the Eye-Witness. "The way Grigory told the story to my agents," Leon said, "he and his brother jumped overboard and swam to shore in a panic, leaving their friend to fend for himself."

"But he wouldn't say why they panicked?" I asked. "Why they jumped overboard?"

"Nope. Whatever scared them was so traumatic, Dmitri couldn't talk about it at all and Grigory could only describe it in Russian." Leon laughed then and played me a phone-video of Grigory talking excitedly in Russian: Лодка для монстров. Мы прыгаем. Мы плаваем, как ад.

"Leon, the video's hilarious but you know I don't speak Russian. What's the translation?"

"It translates roughly as *Monster attack boat. We jump. We swim like hell.* But when we tried to press them about it, we got nothing. Nada. Zero. Bupkus."

Grigory's comment was "puzzling," that is, until I caught up with Jengu a few days later and asked him what he did on Halloween. "Mags," Jengu gloated, "that Halloween scene was totally bitchin'. Me n' Squiggs had a load of fendelin in Michael's boat when some jerkoff dude in another boat shot at us. Prob'ly thought we were hijackin' his stash or somethin' but hey! that's real bad manners."

"Jengu, that's bizarre. Then what'd you do?"

"So Squiggs, he's easily offended, he turbo'd himself up n' over, landed on the jerkoff's boat, tentacles wavin'. An' that's when two guys jumped overboard and started swimmin' double-time toward the shore. Last I saw, the jerkoff dude with the gun was headed out to sea at full throttle, shriekin' like a banshee."

All of this is interesting, of course, but it doesn't explain why, on Halloween night, the Bandushko brothers and their friend the Eye-Witness were anchored off Ponce Inlet. As we'd find out much later, they were waiting there to rendezvous with a boat from Bimini. But we didn't know that then.

In the meantime, the Bandushkos apparently overcame their Halloween trauma enough to talk about it, because the word around town is that Grigory *and* Dmitri are enjoying their new-found celebrity—trading stories about their terrifying aquatic encounter with a Giant Rainbow Squid for free drinks and smokes.

Next, an update about Byzantium. You probably remember that early on, tourists at the Boardwalk were texting and tweeting the folks at home like crazy, saying they were hanging out with Lady Gaga and Elton John? It wasn't true, of course. What happened was, the tourists mistook Semi Sweet Charity for Lady Gaga and the large Tweetie Bird for Sir Elton. Both of whom (Semi Sweet and Tweetie) left the Boardwalk early, heading for the Yum Yum Tree party in South Daytona.

You'll also recall that when we last saw Pan Papanicolaou, he was huffing and puffing in the hot humid darkness of the Master Control Room at Byzantium because the AC and backup generator had blown, causing a total blackout inside. While he huffed and puffed, Pan cursed his brother and son who, like Semi Sweet and Tweetie, had left the Byzantium earlier in pursuit of their own agendas: Petros with a pneumatic girl scout leader at the Bandshell and Prax with Michael at the Yum Yum Tree (it was a big party).

It was indeed unfortunate for Pan that both Prax and Petros were absent when the power blew, because they knew about the scaffolding in the dome, but Pan did not. The scaffolding? Yes, Ben Bulben's scaffolding which he left in place when he didn't finish painting the mural in the dome. The unfinished mural didn't attract attention, though, even though two of the angels looked fuzzy, and the Emperor Constantine was missing one arm. If you happened to look up, you'd assume the angels were flying through clouds, and Constantine was one of those Winged Victory types who are always minus an arm or two.

Anyway, neither Prax nor Petros informed Pan about the unfinished mural or the scaffolding, and both had their reasons. Prax, for one, was sick and tired of Pan's bullshit about *making babies for the honor of the family*. Petros, in turn, had a whole catalogue of grievances against his bad-tempered brother, not the least of which was Pan taking full credit for their designer balls.

Ben, too, could hardly be blamed for leaving his scaffolding in place while he forgot about finishing the mural. After all, when you do remember at some point to get back to work in a hundred-foot-high dome, you'll need scaffolding. And Ben's scaffolding was *smart*—it could be controlled by the artist up in the dome on a hand-held gizmo, moving him smoothly from place to place. And if the hand-held gizmo felt its batteries beginning to fail, it would send a message to the failure-proof-battery-powered-backup-console in the Master Control Room.

So there was Pan in the Master Control Room on the night in question, huffing and puffing and pushing buttons and throwing switches like a crazy person. Unbeknownst to Pan, however, some of those buttons and switches were talking to Ben's scaffolding, prompting the scaffolding to untuck itself. Halloween partiers having fled the Great Rotunda at that point, there was no danger that someone would be injured by scaffold-stuff falling to the floor. There *was* one clear and present danger, however, because the dome itself was not sturdy.

You see, in one of his many cost-cutting schemes, Pan compromised the structural integrity of the dome by purchasing the cheapest materials possible and employing transient labor at way below minimum wage. When Petros pointed out to Pan that this was a stupid way to build a hundred-foot dome, Pan responded in his usual style. *It's a dome on a bowling alley, for Chrissake!* he was heard to yell. *It ain't the fucking Vatican, so who cares if it's built cheap?*

Thus it was that while he pushed buttons and toggled switches on a master console that was arguably smarter than Pan himself, Ben Bulben's scaffolding was preparing itself enthusiastically for his return. Ropes uncoiled, wires strained, pulleys slipped and twisted, slats and boards and baskets swayed and slid, until—

RUMBLE RUMBLE Crash *Slam* BANG!

The hundred-foot dome over the Great Rotunda at the Byzantium Bowling Center creaked and cracked and finally imploded, providing a heart-stopping photo op that looked like someone had bombed St. Peter's Basilica in Rome. Complicating matters was the erroneous information that Lady Gaga and Sir Elton John were on-site witnesses to the catastrophe.

When neither could be found once the smoke had cleared, news went viral that the two *Very Big Celebrities* had gotten blown up. Word went out on a global scale, in fact, and when accompanied by smart-device videos of the dome collapsing, there was no stopping the world media from cashing in.

YET MORE WHIMPERS

During the post-Halloween fallout Slim was a veritable fount of information, especially about Brigadier. "The thing is," she told me, "Brigadier's not crazy. He's been faking crazy ever since an EVAC crew ferried him from the Genius House to a psychiatric ward on Halloween."

"How d' you know he's faking?"

"Because I got the lowdown from an orderly who 'overheard' a conversation between two of Brigadier's VFW friends, basically that Brigadier's faking his 'two headed mushroom' story so he won't get nailed for the fire at the bowling alley."

"Wait," I said, "a fire at the bowling alley?"

"You know," Slim said. "During that so-called 'Cabaret' engineered by Pan's son?"

"But Slim," I protested, "that fire was an accident. It started when a patron knocked an oil lamp off a table."

"Well," Slim said, "according to the geezer-vets, Brigadier *purposely* knocked an oil lamp to the floor, then started the fire with his Zippo lighter. The word is that Pan Papanicolaou found the lighter but didn't report it because he didn't want an arson investigation, so he hid the Zippo in the Pro Shop and forgot about it until the brother—what's his name?"

"Petros."

"Right, Petros. Anyway, Pan's brother found the Zippo, turned it in to the cops, and now the insurance company won't pay up. And the plot thickens because there's scuttlebutt about Pan having a history with 'suspicious fires' in South Florida. Something about being in cahoots with a guy who owns a pub franchise—"

"A pub franchise? *Pig* pubs?"

"That's the one. How'd you know?"

"Oh, I get around."

Slim's disgusted because the arson investigation will be on hold as long as Brigadier keeps on faking crazy. "What a scuzz ball!" Slim said. "The DNA test on the blow-up doll 'sample' came back a clear match for Brigadier which totally creeps me out, but there's no law against playing with a doll in the privacy of your foxhole."

"But who dropped the blow-up doll at Sterling's front door? I mean, that's harassment, isn't it? Like sending a box of poop to someone through the mail?"

"Only if the doll was put there intentionally, with malice aforethought."

"But it wasn't?"

"Nope. The red hairs on the doll came from the Irish Setter that lives at the Genius House."

"You mean Sorrow?"

"Excuse me?"

"The dog's name is Sorrow."

"Of course it would be," Slim laughed. "A dog named Sorrow encapsulates this whole sorrowful business, doesn't it? Anyhow, we figure the Irish Setter crotch-snuffled the blow-up doll out of Brigadier's Foxhole and dragged it around before abandoning it in the front yard."

Slim's Halloween travails weren't limited to Brigadier, however. In fact, the reason Doc Kumagai didn't show up at the Genius House until the next morning was because it took Slim all night to find him, have his car towed, and bring him to the Tower. When Slim told me later about what happened, she said her Halloween all-nighter was exhausting but hilarious.

"Before I could go looking for Doc," she said, "I had to ferry that thug Beebo in my squad car and hand him over for processing. He must've been high on something because the whole time he was in my car he wouldn't shut up about Bigfoot. Kept babbling about a big hairy bear that sat on him and held him down. I asked Trooper about it, being as he's the one who cuffed the creep."

"What'd Trooper say?"

"He said a guy in a bear costume tackled Beebo and held him down. And the guy took a big chance, according to Trooper, because the Beebo creep was waving his rifle around and acting so crazy; it's lucky nobody got shot. Including the guy in the bear suit." I was of course not contradicting Trooper's bear-suit story, just saying "thank you" to Datta in my head, when Slim added the punch line to the Beebo story. "And we got a great outcome, thanks again to Trooper."

"Why's that?"

"Because Trooper's been investigating the dead squirrels and birds all over town, and he nailed Beebo for it. Said the asshole had a squirrel-skin cap stuffed in his pocket and tons of photos on his phone, all showing him and his buddies with their 'trophies.' It's disgusting."

Getting back to Slim looking for Doc on Halloween night, Slim said she was stuck in gridlock for hours. "Finally I made it to where Doc wrapped his convertible around a concrete pelican in front of the Marriott on A1A. He said some twit in a red Miata was driving crazy and ran a stop sign, so he had to swerve to get out of her way."

"Too funny!"

"Except it gets funnier. Doc was doubly pissed off because the bimbo he was with at the Boardwalk abandoned him for some other Batman—"

"Some *other* Batman?"

"Yep, Doc was duded up for Halloween as 'Decapitated Batman,' carrying his bloody Bat Head in a bucket. Said he got the idea from a guy that sells hotdogs off a cart downtown. So when he crash-landed on the pelican, tourists went crazy rubbernecking. Not to mention that 911 dispatchers were flooded with reports about a bloody decapitation—"

"It was ketchup, right? Not blood?"

"How'd you know?"

"I know the guy with the hotdog cart. Anyway, go on."

"Right, so it was practically morning when Doc and I finally pulled in at the Genius House and walked to the Tower. Trooper was right there, said the Fire Chief's crew covered the body with an old red blanket they found on the ground, and he'd stood watch ever since. Here comes the hitch: you ready?"

"As ready as I'll ever be."

"When Doc pulled the red the cape off the 'body,' it was just a fluffy blonde wig, all bedraggled and dirty."

"Uh oh."

"That's for sure. Doc went ballistic, demanded I fire Trooper because he obviously fucked up, said this was the god damnedest mess he'd ever seen, and it was enough to make a man retire."

"Holy crap, Slim, what'd you say?"

"Nothing. If I'd said anything at all, it would've been *Don't let the door hit you in the ass on your way out*."

It's true that before the Fire Chief's crew left the Genius House property on Halloween night, they found a red cloth thing on the ground and, in an act of compassion, used this "blanket" to cover the charred corpse that lay at the bonefire site near the Tower. It's also true that when Slim and Doc arrived the next morning, they were greeted by Trooper who'd been on duty throughout the night, faithfully guarding said blanketed corpse.

Which doesn't mean that Trooper stood at attention all night long and stared at the damn thing, of course. He'd had to relieve himself periodically in the scrub, and he got a nice break from guard duty, talking for a few minutes with those latecomers who wandered over from the Big House to look around. And oh yes, he had to change his uniform pants in his squad car after that crazy video flashed on the Tower.

Clearly, though, none of those brief interruptions counted as derelictions of duty.

Thus, when Slim and Doc finally showed up the next morning, Trooper saw no reason to mention that he might have torn his eyes away from the blanket-covered-corpse for a few minutes. Especially not when Doc Kumagai went ballistic and blamed him—Trooper—for the cockup.

After all, Trooper told himself, he'd spent too many years in dedicated service to have some douchebag pathologist mess with his service record and pension.

THE HOLY HALOS

It remains true that observers were unclear about what happened at the Genius House on Halloween night. You'll recall, I'm sure, that some said Red dove from the Tower into the pile of fire logs; others said he dove but disappeared in mid-flight; still others swore that he didn't dive at all, just went up in smoke. Well, whatever happened on Halloween, no one doubts there *was* a charred body at the base of the Tower—until that body went missing.

Naturally, rumors abounded. Some said trick-or-treaters stole it; others assumed animals got it. There was even a rumor about a horned figure carrying the body and disappearing into the surrounding pine-and-palmetto scrub. I had to admit my astonishment, though, when RonJon came in Geno's store shouting excitedly about his new "church" down at the Inlet.

Always alert for surprises by nutcases, Geno (bless him!) sat RonJon at a table and plied him with stale pumpkin pasticcios to keep him talking while I, coincidentally ensconced in a corner booth, couldn't help but listen in while RonJon rhapsodized over his spiritual awakening.

"It's the real deal, Bro!" RonJon bellowed. "We got us a Temple and a Blind Prophet—drives a train an' wears a white dress like the Pope, says two Angels dressed in silver rainments helped save her Daddy from the clutches of Satan."

"Shut *up!*"

"I'm tellin' you *straight,* man! An' we got us a first-class Relic, swear to God! A shrunken dude in a fuzzy coat and antlers, sits on a gold throne!"

"Real gold?"

"Course not! It's gold candy wrappers, but tourists don't know 'cause it's dark in the Temple!"

"Tourists'll believe *anything.*"

"You got that right! They pay big bucks to ride the train into the Temple, gawk at the Relic, ride the train back out! An' you know what's genius? We're goin' global! Callin' ourselves Holistic Franciscans, honorin' Saint Francis!"

Slight hesitation from Geno. "Uhh . . . Saint Francis?"

"You know, the barefoot dude what loved birds n' shit! We're honorin' Saint Francis 'cause the Prophet saw him in a *VISION!*"

"But . . . I thought you said the Prophet saw two Angels."

"Yeah, but she saw Saint Francis too! It was a fuckin' *TRIFECTA,* man!"

"Right . . . so you call yourselves The Holistic Franciscans?"

"Holy Halos for short! Callin' ourselves *Halos* 'cause Saint Francis had one in the Vision! The Prophet saw it, swear to God!"

Finally a story surfaced in the *Daytona Beach News Journal,* based on a TV interview of three rednecks from Samsula by Reporter Kalley Drum. Here's the transcript of the interview:

Good evening, everyone. I'm Kalley Drum, and this is AROUND OUR TOWN. I'll be talking today with three young men about their eyewitness perspective on the events at Ponce Inlet last Saturday, on Halloween.

Welcome, Gentlemen, to Channel 13. We're excited to have you on our show, so please tell us your story, in your own words.

"Yes'm, so we was at that big house down at the Inlet on Halloween—

—but after the Fire Diver blew hisself up and Darth Vader melted —

You were with Darth Vader?

"Yes'm, it was him, all seven feet tall before he melted—

—so we was gittin outta' there but got turned in the wrong direction—

—an' bust a tire on a train track—

—shouldn't be no train track in the scrub, but there it was—

—so we was fixin' the tire when our girlfriends started screamin' about the Horny God—

You mean the Hornéd God?

"Yes'm, that's it, an' the girls was screamin' that the Horny God was carryin' the Fire Diver to Valholler—

You mean Valhalla?

"Yes'm, it's where the Gods live—

—the Horny God was carryin' the Fire Diver to his funeral pile—

You mean his funeral pyre?

—that's it. Them girls had the whole thing figgered out while the police, they couldn't find their butt with two hands an' a search warrant—

Right, okay! Thanks, gentlemen, for your input. And thanks to our viewers, who've been waiting with bated breath for this story. I'm Kalley Drum, and this is AROUND OUR TOWN, only on Channel 13.

Kalley's TV interview went viral on the Internet, and that's because an astonishing number of people truly believe the Hornéd God Cernunnos chose to incarnate himself on a beach in Florida. Neo-Pagans worldwide, in fact, are joining together into Wikis with the Holy Halos. *It's high time,* these online communities insist, *that the many-and-various pagan denominations are recognized as One Major World Religion.*

I'm told, though, that the Masons are holding out.

Christopher agrees with me that the situation's so ridiculous, it's sublime. "Leave it to Wally," he said, "to put it all in perspective."

"When did you talk to Wally?"

"Right after Kalley's Channel 13 interview with the rednecks from Samsula. Wally agrees that crazy shit's been going down."

"Wally said *crazy shit's been going down?*"

"Of course not. You want a quote or a paraphrase?"

"As close to a quote as you can make it."

"Okay. Wally said *It's fascinating that a figure like the werewolf from Norse mythology has metamorphosed in the popular imagination into the Hornéd God Cernnunos because of anti-hero fantasies promulgated by adulation of the Marvel Comics creature Wolverine.*"

"Wow. Crazy shit, right?"

"You got it. I have to hand it to Wally, though. He's the only person I've talked to who knows how to pronounce *Cernnunos.*"

IN A MIRROR, DARKLY

BOOM! *CRAA-A-CK!* Tinkle tinkle tinkle. Tink . . .
Holy shit!

Son of a bitch!

Christopher and I ran to my front door and I jerked it open, but the landing was clear. Looking down the elevator shaft, we saw Geno and Ralphie on the freight elevator that was stuck five feet below us. They were standing in a pile of broken glass and glaring at a large wooden crate whose side panel had splintered, permitting its contents to fall out and shatter.

"Son of a bitch!" Geno repeated. "Those damn Bandushkos!"

"Yeah," Ralphie chimed in. "And after I told that slob Grigory to be careful. *Build heavy crates!* I told him. *Mirrors are heavy shit, you got to box them up good and strong!*"

"Oh, man," Geno agreed, "those guys are morons. When you're moving big ass mirrors you crate 'em real secure. Now we not only got broken mirrors for which we will be unrenumerated, we also got a mess to clean up." Ralphie peered up at us, shaking his head sadly. "Mags, it's enough to make high class businessmen such as ourselves throw the towel in the bucket."

Back in my apartment, Christopher was falling-down laughing. "Jesus, those two guys are a sitcom, all by themselves. Do they *realize* how funny they are?"

"Not that I ever noticed, but you know what? That mess in the freight elevator creeps me out. It's too many broken mirrors."

"Why? Since when are you superstitious?"

"I don't know. Maybe it's just too much coincidence."

"Coincidence how? You're not making sense."

"Just that I can't get away from mirrors lately."

"How so?"

"For starters, because Wally saved Aunt Sasa's mirror for me all those years, then brought it to me when I moved back to Florida. Why'd he wait so long? I mean, all my other prized possessions went up in smoke in the condo fire in Atlanta. It's almost like Wally knew the fire was coming, so he saved the mirror and waited."

"That's ridiculous, Mags, and you know it. You're not thinking straight."

"Okay, then, what about our opera?"

"What about it?"

"It's all about broken mirrors."

"So? Glad you mention the opera, though. While I'm here, let's clean up the final duet in Act II. I think you're right; it shouldn't be *a cappella* so I want to add a *sostenuto* line for the violins. It'll help the tenor and mezzo stay on pitch."

While Christopher sat down at my piano and started tinkering, I couldn't stop worrying about mirrors. There were things I couldn't mention to Christopher, though, like Kells and who she is and how she was so interested in my mirror that night she and Sterling were here, the night of the Cabaret fire at Byzantium. Kells said *Your cousin Wally did us a big favor by keeping this safe for you.* What the hell is that supposed to mean? Wally did us a "favor"? What kind of favor? And who's *us*?

Christopher was talking at me.

"What? Sorry, I was thinking about something else."

"Obviously. I *asked you* if you're okay with the *sostenuto* underscore."

"Oh sure, absolutely."

"You didn't hear it, did you?"

"Uh, no. Not exactly."

"Mags, you're being silly. Our opera riffs on an all-time great story. Tennyson wrote a lot of poems, but *The Lady of Shalott* is the one everyone knows. People love magic mirrors and curses. And don't forget *you're* the one who came up with the story-idea and title."

"I know, I know. It's a classic story and *In a Mirror, Darkly* is a great title."

"Then why're you upset?"

"It's all so serious. Maybe we should write a comic opera instead."

"I beg to differ, but we don't need to."

"Why not?"

"Because your life's a comic opera."

"Christopher! That's insulting. Opera Buffa's totally farcical, which my life is emphatically not!"

"Really, Mags? Think about it. Your downstairs neighbors are a model train depot and a suspiciously lucrative *wholesale* business, and—"

"I happen to enjoy the hustle and bustle of living downtown."

"—your front porch is a freight elevator, and—"

"The elevator's hugely convenient, in case you haven't noticed!"

"—you love your fire escape more than Mary loved Jesus, and—"

"That's a snarky thing to say! It's also sacrilegious."

"—your apartment has no kitchen, and—"

"Who says I need a kitchen? God? Martha Stewart?"

"—you talk to an imaginary cat, and—"

"I *explained* about Schrödy! I talk to him while he's gone because he'll be back!"

"—you have no furniture to speak of except a sofa and a piano, and—"

"I have all the furniture I need, thank you very much."

"—your piano's a piece of shit."

Sigh. Okay, now we're getting to the point. Christopher's never forgiven me my piano—a white baby grand that I bought from my friend Wesley Ray in Ormond Beach. Unfortunately, this is a conversation that won't go away. *Jesus, Mags,* Christopher always says, *you didn't even try it out. Who buys a piano at an auction? It's like buying a car you haven't driven. And not only that, a white baby grand's so dated, it's absurd.*

I've tried to explain to Christopher that my piano's a Sign. I *know* it's the same white baby grand I fell in love with at the Rainbow Girls. And when the Masonic Temple closed, Merril's stepdad bought it for her. And when Merril quit piano lessons, Peabody Auditorium bought it for concerts. And when I accompanied Kara Andresson at the Bandshell, it's the piano I played. And when I went to Wesley Ray's auction, I recognized it. I knew it was *my* piano!

The thing is, I lost my history when my condo went up in smoke in Atlanta. The only valuable I didn't lose was my Commonplace Box because I had it with me. That's why I still have the book of Irish fairies and a few old photos, because they were in the box.

Now, though, I have Aunt Sasa's mirror from my early years in Pittsburgh, and I have my white baby grand piano from my teenage years in Daytona Beach. Oh, and I have Schrödinger, of course, from my professor years in Atlanta.

If nothing else, arguing with Christopher took my mind off worrying. I hadn't even known he was coming until he showed up at my front door saying he delivered Wally to Geno's model train depot, then came upstairs to get the amp for his theremin. (I'd brought his amp back with me for safekeeping when I drove home from the Genius House on Halloween night, remember?) Anyway, Christopher said he had time for a cappuccino as long as he and Wally got back on the road by sundown, so we walked downstairs to the coffeeshop.

"Why're you in a hurry to get back to DeLand?"

"Actually we're heading to Samsula, not DeLand. To the Cabbage Patch."

"*You?*"

"I know, it's not my usual stomping ground. But it's Cedric's birthday and there's a party for him at the Cabbage Patch. I'll stay a little while, then leave. Wally's letting me keep his convertible until he gets back."

"Gets back from where?"

"After the party's over, Wally and his biker-friend Socrates are going camping."

"I can't even *imagine* Wally on a camping trip."

"Me neither, but that's the plan."

After Christopher left with Wally I couldn't settle down, so I went across the street to the park. I was thinking, musing, when I realized Sterling was sitting beside me. Scared me to death, actually, when she started talking at me. "Sorry I haven't been in touch, Mags. I've been pretty busy, planning for Bimini."

"You're going to *Bimini*? What about the Intervention?"

"You didn't think we'd launch it here, did you?"

"I don't know ... you never said. I asked but you didn't tell me."

"Bimini's our next stop, Mags. We have to check a few Greenhouse-sites before we launch the Intervention. Bimini's one and there are two others. Anyway, our advance party's been on Bimini for a month."

"Your advance party?"

"The three Archies you spotted at Pigs Will Fly. They're—"

"I remember! I called them the Professor, the Confessor, and Rita! They're such perfect 'types,' I had to name them!"

"Well, they're a great team, and we're depending on them. Michael and Prax are already there, too, working with the Archies."

"The wedding's off? Prax and Galatea?"

"It's not off, just postponed until Galatea gets unscabbed from when she and Gigi fell in an aloe pot on Halloween. Jengu and Squiggs left yesterday in Michael's boat, and George and Uncle Billy leave today with his friends Ezra and Tom. They showed up unexpectedly. Uncle Billy's friends, I mean."

"But why—"

"Mags, I don't have time to chat. I meant to give this to you earlier, but I'm giving it to you now. Open the box. It's from the Tutors."

"Wow. It's beautiful." My gift from the Tutors was a pendant on a long chain—a stylized female figure with turquoise stones for eyes.

"Put it on," Sterling said. "It's called a *bennu*. Think of it as a special kind of communicator. I have one too."

"You do? I've never seen you wear a pendant."

"That's because mine's a ring. This ring. The ring you found for me at Blue Spring." When Sterling held out her left hand, I felt a jolt of recognition, like an electric shock. It wasn't just that, though. When I focused on the three turquoise stones in the center, they seemed to flash and sparkle, pulling me toward them with an unearthly pulsating light . . .

Sterling was looking at me sympathetically. "Sorry, sorry," I said. "When I found your ring at Blue Spring I was so excited, I must not've looked closely at it. But now I realize it's so beautiful I guess I got distracted . . . no, it's more like being stunned, or dazzled."

I was trying but failing to tear my eyes away from Sterling's ring and those turquoise stones, so I abruptly changed the subject. "Tell me," I said, "is Kells's ring a bennu, too? That big ring she always wears?"

"No, her ring's totally different. She says it's a photomultiplier, and we know she uses it to manipulate light, but the technology's way beyond the rest of us so we just call it Kells's Bling Ring. The boys have bennus too, though. We each got a bennu when we turned thirteen."

"I remember now. You said you got your ring on your thirteenth birthday. You also said your ring was made specifically for you?"

"Correct."

"So this pendant was made specifically for me?"

"Yes."

I'm not sure how long we sat there in silence. It was unnerving, because even though I refused to meet Sterling's eyes, I knew she was staring at me the whole time. Finally I ventured a comment. "You know what I'm thinking, don't you? I'm scared to take this . . . this thing. If I take it, it means I'm committed. Totally."

"You're already committed, Mags. Remember when you and I talked in the park, the day after you met the Tutors?"

"I remember you showed up out of nowhere, just like today."

"That's not my point, and you know it. When we talked in the park you agreed with me that life should be an adventure. And when I asked whether you'd rather go adventuring in Kansas or in Oz, what'd you say?"

"I said I've never been crazy about Kansas."

"Exactly. And now it's important that you have a bennu, so I'm asking you again to put it on. From now on wear it all the time, just like I always wear my ring."

More unnerving silence. I still couldn't meet Sterling's eyes, but I slipped the pendant's chain over my head while she started talking again quietly, almost as though she was talking to herself. "It's so sad that we're approaching a planet-wide state of anarchy. As long as the worst of us are full of passionate intensity, while the best of us lack all conviction, there's no way—"

"Wait, what did you just say? What—"

Honk honk HON-N-NK! An uptick in traffic noise startled both of us, especially the insistent honking from a black Suburban that had pulled up to the curb. "Time's up, Mags. I gotta go." Sigh. "Okay, but first I need to know—" Sterling was already running toward the Suburban and I was trailing behind. "Sterling, wait! I need to know how my bennu works. You said it's a 'communicator,' right? So how does it communicate?"

"When the time comes, Mags, you'll know."

"That's my answer? What the hell kind of answer is that? Jeez, Sterling—"

"It's all I've got right now, Mags. Sorry—" I was still running but gasping for breath and pissed off because I couldn't see who was driving the Suburban. "Sterling! How do I contact you while you're away? Will your phone work on Bimini or will I get static?"

"Gotta go, Mags. I'll be in touch—"

"Okay, but—" Slam! She was in the car and hollering out the window. "Mags, I promise I'll be in touch. Just remember to wear your pendant when you're out and about."

"But you didn't tell me *why* I should wear it—"

While the Suburban headed over the bridge, I stood at the curb and fumed.

Later, sitting in my favorite window-booth at Geno's with a peppermint latte (the foamy mint always calms me down),

I examined my pendant. My Girl with Turquoise Eyes. It's beautifully crafted, silvery and shiny—a stylized female figure on a long silver chain as fine and strong as monofilament. The most remarkable thing about the pendant, though, is the eyes: vivid turquoise jewels, so deep and multi-faceted, they seem lit from within.

The first time I noticed her ring, I asked Sterling about the turquoise stones. She said Floreans mine them, and they're called *sea diamonds* because they form on the shells of foraminifers, single-celled marine creatures that've lived in the oceans for five hundred million years. She also said sea diamonds are relatively rare.

Sitting there at Geno's, staring into the eye-stones and immersing myself in them, I was in another place, diving into aquamarine depths, feeling the insistent thrum of rhythmic tidal lyres. I was diving down, down, down toward salamandrine fires . . .

"You okay, Mags?" Geno was sitting across from me, looking concerned.

"What?"

"I said, *You okay, Mags?* I'm only askin' because I noticed you over in the park, talking to yourself. Or an imaginary friend."

"Excuse me? I was with Sterling in the park, having a serious conversation."

"Sure you were. And you confabulated your heart-to-heart with a hissy fit?"

"*What?*"

"Mags, I watched you through this window. You were all by yourself, wavin' your arms and hollering like a crazy person, and you almost ran into traffic."

"You saw *wrong*, Geno, so give it a rest. I was with Sterling, all right?"

"Okay okay, I didn't mean to upset you. I'm just sayin', is all." Geno stopped talking, just sat there looking concerned. "*What?* Geno, you're making me nervous."

"I worry about you, Mags. There you are out in public, goin' postal while you talk to an imaginary friend. I mean, it's okay that you talk to an imaginary cat—"

"That's *enough*, dammit! You know I have to be protective of Schrödy." I was trying not to cry. "I thought I'd lost him when my condo burned in Atlanta, Geno. I looked all over for him but he never showed up, and then I had to move to Florida without him except Mrs. McGillicuddy was sure she saw him, but when she called me and I went back to get him, I found that what Mrs. McGillicuddy saw was a different tuxedo cat, not Schrödy after all but then—"

Frak me, I was crying. I *hate* crying in front of people.

"Hey, I'm sorry, Mags. Really. I didn't mean to upset you. Here, use my hanky. It's real cloth, not that paper shit."

"Thanks." Sniffle, blow. "I'll wash your handkerchief for you when I do my laundry."

"Keep it, I got plenty. And while I'm closing up, how's about another latte on the house? Peppermint, right? With chocolate straws?"

That second peppermint latte definitely helped me calm down, and I let Geno know I was appreciative. "I feel lots better, Geno. Thanks for caring."

"No problem, Mags. We gotta take care of our friends, right?"

"That's for sure. And now I'm ready to settle down for a good night's sleep."

"Me too, after I finish closing up. Nice necklace, by the way. Is it new?"

"Just got it. Sterling gave it to me when we were talking in the park."

"Sure she did. *Anyway*, it looks expensive. What do you call those blue stones?"

"They're sea diamonds. Very rare."

"Then they're expensive, for sure. *If it's rare, it's expensive.* That's what my Aunt Jillsy says. The woman has boxes full of expensive joolery, keeps it all in a safe. Me, I'd rather have money in the bank."

ALWAYS NOTICE THE EYES

I heard it first, before I could see it. Somewhere ahead of me I heard a slither, like a snake moving through dead leaves. The sound got louder, and I knew it was coming toward me, but when I tried to back away, I slipped and sat down hard on my butt.

Come on Mags, get up! Get up! Someone was calling me, trying to help me, but I couldn't move.

The slither sound was louder now, scaly, like sheets of paper rubbing together. It was dark all around except for a glow like fire ahead of me, a glow that was moving toward me with the slither, and I could feel heat. Fire was coming closer; fire was coming to get me.

Mags, you have to get up! You have to stand up to it!

But I couldn't stand, I couldn't move. I was hot . . . hot . . . Omigod, *I'M BURNING!*

You're not burning, Mags! It's not real, it's a meme!

Then I saw its eyes, green and reptilian, flashing, flecked with red. The serpent was huge, blood-red and licked with flames. And it was smiling at me . . .

MAGS! WAKE UP! Kells was standing over me, shaking me, calling to me.

"Kells? What're you doing here? How'd you get in?"

"Doesn't matter how I got in. I was worried about you."

"What? You knew I was having a nightmare? How the hell did you know that?"

Kells didn't respond, just gave me one of her big-eyed enigmatic *looks*. Well thanks heaps! is what I was thinking but I didn't say it out loud. Not that it'd matter since she can rummage around in my brain any time she wants to. But was I *pissed*? You better believe it.

I mean, I understand why fire would show up in my dreams. But why would my subconscious mind conjure up a serpent the size of my fire escape—Oh. Damn. I get it. The gigantic coiling spiral . . .

Kells was snapping her fingers in front of my face. "Mags? Come back, Mags."

"Sorry, I guess I was reliving the nightmare, trying to figure it out. But you can't really understand your dreams, can you? I mean, you can't understand them literally . . ."

"That wasn't any old nightmare, Mags. The serpent in your dream was a Momec, a meme-creature from the Great Stream of Consciousness."

"Listen," I said, "everybody has bad dreams once in a while, right? It's no big deal. I'll make some coffee and . . . Shit! I'm soaking wet. I'm a sweat ball. Hang on a minute while I get a quick shower, okay?"

While I showered and changed, Kells poked around in my pantry and fridge. When I came back, she was still poking. "Don't you have any fruit? Any fresh veggies?"

"Um, not exactly 'fresh' veggies, but I have peppers and onions in oil. They go with the leftover meatball stromboli from Sergio's. The stromboli's in the fridge—"

"Never mind. Just make some coffee, and we'll talk."

"Perfect, and I always have MoonPies—"

"Just make the coffee, okay?"

Kells showed up in my apartment in the middle of the night because she had a premonition. "You need to know, Mags, the serpent in your dream was a Momec," she said. "We knew Momecs would be invading your dreams sooner or later. I'm here because—"

"*We* knew? Who the hell are *we?*"

"Mags, we have a lot of catching up to do tonight, *so please don't interrupt.*"

"Sorry, Kells, I'll settle down. Promise."

"Good. *So as I was saying*, we knew Momecs would invade your dreams sooner or later, and I'm here tonight because you need to know that a Momec always brings a message."

"Well, guess what," I said. "This messenger definitely got the message mixed. The snake was smiling at me like it wanted to be friendly, but there was nothing friendly about those eyes."

"Describe the eyes, tell me what you saw."

"They were snake eyes, or what I imagine snake eyes to be: bright green with that red viper-stripe in the middle where a pupil should be. And the eyes were flashing, throwing off sparks like a Fourth of July sparkler." Kells got quiet then, and I was glad just to sit and sip my coffee. Might've been nice to add a jigger of brandy, though. I mean, it isn't every day (or night) you get a visit from a Momec. Lucky me.

Again, though, Kells wasn't finished. "The Momec brought you a message, Mags, and this is it: *Always notice the eyes.*"

"That's it? That's the message? And I'm supposed to know what it means?"

"All in good time, Mags, all in good time. You'll know eventually because you have the Sight. That's why the Momec came to you."

"I have the Sight? It's funny you say that because someone else said it to me a long time ago. What she said to me is, *You're strong with the Sight.*

"Who told you that?"

"Aunt Sasa, the gypsy woman in Pittsburgh. I told you about her, remember? She's the one who gave me my mirror."

It was strange, the way Kells talked and talked and talked that night, like I was her agenda and she had to make sure she covered all her pre-arranged topics. What's the rush? I wanted to ask. I mean, it isn't like I've been deluged with information ever since that day when I agreed to write their freaking "book." More like I got brushed off with a half-answer or no answer at all practically every time I tried to probe.

Then zip! All of a sudden Kells appears at midnight chasing Puff the Magic Dragon, and I get enough info to fill a library. Not just about the Intervention, either. More like what I'd call *The Big Picture*, plus some scary things like why you can't always trust Archies. She even explained more than Sterling did about Flukey Fog, saying Sterling should've taught me way more.

Kells didn't criticize, though, just commented that Sterling had been distracted lately and no wonder.

The major topic on her agenda, though, totally blew me away. "We call it *Einstein's Blunder*," Kells said, "though we mean no disrespect. Einstein was truly a creative genius, and he was moving your Sapient science in the right direction:

think Ptolemy, then Copernicus, then Kepler, then Newton, then Einstein."

"But?"

"But Einstein stopped too soon after he formulated Spacetime. He didn't take that next crucial step and formulate Timespace—the mirror image of Spacetime. Timespace is here, there, everywhere, coexisting with Spacetime. But the closest your scientists get is hypothesizing about a 'shadow world' filled with 'dark matter' and 'dark energy.' Well, Timespace is real and it isn't dark. It's light—an infinity of light that flows with the Great Stream of Consciousness."

"So . . . when you disappear . . . or just *appear* like you did tonight . . . you're moving in and out of Timespace? That's what Sterling does, too?"

"Exactly. And you can learn it as well because you do it in your mind when—"

"Omigod, I know! You 'flip a brain switch. Like Datta said that day when we were meeting in his cottage. Remember? Sterling and I came in when Datta was talking. He and Mercedes were saying something about landing by mistake in the fountain of the Excalibur hotel in Las Vegas. And that's when Datta said to you, *It's simple for you because you just click your brain switch and go blip—and you're where you want to be.* I'm sure that's what he said."

"Good memory, Mags. That's exactly what Datta said, and he was right. You quiet your mind, focus, and flip that switch. Think of the famous optical illusion, the one called *Young Lady or Old Hag.* Both images coexist in one image. When you shift your perspective, you see one or the other, but never both. It's the same with Spacetime and Timespace. They coexist, each with the other, and you can be <u>in</u> one or the other but never in both simultaneously."

Compassionate silence, while Kells let me try to process what I was hearing. Finally I was ready to talk again. "Sorry I interrupted, Kells. You started to say something about how I already do this in my mind?"

"In a sense, yes. It's called mental time travel or MTT, and it's related to dreaming as well as memory. Mentally, we project ourselves backward in time and forward in time."

"Okay, I get that because I do MTT when I have flashbacks, or when I go walkabout. But that's not the same thing as moving into Timespace?"

"No. Moving into Timespace means accessing an alternate reality."

"But I can learn to do it? To flip that switch?"

"Yes, I'll help you and so will Sterling because we'll all know when you're ready. When that happens, you'll need to picture black ice because it's your Timespace imprint. You were on one side of the ice, then you went through it to the other side. Just as you will when—"

"Wait…black ice? You mean when I was a kid and fell through black ice into a lake? But that was horrible, I could've drowned."

"You didn't, though, and when you came back up you were imprinted."

"But I didn't come back up by myself. Some bullies pulled me out, said I was *so heavy* and … no wait, maybe they weren't bullies. Just strange, peculiar. They were little, the size of kids but they looked old … and they sounded old … Oh no, no! Those boys … whoever they were, whatever they were … you sent them? That whole thing at the frozen lake was a setup?"

Kells nodded. "We knew from your DNA that you were special, but you needed a Timespace imprint so we made sure you got one. Early."

By the time Kells was ready to leave I couldn't help wondering whether I was *in* a book instead of writing one. Kells would say she had to go, then remember yet one more thing she needed to tell me, and hours later she'd remember something else.

Finally she left my apartment at sunrise, via my fire escape. I walked down with her, said goodbye, then climbed back up and stood on the landing outside my back door, looking out over the waking-up city below and letting my thoughts wander. It was cloudy and overcast with a chill breeze, the kind of day that fit my mood, bemused as I was by that final unsatisfactory meetup with Sterling in the park. Not to mention middle-of-the-night visits from a dream-snake and my almost-human friend.

Just then the clouds broke overhead, and I stood transfixed, watching the sun's morning rays set my copper-colored fire escape ablaze. Try as I might, I couldn't tear my eyes away while a shaft of sunlight pushed a shadow down the spiral fire escape—gradually, incrementally, until the shadow melted into the alleyway below.

The illusion of motion was mesmerizing. Standing there, I watched the giant spiral staircase come alive, morphing into a strand of DNA, a double helix, spiraling its sentient microcosmic life-force through time. And I watched Plato's spindle, winding and unwinding to infinity and beyond, like the intersecting vortices of Uncle Billy's gyres.

Most of all, I watched a giant copper snake, shedding its skin.

I'm not sure how long I stayed outside on the landing. When I went back inside my apartment, though, reality reasserted itself with a vengeance, to-wit: I remembered I promised Kells I'd do her a favor, and I realized I was starving.

"Schrödy!" I hollered. "I'll be back after I get breakfast at Geno's and make a quick trip to the Genius House."

First, though, I stood in front of my mirror and looked into it as hard as I could. As per usual, all I saw was myself, looking back at me. Well this is just great, I said to myself. All those years ago Aunt Sasa tells me I'm *strong with the Sight*, but all I ever see in this stupid mirror is my own self. Who's looking depressingly elderly, by the way.

"Mags? Why're you talking to the mirror?" Schrödy, of course.

"Because everything's connected but nothing makes sense."

"Uh huh. So, what does the mirror think about that?"

"If you're trying to be cute, you're failing miserably."

"Mags, I'm just trying to help you."

"Help me *how*? All of a sudden everybody wants to help me. First Sterling, then Geno, then Kells. Kells was here all last night *helping me*, and now I'm exhausted because I didn't get any sleep. Zilch. Zero. Bugger all. On top of that, I got sucked into running an errand for Kells."

No comment from the cat. "Schrödy?"

Still no comment.

"Schrödy, I'm sorry I snapped at you, okay? It's not your fault I'm involved in this Genius House craziness. I'll be back in a little while and I'll be in a better mood. A *good* mood."

"Promise?"

"Absolutely."

"Okay, then. I'll get a nap while you're gone."

On my way out I looked one last time in my mirror but saw only my same old face peering back at me. It was a juvenile thing to do, I know, but I couldn't help it—I stuck out my tongue and sneered at my reflection in the mirror. Then I turned around and started walking toward my front door.

That's when I heard a faint rustling sound behind me—like a snake moving through dry leaves.

The favor I promised Kells was this: I'd go to the Genius House, get a small box from the music room upstairs, and give it to Cassandra who'd be waiting for me in the park. I had a zillion questions, of course, but by that time Kells was in a hurry to leave my apartment and cut me off so I let it drop. Especially when she assured me I wouldn't have any unexpected encounters because the Archies and Roomers at the Genius House were expecting me and would stay out of my way.

The box was where Kells said it would be, on top of the piano in the music room, and I got in and out of the house without incident. I tried to open the box, of course—even though Kells warned me not to—but it had no visible hinges or clasp, and when I shook it I couldn't hear anything rattling around inside.

The box defeated me, in other words, and that pissed me off because it was one more mystery that no one bothered to explain. Not only that, the box looked familiar.

Okay, I thought to myself, how can this be? I *know* I've never seen this freakin' box before. It was a conundrum, and I was trying to figure it out when a fog rolled in. That's right, a pea soup fog like you read about in Jack the Ripper stories except it wasn't smoggy or dirty, just thick. Holy crepuscular crap, I thought, what's going on?

I felt dizzy and sick, would've stumbled and fallen if I hadn't already reached Agatha. Feeling for her door handle, leaning against her to hold myself steady, my mind's eye lit up with a vision so real it took my breath away:

> *I'm on an island at night. It's beautiful, verdant, with gray sands glossed by moonlight. Yet a mist of sadness hovers over the island. Ferns greenly weep, dropping tears into the mist that drifts and curls while voices whisper among the rushes. And now I see, disappearing into the distance, a tiny dark-haired girl-child running. She turns momentarily, meets my gaze, then plunges into the sea . . .*

I know this place, I thought . . . I know it because I dreamed it and—omigod, I'm in Uncle Billy's poem and the child is Sterling . . . she tried to tell me she'd been stolen but I didn't believe her . . .

The vision was gone as suddenly as it appeared, and so was the fog. I knew it was Flukey Fog; it had to be. Kells said the Roomers only practice with fog in the middle of the night, but maybe they were giving it a daytime test run? And I was hallucinating because that's what Flukey Fog does to you. That mushroom effluence causes visions.

Mags, I said to myself, get outta' here pronto before they start practicing again with their fog machine. For sure, I answered back, no way do I want to get caught in it and start hallucinating while Agatha and I are on the road.

Agatha started right up, no sputters or hesitations. Good Girl, I crooned to her while we turned out of the driveway and headed north.

I was back in town in no time, and when I got to the park, I heard Cassandra before I saw her because she was tootling "White Coral Bells" on her flute. "Thanks, Mags," she said when I handed her the box. Before I could ask what was going on, though, she sped away from me on her unicycle, the long wispy scarf that she ties around her topknot floating greenly behind her.

Was I miffed? You bet I was! I mean, didn't I deserve more than a perfunctory *Thanks, Mags*? I was still fuming while I walked back through Geno's store and stood in front of the freight elevator, pushing the "call" button. Again and again and again.

"Yo, Mags," Geno hollered from the coffeeshop and started walking in my direction. "I regret the elevator's in a state of disrepair."

"Meaning you haven't cleaned up the broken mirrors yet?"

"Something like that, and you have three messages—"

"And my backup elevator?"

"Also temporarily immobilized. Your messages—"

"Never mind, I'll climb the stairs."

"Which is a good idea for the cardio benefits which I will partake with you while I deliver your messages because as usual, you keep on interrupting."

Sigh. "Okay, talk at me while we walk upstairs."

Geno started with the news that I was in trouble with my editor. "So his name's Ford and he said Fairies are the last straw. That's the message, Mags, which I swear. *Fairies are the last straw*. You wanna clue me in? Because he was not in a mood to be chatty."

"It's about my current project, Geno, an Irish cookery book. I left Ford a message that I'm adding a section on Irish Fairies."

"Why didn't you tell him directly?"

"I did already, and he went ballistic. Ford always overreacts. He'll calm down and I'll finish the book and get paid for it and stay up-to-date on my rent, so don't worry about it. Next message?"

"Right, so your friend in the chair says don't be late for the party."

"My friend in the *wheel*chair? Talisman?"

"Guess so. Sonny, he took the message before he went home sick, so I am parlaying."

"She didn't say where the party is? Or when?"

"Not to me. Like I said—"

"I know, I know. You're just the messenger. And don't worry, I won't shoot you."

"*Shoot* me? Who's talkin' about shooting?"

"*Shooting the messenger* is a metaphoric phrase used to describe the act of blaming the bearer of bad news *for* the bad news."

"As I was preparin' to say exactly. And speaking of shootin' a message—"

"I said shooting a *messenger,* not a *message!*"

"Yeah yeah, calm down. So the last *message* is you should be on the lookout for nutcases. Which will always surprise you, by the way because—" Geno kept right on talking while I unlocked my front door, saying he'd asked the cops to patrol our block again at night because customers reported "suspicious characters" in the alley.

"Well for sure it's not my weirdo friends this time, Geno, because they're all out of town."

"No kiddin'? What'd they do, head for Key West after they blew up the Boardwalk? Me and Sonny, we went to Key West last year and checked it out. Sonny's old boyfriend was gonna be a big deal in the Christmas parade and Sonny'd never been so I said sure, why not."

"Was his old boyfriend the Parade Marshal or something?"

"Naw, his old boyfriend was Mrs. Claus."

"*Mrs.* Claus?"

"Yeah, and don't get me started on those Key West freaky-deaks. We left that night and drove straight through to get back. Sonny, he wanted to stay and party, but I told him over my dead body."

After assuring Geno I'd keep my doors and the fire escape locked, I was glad to get back in my apartment and collapse on my sofa.

"It's about time you're back."

"Schrödy, I've had a remarkably bad morning *so don't start with me, all right?*"

"Apparently this is still the winter of our discontent?"

"Cute, very cute. When did you die and come back as Shakespeare's cat?"

"This morning, around the time you promised to come home in a good mood."

Sigh. "Okay, you want to hear about my morning?"

"Might as well."

"For starters, Ford's ready to fire me."

"Which is business as usual between you two."

"And Geno's on a rant about nutcases loose in the neighborhood."

"Also business as usual."

"*And there's a party somewhere today BUT I'M NOT INVITED.*"

"*Au contraire.*"

"What?"

"Monica's been calling all morning and leaving voice messages, woke me up every time I tried to fall asleep. She's hosting a wine-tasting party at 3:00 today at Three Graces and you're invited."

"Omigod, I'm stunned."

"And I'm sleepy because I missed my nap."

"Schrödy, I promise I'll come back from the party in a *stupendous* mood."

"Oft' expectation fails, most often where it promises most."

"You're impossible. You know that, don't you?"

"Of course I do. And now— *finally*—to sleep, perchance to dream."

Schrödy was right about Monica's voicemail messages. She was hosting one of her famous wine tastings and I was invited! I didn't even care that mine was obviously a last-minute invitation because I was so-o-o ready for a *trés chic* event. Anticipating like crazy, I talked to myself while I planned my ensemble:

Okay Mags, my girl, your best plan is to start with basic black, understated but elegant, then dazzle with accessories. Yes! I'll wear my Fendi black silk shirt with the handkerchief hem and skinny long sleeves. It's perfect for a chilly day. And my Vera Wang leather coat over those great boot-cut pants from Chico's . . . but I need boots. No, not black boots. I need a sensational look. Of course! My Louboutins!

Shoot, where are they? I only worn them once, on Halloween . . . even though the turquoise leather clashed with my red hoodie. This'll be so much better, it's like my Louboutins and my new pendant were meant for each other. The overlay of glazed Python on the boots is too spectacular to be believed, and I love the solid silver bootheels. Dammit, where are they? Okay, here they are and . . .

Uh oh, I. forgot they're platform stilettos . . .

The conversation with myself hit a temporary snag while I rationalized my way out of sensible footwear and into those gorgeous silver-heeled Louboutins. Eventually, humming Carly Simon's "Anticipation" and with fifteen minutes to spare, I was ready to head for the party

Avoiding even a glance toward Aunt Sasa's mirror, I locked my front door and walked *very carefully* down the stairs.

Walk slowly, Mags. Enjoy the swishes of your coat and the clicks of those silver boot-heels on the sidewalk. Yes, ma'am, I am stylin' today. Meryl Streep, eat your heart out, because today I am more fabulous than you.

So I'm almost at Three Graces and there's already a crowd. I see Talisman by the door, and who's the blonde with Talisman? Oh my gosh! It's Slim in civvies, and she's wearing one of Christine's wigs. Which reminds me, I owe Christine for the Red Riding Hood wig. Damn it all, I wish I'd borrowed a cheaper wig for the Boardwalk. Oh, well, live and learn. I thought sure Deirdre would be here, but I don't see . . . no, wait. There she is, standing by the door. Can't mistake that long auburn hair and fabulous figure. Makes you understand why Red would fall in love with her, though, because she's so gorgeous.

Hmm, that's weird. Why's Deirdre holding Phyllo? Diff's across the street in the park, so why . . . I know, I bet the little dickens got loose again and Deirdre caught him for Diff. That's it, she's waving to Diff to come get Phyllo. Okay, she's putting

Phyllo down. She'd better hold onto his leash until the light changes and traffic stops, though.

Wait, what's she doing? No, Deirdre! Don't let him go! Phyllo, get out of the street!

Diff, watch out!

No! NO! *DIFF!*

The accident played itself out like a slow-motion scene in a disaster movie. While Phyllo ran into the street toward Diff, Diff ran into the street toward Phyllo. The black Suburban bearing down on them came to a screeching halt while a string of cars behind it rear-ended each other: *Boom! Boom! Boom! Boom!* Then silence.

Phyllo lay silent and unmoving, crushed under the Suburban's front tire. And Diff—upended and flung onto the hood of the Suburban when it hit him—had rolled like an under-stuffed rag doll off the hood and onto the pavement, where he too lay silent and unmoving. While everyone else froze in place, Cassandra ran to Diff from one side of the street, and Slim ran to him from the other. Seconds felt like hours while an eerie silence hung like a pall, punctuated only by Cassandra's broken sobs.

Finally sirens howled in the distance, jolting onlookers into a low buzz of conversation while people came from every direction to see what all the noise was about. The crowd on the sidewalk was so thick, in fact, that until I located Talisman by her big-brimmed yellow hat, I couldn't see any of my friends.

Omigod, I thought. Where's Deirdre? She'll be devastated. Coming on the heels of that Halloween catastrophe with Red, she'll be a wreck. She didn't mean to hurt Diff, and poor little Phyllo . . . I still don't see Deirdre . . .

No, there she is.

That's okay, then, she's looking my way and ... What? *What? No, oh no no no no!*

No it can't be! Deirdre's looking at me with snake eyes!

Run! I have to run! I'll run ... shit! It's like running on stilts! Gotta get these boots off, carry my boots ... run through the alley ... get home, lock myself in ... My fire escape, I'll use my fire escape—omigod the cops are on my fire escape! How'd they get keys? They see me, they're calling me, can't chance it ...

Mags?

Sterling? Where are you? I hear you but I can't—

Listen to me, Mags. Get back to your apartment, then do what I say.

Okay okay, but Deirdre, she's—

I know about Deirdre, Mags. She's a Pathic, she sucked Red dry, made him crazy. You have to get away from her! Back to your apartment!

Okay okay ... elevators no good, go in the back way and up the stairs before ... Shit! Deirdre's on the mezzanine balcony, why's she with Sammy? Omigod not Sammy too, please please not Sammy ... they'll see me on the stairs ... But they can't see the secret staircase, Geno's secret staircase ... that's it ... I can do it, I can do it ... quiet quiet, okay, almost there ... I'm in! Oh thank God, throw the deadbolts—

Mags?

Sterling? I hear you but I still can't see you ...

I'm here, Mags, and so is Kells. Look in your mirror.

Okay, okay, I see you but how—

Look at me, Mags, look in my eyes. Mirror me, like Kells told you. Our minds have to connect, build a bridge . . . I'll go slow . . . slow . . . That's right, hold my gaze . . . Now grab something heavy and smash the mirror—

What? That's crazy! That's—

Mags! Kells told you about the mirror, it's your portal! Mirror me, Mags, that's right . . . that's right . . . now break the mirror with your boot heel! Use your kill shot!

Okay okay, Kells told me . . . she told me . . . the mirror's like ice . . . black ice was my imprint . . . I have to picture it then go through . . . okay okay, my boot, my boot's heavy . . . the heel, the silver heel I can use the heel to crack the mirror, I'll swing—

BLEEP BLEEP WOO-O-O! WOO-O-O-O-O!

What?!! Sirens and screaming! Someone pounding on my door! Who . . . ???

"OPEN UP, MAGS! IT'S GENO! IT'S ME AND SAMMY AND DEIRDRE!"

You can do it, Mags! Picture black ice, smash the mirror!

Shit, holy shit—no ice, I can't see ice! Only fire, fire's in the mirror, I'm on fire!

"YOU GOTTA GET OUT, MAGS, THE BUILDING'S ON FIRE!"

Mags, you're not burning! It's not real, it's a meme, just a meme!

Okay okay, just a meme, but my boot! I dropped my boot! Where . . .

"LET THE COPS IN! THEY'LL HELP US!"

Do it Mags! Smash the mirror! Dive through!

So hot, burning! Can't do it, can't . . .

"WE'RE COMIN' IN!"

Your kill shot, Mags!

Yes okay okay!!

THWAACK! CRASH! Tinkle tinkle tinkle. . . . tink . . .

THROUGH THE MIRROR

You did it, Mags! You smashed it! Now dive through the mirror! DIVE!

I will, I will! Okay, Sterling, here I come! *UHH!* Oh-h-h, that hurt!

Come on, Mags, get up. That's right . . . now stay low, get your balance! Good!

Ohh, hit my head so hard . . . oh no no! I'll throw up! I HATE throwing up! No, oh no, please no . . .

Sounds of violent retching, slowly diminishing.

Sterling, you're fading . . .

I gotta go, Mags.

Go where? I can't see you, can't . . .

You're okay now, Mags, you're okay . . .

Sterling, no! Don't leave, please don't leave me!

Silence.

Sigh. *Damn* it all, my head's still spinning . . . vertigo's no joke, so dizzy, so dizzy . . . where's the horizon? The horizon shifted, broke apart . . . feels like I'm on Space Mountain after it flew off the track . . . dammit, still spinning . . .

"Control yourself, Mags. First time's the worst, after that it's not so bad."

"*Shrödy?* Is that you?"

"Duh Mags, of course it's me. Do you talk to any other cat? More to the point, does any other cat talk to you?"

"But you look different. You're black all over and you have a tail."

"As per usual, you're not terribly observant. I'm not *all* black because I have a white spot on my chest. See? But I do have a tail again."

"What are you talking about, *again?* You never had a tail, you're a Manx."

"I was a Manx in several of my lives, yes. At this moment, however—

"What? Are you saying it's true? Cats have nine lives?"

Exasperated sniffs. "Mags, will you *ever* learn to stop interrupting and start listening?"

"Sorry sorry, continue."

"So first of all, ordinary cats have only one life, not nine. But *extraordinary* cats—like me—are certifiable Tricksters. As I'm sure you know, Tricksters have been essential figures in every mythology since stories and storytelling began. As I'm also sure you know, Tricksters are shapeshifters. Capiche?"

"Omigod, I get it now. You and Boots and Ranger were always the same cat!"

"Precisely. And now to get back to your rude interruption, I've been a Manx but I'm not one now. Now I'm *The Celtic Cat*. Also known as *Cat Sidhe*, or *Cat Sí* in the new Irish orthography—"

"*What?*"

"Never mind, we'll save the lessons in Celtic lore for later. Right now I'm in charge of beginning your orientation to Timespace, so let's go. *Tiugainn!*"

When Schrödinger yowled *Tiugainn!* while tapping the white spot on his chest, my Amazing Technicolor Dreamcar magically appeared. To say the least, I was flummoxed.

"What are you waiting for, Mags? Let's get in."

"But where will we go?"

"Totally up to you. Use your imagination, pick a story."

"A story?"

"Duh, Mags. You're the one who said *If you don't pick a story, a story picks you.* So pick a story and let's climb in your Dreamcar before it disappears."

"Okay okay, I picked a story and—Oh. My. God. Look at that, Shrödy! It's gorgeous!"

"Not to be a know-it-all, Mags . . . but I *knew* what story you'd pick."

"Hang on to your hat, Shrödy! Or your fur, or whatever cats hang onto! Because we're off to see the Wizard!"

To clue you in: as soon as I picked a story and climbed in my Amazing Technicolor Dreamcar a vista appeared, and not just any old vista. Not by a long shot! Before us lay a road stretching off into the distance, a *yellow brick road* that gleamed and glimmered while it beckoned

Sitting behind the wheel of my roaring multicolored rattletrap with the wind in my hair, I felt the years slipping away and . . . uh oh . . . "Shrödy, what's happening? I'm driving my Dreamcar so we have to be in the past, don't we? I mean, I had this car when I was a teenager."

"So?"

"So look at my hands, they're old-lady hands. Wait, there should be a mirror here on the visor . . . yes it's here, still cracked but I can see . . . Oh! My! God! I look old. I *am* old! But how can this be? My Dreamcar belongs in my past when I was young so how can it be here now in the present with me? I mean, I'm already a *retiree,* for crying out loud!"

"Timespace Lessson #1, Mags. You can't live in two worlds at the same time. You're lucky to be here, but you're just a visitor."

"I'm just a visitor? What the hell does *that* mean?"

"It means you have to go back to Spacetime because that's your reality. *And* you have to go back through your mirror. You can visit Timespace whenever you want, but until you learn to flip the time-switch in your brain, your mirror will be your only portal."

"But my mirror's broken! I smashed it with the heel of my Louboutin and ... omigod ... those boots cost a fortune! Please tell me I didn't ruin my boots!"

"*Tabhair neart dom, a Thiarna!*"

"What?"

"I said *Give me strength* ... oh never mind, it's not important. The important thing is Timespace Lesson #2, to-wit: *Your mirror won't be broken when you go back home.*"

"So it healed itself? You're telling me it's a *magic* mirror?"

"Mags, please don't embarrass yourself. Surely you remember the words of the immortal Sir Arthur C. Clarke about magic?"

"Of course I remember! Clarke famously said *Any sufficiently advanced technology is indistinguishable from magic.* So there!"

"My point exactly. Think about it."

Pregnant pause while I thought about Shrödy's point. *What* magic? I wondered. Boskop technology? Naw, Boskop technology's hugely advanced but it'd be a stretch to invent mirrors that un-smash themselves. Besides that, why would they want to? Boskops live in Spacetime just like Sapients, so a technology so advanced it seems like magic is more likely a Timespace phenomenon—

"Sorry, Mags, I gotta go."

"Wait, Shrödy, don't leave me yet! I'm thinking as hard as I can and besides, you didn't tell me how to *find* my mirror so I can go back home!"

Silence. "Shrödy?"

More silence.

"Well this is just great. *Now* what the hell do I do? Schrödy? Sterling? Kells? Oh for heaven's sake, I know you're out there! *Why won't you help me? PLEASE!!!*"

"Maybe you should follow the numbers."

"What ? Who ...? Miss Fortunato? *Alli???*"

"In the flesh. In a manner of speaking, that is."

"But ... how is this possible?"

"You'll know everything in good time, Mags. All in good time."

"That's what Kells always says."

"I know."

"You know *Kells*?"

"Of course I do, and I'm here now to get you back home because you have a book to write. A very important book."

EPILOGUE

So, Dear Reader, that's my story up to now. Miss Fortunato took me home through my mirror, and Schrödy was right—it hadn't stayed broken after I smashed it. Geno's building wasn't on fire, either. Deirdre planted a fire-meme in Geno's and Sammy's brains, just like she did in mine. I'm not sure about the two cops, though. I don't know if they're Pathics, I mean.

Oh, and it turns out that my bracelet—my silver cuff bracelet with the Fibonacci numbers engraved on it, remember? The bracelet Miss Fortunato always wore and left for me on her last day (with her wig and a note) as a teacher at Mainland High School? Well, the bracelet's a *bennu*. It's like my pendant except it doesn't have any sea diamonds embedded in it.

That bracelet's important, though, because all *bennus* are important. It's like Sterling told me: they're special kinds of communicators. And the bracelet Alli gave me all those years ago is, in fact, how the Tutors kept track of me until I retired from Georgia Tech in Atlanta and moved back to Daytona Beach.

Alli didn't stay long after we got back to my apartment, but before departing she left me with an admonition about traveling back and forth between the two worlds: *While you're in Timespace, Mags, you may feel that you've lived hours, days, months.*

But every time you go back to Spacetime—because you <u>must</u> always return to Spacetime—it will seem to other people that you were never gone at all.

I putzed around my apartment for a while after Alli left, thinking about those amazing conversations the two of us had while we worked together years ago at Mainland High School.

Most of all, I thought about the "what if" games we played. Remember those? *What if homo Sapiens turns out to be Planet Earth's most invasive species?*

Gulp. And this one: *What if our timebound classical universe has a doppelgänger—a quantum universe where time constricts and dilates and runs backward?* Double gulp.

And the one that totally blows me away: *What if Neanderthals are not really extinct, but just hiding out?*

And now . . . here we are.

I could have indulged myself for days, but I didn't because I knew what I had to do. It was time for me to review my notes and start the book I'd agreed to write a little over four months ago. Accordingly, I got my desk in order, made a fresh pot of strong coffee, and began penning the book's Introduction:

This is the story of a book, the first in a five-volume series. The series will be about an Intervention, soon to be launched, to prevent the death of a little blue-green planet whose ape-descended dominant life form is amazingly primitive and stunningly rapacious.

The story in this book begins very simply.

It begins with a house.

ADDENDA

PAGES FROM MAGS'S GENIUS HOUSE NOTEBOOK

Notes re: Working Title of Volume One

Even though I knew it might change, I'd finally decided on a working title for Book One of our 5-volume trilogy. When I told Sterling I wanted to have The Genius House *in the title, she agreed with me because the house is so important in the story; it's practically a character. Other places are important in the story too, like Byzantium and Pigs Will Fly and The Holistic Temple. But when you get right down to it, the Genius House is where the story of our Region started more than a century ago, with a shipwreck and a curse.*

Plus, the Genius House is where everything picked up speed and got complicated—on Halloween. The aftermath of Halloween is when I finally understood that the Celtic Wheel of the Year was turning (meaning the Intervention was well underway), and it was too late to back out. Even if I wanted to.

Sterling and I agree that If we stay with The Genius House *in the title for this first book of the trilogy, we'll also use an important place-name in the title of each of the next four books. As I'm sure you've guessed by now, the title of the next book will include an important place on the island of Bimini.*

Notes re: "Foundational Texts"

Foundational texts are defined by Martin Puchner in *The Written World: The Power of Stories to shape People, History, Civilization* (Random House: New York, 2017) as follows—

"Texts that accrued power and significance over time until they became source codes for entire cultures, telling people where they came from and how they should live their lives" (xxii).

Through history, as Puchner explains, "foundational texts were often presided over by priests, who enshrined them at the center of empires and nations. Kings promoted these texts because they realized that a story could justify conquests and provide cultural cohesion." And, "foundational texts first arose in very few places, but as their influence spread and new texts emerged, the globe increasingly resembled a map organized by literature—by the foundational texts dominating a given region" (xxiii).

Puchner makes it clear that some later foundational texts (such as *The Communist Manifesto*) may be equally as influential as some that are much, much older (such as the *Bible*).

Examples of foundational texts—some arguably more influential than others— include *The Hebrew Bible and The New Testament, The Book of Mormon, Popol Vuh, Don Quixote, The Epic of Gilgamesh, The Communist Manifesto, Beowulf, The Tale of Genji, Mein Kampf, The Constitution of the United States of America, The Quran, The Bhagavad Gita, The Diamond Sutra, Mao's Little Red Book, One Thousand and One Nights, The Origin of Species, The Epic of Sunjata, Omeros, The Iliad and The Odyssey, The Autobiography of Benjamin Franklin*, and many, many others.

Notes re: The Celtic Wheel of the Year

For both ancient and modern Celts, the Wheel of the Year is an annual cycle of seasonal festivals based on a year's chief solar events (solstices and equinoxes) and the midpoints between them.

Names for these festivals vary among diverse traditions, including the holidays known to us as Halloween, Christmas, Groundhog Day, Easter, and Midsummer (May Day).

*The **Wheel of the Year** in the Northern Hemisphere. Pagans in the Southern Hemisphere advance these dates six months to coincide with their own seasons.*

Summary #1 (August)

Some nights, you might as well forget about sleeping. Which is exactly what happened to me the night I got home after meeting Sterling's Tutors. I mean, give me a break here. Three species of supposedly extinct hominins come out of hiding so they can launch a plan to block us worthless Sapients from proliferating like kudzu while we destroy the planet and ourselves along with it? Seriously?

You know how sometimes you wake up from a traumatic real-as-life dream and think, "Oh, thank God it was a dream!" And you're so relieved because you didn't really walk naked into a room full of strangers? Well, just imagine that you wake up from a traumatic real-as-life dream and you say to yourself, "Oh my God, it's true."

That was me. And the truth was horrible because I knew I'd rather walk naked into a room full of strangers than adjust my worldview to encompass the notion that three funny-looking species of people are alive and well and—most astonishing and humiliating of all—smarter and nicer than I am.

You need to understand something here: one of my worst nightmares is walking naked into a room full of people. If you have issues about body image you'll understand where I'm coming from, and you'll know I'm seriously disgruntled when I say I'd prefer the naked dream to the far-out situation I encountered at the Genius House.

Summary #2 (September)

So there I was with a new writing project, wondering how in the world I'd create realistic characters who are humanoid robots called Archies, not to mention a reptilian sub-species of humans called Pathics, plus three supposed-to-be-extinct races of people who look like Wookiees, Hobbits, and Aliens.

I worried and worried, until finally I decided I'll start by telling about Opera in the Park. After all, opera's important to me and I'm "The Writer," so why not? In the meantime, I had the NASCAR balloon fiasco to worry about, and I had questions. Like why was it flying over the Genius House and who were the two dead guys in the balloon-basket? At least I calmed Geno down by correcting the exaggerations in the TV news accounts.

After Geno left my apartment, though, I started wondering about that yellow crime scene tape. Sterling called to make sure I'd gotten home okay, and that's when she told me the whole property was cordoned off. Less than minutes after I left, she said, the place was crawling with law enforcement types—FDLE operatives dispatched from Tallahassee, including the Big Gun himself. I knew the Big Gun (his name's Leon Perez), but before I could ask questions, Sterling said she had to run.

I kept wondering, though, why FDLE immediately launched such a high-powered investigation. Maybe the two dead guys were important in a bigtime ongoing case, but how would investigators have known that right away? I mean, even from where I was sitting in the kitchen of the big house, I could see that the two bodies were burned to a crisp. So how could anyone have known right away who they were?

Summary #3 (Early October)

Geno was right about one thing, that it was nuts at the Genius House. Helicopters buzzed overhead, TV reporters and camera crews stomped all over the grounds, et cetera. It wasn't a dead body, of course. It was a blow-up doll. Geno got a big laugh out of it when it hit the TV news, for sure. Sterling was furious, though, because the news stories implied if you had a choice, you'd lots rather find a <u>real</u> dead body in your front yard than a blow-up doll. Which had clearly been used.

Sterling was doubly embarrassed about it because the blow-up doll was THE big news story for days on end. Plus, once again she had to put up with police and reporters who wanted to talk to Mary and Ben, not the kids, and where the hell are the parents, anyway?

I knew she was worried, too, about local troublemakers. Like the anonymous "tipster" Geno mentioned. Could it have been Brigadier or Lily Amaryllis? Sterling says both of them are dying to make trouble for the Genius House... It wasn't the blow-up doll incident or local troublemakers that Sterling was most upset about, though, it was the nemesis ... no, that's not right. The way she says it, it's NEMESIS in all caps. Like the CIA or KGB. Or better yet, like SPECTRE in the James Bond movies—a global network that's Evil Incarnate.

Sometimes, when Sterling gets a far-off look in her eyes I know she's thinking about nemesis ... sorry, NEMESIS. I know because when she gets like that, she mutters and talks to herself about a "black cloud" that's hovering overhead or a "dark stain" that's spreading. I try to be sympathetic but really, I get tired of the drama.

I have to admit, though, that I've been obsessing about a shadowy presence too, the shadow that followed Kells and Sterling the night of the Byzantium fire after I walked them down my fire escape. While Kells and Sterling headed across Beach Street, the shadow attacked me. Except I thought it was a blanket, a thick black blanket. First I figured the blanket was an Archie-gone-AWOL, because that really does happen. But Diff showed up and chased the shadow away, and anyway I had other things on my mind, so I decided to stop worrying about it.

Summary #4 (Late October)

The only thing I know for sure about the second Chocolate Factory robbery is that Michael filed a police report two days earlier. He'd parked the Suburban in the driveway by the kitchen, but when he came back with a load of recording equipment, the car was gone. No, he reported, he didn't leave the keys in the ignition, plus the Suburban had a state-of-the-art alarm system.

Sterling's convinced that someone who hates her family has to be behind all this—the balloon crash and the blow-up doll and the latest Chocolate Factory heist—because the only common factor is the Genius House. Sterling's totally frazzled, and I don't blame her, but you know what? I've been pretty frazzled lately, myself. By the Roomers.

Meet the Tutors? Un-extinct people like us except they look like Wookiees, Hobbits, and Aliens? Not a problem. And Pathics? A reptilian sub-species of homo Sapiens? Okay, a bit of a problem until you realize that we're used to them by other names: lunatic, maniac, bad seed, sociopath.

And Archies? Humanoid robots with archetypal identities? Again, a bit of a problem until you realize that we have robots too. It's just that ours aren't biological and don't look like real people. Once I accepted the concept of biobots that have mushroom neuralnets for brains, I could deal with the Archies.

But Roomers? Biobots that look like mushrooms? Living breathing mushrooms that walk and talk and sing Sinatra medleys? I was okay about the Roomers while I was at the Genius House with Sterling, probably because I was in shock, but when I got home I couldn't keep my head wrapped around the concept. Right, I'd say to myself, so there I was in a room full of mushrooms. Chit-chatting with a few fungi, basically. Oh, sure, I know some people talk to their houseplants, but they don't invite them to parties and . . .

Wait. I don't freak out about Christopher Robin being best friends with a talking teddy bear. And I love watching Dorothy skipping along the yellow brick road with a scarecrow and a tin man. And it's undeniable that, personally, I am always ready to entertain Don Juan de Marco, should he land on my balcony and invite himself in. So why am I super upset about discussing current events with a two-headed mushroom? This is what I asked myself, and the answer was obvious: it's all about perspective. Otherwise, how do you explain fictional characters who are realer than real? Like Sherlock Holmes, for example?

And that reminds me. Arthur Conan Doyle believed in fairies, just like Uncle Billy, and who's to say they're wrong? It all gets back, again, to what's real and what's not. It's like Hamlet says to Horatio:

"There are more things in heaven and earth, Horatio, / Than are dreamt of in your philosophy." And here's the thing: There's a reason that scene in Hamlet *is so famous. It's genius: Shakespeare sets up that whole scene to make the point that we shouldn't make fun of people who talk to ghosts. Or fairies or houseplants or cats. Whatever.*

Summary #5 (November)

So in some respects I've got pretty good notes for the Genius House book. About Hummalingus, for example. To think that at one time we were all synaesthetes who could see music and hear color but then . . . then we lost it. That's sad. And mind-talking must be like Hummalingus, an innate ability we don't have any more. That's what Sterling says, that we used to mind-talk too until it became vestigial, like an appendix. The best we can do now is be empathetic, and some of us aren't even good at that.

I'm still missing what I call The Big Picture, though. I mean, you can't create a narrative, any narrative, without writing the backstory first. Maybe you don't include any of it "up front," but you have to know what it is. And that's where I'm still in the dark. Oh, sure, I know about the faked extinctions, and how Neanders and Floreans adapted and evolved, and how Sapients got greedy and became the most invasive species on the planet while Boskops were running circles around us technologically. But what about Before and After and Above-and-Beyond?

For example, how are Piper-candidates picked? And by whom? And who invited Fairies to hang out in Florida, of all places? And why does Kells call planet earth "Our Blue Gaia"? Is there another Blue Gaia? If so, where is it? And who—or what—are the Gardeners? And how do George and Uncle Billy fit in this—whatever this is? And for that matter, there are tons of mythic traditions on the planet, so who decreed that our "region" follows the Celts? What about the 41 other regions? Do they all subscribe to different mythologies?

When I try to talk to Sterling about The Big Picture we get bogged down in Quantum versus Cosmic (and don't forget Local) until my head starts hurting and Sterling makes up a reason why she has to go. And when I try to talk to Kells, she just says be patient because eventually All Will Be Revealed. Fabulous.

In the meantime, I'm supposed to be writing "The Book," so what should I do? I can't ask any of my friends for advice because who'd believe me? Not even Talisman, and she's the only one who's serious about alternative realities. So okay, I have no alternative but to settle down and talk to myself. Which I do pretty regularly. Mags, I'll say to myself, you're not making this up, you're telling it. You're just a storyteller, so get on with the job. What's that fancy word? I know—Amanuensis. That's what I am, and I need to remember it.

Okay, I'll say back to myself, our Genius House story might not read like a happy-ever-after romance, but I sure hope it doesn't become a tragedy. And that will be partly up to me as the Writer. The Writer provides the lens, the coloring, the perspective, the tone. That's why I admire Kurt Vonnegut so much. He saw humanity at its worst, but he never gave in to despair. Never. Vonnegut maintained a sense of humor up to the very end. A compassionate sense of humor. That's what I need to remember.

Notes Re: Neander Evolution

Neanders befriended musk oxen, which turned out to be a good deal for both species. The underfur of the musk ox is the densest natural fiber on the planet, eight times denser than sheep's wool and lighter than cashmere. And the outer-fur is coarse and stiff, three to four inches thick. It's such a good insulator, in fact, that radar can't track musk oxen and even sophisticated heat-seeking satellites can't detect them. At first Neanders wore musk ox fur garments to shield them from cold and from detection, but eventually their own skin got thicker and darker and began to grow fur.

Neanders' skin-and-fur development parallels that of the polar bear: black skin, which absorbs more heat than white skin, and a thick fur coat for holding in the heat. A transparent fur coat depends on available light. Sunlight reflected from densely packed transparent hairs makes the fur look white. It's an ingenious adaptation. In fact, Neander fur (like polar bear fur) is made up of hollow hairs called guard hairs. These air-filled guard hairs help transmit heat from sunlight to black skin as a solar heat collector. In turn, the reflection retards heat loss from the skin.

Wow. Who could ever have guessed that Neanderthals—who started out looking pretty much like us—would end up looking like white-furred Wookiees?

Notes Re: My Q&A with Datta

Question to Datta: The black skin and white fur makes sense, but isn't it a disadvantage in sub-zero weather to be so tall and skinny? If your skin and fur is like a polar bear's, why aren't you also low to the ground and padded with fat?"

Answer: *Because we climb mountains, so we had to be lean and limber like the best rock climbers.*

Question to Datta: *But why exceptionally tall?*

Answer: *Tall can be an advantage to a climber, if limber goes along with it. You've seen those rock-climber stretches, arms and legs splayed out, reaching from one finger- or toe-hold to another? The longer you are, the more chances you have of being able to reach those hard-to-find grab-spots.*

After Datta and I talked, I could picture it all: Datta's ancestors braving snow and ice, climbing always higher, always farther, finding slim purchase on rocky outcroppings, keeping the clan together by sending their voices high and far over frozen wastes and sheer cliffs. It's like the aborigines in Australia, always knowing where they are through their Songlines.

"That's it, exactly," Datta told me. "Utilizing our Neander Songnet, we can convene a NEFBO gathering in a matter of minutes."

Notes Re: Timespace
When Kells confronted me with the concept of Timespace during our "all-nighter" in my apartment, I took copious notes. I tried to, anyway. But I was so flummoxed by everything that night— starting with a visit from the Cosmic Serpent—it's a wonder I

didn't write gibberish! Finally, though, I culled my notes and ended up with these "bullets":

- *Time is fundamental in Timespace, whereas Space evolves.*
- *Timespace is a world of "shifting past" where retro-causality may hold sway.*
- *In Timespace, Time is malleable, discontinuous.*
- *The Great Stream of Consciousness flows fitfully through Timespace.*
- *Now and then, a rivulet from the Great Stream makes a backstream connection.*
- *In Timespace, the texture of Time varies.*
- *Most of all, INFINITY is the key to Timespace.*

You know, it's one thing to love alternate-reality stories like "The Wizard of Oz" and "Alice in Wonderland." But imagine learning there really is a shadow world that's coterminous with this one. Gulp. Yet I had to admit, during our seemingly endless all-nighter, that Kells proved herself an incomparable teacher—certainly worthy of the title "Tutor."

By the time she introduced the analogy of the famous optical illusion of the Young Lady and Old Hag, I understood precisely what she meant by "coterminous realities". In coterminous realities, you're in one or you're in the other. It's like the analogy: you can see one or see the other, but you simply can't see both images—both women— at the same time.

Notes Re: Kells's Analogy

Young Lady and Old Hag

I wasn't happy about the title of the optical illusion itself, of course. I mean, "Young Lady and Old Hag"? Give me a break! One more dig at The Older Woman, the way I see it. But Kells had nothing to do with the title of the Illusion, so I didn't object at the time. Anyway, it'll be way too late to bring it up the next time I see her. Whenever that is.

LIST OF CHARACTERS

Agatha—Mags's ancient Volvo.

Alice (Alicia, Alli)—See Miss Fortunato.

Archies—biological robots; humanoid so they don't attract attention (i.e., they "look like us"); carbon-based rather than silicon-based; engineered to be "archetypal" and that's why they're called "Archies." See **Biobots, 'Noids.**

Aunt Betty—Bethie Jean's mother.

Aunt Cissy—Wally's mother; she's skinny like Olive Oyl.

Aunt Jillsy—Geno's aunt who raised him in Pittsburgh (Geno's an orphan).

Aunt Sasa—old gypsy woman in Pittsburgh; gave Mags her antique mirror.

Bandushkos, Dmitri and Grigory—Russian brothers; Geno's transient day-laborers.

Bandushkos, Igor and Ivan—cousins of Dmitri and Grigory, found dead in the NASCAR balloon basket after it explodes over the Genius House.

Bangers—afraid Earth will explode in a nuclear holocaust. (See **Whimperers.**)

Barbara Out Back—Mags's first Florida friend; lives with her mother and little sister Vickie in a trailer park behind the Lyndhurst Hotel.

Beebo, aka Moses—son of Preacher and Lily Amaryllis; loves guns, kills birds and squirrels for fun; Mags dubs him "Sid Vicious."

Ben Bulben—Sterling's adoptive father, husband of Mary Buck; art professor at Stetson University in DeLand; sculped Brobdingnagian statues on the Stetson campus; left his "Sistine Chapelish" mural in the dome at Byzantium unfinished.

Bethie Jean—Mags's cousin in Pittsburgh; takes the stage name "B.J. Smithfield" when she becomes a country music star.

Bobby and Jules—Mags's longtime Atlanta friends; members of her book club; a power couple.

Big Tony DiCicco—owner of DiCiccos' roadside market in Penn Hills; loves to gamble.

Biobots—biological robots, engineered to be "archetypal." See **Archies, 'Noids.**

Bogos—a bogus group, people who don't belong together.

Booker—Mags's high school girlfriend; "always had her nose in a book"; a researcher, Archivist at City Island Library, and private pilot; collaborates with Mags on Kitchen Table Books.

Boots—Joan Reddish's cat in Penn Hills.

Boskops—a non-extinct hominin species: *homo Boskopis* (evolved for millennia in isolation; now look like skinny big-eyed aliens); so technologically advanced, they can manipulate light.

Brigadier—a bogus former officer and fighter pilot; spies on the Genius House; is fixated on General Turgidson in the *Dr. Strangelove* movie; wears one black glove to hide his fake missing hand; hangs out with Preacher at the Holistic Temple.

Casey—Sterling's boyfriend; a student at Stetson University; Talisman's student assistant.

Cedric the Saxon—legendary biker; real name Ralph Palfer (married to Nancy).

Christine—hairsmith, owns Christine's Cottage; costumer, wig-maker, make-up artist.

Christopher—composer-in-residence at Stetson University in DeLand; Mags's former student at Georgia Tech; wrote an opera with Mags.

Cassandra—an Archie; street performer; flautist, rides a unicycle; "White Coral Bells" is her signature song. See **Archie, Biobot, Noid.**

Confessor, The—an Archie: often seen in the company of The Professor and Rita; wears a white linen suit; looks like a cadaver. See **Archie, Biobot, 'Noid.**

Dam Dog Leo—Dalmation who lives with Barbara Out Back, Mags's first Florida friend.

Danaans, The—a race of legendary Celts; part-human, part-fairy; beautiful and long-lived but not immortal; in Gaelic the *Tuatha de Danaan*. They lived in Tara, the Irish Camelot.

Datta—a Genius House Tutor (a Neander): the tall furry one, looks like a white Wookiee; his cottage-mate (and synergete) is Mercedes the musk ox. See **Neander, NEFBO, Tutor.**

Dayadhvam and Damyata—Datta's brothers. See **The Three Das.**

Deirdre—Mags's beautiful friend; looks like a Celtic goddess; Sterling's brother Red is in love with her, calls her his "Deidre of the Sorrows."

Diff—an Archie; street performer, drummer; hangs out in Riverside Park with his pet ferret Phyllo; saves Mags from a mysterious Shadow. See **Archie, Biobot, 'Noid.**

Doc Kumagai—the Volusia County Coroner; often works with Slim.

Dorothy Jane—Pandora's adopted daughter; member of Mags's Atlanta book club; a professional dog trainer (bulldogs); after her Atlanta condo fire, Mags lives temporarily with her.

Dorothy Willis—the maid at the Lyndhurst Hotel when Mags arrives in Florida.

Elizabeth Margaret Magee ("Peg")—Mags's mom.

English Butler— an Archie: a shape-shifting Trickster. See **Archie, Biobot, 'Noid, Trickster.**

Exalted Mother Margaret—plays a white baby grand for Mags's Rainbow Girls procession.

Ezra—Uncle Billy's friend.

Fat Guy—often seen with Preacher; sometimes wears a white monk's robe.

Father Vincenzo Parlapiano—chief priest at Latrobe's Benedictine Abbey; related to the DiCiccos in Pittsburgh; officiated at nuptial mass for Mena and Frankie.

Floreans—a non-extinct hominin species: *homo Floresiensis;* evolved for millennia in isolation; males now look like bald Hobbits with beards like seaweed; they can live on land *or* in water, evolved bioluminescence and swim bladders; "stoners," they get high on fendelin (special kelp).

Ford—Mags and Booker's contentious Atlanta editor; edits their Kitchen Table Books.

Frankie Moose—Geno's cousin; an artist who designed the copper-colored spiral fire escape (with a rooftop gazebo) on Geno's downtown building.

French Maid—an Archie: a shape-shifting Trickster. See **Archie, Biobot, 'Noid, Trickster.**

Galatea Gallimachos—Gigi's daughter; in love with Praxiteles Papanicolaou.

Geno—Mags' Italian landlord in Daytona Beach.

George—Uncle Billy's wife; Sterling's aunt from Ireland.

Gigi Gallimachos—Galatea's mother; is being courted for her money by Max Finklestein.

Gooseberry Fool—Celtic singing group; also Irish dessert.

Groosma—Pennsylvania Dutch for "Grandmother"; Mags's paternal grandmother.

Groupies—"Lysistrata Ladies," "Gamer Gurus," and "Trader Joes"; will eventually be part of the Intervention called "Pay the Piper."

Harem Girl, The—a Boardwalk bimbo; thinks Max Finklestein is Hans Solo.

Harlequin—an Archie; street performer in the park; a mime. See **Archie, Biobot, 'Noid.**

Jasper Junior—Groosma's no-good brother.

Jasper Senior—Groosma's tyrannical father; married Maisie.

Jengu—a Genius House Tutor (a Florean): the short bald one, looks like an orange Hobbit with a skanky beard; his cottage-mate (and synergete) is Squiggs the cuttlefish; adopts Sorrow the Irish setter after Red disowns the dog. See **Florean, NEFBO, Tutor.**

Jim Ed Clifton—redneck who got Mags hooked on MoonPies; later Reenie's partner.

Jitsu—Jengu's Florean girlfriend who periodically goes AWOL; she's much younger than he.

Kalley Drum—a TV reporter for Channel 13.

Kathleen and Bill O'Malley—saved Mags's family from bankruptcy by becoming partners in the Lyndhurst Hotel; former vaudeville performers; she plays, he sings

Kells—a Genius House Tutor (a Boskop); she's in charge of the Genius House tutors; looks like a tall skinny alien; has huge eyes and no head hair, so she wears dark glasses and a wig or headscarf in public; sometimes she glows, has an aura. See **Boskop, NEFBO, Tutor.**

Kara Andresson—a professional opera singer who landed in Daytona Beach; Mags accompanied her at the Bandshell; introduced Mags to opera, a love that never left her.

Lady in the Red Dress, The—Mags sees her going in the Reddish house after Missus dies.

Lady Sennacherib—Cedric the Saxon's wife; crochets chain mail; real name is Nancy.

Leon Perez—FDLE Director (Florida Department of Law Enforcement) in Tallahassee; Slim's good friend; Talisman's former student assistant; known to adoring females as "Hot Buns."

Lily Amaryllis—wife of Preacher; mother of Rose and Beebo, aka Moses; legally blind; hates the Genius House people; honorary mayor of Ponce Inlet (in perpetuity).

Little Wiener, The—Mags's nemesis at Georgia Tech; real name is Arsenault J. Springer.

Luigi—pushes cart with sno cones in downtown Pittsburgh; has horse Pucci and monkey Mussolini with him; gives Mags horsetail hairs for her amulet.

Lynn, Angela, and Phyllis—Mena and Frankie's three daughters.

Mark and Merril—Mags's best friends in high school.

Mary Buck—Sterling's adoptive mother; legendary stunt pilot; math professor at Embry-Riddle University in Daytona Beach until her plane disappeared near Bimini.

Max and Myrtle—live at the Lyndhurst Hotel; befriended Mags's father; Max gigs frogs, Myrtle cooks frog legs.

Max Finklestein—a Harrison Ford lookalike; dresses up like Indiana Jones for Halloween; owner of "Pigs Will Fly," a pub in downtown Daytona where Uncle Billy does a poetry reading.

May Louisa Gottschalk (Maisie)—married Jasper Senior, became Groosma's stepmother.

Mercedes ("Mercy")—a musk ox who is Datta's cottage-mate; they're "synergetic species."

Mena—Big Tony's orphan niece.

Michael O'Duinn Magee (Mick)—Mags's paternal grandfather; Mags inherited his ancient book about Irish fairies, which she keeps in her Commonplace Box.

Michael Robartes Bulben—Sterling's brother; a musical prodigy; has a new girl band.

Miss Fortunato (Alice, Alicia, Alli)—Mags's role model; a one-semester substitute high school teacher: math and physics; Mags becomes her student assistant.

Miss Gatch—Mags's senior English teacher in high school.

Mister Butt Crack—an Archie; wears lots of chains and keys; wears his pants low so his butt-crack shows; Geno finds him suspicious. See **Archie, Biobot, 'Noid.**

Momec—a meme-creature from the Great Stream of Consciousness; always brings a message.

Monica—Mags's dean at Georgia Tech; an expert on French wines.

Mr. and Mrs. Fabrizi—own and run a small convenience store and deli in Penn Hills.

Mr. Fenton—principal of Mainland High School.

Mrs. McGillicuddy—Mags's Atlanta neighbor who spots Schrödy in the woods near her house; Mags has to move to Florida without Schrödy, but she and Mrs. McGillicuddy have a plan: after Mrs. McGillicuddy entices the cat into her kitchen, she'll call Mags to come get him.

Mr. Yoakum—Mags's math/physics teacher for whom Miss Fortunato substituted.

Mussolini—Luigi's monkey.

Muti—German for "Grandmother"; Mags's maternal grandmother who lives with Mags and family in Penn Hills and moves to Daytona Beach with them.

Nancy—wife of Cedric the Saxon; calls herself Lady Sennacherib.

Neanders—a non-extinct hominin species: *homo Neanderthalensis;* evolved for millennia in isolation; now look like white-furred Wookiees.

NEFBOs—acronym for the three supposedly-extinct hominin species: Neanders, Floreans, and Boskops. See **Boskops, Floreans,** and **Neanders.**

'Noids—humanoid and shroomanoid robots engineered by Boskop technology many millennia ago after Boskop roboticists climbed out of the Uncanny Valley. See **Biobots.**

Old Sonny—Geno's cousin; works at Geno's store. See **Sonny.**

Pan Papanicolaou—owner-developer of the Byzantium Bowling Center at the Boardwalk; Geno's longtime competitor and antagonist.

Pandora—owner of Pandora's Emporium in Atlanta; member of Mags's book club.

Pauline—lives at the Lyndhurst Hotel year-round; skinny like Olive Oyl.

Pathics—a sub-species of *homo Sapiens* whose bloodline is reptilian (their ancestors interbred with snakes); called "Pathics" because they're sociopaths and telepaths.

Patty—Mags's childhood friend in Penn Hills.

Petros Papanicolaou—Pan's brother; conceived the genius idea for their "designer balls."

Phyllo—Diff's pet ferret.

Porter—Ford's cousin; member of Mags's Atlanta book club; former hippie, never got over the sixties; drove his "magic school bus" around the USA for 7 years, following The Grateful Dead.

Praxiteles Papanicolaou (Prax)—Pan's son; he's Greek God Beautiful; known to all the Greek mothers in the Halifax Area as "The Catch of the Century"; Michael's in love with him.

Preacher—former Lighthouse Keeper in Ponce Inlet; husband of Lily Amaryllis; father of Rose but adopted Beebo; built Bottle Wall, Glory Hole, and Holistic Temple; drives a big model train into his Temple, to use as the first row of seats; real name is Stanley Clinkscales.

Professor, The—an Archie: often seen in the company of The Confessor and Rita; fiftyish with a mustache and small beard, round black-rimmed Harry Potter glasses, and a bad hairpiece; wears rumpled brown tweed with elbow patches. See **Archie, Biobot, 'Noid.**

Pucci—Luigi's horse; Mags gets three hairs from Pucci's tail for her amulet.

Ralph Palfer—registrar at Stetson University in DeLand. See **Cedric the Saxon.**

Ralphie Marbles the Third—Geno's Florida cousin; often works at Geno's store; inherited a beachfront hotel; loves costume events, dressing up as popular saints like St. Francis of Assisi.

Ralphie Marbles Junior—Big Tony's cousin in Pittsburgh; drives Tony to Florida to gamble.

Ranger—the Lyndhurst hotel cat.

Raymond O'Duinn Magee—Mags's dad.

Red Hanrahan Bulben—Sterling's brother; crazy about "flying"; hangs out at Skydive DeLand; has long wavy red hair; a little guy with a huge voice; crazy in love with Deirdre.

Reddish Family—Mister, Missus, Joan, and Joan's cat Boots; Mags and Muti often visit.

Reenie—Mags's outrageous, big-hearted friend; she builds "Scary Mary," a purple motorcycle, in her granddad's garage; wears blue eye shadow and "Jungle Gardenia" cologne; dances on tables at the Cabbage Patch; hooks up with Jim Ed Clifton so they can help outcasts and misfits.

Rita—an Archie; loves Margaritas; definitely a "type": bleached hair with dark roots, too much makeup, a size fourteen squeezed into a size ten; lots of attitude; often seen with the Professor and the Confessor. See **Archie, Biobot**; **'Noid.**

RonJon—Geno's elderly, tattooed, pony-tailed surfer friend who brings him gossip in exchange for food; he TALKS LOUD, even when he's not excited; is prone to hyperbole.

Roomers—biological robots; "shroomanoid" rather than humanoid (they're mushrooms, and they want to look like mushrooms: it's their *identity!*); they're carbon-based rather than silicon-based; Mags meets Amanita, Chanterelle, Copeland and Mrs. Grales at the Genius House; they're part of a global mycelial network. See **Biobots, 'Noids.**

Rose—Sterling's former best friend; Lily Amaryllis' daughter; Mags dubs her "Jayne Mansfield with double-digit cleavage."

Ruth Winston—mother of Patty, Mags's Penn Hills girlfriend; always at church; doesn't like Italians just "on principle."

Sammy the Sabrett Guy—has a hot dog cart in Daytona Beach, near Geno's store.

Sapients—supposedly the only non-extinct hominin species: *homo Sapiens*, i.e., us!

See **Boskops, Floreans, Neanders, NEFBOs, SAPS.**

SAPS—acronym for us: *homo Sapiens.*

Schrödinger (Schrödy)—Mags's tuxedo Manx cat; shows up one day at her Atlanta condo.

Semi Sweet Charity—drag queen; hangs out at Byzantium and the Yum Yum Tree.

Slim—female deputy sheriff; plays racquetball with Mags; Talisman's former student assistant.

Socrates—a Biker who hangs out at the Cabbage Patch; befriended Wally.

Sonny DiCicco—Big Tony's son; was sent away to military school; surfaced later in Miami; got head-whacked in a melee; rescued by Ralphie and brought to Daytona; then called "Old Sonny."

Sorrow—Red's Irish Setter; formerly called Deirdre, then Dumbitch until Jengu adopted her.

Squiggs—a cuttlefish who is Jengu's cottage-mate and best friend; they're "synergetic species."

Stanley Clinkscales—see Preacher.

Stella—Maisie moved in with her (Stella) after she (Maisie) dumped Jasper Senior.

Sterling (Sterling Silver Buck)—sister of Michael and Red; Mags's young Florida friend and true *alter ego*; an accomplished flautist with an 4-octave singing voice, Sterling loves opera, dressing up like classic film stars, and is already a published poet; she's Casey's girlfriend.

Talisman—professor at Stetson University in DeLand; in a wheelchair (a "Chairperson"); Mags's long-time friend; a psychic who helps detectives solve cases.

Three Graces, The—Princess, Mazie and Mary Fuller; own Three Graces Restaurant in Daytona Beach; all three are chefs.

Three Tribes Council, The—organized 100,000 years ago when Sapients stormed out of the Four Tribes Council, leaving Neanders, Floreans, and Boskops (NEFBOS) to decide what to do about the troublesome Sapients; NEFBOs decided to fake their extinctions and begin diasporas to remote areas of Planet Earth.

Tricksters—Archies who are shapeshifters, so they have fluid identities, like professional actors who get to choose their roles. See **English Butler, French Maid, Schrödinger.**

Trooper—Deputy Sheriff who works with **Slim.**

Tutors—three supposedly-extinct hominins (Datta's a Neander, Jengu's a Florean, and Kells is a Boskop); they've been assigned to the Genius House in Florida where they will prepare for the Intervention called *Pay the Piper*. See **Datta, Jengu, Kells**; also **Neanders, Floreans, Boskops.**

Uncle Billy— Sterling's uncle; George's husband; a famous Irish poet and scholar.

Uncle Jake—Mags's uncle; Bethie Jean's father.

Uncle Walter—Mags's uncle; Wally's father; husband of Aunt Cissy.

Wally—Mags' genius-nerdy cousin; owns BMWs but doesn't drive them, just admires the engineering; but loves driving his BMW motorcycle.

Wesley Ray—auctioneer in Ormond Beach; Mags bought her white baby grand piano from him.

Whimperers—afraid Planet Earth will slowly die and become uninhabitable.

Preview

MAGS
at
HEMINGWAY'S
HILBERT HOTEL

(BOOK 2 OF *THE MAGS CHRONICLES*)

You should never say "never." Not if you don't want to eat your own words, that is.

I said pigs would fly before I'd let myself get involved in one of Sterling's crazy expeditions, yet here I am, wondering when I'll ever learn. "Sterling," I said, "you promised I could stay in the hotel. You *promised.*"

"Mags," she said, "there are some things you have to experience in person. The Bimini Road's famous for a reason. You admitted you've always wondered if the stories and legends are true, didn't you?"

"Well sure, I wondered about it. But that didn't mean I wanted to *go* there."

"Yet if I hadn't brought you here, would you believe it?"

"No," grudgingly.

"Exactly. And that's why you had to come, so you can see for yourself."

I was still annoyed. Actually, I was still terrified, not to mention dizzy and disoriented— the way you feel when you just jumped off a twenty-foot-high dive platform, backward and blindfolded.

I knew Sterling was right, though. If she'd told me I wouldn't have believed it. And I had to admit it's breathtakingly beautiful, especially the music and the colors. And the sense of being free, as if we were flying like a dandelion flies when it releases its tiny parasol of fluff to the breeze. It was indescribable.

Wait, I thought, Someone's coming toward us. Is it Jengu? Yes, it's Jengu! He's waving and smiling that huge smile of his. And he's with someone. But oh my goodness, she's not just *anyone*. She's extraordinary. Silvery, gleaming, graceful. The quintessence of every mermaid story you've ever read or heard about—Undine, maybe, or one of the Rhinemaidens, or Ariel.

They were getting closer, moving through the water like an ephemera, a mirage that shimmers and glimmers.

"Welcome, Mags," the mirage-maiden said, with a smile as big as Jengu's.

"Welcome to Atlantis."

ABOUT THE AUTHOR

©Photo by Booker

While S. O'Duinn Magee pursued a thirty-year career as a professor and literary critic, she was known as "Margaret M. 'Maggie' Dunn." Under that name she earned BA and MA degrees from Stetson University (DeLand, FL) and a PhD degree from Indiana University (Bloomington, IN). She is presently Emerita Professor of English at Rollins College (Winter Park, FL), and she taught at Stetson and the University of Central Florida as well.

As an internationally published scholar, she presented papers at academic conferences both here and abroad, and she co-authored *The Composite Novel: The Short Story Cycle in Transition*. That book, as well as her substantial body of work on composite structure in fiction and film, is cited in numerous articles and anthologies.

Upon retiring from academics, Maggie Dunn chose the pen name "S. O'Duinn Magee" (aka Mags) by which she as a writer would thereafter be known. Subsequently she worked with composer Christopher Weiss on their award-winning opera (*In a Mirror, Darkly*) for which she wrote the libretto. She also self-published her first work of fiction (*Vinegar Pie & Kumquat Ice Cream: A Composite Novel*).

Like her alter ego Mags—the "voice" of all her fiction—she loves strong black coffee, single malt Scotch, and MoonPies (not necessarily in that order); her favorite novelists are Kurt Vonnegut, Douglas Adams, and Margaret Atwood (again, not necessarily in that order); and she generally wears black (blacks always match and they don't show ketchup stains).

Unlike Mags, she does not talk to cats.

For more info about Mags, check out her website:
www.magsthewriter.com